First Edition

ISBN: 9798340025609

Cover art by Mauriziana Gualdrini @itsamau

I dedicate this book to all the amazing people I have met in my travels—for every conversation, adventure, and misadventure; for every laugh, tear, and revelation.

I would also like to give a special mention to Adriel, Kubi, and Loki. Who shared with me the joys of Avalon during my multiple visits these last few years.

1
The Temple of Artemis

The Glastonbury Tor was a hill visible from miles away, with a large tower that sat on top that loomed over the valley like a lighthouse from a forgotten age. Ethan pressed his face against the dirty glass of the country bus, straining to catch a better glimpse of what he hoped would be his future. For the next two weeks, he was running away—from London, from responsibility, from family, friends, and even from himself. He had no idea what awaited him in the small village of Glastonbury. Six years out of university and four years as a data analyst had left him feeling trapped in the big city.

"Fuck off," Ethan whispered to himself, reflecting on the lukewarm reception from everyone he'd told about his journey. "Fuck off, all of them," he mumbled, thinking of his mother, friends, and coworkers who had all laughed at the idea of wasting a holiday in England instead of going to somewhere warmer during the autumn months.

The town of Glastonbury seemed like it was on an island amidst a sea of green fields, surrounded by ridge lines on all sides. The nearest large town was Wells, a cathedral town that had recently been used as a film set for a new action movie. The town had been buzzing with excitement when Ethan stopped there for coffee, waiting for the bus to take him deeper into the countryside. Wells reminded him of his childhood home outside London, with all the expected shops and just enough charm to make it a weekend destination for the elderly and the bored.

Glastonbury, by comparison, was even smaller—little more than a High Street and a large abbey at its center. As the bus climbed the hill, revealing the first few buildings of the town, Ethan sat back in his seat and checked his phone for directions to the Bed and Breakfast he had booked. He sighed as he noticed his service had dropped to a single bar.

"Oi, lad! This is yer stop 'ere," came the muffled voice of the driver, his thick Somerset accent almost incomprehensible to Ethan's London ears.

Ethan glanced out the window and saw that the bus had reached the top of the High Street, at the crossroads of the village. Grabbing his suitcase and backpack, he headed for the doors, which swung open, releasing a thick cloud of smoke and incense into his face. The driver chuckled at Ethan's expression.

"Welcome to Glastonbury. Full o' witches and false wishes."

Ethan gave a nervous wave and nod, then stepped off the bus. The doors creaked shut behind him, and the bus quickly disappeared down the hill, turning a corner and vanishing from view.

He stood at the top of the High Street, absorbing his surroundings. To his left, a rundown pub, it's lights flickered dimly through the dark windows. To his right, a homeless man with a large greying afro gulped down a sausage roll. Ahead, the town's shops, cafés, and churches lay scattered in the distance. The smell of incense, marijuana, and lavender thickened the air, making Ethan cough.

"Well, this is… disappointing," he muttered. "It looks like every shitty village God forgot."

He pulled out his phone, but the service still showed one weak bar.

"Just wait for the next bus, turn back, and go home. No one would blame you," he thought.

He checked the bus schedule again—no buses until the next evening. With a sigh, he mustered his energy and began walking towards the center of town, determined to find his Bed and Breakfast.

As he neared the heart of Glastonbury, the streets slowly filled with people. The first sight that caught his eye was a young woman walking six small dogs, their tiny legs shaking as they bounced in unison down the road. Ethan stared at her for a moment too long, and she caught his gaze.

"Hey! Did you just get in? Welcome to Glastonbury!" she called out in a fading Irish accent from across the street. Before he could respond, she crossed the road with her army of dogs, expertly maneuvering around an oncoming cyclist. Ethan reluctantly accepted her sudden hug, unable to move out of the way in time.

"How's things? I'm Zoe, and these are my little goblins: Peanut, Cashew, Walnut, Pistachio, Bilbo, and Pecan," she said, chuckling as she introduced each dog.

"All nuts?" Ethan asked, bemused. "But why is one—"

"Bilbo? Oh, he's always getting into trouble with the local wizard, that's why!" she laughed, snorting between giggles. "Used to be Almond until he started running off."

"What's she trying to sell me on?" he wondered while backing away slowly. "Well, nice to meet you and your little army, but I must be going."

"What's your name, then? What brings ya to charming little Glastonbury, eh?" she asked, still following after him.

"My name is Ethan. I'm here on holiday."

"Holiday? It isn't that bloody music festival again, is it? No, that's not till summer. Oh! You're here for Samhain, aren't you?" she asked, her excitement growing.

"Uh… yeah, sure. For that," Ethan replied, trying to sound convincing.

"Oh, Glastonbury is the best place in all of England for Samhain! That's why I moved here—not for England, but for Samhain in England! People here are good fun during the festival," she rambled on.

Ethan tuned Zoe out as she rambled on about last year's Samhain festival. As he attempted to lose her in the flow of people meandering through the town, he finally accepted that she was too persistent. She followed along, her dogs trotting after him, so he slowed down, deciding to take in the peculiar town of Glastonbury.

The town, though small, had an eclectic mix of shops and cafés that seemed to amplify its odd charm. Crystals, tarot readings, feathers, bones, and dreamcatchers filled the windows of most of the 20 or so "hippie" stores. Scattered among them were rare bookshops specializing in the occult and New Age philosophies. Glastonbury's peculiarities extended to the erratic operating hours displayed on the shop windows:

8 a.m. - 1 p.m.
11 a.m. - 12:30 p.m.
Sunrise to Sunset
Only open until Beltane, closed until Samhain

Several stores also had signs advertising spiritual workshops and events: Buddhist meditation courses, spirit guide sessions, and runic magic classes. Ethan could hardly believe it.

At the end of the street, the road curved into a charming town square with more oddities: pubs with Celtic-themed signs, cafés with outdoor seating, and yet more shops specializing in obscure spiritual practices. Ethan stopped at the market cross, scanning his phone for directions to his Bed and Breakfast, when Zoe finally caught up with him, her dogs yapping at her heels.

"Isn't it great?" she declared, breathless.

"Uh, yeah. Great. Where's Benedict Street?" Ethan asked, desperate for some peace.

"Benedict Street? Ah, that's where you're stayin', eh? Most folks live off Benedict Street. What's the place called?"

"It's some kind of temple."

Zoe grinned, mischief flashing in her eyes. "Temple, eh? Right, well, you'll see. Just 'round the corner there. Once you spot St. Ben's, you're close."

Ethan gave a hurried thanks and started off, eager to escape Zoe's wild energy. As he turned the corner, he heard her call out, "See you 'round real soon, Ethan!"

He winced at the thought.

The houses along Benedict Street were a motley assortment of colors and designs, some covered in murals. A few bore plaques naming them "temples"—Temple to Ganesh, Temple to Odin, Temple to St. Brigid. It seemed almost every other home in the town was a shrine to something.

Finally, at the end of the street near the park, Ethan found the Temple of Artemis, a dark green house with ivy-like trim framing its windows. The door, painted bright red, featured an iron knob shaped like a wolf's head. Ethan hesitated for a moment before using the bow-and-arrow-shaped knocker to announce his arrival.

He had chosen this Bed and Breakfast solely because it was the only one available when he booked his trip. The fact that it was run by two women had stoked fantasies in his mind about the countryside. As the door creaked open, two stunning women appeared before him. One was blonde with striking blue eyes; the other, a brunette with hazel eyes. Both wore white robes with golden sashes and crowns made of flowers.

"Hello, ladies—" Ethan began, but the blonde raised her hand, signaling him to stop, while the brunette put a finger to her lips in a gesture of silence.

Ethan opened his mouth to try again, but the brunette handed him a handwritten note. The women smiled and urged him to read it:

Our names are Vesta and Cardea, and we welcome you to our sanctuary dedicated to the holy goddess Artemis. This home is a sacred temple, and we ask that you respect its sacredness by following these rules:

1. Always wear white inside the home. We will provide you with a robe, which you should change into before entering the temple. You may wear what you like in your room.
2. No meat is to be consumed unless it is a full moon.
3. Guests are welcome, provided they respect the temple's rules. Extra robes are available for them.
4. Do not enter the private chambers of Vesta and Cardea. These are our sacred spaces and are off-limits, especially to men.
5. There is no television. We encourage you to disconnect during your stay. A landline phone is available in your room, but mobile phones are not permitted.
6. Any personal rituals or ceremonies should be done in your room, unless they are dedicated to Artemis.

"What the fuck? I'm paying to stay here!" Ethan muttered.

The blonde woman glared and flipped the note, revealing the final rule:

7. No profanity is allowed within the temple.

We hope these rules create a sacred and peaceful stay for you. We look forward to sharing in the energies of the huntress Artemis with you during your visit. Additionally, we are participating in a silent fasting meditation until the Solstice. This means we are not speaking until December 21st. You may speak to us, but we ask that you whisper and understand that you will not receive a verbal response.

Goddesses' Blessings,
Vesta and Cardea

Ethan stood there, dumbfounded, turning the parchment over again to make sure he had read it correctly.

"I'm paying to stay here?" he repeated under his breath.

The brunette once again motioned for silence.

"Fine," Ethan whispered, defeated. "I didn't expect all these rules."

The two women exchanged a silent glance, then shrugged with serene smiles. Ethan sighed, resigned to his fate. He'd already checked—there were no other rooms available in the entire town.

"Maybe I can find a room at a pub," he thought, but before he could dwell on it, the women took his bags and ushered him inside. The door closed with a creak behind him, and he found himself standing alone in the entryway, staring at the white robe hanging on a coat peg. His thoughts raced. "This is not what I expected… What have I gotten myself into?"

Reluctantly, he removed his jacket and slipped into the silky robe, which made him look like he was about to join a stag do. His undershirt—a cheeky movie poster tee—was still visible beneath the collar. He sighed again and stepped through the second door into the house proper.

Everything inside the house was spotless. Though the afternoon sun still hung low in the sky outside, the interior was dimly lit, with only a few candles lining the walls. To his left, a staircase wound its way upward, and to his right, two closed doors led to other parts of the house. The silence was so complete that Ethan's own breathing sounded unnaturally loud. He began ascending the stairs.

The walls were painted white, with intricate green designs resembling vines climbing up them. More plants, real ones this time, filled the corners of the hallways. At the top of the stairs, Ethan hesitated, unsure where to go, until a soft tap on the wall caught his attention. Vesta and Cardea were beckoning him towards a room at the front of the house.

His room was simple but comfortable: a large bay window, a small desk, a bed, and a wardrobe. There was an antique feel to the furniture, and the room's centerpiece was a painted mandala over the old fireplace. A glass of wine and a rolled-up yoga mat were placed neatly by the bed.

Before leaving, Ethan turned to the two women. "Wait," he whispered, "which one of you is which?"

The blonde shook her head, indicating she was not Vesta.

"So you're Cardea?" Ethan asked, to which she smiled and nodded.

"Thanks," he whispered, then turned to unpack. As he started to settle in, he watched Vesta and Cardea leave the room, hand in hand. A pang of realization hit him.

"Oh," he thought. "Well, that explains why they're okay with a guy staying here. They're… together. Great. There goes my chance at a cheeky romance."

Ethan collapsed onto the bed, exhausted. "Fuck, what am I even thinking?" he muttered to himself. "I didn't come here for that. I came here to get away." He stared out the window as the rain began to fall softly. The gentle patter of raindrops lulled him into a deep, dreamless sleep.

—

Ethan awoke early the next morning to the sound of a robin tapping its beak against the window. He was still wearing the white robe, his shoes from the previous evening still on his feet. The untouched glass of wine sat on the table beside his bed, and his bags remained unpacked in the corner. His stomach growled, reminding him that this was a Bed and Breakfast after all.

He quickly changed into fresh clothes and threw the robe back on, determined to find something to eat. As he wandered downstairs, he found the kitchen—a lush, plant-filled room where it was difficult to even spot the refrigerator. After rummaging through its contents, he discovered nothing but fruits, vegetables, yogurt, and jams—definitely no bacon or eggs.

"Shit," Ethan muttered. "No meat unless it's a full moon. Brilliant."

Ethan, still starving, rummaged through the pantry but found little more than organic muesli and stale French bread. Frustrated and still hungry, he returned to his room, threw on his raincoat, and headed outside in search of something more satisfying. Just as he stepped out the door, he remembered he was still wearing the white robe. Letting out a small gasp at the thought of being seen in such an outfit, he quickly shrugged it off, leaving it in the entryway. He grabbed the spare key with his name attached and set off down Benedict Street.

The early morning air was crisp and cool, typical for October in England. The rising sun painted the horizon with soft pinks and oranges, though heavy clouds loomed in the distance, promising more rain. For Ethan, the quiet country morning was a stark contrast to the bustling streets of London he was used to. He inhaled deeply, realizing how fresh the air felt—no pollution, no noise. He let out a cough, not yet used to the thin, clean air of the countryside.

As he passed St. Benedict's Church, he noticed a woman in the garden, tending to the flowers. She waved warmly, her strangely familiar smile brightening the morning.

"Good morning!" She said with more excitement that Ethan was expecting.

"Morning, sorry to bother. I'm absolutely starving. Forgot to eat last night before I passed out."

"Oh yes, staying at the Temple of Artemis, are ya? I bet you slept wonderfully there," she said with a knowing smile.

"Wonderfully quiet, yes. But that mattress was bloody uncomfortable. How did you know where I was staying?"

"So many questions, and you don't even know my name" she teased with a wink.

Ethan sighed. "Sorry, yeah. I'm sorry. What is your name?"

"My name is Selene, I tend these gardens. And your name is?" She smiled pleasantly.

"Ethan, I just got in yesterday."

"Yes, I know. I was in my garden when you arrived yesterday. You seemed quit determined not to enjoy my flowers as you rushed by."

"Sorry, was a bit focused on finding my lodging last night. Now, do you know a place where I can find a bite to eat? I haven't eaten since I arrived."

"This is Glastonbury, dear. Most places don't open until ten in the morning. It's barely half seven now," she chuckled.

"What about a Tesco or Morrisons? I just need something quick."

"Nope, not open till ten. And it's Sunday."

"Fuck. What do I do, then?" Ethan's frustration was palpable.

Selene studied him thoughtfully, then her eyes twinkled. "You could help me in the garden, and I'll cook you something after. How does that sound?"

Ethan hesitated. "How long will that take?"

"Until about nine o'clock," she replied with a mischievous grin.

"Maybe some other time," Ethan said, backing away.

Selene laughed softly and shook her head. "Well, I know just the place for you. A new café opened recently, run by a couple from the north. It's called The Andrew's Cross, right by the market cross. They open early. You'll love it and the owners I think."

"Thanks, I'll check it out," Ethan said, already walking away.

The St. Andrew's Cross was just where Selene said it would be. The café, housed in a brick building with deep blue wood accents, featured large glass windows displaying the Scottish flag. Outside, a woman with fiery red hair and bright green eyes was setting out small tables and chairs, the cobblestone pavement still wet from the morning's rain.

Ethan hesitated for a moment, taking in the sight and the smell of meat and coffee wafting from the open door.

"I'm home," Ethan thought as a smile crept across his face.

Inside, a large man with a thick Scottish accent popped his head out from behind a bakery display. "Are ye one o' the hippie types, or are ye here fer a proper breakfast?" he bellowed, his voice as booming as his laugh.

"Sorry, what?" Ethan asked, struggling to understand.

"Are ye a hippie or do ye want a proper breakfast?" the man repeated, even louder.

"Uh, a proper breakfast, please. Does that mean you do full English?"

"Aye, but better. I make a full Scottish breakfast—more meat, more food!" the man shouted, laughing again. "Go on, sit outside. My wife will bring ye a coffee."

Ethan took a seat at one of the tables, and the red-haired woman appeared moments later. "Good mornin', love. Ye alright?" she asked, her much softer Scottish accent much easier for Ethan to understand. "Coffee?"

"Yeah, please. Skinny latte, extra sugar."

"Lovely. Be just a minute," she said before disappearing back inside.

As Ethan waited, he observed the town waking up around him. The hippies the Scott seemed to dislike were loitered near the market cross, smoking and chatting. An elderly man wearing a pirate coat strolled by, barefoot, while workers set up for a small festival in the parking lot of the town hall. Despite his initial misgivings, there was something comforting about the slow rhythm of the place.

"Here ye go," the woman returned with his coffee, setting it down with a smile. "So, whit brings ye tae Glastonbury then?"

"You assume I just got here?" He questioned, taking a sip of his coffee.

"Aye, o' course ye did! Everybody kens everybody 'round here."

"That's going to be hard to get used to."

"Ye'll be fine. Less than 7,000 folk live here," she laughed.

"An' they're all half mad," the man added, arriving with a plate piled high with food.

Ethan's eyes widened at the sight of the massive breakfast. "You weren't kidding—how much does this weigh?"

The man grinned proudly. "Here we hae bacon, link sausage, beans, tomatoes, mushrooms, tattie scones, egg, an' wi' the Scottish twist—haggis, black pudding, an' square sausage!" He suddenly looked sheepish. "Oh, I forgot yer toast. Just a minute!"

The woman laughed as her husband rushed back inside. "I should've introduced us! I'm Isla, an' that's Hamish. We're MacLeods frae Skye—couldn't get mair Scottish if we were red haired coos."

Ethan smiled. "I'm Ethan. Pleased to meet you both. This breakfast is incredible."

"Ye enjoy. Hamish'll be back wi' yer toast in a moment." Isla said, giving Hamish a quick kiss on the cheek as he reappeared with the toast.

As Ethan tucked into his food, savoring the taste of real bacon and linked sausage, he heard a voice from behind him.

"Buongiorno! My friend, I have traveled very far to be here in front of you right now. May I sit and have a coffee with you?" he said excitedly, his faded Italian accent adding charm to his words.

"I'm sorry, do I know you?"

"You do not know me yet. But I know I am supposed to know you. My name is Matteo. I am so grateful to have met you!" He reached out for a handshake, but when Ethan extended his hand, Matteo grabbed him into a hug. "My brother! Yes! Ahhhooooo!" he howled into the morning sky.

"What the fuck is happening right now? Who is this man?" Ethan's thoughts raced, trying to remember if he had met Matteo before.

"I'm sorry, Matteo, I really don't think we have met before," Ethan said kindly, as if he were talking to a man out of his mind.

"Oh. I'm sorry. I have been walking for so long. Yes, you are right. We have not met. But we are meant to meet. I have been told so." Matteo placed his hand over his heart and backed up.

At this moment, Isla came out. "Heya! Ye new here as well? Very good yous met. Can I get you a coffee o' somethin'?"

"Yes, a coffee. Black," Matteo replied, glancing down at Ethan's half-finished plate. "And whatever he was having. I have not eaten in three days."

"O' course! Sit down, an' I will get it right away." Isla pulled out his chair and ran back inside.

"Such a lovely woman. What is her accent? I have never heard such a voice before. It was like listening to English, but like someone forgot how to speak it," Matteo remarked gently, his sincerity apparent.

"She's Scottish. Wait—you haven't eaten in three days?" Ethan replied.

"Ah, yes, not since I was in Brighton."

"Brighton, as in the south of England?"

"Yes, across from France. Where I took the boat."

"You came from France?"

"Si, I mean, yes. Originally, I come from Italy."

Isla returned with the black coffee, and Matteo took a sip.

"Beautiful woman. This coffee—you have no idea. After walking for one month, this coffee is life-changing," Matteo said with deep gratitude.

"You've walked for one month?" Isla gasped.

"Wait, you walked here from Italy?" Ethan said in disbelief.

"Yes," Matteo responded humbly, taking another sip.

"I will gladly tell you my story," he said, looking at Isla. "But for now, I must talk to my brother, please."

"O' of course. I will go check on Hamish an' see if yer breakfast is ready," Isla said awkwardly.

"What do you have to talk to me about? I still don't know who you are."

Matteo took a breath and collected himself. "Yes, I was told to come here to Glastonbury, a town I have never been to before, so that I may find answers."

"Who told you this?"

"Grandmother told me this. She said I would come here only by foot, and I would find someone I was meant to speak to right away. That they would be a sibling to me."

"Your grandmother told you this?"

"Yes, Grandmother Ayahuasca told me this."

Hamish came out with a second plate of breakfast for Matteo.

"Thank you so deeply, my friend. Are you from these Scottish lands as well?" Matteo directed his attention to Hamish.

"Aye, that I am. Hear you walked half o' bloody Europe to have my breakfast."

"That I did. I cannot wait to eat it. Thank you so much for your kindness, your food, and your skills as a chef," Matteo said sincerely.

"Oh, ye will make this wee chef blush. Get t'eating now," Hamish said, going back inside with a new energy in his step.

Matteo smiled at his plate of food, put his hands together, and said, "Thank you, great guides, for this meal. Thank you for the energy it will give me. And thank you to grandmother for guiding me here."

"You keep saying grandmother guided you here. But what does that mean exactly?"

"I do not know. That is why she is mysterious. She tells you so much, but you can only understand parts of the story. The part I understood was that I have to be here and that you and I would help each other. So tell me your name and what guided you here?"

"You don't know my name?"

"How would I know your name? We just met!"

"Are you messing with me, man?"

"No. I do not understand. Why would I know your name?" Matteo seemed genuinely confused.

Ethan looked at him and then let out an awkward laugh. "Sure, okay, yeah. My name is Ethan."

"Your family name?" Matteo asked between bites of black pudding.

"Rivers. My family name is Rivers."

Matteo took a bite of beans and looked at Ethan as if to say, "Continue."

"Yeah, okay. So I came here on holiday to get away from London for a bit. That's really all there is."

"That cannot be it. My brother did not come here for such a simple reason," Matteo said, pausing before speaking again. "What happened to you in London?"

"What happened? Nothing happened."

"Come on." Matteo glared.

"Well, yeah. I worked a job moving files from one server to another. By the time I got done moving the files, another system required me to move them again. I would say that's nothing."

"Do you think your value is based on your job? What did you love about London?"

"Love about London? Shit, I have never thought about what I loved about London. What do people usually love about it? Just say that so he backs off," Ethan thought.

"Uh, the food. The museums are nice. I liked—or rather loved—the theater scene. My friends there are a good laugh."

"Okay, let that be your answer," Matteo said, returning to his plate of food.

There was an extended period of silence. Ethan lowered himself back into a comfortable position in the seat, letting the tension of Matteo's questions release from him. The street was getting busier now; more shops had opened their doors, more hippies had emerged, and the morning commuters were making their way to work. A few more people had sat in the patio chairs around Matteo and

Ethan. Isla was running back and forth out of the café, delivering various coffees and sweet rolls to the customers. The sound of the town was like gentle hummingbirds—a gentle vibration of activity that built with every new person that joined the area around the market cross.

"So, what is there to do in this Glastonbury, anyway?" Matteo asked, breaking through Ethan's drifting thoughts.

"Well, I think the climb to the Tor is supposed to be quite nice."

"The Tor? Oh, you mean the tower on the hill. I saw it from a distance early today as I walked."

"Yes, we do need to talk about that!" Ethan had almost forgotten. "You walked here. Well, shit. How was it?"

"Long. But incredibly beautiful. The mornings in England are something truly special. The nights… not so much. Very cold."

"Why didn't you just take a bus? Or fly?"

"Because Grandmother—"

"Because Grandmother told you," Ethan finished.

"Ha! See? You are getting it now, my brother. Yes, she showed me walking here. So that is what I did," Matteo replied with a satisfied smile. "So, shall we climb to the Tor together?"

After they had both finished their plates of food, they walked up the High Street together. The early morning sun had surrendered to the clouds, leading to a light rain typical for this time of year. The majority of stores were now open to the public, and despite Ethan's initial impressions of the town, a fair amount of weekend tourists were now visiting the various novelty shops available. Matteo stopped in front of one shop in particular: The Nine Realms, a small blue-framed storefront with little visibility inside. The display showcased many figures, books, candles, and oddities.

"Woah, I can't believe the things they sell here. In my hometown, I think they still burn witches," Matteo exclaimed.

"Really? There are a lot of stores in London that sell this crap too," Ethan replied.

"Do you think it's crap? So you've purchased things before?"

"What? No, I just—you know the whole witchy vibe. Ever since those Harry Potter books, it's been all the rage in England."

"We should go in. Let us see some of these things. Experience the town!" Matteo said, smiling, already opening the door to go inside.

Ethan paused, debating whether to follow him in.

Matteo stuck his head out. "Come, my friend. We take today together!"

"Fine." Ethan shuffled in like a child forced to go to church.

Inside, the store was surprisingly large; however, it felt smaller due to the many shelves and displays full of endless items that were indistinguishable between "for sale" and "for display." Upon stepping into the threshold, Ethan was greeted by a familiar noise: the running of many little paws on the floor. Five of Zoe's dogs ran toward him, jumping up and down on his leg.

"Ethan! So good to see you. How's things?" Zoe exclaimed, appearing from around a display of candles.

"Hey. Zoe, right? Sorry, I don't remember all of the little nut names."

"Oh, it's alright! Everyone always gets them confused. Even I forget half the time. Just make up new ones if I do."

"Ethan, you already have such a pretty friend in town? Nice!" Matteo said with excitement.

"Pretty? Oh, stop it. Just a mad bog witch trying to get by." Zoe blushed. "Ethan, one day and already meeting people? Told you this place was wicked good."

"Didn't really have a choice. We just met."

"That's how it works here. You'll be friends for life now. That's a Glastonbury guarantee," she said, putting out finger guns to both Matteo and Ethan while she winked.

Ethan took a moment to study Zoe for the first time in detail. She appeared to be in her mid-to-late thirties, with messy brunette hair kept in a loose bun and a short fringe. She had a beautiful smile that took up most of her chin, and deep brown eyes that carried an innocent depth. Her figure was hidden by unfitting clothing of various sizes—some too small, others far too big.

Matteo interrupted Ethan's appraisal of Zoe. "Is this your shop?"

"Me? A businesswoman? Do I look like one?" Zoe said with sudden seriousness.

"Yes?" Matteo said, unsure of himself.

"Shit! Well, I will need to try harder to look more crazy then. Hate that you had me made! Yes, this is my little shop of wonders, horrors, and everything in between." She made her snorted laugh that was now all too familiar to Ethan.

"Wow! So amazing, you are so young. And with so many employees too!" Matteo leaned down to play with her crazed group of dogs, all begging for attention.

"Alright, alright, stop flirting with me in that cute accent! What are you two getting into today?"

"We will climb the Tor!" Matteo answered, now completely on the ground.

"Yeah, take in the town, I think," Ethan added unenthusiastically.

"What about the White Springs?" Zoe asked.

"What is that?"

"Only the most sacred spring in all of Avalon! Probably. You must go—right below the Tor, on the way. You can't miss it. Near the Red Spring as well."

"Thank you so much, Zoe." Matteo said, coming off the floor to give her a hug. "Will you not come with us?"

"Ah, well, you see, I am this big businesswoman, so I do need to run my shop at least for the morning rush."

Ethan looked around at the morning rush… it was only the three of them in the store.

"How about I join you on the Tor afterwards? Been a while since I climbed the ol' sacred hill myself."

"Yes! We would love that. You can tell me about the history, yes?" Matteo answered.

"Of course. See you in about two hours, right outside the White Spring?"

"Sounds good," Ethan said, feeling claustrophobic and wanting to leave the store, edging slowly towards the door.

"Great. Now come here, you two!" Zoe reached out and grabbed Ethan back in to give him a large hug. Then she hugged Matteo as well, who acted as though he was being hugged by a mother, with a warm smile appearing on his face.

"Oh! I should buy something from you to exchange for the information," Matteo insisted.

"You don't have to! Perfectly normal advice to give new adventurers to our weird little slice of Avalon."

"Please, allow me to support you, so you can continue to be kind to others," Matteo said more seriously, looking deep into Zoe's eyes. She gestured for him to look around.

Matteo studied each item carefully. Ethan was feeling increasingly more uncomfortable, so he made a quick escape to the street to breathe the lighter air. His heart was racing; he couldn't find a return to a steady breath, something he had struggled with all his life. For some time he had been placed on medication for anxiety, but he had stopped taking it before he left for Glastonbury. Learning to deal with his anxiety on his own was something he desired, but feared. Ethan was able to pull himself together just as Matteo walked out with a small bag.

"Such a lovely woman. So happy you got to meet her, are you okay, my friend?"

"Fine. What did you buy?"

Matteo paused for a moment, then smiled. "I will show you when we get to the White Springs."

2
The White Springs

The road leading to the Tor breaks off the high street at the top of the slight hill to the right. The road snakes along several small districts of houses with a few pop-up shops along the way. An old inn is the only business until the Red and White Springs. Upon getting closer to the springs, the walking path becomes elevated from the road and runs right in front of several residential spaces, many with "Temple" advertised on the front windows once again. Near the top of the hill, the walk becomes more dramatic, and the views of the Tor begin to appear behind the trees. On the left comes first the Red Springs, which are tucked away in a world peace garden with a beautiful entrance and small visitor center. Around the corner from the Red Springs is the water-soaked path to the White Springs. There came a moment where Ethan and Matteo can see a dirt path that carries on to the Glastonbury Tor and the path forward that goes to a large square building resting on the side of the hill.

"It's very wet," Ethan remarked while watching a steady stream of water flow from the brutalist square ahead. "Is that the White Springs? It doesn't look as nice as the red one."

"The only way to know is to go!" Matteo said, laughing at his own rhyme.

The pair walked further down the shadowed street towards the source of the water's flow. As they got closer, they could see several people waiting outside of the structure, many of whom were centered around a space between the springs and a small carriage house. Within this space were several fountains pouring forth water from the stone wall behind them. Many of the onlookers outside had flasks for collecting drinking water from a single tap on the side of the main structure. Matteo put down his pack to pull out his own water bottle.

"Come, Ethan. Let us try some of this holy water."

"I do not have a bottle with me."

"Then at least come try it," Matteo replied as he joined the queue of people waiting for a taste of the special water. "Excuse me, friend. What is special about this water?" Matteo asked the man in front of him.

"Pardon. Oh— hi! First time at the springs, I see. Don't know what's so special about it, to be honest. We just all drink the stuff!" The man answered in a thick Dorset accent.

"Ah, the whole town drinks this water?"

"Why, of course! Either this'n or the red water from over there," he said, pointing towards the opposite stone wall with another tap sourcing from the Red Springs on the other side. "To be honest with you, though, I prefer the white water myself. The red water tastes like a bloody penny!"

The man then stepped up and retrieved his water, allowing Matteo to come and fill his bottle. After filling it to the brim, he took a drink. "Woah. This is special water. Here, give it a drink, Ethan!" he said, handing his bottle over.

Ethan took a sip and found it to taste remarkably like water. "Tastes like water."

"Yes, water. But can't you feel its energy? I can feel something in it." Matteo took another long drink, then filled the bottle up once more.

"It tastes like good water!" Ethan said, trying to seem enthusiastic.

"For my time here, I believe I will drink only from these waters for the duration. Then I will be able to tell you if it is truly special."

"And how long is that? How long will you stay?"

"Until I have fulfilled my purpose for being here."

"What is your purpose for being here?"

"That is the best part! I do not know!" Matteo said, laughing deeply. "Come, let us go inside." Matteo went to the front of the square stone structure to find a golden gate half-opened towards an extremely dark room. He looked deeper inside, then turned his head back towards Ethan with an excited, child-like expression on his face and disappeared into the darkness of the springs.

Ethan approached the golden gate with caution. From within, he could hear the sounds of running water but little else. The entrance was that of a dark abyss, swallowing all light that entered from the outside. He heard a man gasp, and then afterwards came a loud splash.

"What have I gotten myself into…" Ethan thought, clenching his fist, breathing in deep, and going inside.

As he walked in, he was greeted by stone stairs that led down into a large central chamber. In front was a large white sign on which several rules were written:

WELCOME TO THE WHITE SPRINGS
NO PHOTOGRAPHY
NO PHONES
PLEASE BE QUIET
RESPECT THE SPACE OR BE REMOVED
NUDITY IN PROGRESS.

The last line caught Ethan off guard, but not as much as looking up and seeing that there were, in fact, several naked people sitting on the edge of a large central basin filled with water. The White Spring was a large central room made up of walls containing brick and stone. The only lighting came from hundreds of candles that lined the walls, adorned all flat surfaces, and hung from small chandeliers. Wax covered the floors and dribbled down every surface. The central basin was around 15 feet in diameter and sat between four massive pillars. The water was being funneled from a waterfall in the left corner of the room that cascaded down into several levels of baths and smaller basins leading towards the center.

The water spilled over the sides of the central pool, creating many puddles and flows of water that led outside, forming the flowing streams onto the street. As Ethan walked down the stairs into the waterlogged stone flooring, he saw a very intense and tall man standing near a wooden hutch. The man was hooded; only his greying beard could be seen under the shadows of the cowl. His skin was dark, which only made it more difficult to make out his features. The man's eyes were shadowed; however, this did not stop Ethan from feeling his gaze lock directly into his own. Ethan averted his eyes, pretending not to have looked. The man did not say a word but bowed gently towards Ethan and beckoned him in.

Ethan's eyes were beginning to adjust, allowing him to see that around the two central pillars were two sides tucked away from initial visions. To the right was a hall that was just as grand and imposing as the rest of the room. More candles lined the walls and carried Ethan's vision to a corner where a wooden gateway had been created to separate a space tucked away from the rest. In the opposite corner came natural light from a gated-off side door that sat across from a small skylight. To the left of the central chamber, a near-identical hall existed where another tucked-away corner was out of sight, and Matteo was standing, taking off his clothes.

"What are you doing?" Ethan whispered in a rushed tone.

"What do you mean? I am taking a dip. Do you not see the others doing it?"

"Yes, but we don't have any bathing suits. It's not proper."

"Oh, I forgot England is not like the rest of Europe. You are still ashamed of your bodies," Matteo replied without remorse.

"It's not that we are ashamed! We are just more, well—proper!" Ethan retorted, raising his voice. "I will not do it!"

"That is okay. I will go in then. I cannot make you," Matteo responded, then took off more clothes, revealing his underwear.

"Christ, Matteo! What is this? Some sick way to see me naked!"

"We are two men. Are you not comfortable around naked men? This is so common."

"Not to us!" Ethan's voice had been loud too long. He felt the firm hand of the hooded man behind him. His presence alone told Ethan to quiet down. "Sorry, I am sorry," he said more quietly.

"My brother, if this is too much for you, we will go. But is there a reason you fear this so much?" Matteo asked.

"I just— it's not proper."

"According to who?"

"To bloody society."

"Society is why we take the medicine for our anxiety. Anxiety caused by society. My brother, this is the medicine of water," Matteo reassured.

"My parents would not approve."

"The water is the medicine, my brother." With that, Matteo smiled and then walked deeper into the dark room to remove the remainder of his clothing and climb into the water. As Matteo entered, his breath was taken from him. He let out a small deep gasp and then went out of sight, leaving Ethan alone to his thoughts:

"Fuck, what if he is right? The meds were shit. I am shit for needing to take them. No, no, no. This dude is crazy. Walking from bloody Italy, taking in the sunrise like some kind of fairy princess. Dad would look at him and be like,

'That's not what men do.' But do men take anxiety meds? Do men smash their computer at work? Do men sit in an office all bloody fucking day to the sound of clacking keyboards?"

He removed his shoes.

"What is he on about society for? Society says it's proper to wear clothes because we are not bloody animals. Pissin' and shittin' everywhere. I am not a bloody animal. I dress nice, I keep my hair up, I trim my beard, I go to the gym, I take vitamins. I am not a bloody animal."

He removed his jacket.

"Of course I am an animal. Look at me. Teeth too big, eyes too small, belly too flabby, arms not big enough. I am just an ugly freak of an animal. This is why I don't have a girlfriend. This is why I will die alone."

He removed his shirt.

"Death. Fucking death. Just waiting around the corner. What will it be? High blood pressure? That got Gran. Cancer? That got Joseph. Car accident? 10,000 a rotten year; I could be next. What's that mark on my arm? Melanoma, probably. What about a knife? Just get stabbed eating a fucking sausage roll these days!"

He removed his pants.

"Food now, that has always been my downfall. Ate a whole Scottish this morning. What did I do that for? Got enough to worry about without packing on weight again. Remember primary school? Everyone laughing at chubby little ugly fuck."

He removed his underwear.

"Fuck it."

He stepped into the water… Silence.

—

Ethan's mind froze as his body went into survival mode. The water was the coldest that he had ever felt in his life. The air was stripped from his lungs; the blood flowed from the surface of his body to deep within to keep his organs warm. He looked up to see Matteo and several others sitting in a circle of the spring— five men and seven women — all closed in and focused on frozen meditation. Ethan's eyes flickered to a beautiful woman with her breasts visible above the surface of the water. But he quickly looked away, feeling no desire nor sexual lust. In that moment, they were all just amorphous humans, pale, shivering, and silent.

Matteo sat up and moved to a deeper section of the pool, fully submerging for only a moment before the temperature drove him out to gasp for the warming air. Ethan's mind was still blank. He could not think of work, family, dying, or any of the other fears that consumed him only moments ago. There was only this moment and only the growing desire to get out to warm himself. He looked around and saw that some were getting out of the water, giving him the cue that he could do the same. His arms felt numb, his feet tingled, and his eyes were fixated on only what was in front of him.

When getting out, he realized he had no towel or other way to dry himself. Ethan looked around in a panic for anyone who might be able to help. No words could leave his frozen lips to plead for aid; he was forced to be still while exposed in the dark room. The glow of a nearby candle attracted him, the warmth beckoning him in to get close. He felt entranced by the flickering light, dancing to a sacred rhythm. He lost himself in the flame, so much so he almost didn't feel the gentle placement of a towel on his shoulder. Mechanically, he reached up, not seeing the person who had given it to him; he began to dry his body. With every surface he rubbed, he could feel the warmth returning to his skin.

Ethan's mind began to defrost, allowing him to turn from the enchanting flame to see that no one around appeared to be missing a towel... Matteo was in the water. All that had gotten out with him were getting dressed in private against the wall. When Ethan was finished drying, he got dressed and placed the gifted towel gently onto a small bench that was tucked against the stone wall— figuring whoever gave it to him would come and collect it. Matteo's paled body appeared over the lip of the well and procured a towel from his large backpack. He, too, was completely silent and stared directly ahead, transfixed in his cleared mind.

The running of the water into the various pools was the only noise that echoed on the chamber walls. Ethan looked around and caught his eyes looking at the small room tucked away in the opposite corner from the waterfall. It appeared to be a dark tunnel with wooden branches woven to create a cylindrical tube that led to a statue of a pregnant woman kneeling with a stoic expression. On instinct, Ethan walked into the tunnel to sit before the statue of the woman, his expression now mirroring that of the statue. Around her crossed legs were flowers at various levels of decay. There were also several candles, crystals, jewels, and half-burned notes left before her visage.

Matteo appeared next to Ethan with the small bag from Zoe's store in his hand.

"Shall we?" he whispered, reaching in and procuring two small candles with notes pressed into the wax.

"What are these?"

"Prayers," Matteo answered, handing the green candle to Ethan.

"What are we praying for?"

"Zoe said that these candles contain sacred words and prayers already within them. Perhaps we do not need to know ourselves." Matteo reached out his arm and lit his blue candle, then placed it on the altar.

"What would I pray for?" Ethan thought, studying his candle. "I never liked church. Boring waste of Sunday." Still, he pondered. Not finding an answer, he lit his candle anyway to expedite the experience and not leave Matteo waiting.

They spent a moment of reflection watching their candles burn before getting up and making their way to the entrance of the spring once more. Beyond the golden gate, the sun could be seen warming the day. This excited the companions, who were still feeling the effects of the spring. They both walked up the stone stairs and looked to leave.

"Healing," came a deep voice directed towards Ethan. He looked behind to see that it had come from the hooded caretaker of the springs, whose face was now visible in the glow of the sun's radiance. His eyes were as dark as his skin; the grey beard only covered his chin, and his aura of intensity sat thick on his expression. He held his gaze for only a moment longer before returning it to the shadows of the chamber.

Outside, Ethan and Matteo allowed their eyes to adjust to the warming sun, allowing the rays to soak deep into their skin. Neither of the two had words to say, nor did they wish to speak through the calm that had been gifted to them. Yet in unison, they stepped out into the street and looked back at the White Springs in gratitude and wonder. Then they both turned and made their way down the water-lined path to the entrance of the Tor.

Zoe came around the stone wall of the Red Spring just as Matteo and Ethan had reached the end of the street.

“Perfect Avalon timing!” she snorted.

“How was the morning rush?” asked Ethan with a peaceful tone.

“Ah, well. A couple of candles, a couple of books sold. Good enough for me today! What about you two? I can tell by your faces that something happened. How was it?”

“Yes, incredible. Thank you,” Matteo answered with a small nod of his head. “Where are all of your little friends?” he asked, looking to see she had none of her dogs with her.

“Little dogs are great companions but absolutely rubbish climbers. I just live upstairs of the shop, so I tucked ’em away with some treats. They’ll be fine for a bit while we climb the Tor! Exciting. Your first time!” Her energy seemed to only increase now that she did not have her minions holding her down. “Shall we?” She put her arms around both Matteo and Ethan, and they walked together up the path towards the hill.

The path was steep at first as they passed by a small sign detailing the history of the Glastonbury Tor.

"Oh, don't worry about that! I will tell you the real history!" she said, scoffing at the aged sign.

"What was the Tor originally?" asked Ethan.

"Well, that's always interesting. Everyone says the Tor, but technically the building is St. Michael's Tower and it sit's on the Glastonbury Tor. But most people will just say the Tor. There was originally a church here after the Saxons came. But in the 1200s, there was this massive earthquake that destroyed the church. Some say a wrath of the old gods."

"So the tower is from then?"

"No, no. Even after this big bloody earthquake, they thought it would be a good idea to build an even bigger church. Then in the 1500s, they started taking down all the old churches and abbeys, and for some reason, they left the tower here. Even though it used to be a church, most people would consider the Tor a very pagan site," she answered with expert confidence.

They now reached the first level of the climb, which opened up to a large meadow that allowed for views of the town below and the continuing rise up. From here, the Tor did not seem so far away, nestled on top of a large hill behind another hill. It did not look very tall or very far from where the trio stood now. They could see they were not alone in this journey to the top; several dozen other groups were at various stages of the climb ahead of them.

"Pagan? What do you mean?" questioned Ethan.

"By the Gods, you really had no idea where you signed up for a two-week holiday, do you?" she jested. "Yes, Pagans. Witches, wizards, shamans, druids, healers, oracles, the whole lot consider Glastonbury to be a holy place. But of course, the Christians believe so as well. Even the Buddhists and Hindus all claim some sort of sacredness to this place. Hell, King Arthur is said to be buried right back in town. Merlin probably cast some of his spells from atop this very hill!"

"You must be joking. Come on."

"Who is King Arthur?" Matteo added.

"You are like two lost boys! Don't worry, Zoe has you covered!"

They continued on their journey up the increasingly steep hill. Zoe shared with them the various legends of the land, from King Arthur to secret cave entrances to the fairy world, and even a story about a sleeping dragon being contained within the hill the tower sat on. The further they climbed, the more the tower became visible to them in the distance, appearing to grow out of the earth, just like the very legends Zoe was sharing. The higher they climbed, the stronger the wind got as well.

"Bloody hell! This wind is insane!" Ethan shouted between gusts.

"Cavolo! Is this the dragon's wings?" yelled Matteo.

"It only gets more intense the closer we get! Hold on to your butts!" Zoe seemed to be enjoying watching them fight the invisible forces of the Tor.

"Who thought this would be a good place for a church?" said Ethan.

"The Druids!" returned Zoe.

They had now reached the second hill that sat before the final path towards the tower. The path now snaked ahead in a way that did, in fact, mimic something similar to the spine of a dragon. Ethan took this time to catch his breath and look around him. The views from the top were more stunning than he could have imagined. Like no other place in England, he had seen such views of the land around him. The Tor sat isolated in the middle of a massive valley of fields and small villages in every direction. To the west, he could see Glastonbury town. He saw the street in which he was staying, St. Benedict's, where he met Selene. The whole of all of his experiences these next two weeks would be confined within his view right now. Matteo came next to him and sat down in the grass to take in the view as well.

"This is the most beautiful view I have seen in this country so far. No, in all of this journey. I can see it now, the reason the druids chose this spot."

"Imagine that only a few thousand years ago this hill was a true island! When the ocean levels were higher, this place would have only been accessible during low tide. Otherwise, it would be protected by the spirits of the sea," Zoe told them.

Ethan could see it now, the legends of this valley. He was not convinced that any dragon was kept in the earth, nor could he see a secret tunnel to the fairy world existing below him, but he could see why people were so captivated by its view.

"Come, come! It only gets better the closer we get."

Matteo and Ethan took in the view for another moment, then continued their way up the snaking path. The tower was completely visible to them; it was, in fact, an old cathedral tower standing isolated in a sky of whipping wind. The structure was hollow, with only a single doorless entry that passed straight through to the other side. There were little markings of Christianity left on the building; it appeared more like an old castle tower, with a turret placement at the top where the roof used to be. The tower was made up of four minor levels of increasingly smaller size that all fused together to create the imposing image that so many people had gathered under. The autumn air was cool, and the wind acted like a hail of arrows coming from the top of the tower, penetrating through the clothing of Ethan and Matteo.

The majority of people were congregated on the north side of the tower, which was shielded from the southerly winds. First, Zoe led them into the open gateway into the center of the tower, where several others were taking shelter. Ethan entered first to a jarring difference in noise. Away from the constant pressure of the wind, he was greeted by the sound of drums and bells being played. The people within the tower were playing music and dancing— many of them younger— there was also an older man whom Ethan had seen earlier in town. He was wearing a pirate outfit, was barefoot, and had a long grey beard. He was dancing in the center, entranced by the music.

"Who is that?" Ethan whispered to Zoe.

"That? Oh, that's crazy ol' Owen! A fixture of this little town. He is almost always up here. Careful; if he catches you, he is a bit mad."

"What do you mean mad?"

"You know, mad. Like a bit crazy. He is always spouting crazy things to new people in town. I bet he stops by if he sees you one day."

"Great, I have that to look forward to now," Ethan thought. "I should also ask her about the man in the springs…"

"Zoe, what about the man in the springs? What's his deal? Kind of a creepy fucker."

"Who? Silus? He takes care of the springs. Really intense man. Hardly speaks to most visitors"

"He spoke to me."

"Really? What did he—" She was cut off by the music changing rhythm and a loud horn being blown.

Ethan looked to see Matteo had now joined the dancers and had a rattle in his hand. Zoe rushed into the fray of growing dancers in the tiny space.

"Come on, Ethan! Join us!" she shouted back at him. The party of dancers and musicians now spilled out into the windswept hill.

Ethan began to feel overwhelmed once again. He stepped out the other gateway of the Tor to the calmer east-facing slope. The music was carried away into the horizon; he was now left with the deadening silence of the wind rushing by him as he looked out into the distance. It was past midday now.

"What the fuck is happening? Ancient springs? Wizards? Towers? Fairies? Italians? This is not London. This is not London… this is not home. But… what is home? What is home?" His mind was racing for the first time since he left the White Springs. He looked around to see that Crazy Owen had broken away from the party and was now dancing his way towards Ethan.

"Fuck, stay away, you crazy bastard. I do not need you messing with me right now," Ethan nearly said aloud.

Owen had now made eye contact with Ethan, who looked away as he did in the springs. This did not stop the old man from approaching with something in his hand.

"Got a loight?" he asked in a thick Somerset accent.

"A what?"

"Tryin' to loight up. You got a loighter?"

"Oh, no, I don't."

"Ah, shit." He then rummaged around in his pirate jacket and found what he was looking for. "Ha! 'ad one in me other pocket, I did." Owen then lit up his joint and stood next to Ethan. "Do ya smoke?" he asked, handing him the joint.

"Well, yeah, but not a lot."

"Where are ye from?"

"London."

"Then ya must give it a try. This 'ere's the finest weed in Somerset. I grows it meself, I do." he said, gesturing his hand out once more.

Ethan reluctantly took it and drew a quick puff.

"Is that how you London lot smoke these days? Come on now, take a proper inhale, hold it, then breathe out like a man. Calm yerself." he said with a surprisingly reassuring voice.

Ethan obeyed, took the joint one more time, took in deeply, held, and released the thick cloud of smoke that was quickly taken away in the wind. As he went to hand it back, Owen put his hand up.

"Keep it, brother. Could tell ya needed it. I'll have a word with ya when you're ready." Owen said, glaring deeply at Ethan as if he was looking at his very soul. He then started dancing, smiled like a crazy person once again, and made his way back to the party on the other side of the hill. Ethan stood there in disbelief, looked down at the joint, shrugged, and took another drag.

"This fucking town, man," he said aloud with a smile.

Ethan walked from one side of the hill to the other, taking in the endlessly stunning views from all sides. The clouds were thick and scattered, leading to moments of sun followed by moments of grey clouds. Occasionally, rain would sprinkle onto his face. He smoked the entire joint and was feeling very light. But not uncomfortable, like he had in the past smoking pot. It had always given him more anxiety, not less, when he smoked it with his friends back in the city. The city that now felt a million miles away from where he was standing right now.

"Hey! You alright?" Zoe's voice came from behind him as he was taking the last puff of Owen's weed.

"Yeah, I just get overwhelmed. Fun party, though, it seems."

"Our Italian friend certainly took to it. He is still over there."

"Is it always like this here?"

"Yes, in a way. The only constant in the lands of Avalon is the fact that we are in a special place. You really never know what you will come across."

"I am starting to get that," laughed Ethan. "Alright, so we did the White Springs. We have climbed the Tor. What's next?"

"What's next? Well, this is about it! High street, Tor Springs. That's Glastonbury!"

"Come on, that can't be it."

"Well, there is also the Abbey, a big park in the center of town. Really nice. You can do the Red Springs if you'd like. Then, well, yeah, a few nice walks around the fields."

"So I have seen almost everything. In one day," Ethan said in despair.

"Ethan, Glastonbury isn't about what you see. It's about what you experience," she said with a gentle smile.

"So what should I experience next then?"

"Well, I hear Isla is having a circle tomorrow. For newcomers, actually. So that would be perfect!"

"A circle? A circle of what?"

"Sharing, of course."

"More hippie shit," he thought. "Fine, yeah, I will go. Where is it?"

"Freyja's Hall. Right in the center; you can't miss it. I will go with you to make sure you actually go," she said, pushing him gently in a joking way.

It was in this moment that Ethan looked more deeply at her, feeling warmth grow in his chest. "Am I starting to like her?" he thought, feeling himself blush. "Yeah, sure. What time?"

"Half past seven. Meet you outside of my shop around then?"

"Yeah, that would be perfect."

There was nothing left to be said, which led to a moment of the two standing alone in the shadow of the Tor.

"Well, I should be going. I honestly have to get some shopping done, unpack, and get myself sorted. Feeling a bit dirty despite my dip today."

"Yeah, get to that, you filthy fucker!" she exclaimed. "I am going to stay up here a bit. Know your way back?"

"I think so. Pretty sure I can see where to go from up here," he gestured to Benedict Street in the distance.

"Oh, wonderful. Well, I hope you have had a good first day in Glastonbury. So happy to have you here!" She hugged him and then left for the party on the hill once more, turning briefly to wave to him.

Ethan took one last view of the panorama of the Tor, collected himself, and headed back towards the path down the hill. As he walked by the group of people dancing at the front, he could see Matteo lost in the crowd, still playing his rattle. He thought of saying goodbye but decided it would be best to make a quick escape before he was dragged into something else. So he took to the path down the Tor alone, back towards the town and his room nestled away in the Temple of Artemis.

—

He was carrying several bags of groceries through the door of his Bed and Breakfast when he saw the white robes hanging in the entrance.

"Fuck," he said aloud. "I forgot about these crazy rules. I will slip in quickly first." He plotted, dashing inside towards the kitchen to drop off his groceries. By the time he had the bags on the counter, he turned around to see Cardea behind him with a white robe in hand. She looked very disappointed.

"Sorry, sorry. Busy day. Had all these bags."

She looked at him, uninterested in his reasoning, gesturing the white robe to him. He reluctantly accepted and went towards the entrance once again to take his coat off and change into the robe. When he returned to the kitchen, Vesta had now joined Cardea in rummaging through his groceries.

"Hey, what are you doing?"

Vesta procured a pack of sausages out of his bag and held them up to Ethan. She, too, looked very disappointed.

"Ah, come on. I forgot. Won't happen again."

Vesta ran over to the corner of the kitchen and threw his sausages in the bin.

"Fuck's sake. I just bought those! I am paying to be here; this is crazy! Are you going to pay me back?" he shouted at them, looking for an answer.

Cardea pondered for a moment, then left for the back garden for a moment and came back with a handful of dirt-covered carrots and offered them to Ethan.

"What, oh come on. Carrots for sausages?"

She smiled and placed them in his bag with grace. Vesta completed her inspection of his purchases, seemed satisfied at no other meats being within, then took Cardea's hand and returned to the adjoining room of the house, leaving Ethan alone in the kitchen.

"Fucking Christ," Ethan muttered, distributing the remainder of his groceries to the pantry and the fridge before heading upstairs with a bag of crisps to be left alone.

"Glad I got something to eat before coming back. Looks like I will need to continue to eat my meat in secret. Away from the vegan Nazis down there."

Ethan took to unpacking his suitcase and distributing the clothes into the wardrobe, pulling his toiletries out to go take a long hot shower. He still felt his bones shivering from the dip in the White Springs. Feeling the scalding water pour down his limbs was the best feeling he had all day. He was also still a little stoned from Owen's weed, which certainly was helping his nerves around the house's strange rules.

After his shower, he came out to see the sun was already setting, and he had little more to do than to lay in his bed wrapped in his towel and think of the day.

"Could use a bloody TV right now. How can they not have a TV in this room? What am I supposed to do..."

He lay there exhausted, high, drained. Thoughts worked their way back into his mind. Thoughts of work, thoughts of his mom, his friends. He looked at his mobile to see he had no missed calls from anyone.

"Fuck. No one cares that I have disappeared, it seems."

He tried calling his mom. She answered but was already drunk. Only talked about herself, what she was doing, and what her latest lover had told her. He didn't speak about his day at all by the time he had hung up the phone from her.

"Fuck. I hate when I get like this. Wish I had more weed. I wish I could jump in the spring again. Silence my thoughts."

He lay there battling himself, hating himself, arguing with himself for what seemed like hours until sleep finally took him.

3
Jai Maa Saraswati

Clack, tap

"Ethan."

Clack, tap

"Ethan, my brother!"

Matteo was on the street below the bay window, throwing small pebbles up towards Ethan's room. After a third rock was thrown, Ethan appeared at the window with a rather upset expression on his face.

"What the hell, man? What time is it?" he grumbled.

"Early. I just came from the Tor. You have to come."

"Why should I do that?"

"Because we are men, with two good legs, and are alive! We must use this time—"

"Use this time to bloody sleep." Ethan went to close the window.

"Come, I will buy you a coffee and we will walk together!" Matteo pleaded.

Ethan climbed back into bed, trying to close his eyes again. But then it hit him, and he went back to the window to find Matteo still below.

"How did you know where I am staying?"

"The woman."

"What woman?"

"The one in the garden, down by the church."

"Selene?" he thought. "And you have been at the Tor all night long?"

"Yes. It was amazing!"

"You are a crazy man! Fine, fine. I am coming down. Only because I think you are a nutter, you hear me?"

"Ha! Yes, my brother!" Matteo's face lit up with excitement.

Ethan got dressed in his normal clothes without putting the white robe on in hopes that he would be able to slip out quickly without being noticed. Luckily, it appeared everyone was still asleep at "six in the bloody morning," Ethan thought as he looked at his watch while putting it on. The day looked gray and cool, so he grabbed his raincoat on the way out the door to be greeted by a hug from his Italian companion.

"Buongiorno, amico mio! Tell me, who do you stay with here?"

"Two sirens."

"As in, the stories of Odysseus sirens?"

"Yeah, but these don't talk and just stare at you till your soul is ripped out of your body."

"Woah. Sounds intense. Are they beautiful like sirens?"

"Sadly, very."

"Then I am happy to save you. Come, come." Matteo gestured towards the town center.

"Where are we going so early anyway?"

"You will see."

"No, I will go back to bed."

"No, you won't. And you will enjoy yourself. I promise."

"He is right; already up, might as well get coffee," thought Ethan. "So really, no sleep last night?"

"No, I slept a little on the Tor. We sang and danced until the moon came out. It was beautiful. So many great people."

"Had to be freezing up there, man!"

"Yes and no; there was a small camp at the bottom of the hill in the forest. We had a small fire and a place to sleep," answered Matteo.

They were walking up to the church gardens where Selene was already starting her morning routine. She saw them and waved.

"I see you found him," she called.

"Yes, yes, I did. Thank you for your assistance, lady of the garden!"

"My name is Selene," she corrected.

"I would appreciate it if you didn't tell everyone where I slept at night," Ethan butted in.

"Oh, I am sorry. I didn't know it was a secret."

"Of course it is! It's common privacy."

"Your friend here seemed to be of a good sort, and I have excellent judgment of character. That's why I am so happy you two met. You need each other." She released the smile at the end while looking towards Ethan.

"What does that mean?" he asked.

"You will see. Now go get your coffees. I need to tend to the garden."

Ethan and Matteo finished their walk to The Andrews Cross, where Isla and Hamish were already beginning their morning routine. They ordered coffees inside, and Matteo asked them for take away.

"Whit are yous getting intae today then?" asked Hamish.

"We will go to the Tor to see the sunrise," Matteo responded.

"Aye, you better hurry then, lads. Sun will be up soon," Hamish replied, getting to work on their coffees. "Whit about ye, Ethan? Any plans?"

"Oh, yeah, actually. I got invited to some kind of sharing circle?"

"Ye're comin' tae my circle the night?" Isla came in from outside with a smile on her face. "Oh, good! I'll be chuffed tae see ye both there. It'll be grand tae see so many new faces the night."

"I had no idea. When were you going to tell me, Ethan?" Matteo jested.

"I wasn't," Ethan thought. "After the coffees, naturally."

"Wonderful. Isla, should we bring anything with us?" asked Matteo.

"Jist a willin'ness tae share. An' a journal if ye fancy it."

Hamish placed their coffees in front of them. "On me today. Thanks for supporting my wife in her group tonight."

"Will you be there?" Matteo asked.

"Fuck no. Not my scene. Bunch o' people cryin' aboot their problems. I havenae the stomach for it. Would shake every one o' them…" Isla glared at him from across the shop. "But! I hope you boys like it, and I'm sure it'll be grand!" He leaned in as if not to be heard. "Jist don't let them talk aboot boyfriends an' the like. Ye'll be there all bloody night." He winked.

"See you tonight then, lads! So looking forward tae learning more about yous!" Isla said as they left the building.

The morning air was cool with a slight breeze from the west. The coffee invigorated Ethan enough to carry him up the now familiar path towards the Tor. Matteo spoke with him nearly the whole walk about the various people he had met the night before. Ethan nodded lifelessly and paid little attention to what he had to say. His mind was foggy and lacked interest in anything besides getting the caffeine faster into his bloodstream.

There were very few people awake at this hour; a few homeless were sleeping in the nooks and crannies of the shops and side streets. As they rounded the corner, they came across a large mural on one of the sides of the building. It was of a winged woman with golden hair riding a horse.

"Holy shit." The sight snapped Ethan out of his sleep coma. "This wasn't here yesterday."

"No, I did not see it either. Someone must have made it last night. It is gorgeous!"

"Why does that woman look familiar?" Ethan asked.

"I am not sure. I think the same. Perhaps a famous artist lives here?"

"Must be; this is some serious commitment. What are those letters?" Ethan said, pointing out the etchings below the picture's frame:

ᛊᛖᛚᛚᛖᚾᛖ : ᚺᛁᚾ : ᚠᚨᛚᛚᛖᚷᚨ

"I have no clue. It is like the Greek, but different?" Matteo responded. The pair studied the drawing for a moment longer and then continued on their brisk journey towards the Tor.

—

When they reached the path leading up to the top of the hill, Matteo led them towards a side route into a small patch of woodland. The trees were small but dense, covering the view of the Tor and its tower quickly from their sight. The leaves were turning bright shades of yellow and orange as time moved deeper into October. Small trees gave way to larger neighbors the closer Matteo and Ethan got to the base of the Tor. There one trail became many, going in several directions along the woodland and into the fields beyond.

"Where are we going?"

"There is an orchard just past here. Apples just falling from the tree for us to eat."

"We came all this way to eat apples?"

"Yes and no! There is something else. Almost there now."

The orchard Matteo was mentioning came into view on the downward slope coming out of the forest. Beyond the orchard were several distant farmhouses; within it, there were several people moving around the center of the grove. Many of the people seemed to be carrying various musical instruments and boxes with them. Each person was in a completely different costume; some were dressed as hippies, others fairly normal, and then the few in the center of the growing circle were wearing Indian-styled costumes; despite the lack of Indians present.

"What are you dragging me into?"

"These are my new friends!"

"Are they supposed to be Indian?"

"I do not know if they are Indian. But I believe they said they are Hindu."

The group was setting up a small altar in the middle of the circle, with images of several of the Hindu deities who were unknown to Ethan. Their instruments were finely crafted, covered in gold and silver, made of finely treated wood, and all well-maintained. In total, there were 32 people in the orchard, all eating the apples and discussing politely amongst one another. One of the finely dressed musicians moved forward to address everyone.

"Last week we celebrated the end of Navaratri. Our beautiful women ended their fast and joined us in a great feast to Durga. Today we are here to—"

"What the fuck is he talking about?" Ethan whispered to Matteo; they were now sitting under an apple tree on the edge of the congregation.

"Shhh," Matteo responded.

"I do not know what anything he is on about," Ethan said to Matteo, who had stopped listening.

"— our music will be to the Goddess Saraswati. May she guide us in the coming winter!"

Light clapping followed by instruments being tuned, and then a warmth began to spread across the orchard as the sun pierced through the thick morning clouds. The faces of the musicians lit up with smiles, and then they began to sing:

"Saraswati, Ma Saraswati,
Veena Vadini Var De,

Jnan Ki Jyoti Se Humko,
Gyaan Ki Disha Tu Dede."

"Fuck, I hate singing," Ethan muttered.

"Everyone now!" cried the presenter.

"Jai Maa Saraswati,
Jai Maa Saraswati,
Vani, Vidya, Vardhini,
Shubh Buddhi Tu De De."

"What are they even saying?"

Matteo looked over to Ethan, sensing his unease. "My brother, relax."

"This just isn't for me."

"Maa Vidya Ki Devi,
Sada Sahayak Rehna,
Hath Mein Tere Veena,
Aur Kitab Rehna."

"We are human. Humans sing. It is a part of our souls." Matteo joined in the next chorus:

"Jai Maa Saraswati,
Jai Maa Saraswati,
Vani, Vidya, Vardhini,
Shubh Buddhi Tu De De."

"I have only ever sung in church. I hated church," Ethan said during an instrumental interlude.

"Church does not own the right to sing."

"I do not know who they are singing to or what they are saying."

"Neither do I. But that does not stop their words from being beautiful."

"Bhar De Humare Jeevan Ko,
Gyaan Ke Ujala Se,
Chir Sukh Shanti Ka Var De,
Apni Kripa Ki Varsa Se."

"What if I say the words wrong?"

"This does not matter. Watch, I will not say them correctly. But my heart, my heart still feels the words."

"Jai Maa Saraswati,
Jai Maa Saraswati,
Vani, Vidya, Vardhini,
Shubh Buddhi Tu De De."

"My brother. Close your eyes. Do not look at me, or the others. Do not think of us here. Only see yourself and feel the words."

Ethan opened his mouth to argue but was cut off by the return of the vocals.

"Saraswati, Ma Saraswati,
Veena Vadini Var De,
Jnan Ki Jyoti Se Humko,
Gyaan Ki Disha Tu Dede."

"I can't, I won't, this is embarrassing."

"Watch me!" Matteo comforted and proceeded to sing the chorus loudly and proudly:

"Jai Maa Saraswati,
Jai Maa Saraswati,
Vani, Vidya, Vardhini,
Shubh Buddhi Tu De De."

Ethan looked away towards the horizon to see the sun's rays continuing to spread across the picture-perfect morning.

"Maa Vidya Ki Devi,
Sada Sahayak Rehna,
Hath Mein Tere Veena,
Aur Kitab Rehna."

"It is a beautiful day." Ethan closed his eyes and prepared to sing:

"Jai Maa Saraswati,
Jai Maa Saraswati,
Vani, Vidya, Vardhini,
Shubh Buddhi Tu De De."

He could feel his face turning red, his heart racing, and his palms beginning to sweat. "Fuck, what am I doing?"

"Bhar De Humare Jeevan Ko,
Gyaan Ke Ujala Se,
Chir Sukh Shanti Ka Var De,
Apni Kripa Ki Varsa Se."

He kept his eyes closed, forcing himself to sing the chorus again:

"Jai Maa Saraswati,
Jai Maa Saraswati,
Vani, Vidya, Vardhini,
Shubh Buddhi Tu De De."

The tempo changed, becoming quicker, encouraging some to stand up and sway to the music. Matteo stood up and looked back towards Ethan to encourage him to do the same.

"Absolutely not, mate. I will sing, but that is all you are getting," Ethan was quick to say. Matteo seemed satisfied with what he won today. The singing continued for one more round of fast-paced celebration to the sun above, leaves shook in resonance with the melody, and birds sang along with the chorus. Ethan kept his voice low, his eyes closed, but he began to feel himself sway to the rhythm of the final set.

"Saraswati, Ma Saraswati,
Veena Vadini Var De,
Jnan Ki Jyoti Se Humko,
Gyaan Ki Disha Tu Dede."

"Jai Maa Saraswati,
Jai Maa Saraswati,
Vani, Vidya, Vardhini,
Shubh Buddhi Tu De De."

"Maa Vidya Ki Devi,
Sada Sahayak Rehna,
Hath Mein Tere Veena,
Aur Kitab Rehna."

"Jai Maa Saraswati,
Jai Maa Saraswati,
Vani, Vidya, Vardhini,
Shubh Buddhi Tu De De."

"Bhar De Humare Jeevan Ko,
Gyaan Ke Ujala Se,

Chir Sukh Shanti Ka Var De,
Apni Kripa Ki Varsa Se."

"Jai Maa Saraswati,
Jai Maa Saraswati,
Vani, Vidya, Vardhini,
Shubh Buddhi Tu De De."

The song and music concluded with the chant:

"Om Shanti Shanti Shanti."

"Wow, such beauty in these words. I feel them," Matteo said with tears down his face.

"Right. Well, you got your wish. I sang along. Can't say I know what I have said."

"That is not what's important. What is important is that you sang, you felt, and you are here. Better than sleeping!" Matteo laughed and sat back down next to Ethan.

Food was now being passed around from various baskets and trays. One man approached Ethan with a tray of fruit and nuts who looked like he had not bathed in a very long time. His hair was knotted and dry, his beard was rough and patchy, his complexion rough and greasy. Matteo saw him and greeted him:

"My friend! Good to see you."

"How did you enjoy it? Told you it would be good, mate!" The greasy man responded. "Who did you bring here?"

"This is my brother Ethan, the one I was telling you about last night."

"You mean the one from your vision?"

"Yes, yes, the very same."

"And you are?" Ethan stepped in, not liking that others talked about him. "What were they saying?"

"My apologies, friend. I am Jasper. But you can call me Ravi. It is my soul name."

"Jasper— I mean Ravi. How long have you been here in Glastonbury?" Ethan prodded.

"Oh, gosh. At least five years now, I think. It's great. Best choice I made for myself. Came from London with serious depression. City was eating me alive—"

"Bet he took showers in the city. Can barely look at his face," Ethan thought, leaning back from Jasper's smelly aura.

"—yeah, and then I found my way to the Guild of Shanti here. Haven't looked back."

"Ethan is from London! Perhaps he will stay here forever as well!" Matteo laughed, clasping Ethan on the back. Ethan laughed awkwardly in return, deeply imagining himself living as Jasper was: filthy, unkempt, sun-scorched, and destitute; he shuddered at the thought.

"You are from London, Ethan? What finally broke you? For me, it was the tube; couldn't take it anymore," asked Ravi.

"Um, it was the tube for me too. Tell me about this Guild?" He deflected.

"The Guild of Shanti? Oh man, what an amazing group of people. We all live together here under the embrace of Kamadeva. We sing, we laugh, we love, and we follow the winds of our great creator to where we need to be."

"So, you all live together?"

"Yes."

"Outside?"

"Where else would we live?"

"In a house?"

"Where all our problems come from, you mean?"

"Yeah, sure."

"No, no, the roof holds back the rays of love sent to us by —"

"By Kamadeva, yes, I get it." Ethan put a stop to the conversation. Noticing his stomach was feeling a bit off from just having coffee, he reached out to grab nuts and fruit from Ravi's tray. He looked around to see if there were any trays of bacon or sausage— but no luck— only fruits, cheese, and nuts. He grabbed a handful of cashews from a nearby tray and sat back down to Matteo and Ravi talking; their attention was, however, drawn back towards the center where the man who led the singing was preparing to speak once again.

"Thank you for that beautiful message to the Gods above us. Now we will sing a song for our family members, alive and long passed," he announced.

"Great, more singing," Ethan droned. But then his pocket began to vibrate, a phone call. "Thank whatever God is saving me," he thought, running to the top of the orchard to answer.

"Hello. Who is this?" he asked excitedly.

"What do you mean who's this? It's your bloody boss, that's who. Don't you have my number saved?" The sharp voice of his boss came through the receiver.

"Sorry, yes, sir. Yes, I have it saved." The light left Ethan's face.

"How's your vacation with the sheep and pigs going? Where are you again? Lincoln?"

"No, sir. I am in—"

"I couldn't give two fucks where you are. What I am calling for is you need to—" He was cut off by the loud singing that began down in the grove:

"Saanjh ki komal god mein,
Yaadein tumhari basti hain,
Purvaj jo maarg dikhate,
Hamaare dilon mein rahte hain."

"What in the hell is that?"

"It's singers, sir."

"Well, they are bloody awful! Anyway, what I was saying is that you are going to need to cut your holiday short in the country. We need you back here."

"Sir, I requested two weeks holiday."

"Two weeks too fucking long. We need you back tomorrow."

"But, I really need—"

"I really need you to stop being such a fucking bender. Time to wipe your tears with your bleeding tampon and get back to it."

"But… I… I…"

"No, it's all sorted. See you in two days, back in this office. Am I clear?"

Ethan's eyes were swelling, his throat was clenched, and his hands were shaking. "Yes, sir," he coughed out.

"Good. Take a fucking shower before you get in too; I bet you smell of—" Ethan slammed shut the mobile. The world was spinning, his heart was racing; he needed to get away. He started walking towards the forested path away from the orchard when Matteo approached from behind.

"Brother, what is wrong?" he asked.

"Nothing. I just have to get out of here. Tired." Ethan began to walk off.

Matteo paused and examined Ethan's eyes: "Okay. I will come with you."

"I would rather walk alone."

"Then I will walk alone but in the same direction. Come." Matteo looked back and waved to the group in the orchard. They walked together down the path towards town, the chains of the Guild of Shanti fading slowly into the distance.

—

"Do you want to talk about the phone call?" Matteo asked after they had walked in silence all the way back to the base of the Tor.

"Not really."

"That is understandable. But it may help if you do."

"I have to leave town is all."

"What! What do you mean? I thought you had two weeks."

"Not anymore; I am needed in London."

"No, this cannot be! Did they say what for?"

"It is my job; they do not really need a reason to ask me back."

"But you have a reason to stay as well, yes?" Matteo asked.

"It's been great. I have already seen the town, though. Isn't much left for me to see."

"Of course, there is! And my brother, Ethan, I must be honest with you. Here, stop." Matteo said as they were now back at the crossroads of the Tor and the White Springs. "Ethan. You are fucked up. You are broken. And to save your life, you must stay here. Otherwise, you will die."

"What the fuck are you on about? What gives you the right to say that?" Ethan was furious.

"I see you; I know you and how you feel. You are broken; that is why you have come. To pick up the pieces and find out who you really are."

"And how do you know this, then, huh?"

"Because I am here for the same reason. If I received a phone call now to return home to Italia, I would have to say no. Even if my own mother told me so. You know why?"

"Why?"

"Because if I were to leave now, I know I will have no purpose and I will die. A man without a purpose is a dead man."

"That's harsh." Ethan felt his words deeply.

"It is the truth. He may walk around, he may play video games, go to the pub, fuck his girlfriend. But a man without purpose cannot truly live his life. Until I find my purpose again, I must stay here. And I hope you will too. By your own choice."

"You don't understand. I need this job. If I don't have it, my life will be over."

"A job is not life; do not think your job is your purpose. It is only a vessel of purpose." Matteo insisted. "I tell you what. Come to the White Springs one more time. Dive into the waters and seek your decision there."

Ethan looked in the direction of the springs and then back to Matteo: "Fuck, that water is freezing, man."

"Yes, it is truly horrific. But the water is honest. And you need to feel honesty."

"Fine. But no promises."

They walked to the White Springs together; there was hardly anyone there this early in the morning. The gate was locked, but Silus could be seen inside, noticing Matteo and Ethan standing outside. Silus approached and pointed towards the CLOSED sign.

"Yes, I know. But my friend here needs the water badly. You see, he has lost his purpose, and he needs the waters. And so do I," Matteo responded.

Silus studied them both for a moment and then opened the gate, allowing them both to slip inside the dark chamber; only a few candles had been lit in the central basin, otherwise the room was pitch black. The well-keeper came in front of both Matteo and Ethan, raised a hand to tell them to wait, and then disappeared around a corner. A moment later, he reappeared with a small iron pot with a handle and a small leather bag. He produced a small piece of coal from the cabinet, warmed it over a candle's flame until it was smoldering, then placed it in the iron pot. From the leather bag, he pulled a handful of leaves to scatter onto the coals to create a thick smoke. This smoke he blew carefully over the two companions.

The air was cold, wet, and charged. Ethan could see his breath mix with the smoke coming from Silus' hands. Matteo's eyes were closed and his breath shallow; he stood with complete calm. Ethan, on the other hand, was shaking. Silus stopped in front of Ethan and blew more of the sweet-smelling vapor across his head and his body. He stopped to lean down and replace the iron incense holder with a small rattle that made a noise like that of a coffee can filled with rice. He shook it towards the sky and around both Matteo's and Ethan's heads. He raised the rattle to Ethan's forehead and began to travel with the instrument down towards Ethan's belly, stopping at his heart. Silus grumbled and began to shake the rattle with great speed over Ethan's chest.

Ethan thought the rattle was about to break from the ferocity that Silus was shaking it when all of a sudden he stopped, looked Ethan in the eyes, and asked:

"What do you fear? Ask the water."

"What—"

"Water, go."

Silus then turned his attention to Matteo, who he had sit down on the stone steps to rattle above his head. Ethan turned to approach the central basin and began to remove his clothes in apprehension. He was about to step into the well when he heard from behind him:

"No. Deep water."

"Deep water? He can't mean up at the top of the spring, can he? Shit, he does," Ethan thought, looking towards the abyss surrounding the mouth of the spring where the water was pouring in from the hillside, supplying the tiers of water leading to the central basin. He let his eyes adjust and then walked carefully along the stone wall to the wall of wells that he had to climb to reach the deepest section of water. Ethan could see nothing further, so he grabbed a small candle holder bearing a lit flame and carefully carried it along with his naked body up the wet steps of the fountain. A small shrine to what appeared to be the Virgin Mary greeted him at the top; the black pool now visible to him as well. Ethan could also see now the water gushing in from under the Tor; the waterfall produced great force and slammed against the water.

"What do you fear? Ask the water?" Silus said to Matteo, who was now undressing at the entrance.

"What do I fear? Right now? This fucking water," Ethan thought.

"Yes, I am water. I am a part of you. I will always allow you to flow."

"I want to live without fear of being trapped." he whispered.

"Then free yourself."

Ethan dove in…

He then shot out of the water, knees shaking, breath bated, ears ringing, blood pumping to every muscle. He reached down to find his footing to return to the entrance and find his clothes. When he pawed around and found them, he first reached for his mobile, flipped it open, and walked outside of the Springs.

Brrrrrriiiinnng… Brrrrrriiiinnng… Brrrrrriiiinnng.

"Hello, calling to cry again?" came the familiar voice of his boss.

"Listen here. I have worked for you ever since I got out of fucking school. I have a degree in psychology, and I punch your fucking numbers all day like a good little robot. I take your abuse, I coddle your insecurities, and I make you far more money than I ever make. I live in a shit flat, with a shit roommate, in that shit city. For too goddamn long, I festered. Now I need a goddamn break from the goddamn city, and your ugly fucking mug. I am owed two weeks PAID leave, and I will get it, or I will not come back at all!"

"I—"

"I am fucking talking right now. I will be back in two weeks' time; I do not want to hear another word about work, data, my performance, none of it, you hear me? I said, do you hear me?"

"Yeah, I hear you. Two weeks."

"Good."

"Glad you grew some balls, kid." *Click* The line closed.

Ethan was left with the burning energy pulsing through his blood, naked in the morning light. He was shaking with what he had just done. Silus came out with a towel for him to cover up with.

"Good water?" he asked.

"Good water," Ethan replied, taking the towel and covering up his pale body that luckily only a squirrel, two birds, and Silus had to see. Ethan took a moment to calm his heart before going back into the chamber and getting fully dressed once more. Matteo was just then descending from the deep well, a blank expression left on his face, his eyes red and puffy from tears that were coming down his cheeks. Silus approached Matteo with a towel and helped him down from the stone wall that lined the central basin.

No words were exchanged with Silus; both Ethan and Matteo looked to him as they left and nodded their heads in gratitude. This seemed sufficient to Silus, who escorted them out and then closed the gate behind them.

"I will stay," Ethan said right away.

"Good, I will leave."

"What?"

"I am just messing with you!"

They stood in the morning light in silence for some time. Only the chirping of autumn birds broke up the serenity.

"So, are you hungry?" asked Ethan.

4

Freyja's Hall

The remainder of the day, Ethan and Matteo passed time at the cafés and bookstore of Glastonbury, talking for the first time as genuine friends. They discussed their favorite movies, funny exploits from their time in university, and made jokes about the everyday; the one thing they did not discuss was what had occurred at the White Springs that morning. There seemed to be an invisible block between them that stopped them from diving deep. Perhaps it was the memory of the cold, the caffeine from the four cappuccinos each, or it could have been their subconscious preparing them for the night to come at Isla's sharing circle.

They waited outside Zoe's shop as Ethan had been instructed, the time growing close when Zoe finally emerged with only one of the dogs.

"Hey, guys! How's things? Just me and Bilbo today. He has a nasty cold and needs some extra attention."

"Has he been hanging out with wizards again?" Ethan joked, hugging Zoe when he saw her. She was looking more lovely to him with every meeting.

"Ha!" She snorted. "He better not have been. No, I think he has been playing with that dirty poodle at the park."

"What makes her dirty?"

"She's the town doggy mattress, always floating around flaunting her poofs! And so is her owner!" She looked to Matteo. "Hey, you alright? You seem calm today."

"Yes, we had such a beautiful day. We talked about everything. Did you know that Ethan is a psychologist?"

"Well, I have a degree. Need more school to be licensed," Ethan corrected.

"No way! I wanted to be a solicitor," exclaimed Zoe.

"I absolutely cannot see that," Ethan jested.

"Yeah, neither could I! That's why I just did a load of ketamine and didn't show up to any of my classes. Really upset Daddy with that one." She cringed, still maintaining her aura of humor.

"Right, so where are we spilling our guts for all to see then?" asked Ethan.

"Isla has the Freyja Hall rented out for us. Lovely little space, just—well, right there actually." She pointed across the street at a door with the small sign *Freyja Hall* painted on the paneling above the golden knob—which so happened to be in the shape of a knob.

"Right, small town."

"Is that Ravi?" Matteo asked, squinting his eyes to see their morning acquaintance walking toward them. He waved.

"Great to see you guys! Where did you go this morning?" he asked, giving them a long, smelly hug.

"Ravi! Yes, we went to the Springs. Had a good vision," Matteo answered.

"Just call me Jasper."

"What? What happened?"

"The energy didn't feel right. I left the Guild. They just don't have the answers I was looking for."

"How long did you last at that one, Jasp? Two weeks?" Zoe asked.

"Hey, I was with the Guild all summer. Since August."

"That's not the whole summer," Ethan protested.

"Felt like it. Have you heard their songs? Bloody awful," Jasper answered. "It was good though—great drugs and parties. But time to see what new things await this new version of me!"

"Oh, you are coming to Isla's circle?" asked Zoe.

"Yeah, haven't been to one of them yet."

From across the street, Isla was walking toward them with a small bag under her arm.

"Hey, everyone! Thank ye so much for comin'. It's such a treat tae see all yer faces. Come on, I've got the key. Let's head in."

"Is Hamish coming?" Jasper asked.

"Gods, no. He hates this sort o' thing. I'm sure he's at the pub watchin' the game right about now. Come along!" She grabbed the golden knob and shoved her way into Freyja's Hall.

The door opened up to a stairwell that led the group up into a second-level studio space that was decorated to look like a Viking long hall. Small fake shields hung from the walls, with plastic dragon skulls adorning the floor lamps. The space was completely open in the center, with many cushions, blankets, and yoga mats piled in one corner. A small partition separated the main space from a small kitchen nook in the back of the room, where a small toilet was tucked away as well. The room was painted very dark, and a big bay window let in the only light in the space before Isla began to light various candles around the hall.

"Mind helpin'? Spread out some o' the cushions fer everyone tae sit around the center here, would ya?" Isla requested. "Maybe fer ten or so? No sure how many will show."

Matteo, Zoe, Ethan, Jasper, and even Bilbo helped set up the space as requested. Isla brought out a small table to place in the center with more candles, incense, and tarot cards laid out for people to take. Against the partition, she displayed a small array of unused baked goods from the café, along with a pot of coffee as well.

It wasn't long before others began to arrive: an older man with dreadlocks who went straight for the coffee and cakes; a younger woman with thick eyeliner, pink hair, and piercings all around her lips; a couple, the woman was pregnant and appeared only moments away from giving birth; another woman with thick dark hair and one arm covered in a variety of tattoos walked in, who seemed to know Zoe as she was greeted by a quick hug; and two men Ethan had seen on the Tor the previous day also arrived, followed by a gorgeous woman in her forties with violently blue eyes, who caught Ethan's eye right away.

"Hey, Zoe? Who is the blonde?" Ethan whispered.

"Fucking mattress."

"What?"

"That's the one with the poodle I warned you about. Stay away from her, Ethan. Promise me?"

"What, you jealous?" He attempted to flirt.

"Hardly. I would pity you if you were attracted to her," Zoe replied with much seriousness.

Jasper had found his way to speak to the blonde and was preoccupied, leaving him the last one standing as Isla sounded a bell asking everyone to sit down.

Zoe was next to Ethan, who was next to Matteo, followed by Jasper, the blonde with blue eyes, the couple, the two from the Tor, the old man with dreads who snaffled all the cakes, the lady with pink hair, Isla, and then the woman with thick hair and tattoos, who finished the circle next to Zoe.

"Thank ye, everyone, for joinin' me in this sacred space o' healin', sharin', and community," Isla began. She procured a small bell that she rang three times to quiet the chatter. "This space is yours fer the duration. But don't think o' time. Don't think o' work. In this space, I want us tae focus on ourselves and one another. In ma hand is the sharin' stick. It must be respected."

She held out a small piece of wood decorated with crystals, ribbons, and flowers.

"The sharin' stick is passed around clockwise. Whoever holds the stick holds the right tae speak and be heard. At no point should the holder o' the stick be interrupted until they've said their piece. If ye have somethin' tae say, please raise yer hand and ask permission first. The holder o' the stick has the right tae accept yer words or decline them. This isnae a space fer debate or argument, but for listenin' and understandin'. I, as the space holder, bear the ability tae end a conversation if it insults the sacredness o' the circle. I hope tae never have tae dae this. Does anyone have any questions?" She paused, lookin' around wi' owl-like eyes.

"Yes, what if we need to use the toilet?" asked the woman who was pregnant.

"Wonderful question! If ye need tae use the toilet or grab a biscuit, ye can dae so in silence. But please try tae wait until someone's finished speakin' before ye dae. Thank ye for askin'. Any other questions?"

"Yeah, will there be time to talk with you afterwards?" asked Jasper.

"Of course, but I hope anythin' ye wish tae share is brought up in the circle. That's the nature o' the circle. Okay, aye, any more questions?"

Silence.

"Very good. Okay, now. Since we have many new faces here, I'd like tae start wi' introductions, so ye can learn each other's names. I'll begin as a demonstration…" She paused to collect herself.

"My name is Isla Macleod. I came tae Glastonbury on a beautiful spring day wi' ma husband, Hamish. We own the Andrew's Cross café, where ye can find us most days. I fell in love wi' this lovely wee town when I visited years ago. It healed me in such amazin' and beautiful ways. Now I've come back tae see what more this town can dae tae heal me and ma connection tae the feminine. Thank ye." She bowed with the stick and passed it to the left.

"Hey. My name is Star, or at least that's the name I have chosen for myself. I am from Cardiff. So, yeah, Welsh or whatever. I never fit in at home. Dad's a minister, mom's a bitch, and they hated having a non-binary fag for a child. So I came here. Or whatever." They passed the stick.

"Aho," replied Jasper.

"The fuck does that mean?" thought Ethan.

"Hello, my name is Dex. I uh, live here in Glastonbury. I have been a farmer for close to four decades. Hate the communists who run our government. Hate the chips they put into our brains. Hate these bloody phones in our pockets. And yeah, wanted to come here and share."

"Thank you… yes," Isla said, seeming thrown off by his attitude. "Next, please."

"Aho," Jasper again.

"The fuck does he keep saying that?" thought Ethan.

"Hi, my name is Mark. I am here because—"

"Jesus Christ. We are not even halfway done with the introductions and I am already bored," Ethan thought, looking around for something interesting to look at. He studied the shields and their details, looked towards the snack table. "I will get up soon and grab a biscuit," he decided.

"Hi, yeah I am Mark's brother, Fredrik. We come from Germany together to find peace here in Glastonbury. Ya." He passed the stick quickly to the couple.

"Aho."

"Why the fuck does he keep saying that?"

"Hello, my name is Rasmus. This is my wife Claudia, and we—"

"Sorry. But please refrain from talking for one another. You must approach this space as individuals first," Isla kindly interrupted.

"Oh, sorry. Yes. My name is Rasmus. We have come from Estonia. My country is very… uh. Tense. We… I lived very close to Russia, and with the wars, we… I thought we should move to Claudia's home country to get away. To raise our son. So we are here." He handed the stick to Claudia.

"Aho!"

"Fuck's sake."

"As my husband has said, my name is Claudia. I grew up here in the UK; however, I was born in Poland. While visiting home, I met Rasmus, who was in Warsaw on holiday three years ago. We have been in love ever since.

Now we have moved here, as he said. This will be our first child, and we want to raise him someplace free of the city and free of the wars. I grew up in Wells; that is where we live now. But we heard of this group from Isla and her husband recently. So we are here."

"Aho."

"My name is Christine. I live in Glastonbury now. I moved here because of my coven. They have all left to be with their boyfriends in the city. Now I am here, alone. I went from a large group of friends to now just me and my adorable dog daughter, Apples. I am looking for new friends, community, and perhaps even love. Thank you."

"She seems quite nice, actually," Ethan thought. He felt Zoe shift disapprovingly at Christine's story.

"Aho!" It was now Jasper's turn. As he gripped the stick and settled in, he appeared to be gathering energy for something, closing his eyes and taking in several deep breaths. Jasper then opened his mouth and proceeded to flood out every problem that had ever plagued him since the time he was five years old. From the bullies who picked on him for being short to the time his mother left him at Tesco's on accident for five hours alone, and then to his time at university where he was caught stealing food from the cafeteria after he lost all of his money to an online dating scam.

Jasper spoke for nearly forty-five minutes before taking a singular pause in his speech.

"That's it, I want to die. I want to fake death so that I can be taken away by emergency services, brought back to life, and then die again so that I do not have to live in a world where this is happening." Ethan screeched in his mind, ready to tear out his hair. He looked around to see if anyone else was bothered by this obvious cry for attention. What he found not only disappointed him but shocked him, as every single person sat with complete focus and stillness at every word Jasper said. Even Matteo was fixated, nearly without blinking toward Jasper. "What is wrong with these people? Well, he clearly has no more of his life story to share, right?"

"Wow, I have talked for a while, haven't I?"

"No, really, mate? You don't fucking say?"

"Please, Jasper. Take as much time as ye need," Isla said with a calm, unwavering voice.

"Kill me."

"Thank you, Jasper. Your story is powerful, and you are brave for sharing it." Isla began again.

"Sorry, I always lose track of my words. Apologies, so many apologies. Yes. Aho." He put his head down and passed the stick to Matteo.

"Thank you all for your words so far. I can tell this is a magical circle of beautiful people already. My name is Matteo. I am from Italia, my journey here to Glastonbury began when I took the medicine of the Grandmother. She told me to come here by the power of my own two feet. And it is here that I would find the key to healing myself. So far she has answered me well. I have loved every moment with the magical places here. I look forward to learning more. Aho!" Matteo said, smiling toward Jasper, then to Ethan, who he was now holding the sharing stick toward.

"I am Ethan. I've been here two days now. And yeah, it's been a great holiday so far. Cool people, good coffee, and nice views of fields and sheep," he joked, passing the stick to Zoe. He then got up to grab a biscuit and a coffee. Matteo approached him from behind.

"You must share. Do not deflect," Matteo whispered next to him.

"I just did."

"No. Really share. We've been through too much for you not to have more to say. Trust me."

"Fuck off," he thought. "Okay, yeah, fine," Ethan replied. Matteo grabbed a biscuit and returned to his cushion.

"… love this town. Love my dogs. And I'm happy to be here to support my new friend Isla in her exploration as a space holder. So thank you for being here to support her as well," Zoe concluded, passing the stick to the tattooed woman.

"Hey. My name is Lila. I'm from America originally…" Ethan now noticed her American accent, "… I came here about a year ago. And since then, I haven't really managed to leave. Keep to myself mostly. Zoe has become a good friend. She invited me here to get me out of my shell. So we'll see how it goes. Thank you." She passed the stick back to Isla.

"Aho," called Jasper.

"Aho," joined Matteo.

"Great, they're both doing it now," Ethan thought.

"Thank ye all for yer introductions. Yer words are heard. Now we move on tae the depth o' our conversation—sharin'!" Isla said enthusiastically."So please, take the stick one more time and let it all out. Don't stop until ye've squeezed every drop out o' yer bucket, so we can go into the new world wi' an empty spirit, ready tae receive all that life gives us!" She then handed the stick tae Star.

"Uh, wow. I don't know how to start."

"Would you like me to go first?" asked Isla.

"Yes, please!" Star quickly handed back the stick.

"Okay. Wow, so much tae share. First, I'd like tae express gratitude for this space. Gratitude for all o' ye, for all yer time and energy. I'm feelin' quite light today, like there are two clouds beneath ma feet. Our business is goin' well. I'm worried about ma husband; he's sacrificed so much for me tae be here. I've never met a man more passionate about his country than he is. We met in the Highlands, both havin' climbed Ben Nevis at the same time. We were lookin' out over the mist-covered valley when we caught each other's eye. Little did I know that we'd end up married a year later. I'm more o' a free spirit, always lookin' for fairies under rocks and shrubs, while he's busy pushin' himself physically. Always workin', ma husband. Always movin' forward… and now he's put himself in this place… for me… I only hope that blessings can… can give us a child. I've prayed. I've prayed so much for the goddess tae bless me wi' a full womb. We've tried for so many years…"

Ethan began to lose focus. "Fuck, I feel bad. She seems really emotional. And she's super nice. But man, how long will this bloody take? Shouldn't have had that other coffee; I'm completely wired," he thought impatiently. He tried to focus on what Isla was saying, but he kept getting distracted by his own thoughts.

Isla eventually finished, drawing Ethan's attention back. However, before she could pass the stick, Claudia raised her hand to offer support. She was crying.

"It took us so long to get pregnant. Everyone makes it seem so easy, especially when you're young. We lost several children to miscarriage before this one. And now… now we couldn't be happier. Keep trying, my love. You will succeed. Would you like a hug?"

"Yes!" replied Isla, who shuffled over to Claudia across the circle, and they embraced in a tear-filled hug.

"Oh… Hamish wasn't joking. I should've listened to him. Might be able to slip away to the pub and see what he's up to, actually…" Just as Ethan was plotting an escape, the stick had moved to Star.

"I don't want children," they began.

"Oh, yikes. This might be good…" Ethan sat up at attention.

"I don't want children. Because I know that I'd only fuck them up like my parents fucked me up. I don't have a good role model of a father, or a mother…"

"Christ, another crier for sure," Ethan rolled his eyes and adjusted his position on the floor. He tuned out for most of Star's share, trying to find something interesting in the room to look at. Then he peered over at Zoe—completely enthralled with Star's story—and he began to daydream about her. "Yeah, I could see it. I mean, she is quite cute, funny, witty…"

"… the first sign of abuse was when my father would hit my mother for not listening to him about how he liked the laundry folded…"

"Oh shit, this escalated quickly."

Ethan, feeling embarrassed for tuning out, tried to focus again. He managed to make it through most of Star's story without distraction, but there were still several more to go before he'd need to speak. He half-listened as Dex complained about the government destroying the country. Dex got quite animated, even yelling as if he were talking to the Prime Minister himself. Somehow, the conversation turned to Dex ranting about his neighbor using sheep manure to fertilize his fields, when apparently horse manure is the best. Ethan learned something new about farming.

Ethan went to use the bathroom during Mark's story and returned to hear Fredrik grieving over the loss of his grandfather, who had escaped Germany before Hitler invaded Poland and worked as a runner for the Allies under a fake identity. He had learned French to impress the women of Paris and later returned to Germany to help rebuild Munich with his new French bride by his side.

The stick then traveled to Rasmus, who shared about growing up near the Russian border in Estonia; how he had dodged the armed services as a young adult; and even his first time trying McDonald's. His story ended with how Claudia helped him recover from drug addiction, which he had fallen into through the Eastern European rave scene, and his newfound connection to God now that he was clean.

"Russia… wonder what the rave culture is like there…" Ethan's mind continued to drift.

Then Claudia—still wiping tears from Isla's comments—shared about losing her mother at a young age. She explained how she was raised by her father and three brothers, always last in line. She mentioned her time working for the Royal Air Force as a translator, and then meeting Rasmus. She opened her arms, crying that she hoped her child would be a girl, so she could make up for her lost girlhood.

"Aho."

"Aho."

"Aho," echoed the room.

Christine took the stick next and talked about how her coven had helped her after a divorce. She quickly segued into discussing an event she was hosting the following week.

"…my trauma after Henry left me led to a profound connection with grief. That's why I became an energy healer, to find blockages in others who've felt the loss of love. I offer all services to those in this room at a discount of 50% should they come and use my services to connect to their true selves," she said, forcing tears. "I am also so thankful to have met my current lover, Joshua. He is an angel sent to me from the stars above!

"Who believes this shit? Didn't she just say she is looking for love? Then who is this Joshua?" He continued to think judgmentally.

"Are you alright?" Jasper asked. "That was powerful stuff, Christine. I can't believe a man would treat you so poorly…"

"Oh, he does," Ethan chuckled to himself.

"Thank you, Jasper. I'll be okay as long as I can help others heal from their traumas. I hope to see anyone who needs it tomorrow at 8 p.m. in the Goddess Garden off High Street. Donations welcome." More fake tears followed.

The stick passed to Jasper…

"Thank you, Isla. Thank you, everyone, for listening. Opening up in spaces like this is the only thing that keeps me together. I came to this town with nothing, with no one. After my time in London, I felt so frustrated, empty, and lost. I always disappointed my father, never found an honest lover, and only had friends of convenience. My boss called me as I left for Glastonbury to chew me out for skipping work, threatening to sack me if I didn't turn around. I told him to go fuck himself, and I haven't looked back."

"'Oh, shit. That sounds… familiar,'" Ethan thought, feeling a pang of guilt for being so judgmental. "Still… he could have said this a lot quicker," he justified to himself.

"I still feel a bit lost, I'd say. But every day, with every word and every person I meet, I find another piece to the puzzle that gets added to my own. And one day, I know what the puzzle will show me, and I'll be complete again." Jasper took a deep breath. "And I believe that's all I have to say."

"Aho!" The room echoed as everyone responded in unison.

"Now they're all bloody doing it."

"Thank you for your powerful story, my friend Jasper." Matteo took the stick from Jasper. "Wow, I feel the power now in this stick. It holds all of our stories, all of our feelings and intentions. This is such a powerful group of people we have here today. Now, I must think of what to add to this story…" He paused for almost two minutes, while everyone, even Ethan, waited patiently for his words.

"Yes. This is what I must share with all of you. It is a story of anger and great pain, of love and loss. You see, my brother was taken from me. His name was Leo. He was so smart, so funny, such a good brother. A good son too, better than me. Talk about the golden child… my brother was killed by a drunk driver in our hometown at the age of fifteen. The man did not stop; he kept driving. We did not know his name; we did not know how Leo died, only that his body was left on the side of the road like trash."

Matteo paused, his eyes red and brimming with tears.

"My brother… he was so young. He was just out for a walk to… to find me. I had an argument with my mother, so I'd left to go and find a place to be alone. But Leo, oh, Leo knew where I'd go. I went to this old Roman temple to look over the village. It was late, the sun was setting… the last sunset my brother would ever see. I cried for days. But it wasn't from sadness or guilt. No, no. These were tears of anger at the man who had done this. After my brother was buried, I did not stop until every person in the village told me everything they'd seen that night. I asked and asked. I began to beg. 'Please!' I would say. 'Give me something, God!'

"Then, I received a sign. The police had finally found footage of a car speeding away at the time of the accident, the model of the car visible. I began to hunt the village for one like it. I searched every house, every alleyway, and then I found it. A yellow car with a cracked windshield, blood still visible on the paint. My brother's blood. Leo's blood. The car was parked outside of a dirty old house, long past its prime. I knocked on the door, my fist clenched like iron, ready to take this man's life. And who answers the door? A woman, maybe forty years old. I asked her:

"'Where is your husband? The man who owns this car.'

"She said, 'I have no husband. This is my car.'

"I looked at her and said, 'You hit my brother? You were the drunk?'

"She began to cry and beg, 'No, I wasn't drunk! I dropped my purse on the seat. I looked away just for a moment. When I looked up, I had already hit him. I'm so sorry! I didn't mean for this to happen. I swear to God this was an accident.'

"The woman… she was so sorry, so sad, so full of guilt. She fell to the floor in anguish, telling me how she felt, how she'd looked back to see my brother's bloodied face, looking back at her. How she hadn't slept in weeks. How she would never forgive herself. In that moment, I fell to the floor and cried with her. There I was… crying with the very person who killed my brother."

"What happened next?" Isla broke her own rules, captivated by Matteo's story.

"Next… that's why I'm here. When I left the woman, I felt so lost. I had personified my anger and grief as this drunken man who did not exist. When I found out it was her, the illusion faded away. I then felt the true loss of my brother; I knew then that no matter what I did, I would never get him back. And so, I did what I always did to solve problems: I walked. I walked across Italy, then to Spain, then to Romania, then back to Italy, all to be told to come here."

"Who told you to go to these places?" asked Star.

"My brother told me. Well, in his own ways," Matteo smiled.

"I thought he said his grandmother told him to come here?" Ethan pondered.

"Now… wow. I have spoken too much and too deep. Please, my new brother Ethan, take this from me. And thank you, everyone, for hearing my words. Thank you, thank you." He bowed.

"Aho!" came the room's response.

"Aho," Ethan whispered under his breath, now holding the sharing stick he was completely unprepared for…

He stared at the finely decorated sharing stick, searching for the words to begin. His heart rate began to increase, anxiety climbing into his throat.

"I…"

A knock, knock, knock rattled from the door right as Ethan began to speak.

"What in the name o' the Goddess," Isla stormed to the door, swinging it open with fury. "We are in the middle of a sharing session. What is it!"

"Sorry, Isla. It's half past eleven. Your booking ended nearly two hours ago," came the voice from the other side.

"Can't we go just a while longer? I have three more people tae share," she pleaded.

"Sorry, it's already nearly two hours past. I am just following the rules of the building owner. He's from the city after all. No bookings past ten he said. If he finds out, he will sack me for sure this time. Not to mention, Ms. Isla, I have to stay awake as long as you are here. I would very much like to get to bed."

Isla negotiated for another moment but returned defeated.

"I'm sorry, everyone. But it appears we'll need tae conclude this circle for now. Ethan, Zoe, Lila, I'm so sorry for this. Please come back tae the next one, and we'll gladly start wi' you three. Also, stop by tomorrow for free coffees and cakes! I'll be sure tae take care o' ye."

"It's okay. Thank you for tonight," Ethan responded, feeling slightly relieved.

"Yeah, it's alright, my love! We are just happy to have heard everyone speak," Zoe added.

"Yeah, it's fine! Didn't have much to share anyways," said Lila.

"Right. Well, again, please accept ma apologies. But for now, the evenin' is concluded. I wish ye all pleasant rest! Don't worry about cleanin' up; I'll dae it. And I'll have some words wi' this building owner in the mornin'." Isla began to pick up the pillows and blow out the candles.

Everyone thanked Isla and said goodbye to one another, beginning to funnel out into the cool night air. Matteo, Jasper, Zoe, Lila, and Ethan were the last to step out, the door promptly being closed behind them by the building attendant.

"My friends, it has been lovely, but I do think I should see that Christine gets home. You know how it can be at night. Bit dodgy. And I was wanting to see if her and Josh would let me move in with them again after the whole 'leaving the guild' thing today." Jasper said before quickly heading after Christine, who was already halfway down the high street.

"Ethan, I am absolutely shattered that we didn't get to hear what you had to say," Zoe said while hugging Ethan and pouting against his chest.

"Well, yeah. Would have been good. Was really winding up for a big one," he joked.

"Why don't we continue the sharing circle then? I wouldn't mind sharing in a smaller group anyways," Lila suggested.

"Yeah, but where is going to be open this time of the night?" Matteo questioned.

Ethan sighed, knowing the answer already.

"The pub, of course!" Zoe exclaimed.

—

The Monk's Arms is the oldest pub on the high street, sitting directly behind the market cross. The building itself was not entirely level; each of its four floors appeared slightly more warped than the previous. The interior, however, was as cozy as pubs come: warm lighting, stone walls, dark wooden benches, and a well-aged bar counter right at the entrance. Some rooms were still rented above, and like most pubs, there was a small kitchen in the cellar that cooked up various pub classics that could be smelled throughout the building. Zoe, Matteo, Ethan, and Lila found themselves in the back corner near the fireplace, as the night had turned quite cold and wet while they were within Freyja's Hall.

"Cheers to a wonderful sharing circle and to Matteo and Ethan! Welcome to Glastonbury!" Zoe started, Guinness in hand. They all followed suit and raised their glasses, then took a drink of their crisp drinks. "Ah—still not quite like home, but it'll do," Zoe said in reference to her drink.

"I have never had a drink like this; what did you say it was?" Matteo asked, taking another drink of the red liquid in his pint glass.

"Ah. That right there is a Somerset Cider. You won't find its equal. Trust me, I have tried," Lila answered.

"You are American?" Ethan asked.

"Yes, most people have trouble telling."

"You do have a bit of an accent, but it isn't as pronounced as most here."

"My father was in the military when he was stationed here in England. When I was born, we lived here for ten years before I moved to the states for the first time. Leaving the streets of England for the swamps and heat of Georgia was… hard to say the least."

"Well then, Lila, seems you are already starting the sharing!" added Zoe.

"I guess I am, but please, none of this formal shit. Just talk like normal people. I hate the uncomfortable silence of those circles," replied Lila.

"Yes! Oh my God. Glad I wasn't the only one losing my mind in there," Ethan was excited to finally get it out.

"That was your first one?"

"Yeah, absolutely mental that. Don't know how you can do more than one."

"I quite enjoyed it," Matteo said with a warm smile. "To hear so much of people's lives. It is a true pleasure."

"Oh, come now, even with Dex's mad ramblings about the government and how they are controlled by lizards from under the earth? That's madness." Ethan pushed, feeling the liberation of alcohol warming his face.

"Well, perhaps there are lizards running the government. Have you met these politicians?" Matteo answered seriously.

"I mean—no, I haven't met a politician before."

"So, how would you know they are in fact not these lizards?"

"Because—that's just bullshit."

"Your boss sounds like he could be a lizard person. How do you know he doesn't crawl back into the sewers and meet with the other lizards, plotting how to ruin your life?" Matteo kept a straight face at first, but then began to break.

"Oh, you are fucking with me, aren't you?"

"Ha! Yes, I am, of course there are no lizard people running the government."

"They are actually just aliens."

"To the aliens who run the government!" Zoe cheered, raising her glass high once again.

"To the aliens!" They all laughed together.

"Okay, yes, some people had some wild stories. But still, they are human; these are their stories and experiences, and no matter what, that is powerful." Matteo returned to his serious tone.

"Fine, fine. But what about that Jasper character then? Does he always share that long?" Ethan prodded.

"Jasper… he has such a kind soul… but he is… a bit…" Zoe struggled to find the right words.

"A bit of a bum? Bit of a loser? Bit of a burnout?" Ethan filled in the blanks with his thoughts.

"—a bit lost," Lila finished for Zoe. "I have known him since I have been here. Even dated him for a bit."

"Avalon, she will heal you in time. But she is a demanding place, and some people never seem to get away from her," replied Zoe. "How long have you been here now, Lila?"

"Three years now. Can't seem to break away myself. Avalon is a cruel bitch like that."

"You were saying about Georgia?" Matteo changed the subject.

"Yes, Georgia. Well, I lived there till I was a teenager. Never really fit in. I was too British to be American. Then when I would visit back here, I was too American to fit back in here. I have always felt in between it all."

"Why did you come back to England?" Ethan asked.

"By the time I was in my twenties, I decided coming back to England for university was the right choice. Got me out of the house, away from Dad and Mom. I still went to become what they wanted me to be, a bloody solicitor—"

"That's where we met," added Zoe.

"Yes, that's where I met my stunning Zoe. The greatest blessing of my life. She invited me here to Glastonbury when I was in a rage out in Bristol. So here I am. Poor, miserable, but at least I am out of the city. Now, raise a drink with me to fucking Bristol; may I never see that shithole again."

"Ethan, sounds like the ball is getting passed to you. Come then, tell us your story." Zoe nudged him in his side.

"Fine, if you want me to open up. We need to get another round of drinks."

Three ciders, a Guinness, and an order of chips in curry sauce were ordered and brought to the table to fuel the ongoing conversation. Ethan drank down another half of cider before feeling loose enough to open up.

"Alright, so here is me in a nutshell. I grew up in the countryside originally. Dad was a tough son of a bitch. Mom, a kind woman, but she always drank her problems away. Felt like the only time we got together as a family was when we were drinking or watching football. When I got older, I went to London. Got a shit job. Now I am here. That's it really."

"Brother Ethan, did you not say you were in university to be a psychologist?"

"Well, yeah. Did that. But I need a few more years of education to really do it. And honestly, I am not sure I have what it takes to do another few years."

"Why not?"

"Because I hated it, man. Hated my professors, hated my classes, hated my assignments. I made it through with average marks and a disdain for people's problems. The human mind, it's really quite a fucking crazy place." Ethan finished his cider.

"Why did you want to be a psychologist in the first place then, Ethan?" asked Lila.

"Why? Well, I guess my parents?"

"Why your parents?"

"So I could understand them," he thought. "Because they wanted me to be," he said.

"What did you want to be?" asked Matteo.

"Not a fucking data processor like I am now," Ethan deflected.

"Come on," Matteo pushed.

"I guess I wanted to be a therapist."

"Why?"

"To help people?"

"Why do you want to help people?"

"Because… no one helped me…" Ethan looked down at his glass. "Wow, cider makes me honest, I guess. I never… yeah, I would have never said that before. Yeah, I wanted to help people."

"Then you can still do that," Zoe reassured.

"I don't know. I couldn't have helped anyone in that room tonight."

"You helped by being there," Zoe said, putting her hand on his leg, causing Ethan to feel his cheeks turn even more red than the alcohol already had.

"Well, yeah, I guess. But alright! You all and the cider have gotten a lot out of me tonight. Zoe, how many dogs do you actually have?" Ethan changed the subject quickly.

"Honestly, I think I have bloody lost count!"

The group continued into the night, laughing and joking through two more rounds of drinks. Matteo remained quiet and had switched to water after his one drink; he smiled as he usually did but rarely added to the conversation unless directly called upon. Ethan was taking his confidence in drink and using it to flirt with Zoe, seeking her attention. Lila had left first after nearly falling asleep at the table. The barkeep came to announce the closing of the pub some time after, leaving the trio out in the cool of the night air to say their farewells.

"I have left those poor little peanuts alone way too long. I bet they have torn up the flat. Well, thank you, boys, it was a good night. And honestly, I haven't seen Lila that social in a while. So it did her some good," Zoe hugged them both.

"Yeah, it was a good night," Ethan searched his mind for any last-minute words to leave Zoe with to make sure she thought of him, but the alcohol left his thoughts clouded.

"Thank you for joining us, dear Zoe. And know I have not lost sight that you have not shared with us. I hope we can hear your story in the future," Matteo said warmly.

"Best not be stepping into the ring for her, my Italian friend!" Ethan thought jealously.

"Maybe one day. Now, to my little beans!" she replied. "Good night, you two." With that, she went up towards her shop and her apartment above.

"Ah, what a free spirit of a woman," Matteo said softly.

"Hey—you should know. I am into her," Ethan said drunkenly.

"Are you really?"

"Well, yeah. I think so."

"Why are you into her?"

"Stop asking fucking questions like this, man."

"Why do you not like my questions?"

"Because, I am fucking wasted, man."

"Ah, yes, the only time you open up?"

"Not the only time."

"I hope it is not. But my brother, I will stop. But I want to be direct with you. Will you allow me this?"

"Whatever."

"You must change how you look at women."

"What do you mean how I look at them?"

"They are not all here to possibly be in love with you."

"Fuck off."

"Just think about it. Now, would you like me to walk back with you? Are you safe to get back?"

"Yeah, I am fucking fine. I will go back on my own."

"Okay, my brother. I love you. Now be safe. I will see you tomorrow."

"Fucking weirdo, alright. See you tomorrow." Matteo hugged him and then disappeared down the high street, leaving Ethan alone to walk back to the Temple of Artemis.

"Fucking Italian. Probably just wants her for himself. Telling me stuff, asking questions. What does he know? Fucking Romans lost Rome then became Italians," he argued with himself.

Ethan continued rambling—both out loud and in his mind—as he walked past the church garden where Selene was no longer sitting. From the corner of his eye, Ethan caught a glimpse of Owen leaning against the wall of the garden, staring into the distance.

"What a creep."

Owen paid no mind to the drunken form of Ethan shuffling by him, his attention solely focused on the shadow of the Tor, illuminated by the moon from afar. Songs of sweet singing poured quietly from the distant monument, songs that Ethan could not hear as he crawled into bed and faded into a thick and restless sleep.

5
The Heron

"Ye look bloody rough, mate."

"Just give me another full Scottish. Extra tattie scone."

"Feel bloody rough too, I see," Hamish laughed. "How was the sharin' circle?"

"Well, I didn't ask about the boyfriends."

"Good."

"But that didn't stop them from whinging for four hours."

"Christ. That right there is why I'll never go again. Despite ma deep love for ma bonnie Isla."

"Where is she?"

"Oh, restin'. We take days off separately tae keep the business open as much as possible."

"How is it? The business."

"Not too bad. Glastonbury may be wee, but she's mighty in tourists lookin' for a decent overpriced coffee."

"So, since I am not a tourist, does that mean I get a discount?"

"Course ye're a tourist. And ye got a free coffee just the other day!"

"How do you stand it here?" Ethan changed the subject.

"Whit do ye mean, lad?"

"Stay here, in this town. It's a bit mad, isn't it?"

"Can be. But when ye've been where I've been, ye're happy tae be wherever ye are as long as it's no back there."

"Didn't know you hated Scotland so much."

"No. I was at the bottom o' a bottle o' whisky," Hamish replied, giving Ethan a plate of food at the small counter near the display cabinet.

"You live in the bottle long?"

"Aye, ever since I was young. Thirty years I lived in that bottle. And I wouldnae have thirty more years if I hadn't crawled out o' it."

"Yeah, fear that sometimes," Ethan reflected, taking bites of grease-filled meat to calm his filthy stomach.

"I tell ye, lad, alcohol is a memory-stealin' heron. Every time ye sleep wi' that stuff in yer liver, she comes tae peck away at yer mind. But only while ye're sleepin'. When ye wake, that's why yer head is poundin'. From that bloody heron peckin' away at yer memories."

"I thought it was from dehydration."

"No. It's that bloody heron! I didn't live a life worth rememberin' until I met that incredible woman sleepin' upstairs right now. Can ye believe it? I want tae live a long and happy life wi' her. That witch even got me tae start doin' yoga."

"You? Yoga?"

"Aye, I might look like a Viking warrior, but I've got the grace o' a fuckin' ballerina."

Ethan continued to eat while looking out the window. "Another rainy day. Keeping away the customers, it seems."

"Eh, hard tae say. I cannae complain. Samhain time, I'll be up tae ma hairy nipples in hemp jumpers and goblin masks, all wantin' vegetarian sausage rolls and skinny lattes." He shuddered at the thought. "Anyways, what's the plan today then, Ethan?"

"Don't rightly know. Feel like I have done everything there is to do in this town." Ethan scarfed down a forkful of beans.

"Well, there's only one thing tae dae in Glastonbury when ye've seen it all…"

"What's that?"

"Do it all over again!" Hamish laughed deeply. "So, will that be a skinny latte to go for ye today, princess?"

—

Ethan stepped out of The Andrew's Cross with his skinny latte in hand, reflecting on Hamish's words.

"Memory-stealing heron, bollocks. Although last night is a bit fuzzy. Bloody ciders have a serious back end to them. Now, I guess I will see what else there is to get into here."

He started up the high street, looking into each shop slowly as he walked by, trying to spy anything he may have missed on previous walks through the town. In one shop, he saw Jasper playing a drum on display while talking with the owner of the shop, whom Ethan had seen at the Tor on his first day. He then walked to Zoe's store only to find it had been closed, a sign hung from the door:

Drank too much. Open tomorrow during usual hours.

Ethan chuckled to himself; the note was horribly written and was clearly made last night before she had even gone to bed. He continued up the street to St. John's churchyard, where he saw the two brothers from last night, Fredrik and Mark, coming out of the entrance in a small tour group led by Christine from the sharing circle as well.

"She must have sold them on a tour after the night ended."

Across the street, at the small grocery, Vesta and Cardea walked out hand in hand, still wearing their white robes despite the rain, their breasts showing through due to their lack of bras.

"God, I wish they were straight." His mind then wandered to Matteo, last night lecturing him on how he looked at women. "Maybe he is right?" he thought for a moment, then pushed it aside.

Further up the street, he saw a group of older men walking together in serious discussion:

"—the bones have to be in the shape of the tree sigil. Otherwise, the ceremony will not call to—"

"What the fuck?"

Ethan looked back to see it was Owen, Dex, Silus, and three other men he did not recognize, walking by. Shrugging it off, Ethan approached a store that had many books on offer when the rain began to come down even harder. He headed in for shelter.

Right as Ethan turned around to study the room, he met eyes with Matteo, who was thumbing through a book from a chair in the center of the room.

"Hey! I told you I would see you at some point!" Matteo exclaimed excitedly.

"I am learning more and more that this town is truly small."

"How are you feeling?"

"Better after another full Scottish," he patted his stomach, satisfied.

"That was a once-in-a-year meal for me! So much pork, I think it is still in me."

"Hey, about last night. Sorry if I—"

"No need to apologize for alcohol, my brother. I have been around it all my life. I know it does not represent the best of ourselves."

"Thanks. By the way, where did you sleep last night?"

"Oh! Yes, that is a funny story. When I left you last night, I had forgotten that I came to town without a plan. So I was actually quite worried about finding a place to stay. I was coming to the Tor when I ran into the Lady of the Garden, Selene. She had just been up to the Tor for the moon. She says it will be full tonight. Anyway, I was telling her I had no place to stay, so she let me stay in the old church dorms. When I told her what I owed her, she said that I could help her with the church activities two days a week."

"How long will she let you stay there?"

"Oh, we did not have a contract or anything. But she made it seem like time is not something she thinks of often."

"That's lucky. I have to pay a pretty price to stay with the silent lovers at the Temple of Artemis."

"Yes, this whole journey has been very magical. Everything has been delivered to me when I need it most. I wish you could stay longer."

"Yeah, me too," Ethan lied. "But, honestly, not sure how much there is to even do here."

"Again you are on this. Look around you! In this shop alone, so much knowledge and wisdom in these books. Look at these," Matteo pulled out a large stack of books:

Britannic Mythology
Ancient Wizards and The Druids
Avalon Awakening: Unlocking the Power of the Self
Norse Mythology: Gods and Heroes
Satan and Sumaria
The Occult of Oculus
Necromancy for Beginners

The Lost Book of Loki
The Hyperborean Cover-Up
Singing to the Stars: A Cry to Orion

"You are going to buy all these?"

"Buy? No, this is a library. All of this knowledge is free for us to learn! And you speak of boredom. Pick up a book!" Matteo handed him *Singing to the Stars: A Cry to Orion*.

"Fine." Ethan grabbed it and sat down on one of the couches near the window. His skinny latte was long cold from his time outside, so he opened the book and began to read. *Singing to the Stars: A Cry to Orion* was about a man who had memories of the ancient Atlanteans and how we have all been reincarnated from those times. That our friends, family, and even adversaries are all part of our past lives from Atlantis.

"Load of shite."

Ethan continued to read, diving deeper into the writings of a person who claimed to be able to communicate directly with the stars through the power of his voice. He could also recover information from the stars through a form of "channeling." There was a large section on personal accounts from his followers who had recovered their lost connections to their Atlantean past. The book was written only ten years ago, and the writer seemed to hold retreats where he would guide people to the stars through his specific meditation techniques. When Ethan reached the section about how to reconnect with lost loved ones through astral sex, he put the book down.

"That's enough for now." He looked outside to see that the rain was beginning to slow down, allowing him to plan his escape. Matteo was engrossed in *The Hyperborean Cover-Up* in the center couch.

"Hey, I think I am going to head out," Ethan announced.

"Oh, I will come with you!"

"Actually, I think I want to be alone today, if that is alright."

"Of course, of course. Is everything okay?"

"Yeah, fine. Just not used to this much… socializing."

From the stairs on the side wall, someone emerged from above.

"Finally stop raining?" came the voice of Lila.

"What were you doing up there?" asked Ethan.

"She lives here! Well, above here."

"For the last year or so, yeah I have. Was about to head out."

"So was I."

"I—" Ethan started.

"I will stay here then. I am really enjoying this book! And my Italian blood is not fond of these rainy days. I think I will rest. I have barely slept since coming to Glastonbury," Matteo interrupted.

"Enjoy your rest then. Come on, Ethan." Lila opened the door and gestured for Ethan to come along.

"So much for being alone…" he shrugged, put on his raincoat, and headed outside.

Lila and Ethan paused when they stepped out into the cool autumn air.

"Where are you off to then?" asked Lila.

"Not really sure. Running out of things to do here."

"Tell me about it. I have done about everything you can do here a few dozen times."

"Do you like it here?"

"I go back and forth. Some days I think it's the most magical place in the world. Others… well, it can feel like an insane asylum."

"Complete with the crazies in the straight jackets," Ethan joked, looking across the street at one of the town homeless singing at the top of his lungs.

"No kidding," she laughed. "Come on, let's go to the Tor. Need to stretch my legs."

She started walking; Ethan followed, the route was now all too familiar to him. They walked in silence all the way to the crossroads where the Tor loomed to the left, and the road to the grocery store was to the right.

"You know what?" Ethan asked.

"What?"

"You might be the quietest person I have met here so far."

"What makes you say that?"

"We just walked for five minutes in complete silence. I feel like I haven't had silence here since I arrived."

"It gets like that sometimes. People come and go, bringing their problems and complaints with them. They either get what they want, get frustrated, or too fucked up, then they leave. The cycle then continues with the next wave of attention seekers." Lila droned.

"Wow, you and Hamish would probably get along."

"The coffee shop owner? Yeah, we met at the pub a few weeks ago. Beautiful singing voice that one. He gives me sanity when we talk... What about you, Ethan? Are you captivated by the magic of this place?" she asked while walking them closer to the Tor.

"Maybe the better word is intrigued by it. I can't deny it's not what I expected in any way."

"What did you expect?"

"I expected to be high a lot more."

"Careful what you wish for. The drugs are here, and they will take over quick. Have you been to the camps around town?"

"Not really. A little the other day for the Hindu prayer circle thing Matteo dragged me to."

"Well. That is where people go when they can't afford to live in town anymore. Also where you find the most drugs. You think the people in town are crazy? Wake up a few times there and you will be begging for the high street."

"Oh yeah? Happen to you a few times then?" Ethan asked in a joking way.

"More than a few times…" she answered grimly.

"Oh…"

"Well, Ethan, I am happy you are here. It's nice to have someone from the outside who doesn't seem to be a complete burnout."

"Thanks. I think?"

"You going to Samhain?"

"Probably. Not quite sure what it is yet."

"You know Halloween, in the States?"

"Yeah, of course."

"Think Halloween, but way more real. Honestly, it's one of the few times of year I truly love living here. Definitely make sure you come."

"Yeah, I definitely will—" Ethan stopped in his tracks. They had just begun to ascend the Tor when, from the corner of his eye, he spotted a heron in a tree. Its eyes were locked directly onto Ethan. "Fucking hell."

"What is it?"

"A fucking heron."

"A herring?"

"No, the fucking bird. The big one!" He pointed.

"I don't see it."

"It's right there! It's massive."

"Follow me," a voice rang in Ethan's mind. The heron then dove into the woods.

"I think… I have to follow that bird," Ethan said, transfixed.

"Bird talking to you?"

"Yes, how'd you know?"

"It happens. Well, better go catch it before it curses you or whatever. I will see you around, bird boy." She continued her walk up toward the Tor.

"Cursed?" he said, looking after her.

"Follow me," the voice came again. Ethan responded by walking towards the tree line and the hunt for the bird beyond. He followed the tree line until it led to a small stream where the heron was standing, vigilant, waiting for him.

"Hey, what do you want? Are you stealing my memories?" he shouted.

The bird stood stoic in response. Then it opened its wings and began to fly through the pass of the small stream. Ethan followed as closely as he could, even as the trees grew dense, blocking his vision. The heron flew up towards two large spires in the distance; the Tor still visible in the background. The heron landed in the branches of the spires, which appeared to be massive oak trees. At the base of the oak trees was a man with his arms raised in the air toward the trees; the heron gestured its head towards the man. Ethan approached cautiously but quickly saw the man was Owen, this time wearing a dark green robe with many necklaces dangling down.

"Owen?" asked Ethan.

He turned to meet Ethan's gaze. "Curious meetin's," he said before looking back towards the tree.

"I was following a bird."

"What bird?"

"The one above you," Ethan pointed up, now seeing the heron was no longer there.

"Disappeared, didn't it?" Owen asked, seeing Ethan's confused face.

"Yes—how did you know? And what are you doin'?"

"Preparin' for the festival."

"Samhain?"

"Yes."

"What was the bird?"

"A spirit, I'd guess."

"A spirit?"

"Yes, yer spirit guide."

"My what?"

"Yer spirit guide. Ye do have one, don't ye?"

"Don't believe so."

"Well, I'd imagine that heron's yer guide. Especially if it led ye to me, at this spot, on this day."

"What is this day?"

"The full moon before the liftin' of the veil. And ye stand on the old entrance to the Isle of Avalon. The one the druids would've used two thousand years ago. These are Gog and Magog."

"The trees?"

"Yes, the oldest oaks in Glastonbury. These are old friends to me and them what came before me. Soon they'll no longer be with us. But 'til then, they serve as a very sacred place for the isle."

"Why did the bird lead me here?" Ethan asked.

"Why d'ye think it did?"

"Wouldn't rightly know. I just heard it speak to me… somehow."

"Tricky birds. Very loud, very talkative if ye're not careful. Ethan, that's yer name, yes?" Ethan nodded. "Well, young Ethan, that bird led ye here to me, which means ye must be needin' to heal."

"Heal? You mean like you are fucking doctor?"

"No, I mean like the druids that once used these trees to commune with the spirits."

"Load o' shit. This town is mad crazy."

"Is it no more crazy than London? No more crazy than the way we treat this planet? We take, consume, and destroy everythin' we touch. But these trees? This isle? It's withstood the madness more than most places."

Ethan felt his heart begin to pick up pace; the pressure in his mind began to rise. "Do you at least have any more weed if you are going to be talking crazy like this?"

"Weed is a fool's medicine."

"You gave it to me just the other day!"

"Yes, on that day I was a fool. To this town, I'm but a fool. But today is not the day of the fool. Are ye a fool, Ethan?"

"I don't fucking know!"

"Do ye know who ye are, Ethan?"

"Fucking get off of me!" Ethan broke away and fell onto the grass-covered earth, his breathing broken and raspy. Owen lowered himself to the ground and onto his knees.

"Breathe. Focus on yer breath. In through the nose, out through the mouth. Slow and steady. Let it be natural. Calm yer mind," he said calmly.

"Fuck you, man. Ye did this to me."

"Breathe, motherfucker! Just breathe!" Owen cut through Ethan's thoughts with his directness.

Ethan stared him down but then gave in and did as he asked.

"In through the nose, out through the mouth. Slow and steady. Let it be natural. Calm yer mind," Owen repeated. Ethan found a rhythm and continued.

"Good, now keep goin'."

Ethan felt his heart calm, the pressure in his mind slowly come to focus.

"Ethan, that bird led ye here for a reason. It led ye here to heal."

"How can you be so sure? It was just a bird, just a coincidence."

"Because, Ethan, there are no coincidences in Glastonbury. Everythin' here happens for a reason. Do ye know tarot cards or the runes?"

"That witch shit? Not really."

"Yes, well that witch shit has meanin'. They're powerful symbols that can direct us in life when we're lost. People can also be this symbol. When we're drawn to them, we're seekin' somethin' that they symbolize."

"So what do you symbolize then?"

"Sacrifice."

The word echoed in Ethan's mind and soul.

"What are ye willin' to sacrifice to learn who ye truly are?" asked Owen.

"Anything." Ethan said without thinking, his head looking down into the mud-covered earth, tears streaming down his face.

"Everythin'?" Owen asked.

"Well, maybe not everything."

"We shall see… do ye wish to take that first step?"

"What does that first step look like?"

"Simply walk between Gog and Magog, walk between the portal of our world and the otherworld."

"Just walk between the trees? That's it?"

"Yes." Owen replied with a smile.

Ethan studied him cautiously, then looked at the two great oaks beside him; a small path lay between them. He took himself off the ground and walked to the massive trees, Owen raisin' his hands to the trees once more as rain clouds darkened in the sky. Ethan stepped between Gog and Magog.

"Now what—"

Lightning struck the earth behind Owen, followed by a loud roar of thunder, causing Ethan to slip in panic, grabbing hold of a nearby holly plant—his hand now bleeding from the sharp spines of the holly leaf—

"Fuck, I cut my hand."

"Place yer hands on the tree," Owen called out. In his hands, he began to play a large drum in a way that mimicked the thunder. Rain began to pour down around them. Ethan placed his bloodied hand on the tree.

"Now what, old man?"

"Speak to the trees. Tell them yer wish."

"My wish?"

"Yes! What ye desire." The drum picked up rhythm and grew louder with the rain.

"What I wish? A million pounds? Love? Loads of sex?" His thoughts rattled on. The lightning flashed once again, causing him to think of his time in Glastonbury: Zoe, Matteo, Hamish, the sharing circle, the Hindu singing, the White Springs, Sulis, Lila, Jasper, the Temple of Artemis, all of it…

"I wish… to know who I truly am."

"And what will ye give?" asked the tree with the voice of Owen.

"Anything."

"Everythin'?" The heron asked, which appeared above him once again.

"Everything," he confirmed. Owen's drumming increased to a climactic intensity, overcoming a final boom of thunder. The rain lightened up, and the heron disappeared once again. Ethan lifted his hand to see that little blood now came from the small cut that the holly had made. He looked over to see Owen was now on his knees once more.

"Can I leave the tree now?" asked Ethan, who was answered with Owen's hand motioning him to come back over.

"See? Easy?" came the exhausted voice of Owen.

"How did you do that? Cause the storm?"

"Cause a storm? I cannot do that. What d'ye think I am? A wizard?"

"Well… maybe."

"Wizards are not real, Ethan."

"A druid then."

"I'm no druid. Only an old fool who speaks to their memory," he joked, lifting his head up to reveal a joint in his mouth.

"Oh, so ye've been fucking with me this whole time?"

"I joke about many things, Ethan. But when it comes to this, I do not joke. What ye just did there is a sacred bond. The spirits will help ye as long as ye listen."

"How do I listen?"

"By clearin' yer mind and always bein' open to receive."

"Well, I'll do my best the last few days I'm here."

"Last few days? Ye cannot leave now."

"I have to; I'll return to work on the first of November."

"So ye think. We shall see. But ye will stay for Samhain then?"

"Yes, I guess since everyone keeps asking me to go."

"Ye will see me there. Ye should help me in the procession."

"That will not happen. Not my thing."

"Keep an open mind, young Ethan."

"Give me a puff of that weed and we can see if it opens my mind any." Ethan reached across.

"Not going to happen."

"Why not? Spirits say I can't?"

"No, this is just ma last joint," Owen laughed. "And I'm tired. I must prepare myself more; the festival is closin' in. Ye should rest as well."

"Yeah, alright. Well, I'll leave ye to yer preparations," Ethan said sarcastically, standing up and beginning to walk away.

"Ethan."

"Yeah?" He turned around.

"Excited to see what ye learn from the heron," he said with another sly smile.

"Yeah, me too." He turned to leave. "What the fuck?" he thought to himself as he walked back towards the base of the Tor.

—

Ethan had good energy at first, but he was quickly struck with exhaustion as he drew closer to town. His eyes became heavy, and his legs felt weak carrying him. He passed by the library where he had met Lila and Matteo earlier. He looked inside to see Matteo asleep on the couch, a book placed over his chest.

Walking by Zoe's, he saw that she too had not left the shop or the flat, the sign still hanging undisturbed in the window. Even The Andrew's Cross was shut up. All around town, it appeared that the majority of shops were closed early, and the entire town was quiet; hardly anyone was in the streets. Walking by the garden where Selene normally was, he saw that she too was not out working. The time was just past two in the afternoon when he arrived back at the Temple of Artemis, where he quickly made his way into his white robe and upstairs. He barely made it to the bed before he collapsed into a deep sleep.

—

A loud noise came from the main floor, waking Ethan from a deeply enriching sleep. The moon was now out and visible through the bay window.

"What the hell was that?"

Another loud noise came from below; this time it sounded like shattering glass. He ran out and down to see what was happening. Ethan barged into the kitchen to find Vesta and Cardea wrestling with a large animal in the middle of the kitchen. Blood was all over the floor and covering their dresses. The animal was a deer that was being skinned and cut up by the two insane-looking women.

"What the fuck!" Ethan shouted.

Cardea turned to "shhh" Ethan. Vesta was struggling to hold back a gag reflex from the spitting blood.

"Fuck off with the silence. Why is there a deer in the middle of the kitchen?!"

Cardea pointed out the window to the full moon.

"Oh, no meat unless it's a full moon? Is that what it is?"

Cardea nodded; Vesta put her hands to her mouth and ran outside to vomit. Cardea let out a sigh with a large knife in her hands. She looked to Ethan as if to ask, "Help out?"

"You have to be joking?"

She shrugged and handed him the knife.

"Fuck it." Ethan grabbed the knife and helped Cardea process the deer. Ethan had no experience doing so; however, Cardea seemed to know exactly every step, showing Ethan and communicating without speaking. The deer was cold to the touch but was clearly hunted with what appeared to be arrows. Another woman came in from the garden, who was also wearing white.

"Oh hello, my name is Maddie. You must be Ethan," the woman responded, presenting a bloodied hand to Ethan to shake.

Cardea motioned for them to be quiet.

"Right, well let's cut up this deer and get to cooking. You can ask me questions if you want afterwards. Deal?"

"Yeah, deal I guess. What do you need?"

Maddie then had Ethan wash up and begin cutting potatoes and other veggies for several stew pots that were on the hob already. Meanwhile, Maddie and Cardea prepared several cuts for Ethan to add to the growing stews. Much of the deer was wrapped in parchment paper. The skin was taken outside and hung to dry by Cardea, leaving Maddie and Ethan alone in the kitchen.

"Should be safe to talk; just be quiet. How's the stew coming along?" Maddie whispered.

"Oh, you know, could use a bit of salt. Think the potatoes are coming along nicely, also… what the fuck just happened?"

"Bet it has been a bit of a shock with the whole silence thing, yeah?" she said with a thick northern accent, smiling to cut the tension.

"To say the least."

"Bit posh, aren't you? London then?"

"Yes."

"Well, welcome to the country," she held up a hoof of the deer to her face with a crazed look in her eye.

"You the hunter?"

"Yes, brought this beautiful creature from the Highlands today. Barely made it for the full moon."

"Is this legal?"

"Legal enough. But it is for religious reasons regardless."

"What do you mean?"

"We worship the Goddess Artemis, the hunting goddess. Our temple believes that we must only consume meat that has been hunted in a way that honors the animal. This animal was hunted with a bow, killed humanely, and we will honor every part of her."

"I don't think this is legal."

"It's a gray area. But think about it. Do you like sausage rolls? Bacon? All of these things we eat daily that we are so disconnected from? Over ten million pigs are killed a year in the UK, and we never bat an eye. We kill one animal a month in a way that honors her. What is worse?"

"So you are an activist then? Throw pigs' blood on people in Piccadilly Square often?"

"Someone is uptight. No, we simply wish to live a different way."

"What is with the whole silent thing?" Ethan changed the subject.

"Oh, that is just Vesta and Cardea's thing; we all just go along with it until they are done. Most of us don't live here in the temple any longer; we all have moved on."

"Where are you from? The north, obviously."

"Yes, the north. Yorkshire area. We have a small group around there that do ceremonies. But we all come back to Glastonbury and the first temple as much as we can."

"How long will the stew take?"

"At least two more hours. But we will make other things once Vesta gets her stomach back. Then we will feast all night in Artemis' honor. Will you join us?"

Ethan looked at the blood-covered floor. "Lost my appetite, believe it or not."

"Well, we will save you some of the meat since I am sure you miss it staying here. Won't have any more until the next full moon. Also, I will be back to Yorkshire in the morning."

"I think I will leave you to your stew and your rituals then." Ethan said tiredly.

"Hope you enjoy your stay here. Vesta and Cardea are wonderful when they actually speak. Even better when they are quiet, if you asked me," she winked.

"Don't plan on being here that long."

"Shame, then just enjoy your time in Glastonbury. Staying much longer?"

"Till the first, and yes. I know of Samhain, and yes I am going." Ethan answered, predicting her next set of questions.

"Magical night, Samhain. Well off to bed then. We shouldn't make much more noise. Pleasure meeting you…?"

"Ethan, my name is Ethan."

"Pleasure, Ethan. Stop by if you are ever up in York." She gave him a hug, forcing him to look down to see both of their white robes were now stained red. "Oh, leave the robe down here. They will wash them for you after the ceremony."

"Yeah, right. Good night then." Ethan took his robe off and walked back up to his room to his bed once again.

"I honestly don't know what else can surprise me about this bloody town," he said aloud as he looked out towards the full moon. "Maggie was pretty hot… fuck, there I go again. Fucking Matteo in my head. Heron in my head, Owen and his bloody trees. Place is fucking with me."

A cold draft was coming from the open side window. Ethan got up and studied the wet and shimmering street below him.

"Just ten more days, that is all you get from me. Then I am gone," he whispered to the Tor before closing the window and heading back to bed. He dreamed of London, then of ancient Atlantis, and then of nothing else.

6
SAMHAIN

Over the next nine days, Ethan found himself in a familiar pattern that he did not stray from: in the morning, he would wake up and make a quiet breakfast in the Temple of Artemis, a place he very much did not like being in after the full moon incident. He would find his way to the Andrew's Cross Café, where he would share brief conversations with Hamish and Isla about the weather, business levels, and different flavors of coffee. Hamish even convinced him to switch from a skinny latte to a full-bodied cortado. Afterward, Ethan would sit outside near the market cross until he spotted one of his various acquaintances from around town. Typically, this was Matteo, who woke up early to watch the sunrise every day; however, on two occasions, the first person Ethan encountered was Zoe, who would walk several of her ever-rotating collection of dogs early in the mornings.

Ethan would then repeat similar routines with Matteo, Zoe, Jasper, or Lila around town: there was always a walk up to the Tor, which was getting more difficult every day with the cooling temperatures. They would then walk down to the White Springs, where the group would take a quick dip in the freezing waters before wandering back to a café or library to spend the afternoons talking, reading, playing board games, or eating finger sandwiches until the sun began to set. In the evenings, they would occasionally go to the pub, where a few pints would be shared along with more conversation and board games.

On the final Wednesday afternoon, the sun came out and warmed the town to a summer-like quality. Zoe recommended that everyone hang out in the Glastonbury Abbey gardens—where Matteo and Ethan had not visited up to that point. The gardens were built around the old Abbey that had long since been decommissioned and turned into a place for folk to meditate and smoke weed among many old and wondrous trees. Supposedly, the body of King Arthur was buried in the gardens; however, Lila said this was unlikely and was instead a tactic used to attract tourism to the area. Regardless, it was a good place to spend the day with friends among the company of ancient yews, oaks, and apple trees.

Matteo had requested to visit the Red Springs that same Friday, which Zoe was happy to oblige with a tour. The Red Spring was a much more manicured experience and featured a large wellhead with a decorative cover on display. Water flowed from a waterfall and wove its way through the walled-off grove; however, Ethan felt little special about the space. Matteo, of course, found it deeply moving and spent the entire day asking Zoe questions about its history and legends. Ethan only stayed because there was nothing better to do, he had paid to go in, and he was becoming increasingly infatuated with Zoe.

Her light and joyful Irish accent, her goofy smile, and her ever-snorting laugh were becoming increasingly endearing to him. He found himself getting excited any time she was a part of their daytime group but was also saddened whenever she had to leave early or work in the shop rather than gallivant up and down the high street.

On a few occasions, Ethan saw Owen around town talking to various people, and each time, Owen would pause to look Ethan in the eye from afar. This provided a sudden and serious reminder of the moment he spent between the two ancient oaks, listening to the drums and thunder produced by Owen. Ethan would quickly try to shake off the feelings of responsibility and guilt that came from the fact that he was merely trying to enjoy his time in Glastonbury before returning home to London at the end of his holiday. Despite his grumbling and constant complaints about the lack of activities in the town, he had to admit to himself that he was steadily growing fond of the peaceful and laid-back lifestyle he had created with his new, dear friends in the little town of Avalon. Each night, he would go back to his small room wishing for a TV to ease his ever-running mind before bed. Besides one pub on the edge of the high street, there was nowhere to catch up on shows, news, or sports in the whole town. This left Ethan feeling isolated from the world beyond. It didn't help that his mobile phone stayed silent most days; outside of one drunken call from his mother, he felt forgotten by the world he came from. This was all about to change as time marched on to October 31st, the night of the Samhain festival and Ethan's final evening in Glastonbury.

"I do not understand; why must you leave tonight?" Matteo asked as they walked toward Zoe's store on the afternoon of the 31st.

"Because I have to be back in London tomorrow to start work. I have a half day."

"You should not go. Call in sick."

"I can't do that; living here hasn't been entirely free, you know."

"Call in sick for the rest of that job. It has been too good this time here in Glastonbury." Matteo had a sadness in his voice.

"Yeah, I have enjoyed it too. But real life is calling me."

"Pffft, real life! This is real life! Tonight we have this amazing festival to look forward to."

"What time did Zoe say to meet at her flat?" Ethan asked, looking down at his watch.

"Just past three; the festival starts at four."

"And my bus leaves at 9:50 PM tonight."

"I heard the festival goes all night! You will miss some of it! You see, you should stay," Matteo pleaded.

"I am sure I will see all I need to see. I also have to leave around nine to grab my luggage, then back to the bus station."

"The bus will run tonight?"

"I bloody well hope so. Come on; Zoe should be waiting."

They reached the door to the side of The Nine Realms and knocked three times to get Zoe's attention. On the other side, they could hear the barking of several dogs already excited at the prospect of visitors. Then they heard a faint voice from within:

"Come in! My hands are full!"

The door opened to a staircase that led to the second-level flat that Zoe occupied. The space was made up of five decent-sized rooms with a small central hallway connecting each of them. Zoe was in what Ethan assumed was her bedroom; she was obscured by the door when they reached the central hall.

"Sorry! Still getting ready; head into the sitting room and have yourselves a snack. I will be there in a minute."

Matteo was the first to peek his head into the far room facing the high street. Ethan followed to find that all twelve dogs were waiting for them on various soft cushions around the living space. Despite their cries for attention, they all stayed in their designated spaces and awaited the two men to greet them with pets and affection. After completing the rounds, they sat on the open couch before a heavy wooden table that held an assortment of "Samhain" themed snacks —essentially Halloween snacks from what Ethan had seen in the States. They both helped themselves to pumpkin cookies and fresh cider while looking around the space.

As with most flats in the UK, this space used to have a working fireplace that was now bricked up and reclaimed by Zoe to hold candles. There were various plants around the edges of the windows, illuminating the space in a pleasant green hue. There was no TV, but plenty of bookshelves bore far more than just books; various jars lined the shelves, containing labels and mysterious ingredients inside. There was a small desk against the central wall with a very thick laptop resting upon it. While the space was fairly organized and tidy by Glastonbury standards, the desk had a myriad of papers and post-it notes scattered about, revealing Zoe's business practices. Hidden away on the floor by the desk were a series of law books that now held plants and old coffee cups upon them. The space was well-lived-in, but cozy, and Ethan felt at ease while they both waited for Zoe to finish up.

"Who else is coming with us tonight?" Matteo called down the hall.

"I invited Isla, Jasper, and Lila to join us here tonight. But Jasper and Lila will be going later to help with the procession," came Zoe's voice, now closer from down the hall. "What do you think?"

Zoe came through the doorway wearing a long black dress made of feathers and emerald stones; her usually messy hair was now tucked away behind a black masquerade mask in the shape of a crow's beak. On most days, Zoe wore many layers, and they were generally quite large for her size. Now this dress revealed to Ethan that she had an incredibly beautiful frame that made his heart race at the sight of her. He was completely enveloped in her image.

"You look incredible!" Ethan stood, followed by Matteo.

"Wow! You are like a big black bird!" Matteo said with goofy excitement.

"Not just any big black bird, but a big black crow! Caw!" she cried!

"Won't you get… you know—cold?" Ethan asked, looking at her slender shoulders that were exposed, along with the top of her collar revealing her previously invisible cleavage.

"Yes, I thought of that, which is why I have this!" She produced a thick shawl made of more feathers, as well as several small bones that dangled from the shoulder piece like Christmas ornaments; it also completely covered her cleavage from view.

"Bloody shawl!" He thought.

"Wow! Are those bones? And emeralds?" asked Matteo.

"Yes, real bones. No, fake emeralds. I like looking good, but I am, in fact, still a very poor witch," she snorted with a laugh.

"I feel very underprepared for tonight," said a still-blushing Ethan.

"Yes, you are right! Do you have anything for us to wear, dear Zoe?" asked Matteo.

"Well, it is all for women, but you are more than welcome to snaffle something from my wardrobe should you take good care of it."

"Yes! Ethan, come, let us get dressed."

"You know what? I think I feel spooky enough in Zoe's company, thank you."

"Ah, I will find something for you too!"

"That won't be—" Ethan tried to say; however, Matteo was already skipping down the hall, choosing not to listen. Thus leaving Zoe and Ethan alone… along with the dogs, who were all very excited to see a dozen dangling bones from Zoe's shawl.

"Zoe, you really do look incredible."

"Aw, thanks, Ethan. You look quite good yourself. What are you supposed to be, then?" She joked while looking at his wool jumper, jeans, and set of old trainers.

"Oh, well clearly I am a zombie, recently come from the grave to eat the brains of the hippies of Glastonbury!" He mimicked the arms of a zombie on the march.

"That was horrifically cringe, but maybe that will keep away the evil spirits tonight as well! Here, let me help your look." She dashed over to the desk and found a small tube of red paint, which she squirted onto a small brush and began to apply to Ethan's face. This was the closest the two had been; Ethan looked deep into her eyes and saw the focus on her expression as she painted unknown symbols onto his face.

"You know, Zoe—"

"Hold on! Almost done; need some darker red to add depth," she grabbed more paint and continued working now on his eyes. "What were you going to say, then?"

"Tonight is my last night and—"

"Shit, no! I forgot. This is horrible news; I really wish you could stay longer," she pouted.

"Yeah, I am starting to wish so too."

"You know, I don't normally like getting close to new people in town. Because usually they leave, just like you are about to now. It's a shame."

"Why is it a shame?" Ethan pressed for some flirtation.

"Because this town is bloody awesome. Speaking of bloody, I think I am done. Look!" She pointed him towards a mirror on the wall. He looked over to see that she had painted fake blood running down from his eyes and pooling just below his lips.

"For something you just came up with, not bad at all."

"Wait till you see what Lila and Isla do! They are both fantastic artists. Me? I am just the village hag," she danced in a circle, showing off her feathers.

"Far more than a hag! What exactly are you dressed as, anyways?"

"This Samhain I decided to be the Goddess of War and Death! The Morrigan!" She raised her arms up fiercely.

"The Morrigan?"

"Yeah, that's right. She is from Irish mythology. It is said that seeing her on a battlefield is an omen of death. But she has many aspects, and not all so grim. There is a lover hidden within her as well."

"A lover hidden within, eh?"

Just then, Matteo came down the hall and gallivanted into the living room. "What do you think?" he declared, revealing that he had found a robe that fit his slender frame, completely red, with a fox mask that barely fit over his face.

"What are you supposed to be?" Ethan asked.

"I don't know, something spooky!"

"Foxes are spooky?"

"Well, to chickens, they are pretty scary!"

"You are the perfect fox spirit, Matteo," Zoe laughed and clapped for him.

"Ah, I see you have been killed," Matteo noticed Ethan's fake blood.

"And brought back from the grave!" Zoe added with a dramatic voice. Ethan raised his arms like the risen dead once again, just a little less enthusiastically.

Knock, knock, knock!

Came the door below. "Come in!" shouted Zoe. Jasper came up dressed in a simple dark green robe and a massive set of antlers that were strongly fashioned to a hat and harness—he had to walk sideways to get into the room. He was followed by Isla, who was painted blue, including dark blue-dyed hair, and an elegant dress that had been tattered in strategic places.

"Oh, let me guess!" Zoe pondered Jasper first. "Cernunnos?"

"What gave it away?" He joked, pointing at his horns; he held a small fake snake in his right hand.

"Now Isla, I must admit you have me completely stumped. Mermaid Barkeep?"

"Close, actually! I tried tae make a spooky selkie. Not sure how successful I was. Didnae want tae go the full half-seal look; figured it would be too hard tae get around," she replied.

"I can see it now, actually! Well, we have Jasper the Horned God, Isla the Selkie, Ethan the Zombie, Matteo the Fox, and Zoe the Morrigan!" Zoe declared victoriously. "Now we just wait to see what Lila has made for us."

"I talked tae her earlier at the café; she said she might not make it to the party because she was still working on her costume. Ye know how she gets about these things," said Isla.

"I hope she's doing alright, poor thing. Well, please sit down, but be careful with those antlers, Jasper! Peanut and Cashew might try to bite those bad boys if you get them too low," she snorted, the two dogs already eyeing the horns from afar.

"Perhaps I will stay standing then… to avoid any collateral damage as well."

"We have a little while longer, yes?" asked Matteo.

"About an hour before people will start gathering down at the festival grounds," answered Zoe.

"Good, then may I ask what is happening tonight? You have been very secretive this week about it!"

"We didn't want to spoil the surprise," replied Jasper.

"This is only ma second Samhain festival here," said Isla, "and I really couldnae tell ye how magical it is. It's only beaten by Beltane in the spring for the magic it brings forth in the town."

"What is the history of it?" Matteo asked further.

"Come now, Zoe; this is yer thing. Ye're the storyteller!" Isla insisted.

"Okay, okay. Come 'round the biscuits, and I will tell the wee ones about Samhain!" She motioned her hands around the center table, and everyone, except Jasper, sat down and watched as Zoe the Morrigan told her tale:

"Samhain is a festival that goes all the way back to the times of the Tuatha Dé Danann when—" Ethan raised his hand. "Yes?"

"Who are the Tuatha Dé Danann?" Ethan asked, genuinely confused.

"The Tuatha Dé Danann were the first inhabitants of Ireland before the Milesians came to the isle, often considered gods by us today. Now, no more questions till after! Now, the Tuatha were said to live within the caves, hills, and ancient sites of Ireland. Now we in Ireland call this the Otherworld, and it is said this is where the Sidhe lived… and I can tell I am losing Ethan again! The Sidhe, pronounced like "Shee," are the fairies of Ireland, the wee people who live in nature; we consider these to be the spirits of the Tuatha as well. Now, Samhain is the time of year when darkness and winter is said to take over; it is also when the veil that separates our world from the world of the Sidhe, the world of the gods, thins. During this time, we can more easily connect with the spirits of the land and, by extension, the land of the dead. There is also a story about a man going into a small cave named after, you guessed it! The Morrigan. This cave was one of the entrances to the Otherworld, and it is where a man named Nera went to receive a prophecy about a war against his queen. This cave is said to be the origin of Samhain; however, I have been to this cave, and I have been to Avalon—and to you, my dear Ethan, Matteo, Jasper, Isla—this is the most magical place to feel the veil thinning. This is where we feel the Sidhe more than anywhere else in the world." She leaned back, exhausted from saying all of this in what seemed like one breath of air.

"Wow! You are such a great storyteller!" Matteo exclaimed.

"Thank you, thank you!" She bowed to a small applause from her audience.

"So what will happen tonight?" asked Ethan.

"Mischief!" Zoe responded while moving her fingers like a spider's legs.

"No, I mean, like, what will the festival be?"

"Oh, that! I am not sure. It's different every year. Jasper? You are on the inside; any insights?" Zoe asked.

"Well, I have been let into the inner circle of Owen and his troop—" Ethan's ears perked up at Owen's mention. "I cannot say too much, as I am being initiated as fire keeper, which is a great honor that I am so ready to be tasked with. But I can say that the ritual tonight involves the Cailleach and the return of the winter hag!"

"Who is going to be the Cailleach?" asked Isla. "Wonder if it will be Lila! Maybe that is why she is so secretive today."

"That I really don't know. I know that the May Queen from last year, Christine, will be involved in some way… I am saying too much. I must be silent! Actually, what is the time?"

"Half-past," replied Ethan.

"I should get going; I will swing by Lila's and see if she is ready too. We are needed earlier for preparations. Excuse me," he got up, knocking his horns on the lamp on his way out. "Shit, sorry! Well, I look forward to seeing you all tonight; enjoy the festival!"

“Good luck, Jasper!” called out Zoe.

“Keep that fire!” shouted Matteo. “How one keeps a fire, I do not know,” he joked to those still in the living room.

“Half-past; I should probably check on Hamish at the shop one last time before we head tae the festival grounds,” announced Isla.

“Why don’t we join you? We can all head over together afterward,” suggested Zoe.

“And we can all get a hot drink before the cold sets in tonight,” added Ethan.

“Yes, please! Even as a fox, my blood is still Italian!”

“Right, everyone head downstairs. I will sort the dogs for the evening, and we can all meet on the street,” Zoe clapped her hands to excite the dogs, and everyone else headed down the stairs to wait for her outside in the brisk autumn air.

—

The group stopped by to see Hamish briefly; however, the narrow streets of Glastonbury were beginning to fill up with tourists and locals alike, all clamoring for skinny lattes. The Andrew’s Cross was the only café open in town—likely due to the fact that all the other cafés were owned by people who were now preparing for the festival. Isla snuck behind the milk-covered counters to make drinks for Matteo, Ethan, and Zoe. She gave a quick kiss to Hamish, who stopped for a moment to look at his wife with a smile before getting back to work.

"He really loves you. That look he gave? That was powerful," said Matteo as he was handed his large chai.

"I'm the luckiest woman in the world. I asked if he needed help, but he told me tae go enjoy the festival. He'd stay open for as long as he could stand. Luckily we were so busy, he didn't mind that I stole these drinks for us," she winked, handing a hot chocolate to Zoe, then the cortado to Ethan.

They then moved through the quickly crowding street to the small town hall parking lot, which had been converted into a place for various vendors, food trucks, and small canvas tents for activities such as tarot readings, face painting, energy realignments, and the chance to hold an owl on your arm. Most of the people running the booths were not recognizable to Ethan, as many of them had various costumes on, hiding their identities. There were witches, skeletons, fairies, beasts, and all manner of painted people running around the small festival grounds.

"So, this is the festival?" asked Ethan.

"Not exactly; the procession will start from the Abbey next door and then will come by here and travel up to the Tor," answered Zoe.

"I wonder what the ceremony will be this year? Owen is mad as a hatter, so I'm sure he's got somethin' magical planned,"commented Isla.

Matteo ventured off from the group to talk with one vendor selling necklaces made of bone and crystal. Ethan was beginning to feel the amount of people get to him; he hid close to Zoe for some comfort in known company. Many young men were approaching her to look at her outfit with wide-eyed expressions; some stopped to compliment her, and half of them actually seemed genuine. Ethan saw the two brothers from the sharing circle walking around without intricate costumes. They saw Ethan from afar.

"Hello! Your name was Ethan, ja?" asked Mark.

"Yeah, that's right. Mark and Fredrik, right?"

"Ja. What do you think of the festival?"

"It's something. Alright so far. No costumes?"

"Had we known, we would have brought our Krampus suits," said Fredrik.

"Krampus?"

"Ja, you know, Krampus. Big scary goat man, whips those who are bad—"

"—or those who do not give good schnapps!" They both laughed. "How much longer will you stay, Ethan?"

"Just till tonight."

"Ah, same. We leave on the bus tonight as well."

"Then I will see you there. Glad I am not the only one cutting out early."

"So sad. To leave such a town; it has been a very magical place. Well, we will see you later then; it will be good to have company on the ride to Bristol. See you later!" Fredrik and Mark left toward a truck selling beer. Ethan looked to see he had gotten separated from Zoe and Isla; luckily, Matteo was still at the booth buying something from the vendor.

"Matteo, what are you getting?" asked Ethan.

"I am buying us necklaces! To always remember tonight. Now, which one do you like?" He held up four necklaces with strange symbols drawn on them: ᛞ, ᚷ, ᛈ, ᚺ, ᚢ, and ᛚ.

"Do they mean something?"

"Pick one, and I will tell you," Matteo smiled.

"Fine, the first one." He pointed at the one with the ᛞ carved on it; it also had a blue crystal bead. "So, what does it mean?"

"Ah, you have chosen what is called the Dagaz—" Matteo looked back toward the vendor, who nodded in confirmation. "—it means new day, or the dawn. It is a good one, I think!"

"Thanks. What about the others?"

"For Zoe, I will give the one that is associated with gifts and exchanging because she has been such a gift to us. That is the ᚷ. For Isla, I will give the ᛚ too because it is connected to water. Her name means island, yes? And her personality is very water-flowing!"

"And she is dressed as a mermaid."

"Yes! Perfect!"

"And the other two?"

"For Jasper and Lila. But I will not know which to give to whom until I see them, I think. Now, where did our beautiful companions go?"

"Not sure; I lost them when I ran into the Germans."

"You saw the Germans? From the circle?"

"Yeah, they are leaving tonight as well."

"Good, good. I am glad you will not be alone when you leave us! Come, let us find our friends." Matteo put the ᛈ around his neck and wrapped his arm around Ethan, then they both headed into the crowd. Luckily, Isla's blue hair was noticeable in the sea of black clothing that was the primary color of Samhain. The crowd was now beginning to part from the streets, and drumming had begun towards the Abbey.

"Glad ye both found us! We got great spots," said Isla. "Zoe knew exactly where they'd be comin' from."

"Insider trading knowledge," Zoe winked.

"I have these necklaces for you!" Matteo said excitedly, putting the small pendants around their necks.

"Thank ye so much, Matteo! Wow, ye gave me laguz? Is it because I am a mermaid?"

"Yes, of course. I knew exactly what these mean," Matteo said sarcastically, clearly having already forgotten what the vendor had told him of their meanings.

"They are runes, old magic symbols. But you chose good ones; thank you, Matteo," Zoe hugged him. "Now, Ethan, don't leave me again. You help keep away all the ghouls and vampires who are hitting on me." She said, putting her hand on his chest, making him feel more comfortable right away.

"I will not leave you again, my lady," he bowed.

"Until tonight!" she jokingly frowned in return. "Oh! It's starting; everyone look!"

At the end of the street, a group of men had now appeared on horses, each one dressed in tattered robes and chains. Even the horses looked ghostly in appearance. The rider in the front wore a crown made of bones; his eyes painted black revealed ghostly pupils—one white, one blue—his beard was bright white around painted black lips. Ethan immediately recognized him as Owen, his foolish and hippie exterior now replaced by something truly scary to look upon. Behind the host of nine men on horseback was a procession of torches carried by around a dozen men and women, one of whom was Jasper, who now was no longer wearing his robe, revealing a bare chest adorned in thick gold necklaces.

"Is it the Jasper? Woah! Look at him; he looks like a beast!" Matteo declared.

"The God of the Wilds, to be precise. They went with a Wild Hunt theme this year, I see," Zoe analyzed.

"I am in love wi' it!" Isla added.

"I am confused," thought Ethan.

Each person in the torchbearers had much less of a theme than the rest: some were skeletons, others goblins, and a few were even dressed and painted as cats, complete with "meowing." Ethan saw one of the cats begin to lick itself while waving to the crowd.

"Are those bloody cat people?" Ethan finally asked.

"Yeah, sorry 'bout them. Every year they try to hop in, and everyone has problems telling them no. Bit too nice here in Glastonbury at times. But they don't cause any harm," answered Zoe. "Unless you count the number of hairballs that are left in town the next day," she said with complete seriousness.

"Fucking what?"

"Joking with you, Ethan! Now come on; we have to make it up the street. We will sneak down the side streets. Watch out for hairballs!" Zoe ushered them through the crowd into one of the alleyways that ran along the high street.

"The Wild Hunt? What is that?"

"It's a legend from the Germanic countries, but popular here in the UK as well. It's said that a host o' riders carry forth climatic change on horseback. They're out for a hunt to prepare for the Yule feast. If ye're caught out while they're huntin', it's said they'll trample and kill ye! Or even take ye to be one o' their servants,"Isla told the group.

"And this is a family-friendly event? Cat people and demon riders from hell?" Ethan pointed out.

"I quite like the cats," said Matteo.

"What? Why?" Ethan countered.

"They make it more fun. You have these very serious riders with their horses, the fire, all very scary. Then you have the cats to tell you everything will be okay!"

"Right on, Matteo! That is the Glastonbury spirit!" said Zoe.

"Won't catch me out at night with either the riders or them cat people running around," said Ethan, no one seeming to catch his comment.

The group exited at the top of the high street just in time to see the procession take the turn towards the Tor. They were even closer now, as the street had narrowed once again, the horses now going single file to fit without brushing into the crowd. Owen spied over the crowd, looking quite menacing at everyone who made eye contact. Ethan kept his eyes down when he passed over them, only raising his eyes again once all the riders had passed. Jasper was now so close they could feel the flames from his torch on their skin. He kept a serious expression until Isla and Zoe attempted to break him:

"Carry me away on yer antlers!" shouted Isla.

"Wonder what he's packing under them furs!" yelled Zoe.

It wasn't until Matteo shouted, "Are you the God of Horniness too?" that he broke his expression and laughed, extending a hand out to shake that of his friends.

"Wait till you see Lila," he whispered to them as he passed by.

After the torchbearers and cats had passed by, there was a much more somber group of white-robed women with stoic expressions carrying a large ornamented box. Hidden among their group was a figure completely shrouded by a thick black garment. The final group was that of ushers with face paint and hats that signified they were officially with the festival, their job clearly to keep back the crowd some distance. There were several drummers among the crowd, cheering everyone on in chants and shouts; some were even singing in deep low voices that could only be heard when they were close by.

"Does anything else happen?" asked Ethan, who was now checking his watch for the ever-closing bus schedule.

"What do you mean?" asked Zoe in return.

"There is so much happening; canae you feel it?" Isla added.

"Yes, I feel the energy. It is more available to us; the veil is certainly thinner," answered Matteo.

"Load of bollocks," thought Ethan, who realized he was in the minority of the group, so he decided to speak no further on his growing boredom.

The cadence of the drumming began to change as the horses ascended the path onto the first hill of the Tor. As the procession and audience emerged onto the flat grassy hill under the Tor, they were greeted by a display of fire and light that lit the entire layered hill before them. The three tiers of the Glastonbury Tor were lit up by dozens of torches and braziers, accompanied by over thirty people in white robes overlooking the entering crowd. At the peak of the Tor could be seen a yellow figure that almost looked to be glowing from the orange rays of the setting autumn sun.

The figure was a woman with her arms raised high to the sky, the white-robed figures on the hill mimicking her movements. The Wild Hunt stopped the procession at the foot of the second path to the Tor, the drums coming to a dead stop with the final beat of the horses' hooves. The air became still with anticipation; whispers began to form in the audience, and then Owen produced a large horn from his cloak, signaling the other eight riders to do the same. Silence returned to the crowd in time for a loud, low blast from the horns of the riders that shook the earth and sky in a way that reached the core of Ethan's soul. Isla and Zoe lowered themselves to the ground in reverence for the occasion; so did many of the other onlookers who felt the power of the horns—Ethan was left standing, mesmerized by the display.

After the numbing sound of the horns had left their ears, the angelic sound of singing now rang out from the Tor; each of the robed individuals were now singing an angelic tune that radiated from the Tower like a radio signal. Ethan felt the music pierce his heart and begin to produce tears in the corners of his eyes; he sucked in the tears to not allow his companions to see that he was feeling the experience after just feeling boredom from the procession. Matteo, on the other hand, was completely sobbing. Isla and Zoe rose from the earth and raised their hands to the sky to sing in unison. Soon the entire valley was singing in unity with the radiance of the hill. From the top, the golden figure could now be seen descending the Tor with several red-robed companions following behind her. The singing rang out in a constant, unbroken harmony for the duration of the descent down to the base of the Tor, while the path the riders now waited in remained completely silent. Upon reaching the final level of the hill, it could be seen that the golden figure was, in fact, Christine, Zoe's adversary, dressed in golden-wrapped cloth. Her face painted white, black, and red eyeliner made her eyes appear like that of sparrow feathers. Even through the known animosity, Zoe seemed unchanged in her deep reverence for the moment, even as she too saw the person descending before her. Christine had a large golden set of wings in the shape of the sun's rays upon her back, each ray reflecting the ever-dimming sun in a truly spectacular way. The red-robed entourage numbered eight, each one wearing a similar face paint to that of Christine, throwing back their hoods to reveal intricate golden circlets upon their heads.

"Holy shit, there's Lila!" Isla gasped.

Sure enough, in the second row of maidens was Lila, whose normally dark eyes had now been turned bright orange by contacts that all the maidens seemed to be wearing. The singing stopped as Christine and the Maidens arrived in front of the starkly contrasted riders in all black. Luckily, the riders were slightly lower on the hill, allowing everyone to see what came next:

"The wheel continues to turn! The golden light of the sun and her energy are leaving our earthly home. The fires of Beltane have kept us safe since the summer celebrations began. Now they must be extinguished for the winter to come!" Christine orated, now raising her arms and lowering them quickly. Following this, one by one, the fires of the hill behind her began to be extinguished, starting with the Tor itself and then vanishing one by one until the braziers she stood between were put out by the Maidens. They then approached Christine and removed the sun rays from her back. Next came the torchbearers, led by Jasper:

"With the fires of Beltane extinguished, the fires of—" he stuttered, clearly nervous. "—the fires of the wild return to heat our homes. From the spirit of the forest, the fallen trees, the furs of the animals we stay warm. We, the spirits of the wild, bring forth the flames of winter!" They then brought their torches forward and began to relight the fires of the Tor, starting with the braziers around Christine and the Maidens, then working their way up the Tor in silence. The final group of white-robed maidens now made their way forward, led by the black-veiled figure from earlier. The ornate box was brought forward and placed before the Wild Hunt, and opened to reveal several grey-wrapped rolls of fabric.

The black-veiled figure approached the position right before Christine, cast down her hood, and revealed herself to be Selene, her face painted white and hair dyed a deep grey.

"The time of the May Queen has come to an end! The time of winter, of cold and death, is upon us. The throne of Avalon no longer belongs to you, dear sister! I present to you these unholy veils; you and your Maidens will be wrapped in deep slumber, guarded by my fierce warriors till the light returns. My reign brings forth the dark spirits, the deep magics, and the powers of the shadows upon this land of Avalon!" Selene's voice was no longer pleasant warmth from previous encounters; it was heavy, gravelly, and felt full of malice.

Selene's servants then approached Christine and began to wrap her loosely in the veils produced from the chest until she looked like a mummy, only her mouth left exposed. One by one, the Maidens in red, including Lila, were wrapped in similar fashions. While this was being done, the Wild Hunt dismounted and stood before the audience. Owen spoke:

"We, the Wild Hunt, are not to be feared by the mortals of this world. Unless you cross us in the dark of the night, we will not harm you. We receive these gifts of the sun maidens with gratitude. We swear by our oath rings that we will protect the peoples of Avalon from the evilest of spirits for the duration of the winter months. Fear us not, but cross our generosity only once and feel the wrath of winter and her host of riders! Hail to the Cailleach!" His voice echoed deeply.

"Hail!" shouted his riders in return. Each one now taking a wrapped maiden in their arms to place upon their horse's saddle, Owen receiving the wrapped form of Christine, the May Queen, for his own dark steed. After securing the hostages, the horses were reared back and then rode gently into the darkness, horns blown once more on their exit. All that was left before the audience now was Selene, the Cailleach, who now produced a torch of her own from the brazier.

"You will see darkness and winter as a good queen. You will not miss the warmth of the sun and her fair maidens once you see the gifts of winter. For I bring together families; I bear gifts of fellowship to your homes. I set forth feasts at your table!" She walked toward a large pile of wood in the center of the lower hill. The sun had now completely descended into darkness behind the distant horizon. "You will soon see me, a most benevolent queen, for I bear the fire of the dragon!" she threw the torch onto the pile of wood, erupting it into a roaring bonfire! The crowd cheered. "Happy Samhain!" Selene shouted over the valley.

"Happy Samhain!" the crowd shouted in return, the drums now picking up to a fast rhythm, breaking the audience from the static state they were in to now quickly circling around the bonfire. Jasper and his companions were also rushing down from the re-lit Tor to the warmth of the fire, many stopping to hug loved ones. Zoe and Isla ran to meet Selene, who was receiving a large amount of love and praise from every direction. Matteo and Ethan followed suit in hugging Selene.

"That was so beautiful!" declared Matteo.

Ethan, on the other hand, was even more confused. He looked to Zoe for explanation. "I am so lost. Why are we celebrating now? Was that not a bad thing?"

"It was wonderful, wasn't it? Such a great way to bring in the darker months."

"Yes, but what about the women and the whole—being taken away by scary horses thing?"

"That? Oh, all for show. There has to be a touch of the dramatic to keep everyone's attention; had you captivated, I saw!" she joked, nudging him in the ribs. "Did you actually think we hurt people at these festivals?"

"Well, no. But this town doesn't seem to run out of surprises, both good and bad."

"See, you are starting to get it here! Now look, the riders are already coming back. Maidens safe and sound," she pointed towards the distance where the horses were being fitted with warm blankets and the riders were now approaching the bonfire, tankards in hand.

"Happy Samhain!" shouted Owen, raising his drink high to a rousing return from those around him. Lila broke away from the other women towards their group.

"Lila, ye did so incredibly!" Isla congratulated.

"Yeah, wow! So amazing, Lila!" Matteo added.

"Yeah, I think it was shit," she responded, head low.

"What do you mean?" Zoe asked.

"The fires were too dim; the sun wasn't bright enough, and the contacts were a stupid idea."

"Wait, you planned all of it?" Ethan asked, stunned.

"Yeah, well some of it. Just the singing, outfits, the face paint, and the bonfires. Otherwise, it was all Christine."

"So, she did nothing then?" Ethan said directly.

"Yeah, she might have looked good, but I know you were the one who did it all!" Zoe comforted.

"Whatever, I need a drink. Then I need a smoke; then I need to get the fuck out of here," replied Lila.

"I can help with the drinking," Jasper emerged with a few cans of beer. "Had them stashed away behind that tree. Kept nice and cool."

"Jasper, great job being the wild man."

"Great job distracting me! Didn't break character the whole time till you lot started catcalling me!"

"You liked it!" said Zoe. "Think you will return for Beltane?"

"I nearly froze to death with my shirt off. I don't think I will be doing that again. Maybe something closer to the big fires. Anyway, Owen is a mad dog; I might try and work with Silus some after this."

"Always on the move, aren't ye, Jasper?" asked Isla.

"Can't keep my spirit in a box. Now, before my nipples fall off from this cold, let's get pissed!" He raised a can high and began to down the beer.

"Beer, Ethan?" asked Lila.

"I really shouldn't; I need to be going soon. But really, good job out there, Lila. You were incredible."

"Glad you were able to stay. Maybe you can come back for Beltane?"

"Yeah, maybe. Well, let me say goodbye until then; I think I am going to start making my rounds to everyone," he offered up his arms for a hug, which Lila took quickly.

"Bye, Ethan. Don't let London eat you up, alright?" She then ducked back into the crowd. Next up for Ethan to say goodbye to were Isla and Jasper, who were talking near the bonfire about the lineup of the procession.

"Heading out. Pleasure meeting you both."

"Awe, man. Hate for you to leave us; it really has been so wonderful having you in Glastonbury. Happy we met. Come back and see us sometime, will you?"

"Yeah, for sure. Some day. Goodbye, Isla; thank Hamish for me when he recovers from the skinny lattes today, will you? Really great way to start my days."

"Ye've been our favorite customer! And that's sayin' a lot, considerin' ye've only ever paid for half o' yer drinks. I hope ye crave a full Scottish and return tae us real soon." She hugged him tightly.

Matteo and Zoe were on the edge of the circle when Ethan emerged. "Well, time for me to head off. Saying goodbye to you two is going to be the hardest, I think."

"My brother! Do you remember what I did when we first met?"

"You howled—" Matteo began to howl like a wolf once more, which prompted several partygoers to do the same.

"Yes, and I will howl with sadness until we see each other again. We have each other's mobile phone numbers, yes? I call you every day."

"Once a month."

"Once a week?"

"Fine, once every two weeks."

"Deal!" Matteo embraced him and held back a few tears before finally letting him go, leaving only Zoe before him.

"Well… goodbye, I guess?" he said awkwardly.

"Oh, fuck off with that shite!" She grabbed him even harder than Matteo had before. "So glad I got to be your Glastonbury tour guide."

"Yeah, wish we had more time," Ethan was now feeling the reality of leaving his new friends, especially Zoe.

"Well, I should honestly be getting back to the dogs myself. Why don't I walk with you?"

"Splendid! Couldn't imagine better company," his heart lept with excitement. "Why would she come with you unless she liked you?" he thought.

"Perfect, Matteo. Don't stay up too late. And watch after the others, will you?"

"Yes, I will!" Matteo waved to her and hugged Ethan one last time before the two walked back down into the village together.

—

Zoe did most of the talking: first about the procession and how it compared to the previous year, then to Christine and how she had gotten fatter since the first time she was the May Queen. Eventually, they were sharing some of their favorite memories of their time together in Glastonbury. Ethan's thoughts began to wander more and more to the final night and an opportunity to make a move on his ever-growing feelings toward Zoe. Sadly for him, the walk back to her flat was not long enough; they now stood before the door.

"Shit, I really do wish we had more time," he said.

"I know, but it was so nice of you to come back from the dead one last time to be with us here."

"What?"

"You are a zombie, remember?"

"I honestly had forgotten," he was now leaning against the wall of her building, debating his next move. "Tell her how you feel. Say that you like her. Kiss her, something!" He thought.

"Well, bit chilly out here. I am going to head in. You better call me too. Don't let Matteo steal all of you from the rest of us!" she snorted.

"Your laugh has always been the craziest thing."

"What do you mean by that then?"

"It's adorable," he blushed.

"Oh, thanks, Ethan." He got closer to her.

"I think you are adorable." He leaned in and kissed her gently. What he felt in return was not what he had imagined; her lips were shut like iron doors. She gently pushed him back.

"Ethan, oh no. I am so sorry."

"Fuck, shit, what have I done?"

"Ethan, you are such a good guy, but—"

"I fucked up; I am so sorry. I thought—"

"You didn't think anything wrong. But, it's the cliché of: it's not you; it's me."

"Shit, that hurts," he thought, but his expression said it all the same.

"No, Ethan. What it is—it's not just you—I should say. I don't date anyone; I haven't for a very long time."

"Why not?"

"The same reason you give up a successful law practice to move to the countryside to make next to nothing while hanging out with all your hippie friends."

"I am lost on what you mean."

"No, I was lost. I came here to heal, Ethan. From a broken heart. And until that healing is done, I will not date again. No one."

"Who broke your heart? What did they do that was so awful?"

"It's complicated."

"You can tell me," Ethan edged closer again, but she recoiled and paused in her thoughts.

"Your bus is soon; you should get ready for it."

"Zoe—"

"Please, let's not ruin our goodbye. I have really enjoyed having you in town. And I do hope you come back. But not all who smile are healed. I need more time to do that before I am ready for anything. With anyone." She reached her arms out and embraced him. "Good luck out there, Ethan."

"Goodbye, Zoe. Take care." The door closed, and he was left in the cold of the autumn night, drums still echoing from the celebrations on the Tor beyond the darkened buildings of Glastonbury's streets. Ethan walked slowly back to his home at the Temple of Artemis; he looked into the window of The Andrews Cross to see Hamish asleep in one of the booths, cups all around him.

"At least Hamish seemed to have a successful evening. Fuck, what did I do that for? Well, you like her. Liked her? I don't know. I just need to get my things and get out of here. I can fuss with myself on the bus out of here."

His thoughts continued to ramble, evolve, and throttle his mind every step down the street. As he carried out the last bag, hung up his white robe, and said goodbye to the empty rooms of the Temple of Artemis, Ethan found himself both angry and sad at his leaving. He was sad that it had to end with a rejection and angry at himself for putting it till the last night to make a move. The walk to the bus station in the town center also gave him no peace; when he arrived, Fredrik and Mark were not there, the time now closing in on the bus's scheduled arrival. The streets of Glastonbury were empty outside of a few smokers outside of the pub; Ethan was alone under the bright fluorescent light of a singular light outside of the tarnished bus stop. His watch ticked five past the scheduled time, then ten past, finally half past. The bus was late.

"Fuck me."

Another ten minutes passed; Ethan was growing steadily more anxious and was about to give up and try to call a cab when finally, the bus could be seen rounding the high street curve. The distantly familiar face of the same bus driver from his arrival could be seen in the glow of the window. He hailed the driver and waited for the creaking doors of the entrance to slide open before him. The driver was half-awake, it seemed, and uttered no more than the cost of the fare to Ethan, who quickly exchanged cash for the paper ticket, then took his seat on the first level.

"Glastonbury, what a time it has been. From Italians, cold springs, boredom, and sharing circles. Thank you, I think. But, it is time to face normal life once again," his thoughts rattled on as the bus carried on with no other passengers besides himself. The bus turned at the roundabout towards the A road, which would carry them through the countryside to Bristol, then a night train to London for his arrival back in the big city.

"Maybe I should get a cat and name it Avalon. That would be nice." Ethan was feeling sleep come over him; he rested his head against the glass and nodded off...

—

Ethan awoke to the bus stopping suddenly; he had not been asleep long.

"Already here?"

He looked out the window, expecting to see the busy streets of Bristol, but was instead greeted by the familiar sight of The Andrews Cross and the rest of Glastonbury town center.

"What? We must have needed to come back for someone." Ethan stood up to look out the window to see that no one else was coming and no one else had boarded the bus.

"Driver, why have we come back 'round?" he asked, but got no response. The door then closed, and they were back on their way. The route was the same: right at the roundabout towards the grocer, right at the next for the A road, then left at the next traffic circle towards Bristol. But instead of seeing the road to Bristol, Ethan saw the top of the high street and the silent streets of Glastonbury.

"Right, here we are, Glastonbury. Off ye go."

"No, I am going to Bristol!"

"Bristol then? Aight, ere we go." The driver started off again, and the same thing happened. The doors of the bus swung open on the Glastonbury high street, right outside the central bus stop. "Aight, ere we are! Glastonbury."

"Fine, I will not play this sick joke again. I am getting off!" Ethan stormed off the bus with his backpack on his back and planted his feet on the street when he realized his suitcase was still in storage on the bus. "Hey! I need—" the doors of the bus closed shut, and it began down the road towards the roundabout. Ethan ran after the bus for a few yards before realizing it was not coming back.

"Fuck! What the fuck is happening!" he shouted. "Right, well he will just come back 'round again!" Ethan ran back to the bus stop to wait. He waited for twenty minutes; the bus never came back. He was now alone with only what his backpack contained, and he needed to reach London by morning.

"My only option is to hire a cab. That'll cost me more than a flight to New York and back, I'd imagine; fuck." He needed a number for a service, so he walked to the nearest pub and headed inside. The Monk's Arms was crowded due to the increase of visitors for the festival, making it difficult to reach the barkeeper to ask for a number. Eventually, he was pointed to a notice board with several cabbies' numbers scrawled on business cards.

Raj's Car Hire

"Hello, I need a cab to Bristol tonight… yes… where from? Glastonbury… what do you mean you don't service Glastonbury? Your number is in the bloody pub!" *click*

Malory Car Hire - Glastonbury

Ring. No answer.

Ring. No answer.

Ring. Picked up: "Hello, is this Malory Car Hire? I need a car to Bristol or London. I will pay whatever—oh… your husband is the driver… oh, he died. Sorry to hear that… will you drive me then…" *click*

Ethan called all five numbers left on the pub notice board, and not a single one was able to service the ride, nor seemed interested. Ethan was now entering an extreme panic:

"No cab, crazy bus drivers, no bloody suitcase, and I haven't a place to sleep now either. Long story short, I am fucked."

"You look stressed, mate; need a drink?" asked the barkeeper.

"Yeah, I am pretty bloody stressed right now, thanks. Got a way out of Glastonbury?"

"Aye, of course. I have a car."

"Can I pay you to drive me to Bristol, or even Wells for that matter?"

"Drive on Samhain night? Are you daft? Asking for trouble. Stop by in the mornin', and I will see what I can do. You can pay for such services?"

"Yes, I can pay."

"Lovely; now pour you a pint? Ain't going anywhere till' the morning anyways."

"Fine, give me a dark one. What's your name for the ride tomorrow?"

"Luther; Luther Groggins is my name." He then poured him a pint of a dark black stout and quickly returned to his duties. Ethan took the pint to the seat against the window and sat with his running thoughts, trying to drown them in the glass of bitter.

"Right, ride in the morning; half day tomorrow. I'll call the boss and explain the bus broke down or something. Yeah, that's it; the bus was on the fritz was all." He took a sip of his beer and looked out the window to see many more people coming down from the Tor to the warmth of the several open pubs in town. Many of the faces were still covered in face paint, costumes—or now—warm winter hats. One face caught Ethan's eye: Matteo.

When Matteo realized he was looking at the face of Ethan, his eyes widened and his smile grew to the extreme. Ethan could hear him from inside the pub: "Ethan!" He sprinted inside and rounded the corner quickly. "Have you decided to stay?"

"Against my will, I am afraid."

"What happened?"

"Crazy bus driver, stolen suitcases, and mysterious circumstances?" He thought. "The bus never showed!" he answered, hands in the air with a campy surprised look.

"Well, it is not all bad. You can hang out with us for one more evening! This is perfect!" Matteo shouted with joy. "I will grab a cider as well!" He rushed off to join the queue for the bar. Behind him walked in Lila and Jasper, who noticed Ethan sitting by the window as well. Lila approached first.

"Ethan? What are you doing here?"

"Bus never showed."

"Really? Well, that happens all the time. I am sure Matteo is happy. He honestly hasn't stopped talking about you since you left."

"Yeah, he already found me," Ethan said, looking towards the bar, seeing Matteo waving at him.

"Do you think he is gay?" Lila asked boldly, causing Ethan to choke on his drink.

"What?"

"Matteo; is he gay? He seems obsessed with you."

"Honestly, I haven't given it much thought. I think he is just friendly. He does call me his brother all the time, so that would be weird."

"You might be right… what about you? Gay? Straight? A little bisexual then?"

"What? You are direct. What about you then?"

"I am not sure. I think I am straight; although nights like this… Sorry, booze makes me honest. Right then, another beer for you?"

"Don't ye dare!" came a voice from the entrance. "The lads are drinking whisky tonight!" Hamish walked in with Isla.

"Hamish! Wow, this is a party now!" Matteo rejoined them from the bar.

"I thought you didn't drink?" asked Jasper, who had walked up as well.

"I don't, but anytime I can be around friends and whisky, it leads tae a good night. Plus, I need tae talk to some friends after the day I had. Christ, I think I might hate the smell o' coffee now!"

Two tables were brought together for Isla, Hamish, Lila, Jasper, Matteo, and Ethan to sit together at the edge of the pub next to the window. Ethan kept quiet, still trying to process all that had happened to him and figuring out his plan for the return to London. Isla was wrapped around Hamish, who was telling old stories of Scotland and his time in the Highlands. Matteo and Lila sat next to Ethan, catching him up on the party that happened after he left. Once the bonfire had died down, a group of them had all run up the Tor to see the night sky and flickering flames from above. Owen and the Wild Hunt played songs and sang old folk tunes to everyone before it got too cold. Selene had made herself scarce after her congratulations and affectionate hugs were given. The town now had people crowded all around the pub, both in and out of costume. Hamish was pouring small tastes of whisky for everyone to try; slowly the sharp taste got to everyone's heads, and Ethan felt his eyes getting heavy.

"Where will you sleep tonight?" asked Matteo.

"Yes, will they let you back into the Temple of Artemis?" added Jasper.

"I don't know. They were not there when I left early tonight. Do they actually have rooms for rent in the pub?"

"Aye, they do. But don't let them swindle ye! Come, stay the night wi' us. We've got a spare room wi' a couch. Ye'll sleep there," said Hamish, who patted his back with his large hands. "Speakin' of, what's the time?"

"Half two," answered Jasper.

"Christ! None of us will get any sleep tonight with this noise outside," said Hamish, rubbing his face.

"Do ye want to stay wi' us tonight, Ethan?" asked Isla.

"If you'll have me. But I do need to leave early; the barkeep is going to take me to Bristol tomorrow."

"Didn't know he could drive, let alone had a car… well, a place to sleep will dae ye good,"said Hamish.

They had two more tastes of Hamish's whisky before the streets started to quiet down and everyone began to return to their homes for the evening. Hamish, Isla, and Ethan were some of the first to leave and say their goodbyes. The apartment above The Andrew's Cross was similar to that of Zoe's; each room was fairly small and sparsely decorated, besides that of the living room. Isla prepared the couch in the spare room for Ethan before heading off to remove her make-up and change clothes. Ethan placed his backpack on the floor and examined what was within:

"My toiletries, my mobile charger, water bottle, raincoat, two pairs of underwear, and wallet… everything else is probably in Bristol by now on that bloody cursed bus. How in the world am I going to find it tomorrow? Fuck, I need to call work. Find a way to wiggle out of this. What time is it? Wake up early to get the lift. How much money do I even have? Fuck, Zoe. I had almost forgotten. I should call her; apologize for everything. Maybe I will see her tomorrow walking the dogs before I leave. Have to explain." His thoughts rattled on as he settled in on the sofa. The noise from the streets was quiet, besides the faint noise of people drumming on the Tor. The gentle thumping in the distance rang in Ethan's ears as his mind tried to justify what had happened to him. He was fully convinced that all that occurred was explainable, with little sight of what would be proven to him in the following days…

7
The Lighthouse

The pub's doors opened at ten in the morning. Ethan had several missed calls already from the office in London, one of which he answered to explain he would be in later that day. When he arrived at the bar, he was greeted by a woman in her forties.

“Mornin’, love! What can I do for you?”

“Is Luther working?”

“Luther?”

“Yes, Luther Groggins was his name. Said he would give me a lift this morning.”

“Well, you must be mistaken.”

“Why is that?” His blood pressure rose.

“Luther Groggins hasn’t worked here in over ten years.”

“Well, perhaps he was just helping last night?” His mind began to fuzz over in panic.

“No, dear. That wouldn’t be possible.”

“Why not?” He was panicking.

"Because Luther Groggins died ten years ago."

The world around Ethan closed in. His thoughts raced so much that his brain seemed to only exist in the blur they created. "Who did I speak with last night then? Can you drive me? Who can drive me?" All the things he wanted to say, but he could not seem to produce from his mouth. Instead, he grabbed his one bag and walked out into the quiet streets still littered with the rubbish of the evening. Reacting on instinct, Ethan began to run up the High Street toward the exit of town. He ran for twenty minutes until he reached the traffic circle where the bus had turned several times the night before.

Wells (6.5 Miles)
Bristol (26.7 Miles)

He read the white letters on the road sign, pointing toward the northern A road. His pace was steady as he continued to run along the sleepy roads of the Somerset countryside. The road took a bend to the left around an old farmhouse. As he rounded the corner, he was greeted by a sinking feeling in his gut and a low hum in his ear. What followed was the familiar sight of the road leading toward the High Street in Glastonbury, the Tor standing ominously in the distance… he had rounded the corner and found himself back in the village!

"What the fuck!" he shouted, turning in the opposite direction to run south toward the town of Street, less than three miles from Glastonbury. He was growing tired and panting deeply as he passed the few industrial buildings that lined the southern streets of Glastonbury. He reached the traffic circle that led to the brief stretch of farmland before the buildings of Street began. Just as before, he felt a low humming in his body as he rounded the edge of the traffic circle and then appeared on the edge of the High Street, looking directly at the Glastonbury Tor.

"Fuck, fuck, fuck! What is happening!" He was now drenched in sweat despite the cool morning air; his breath was now visible, his legs sore, and his hands were shaking, braced against his knees.

"What do I do? What do I do? What is happening?"

He walked briskly toward the High Street shops, where people were beginning to emerge from their flats from the night before.

"Do you have a car?" he asked the first person he saw.

"No mate, sorry. Don't believe in them."

"Useless!"

"You there, do you have a car?"

"I do…"

"Can you—"

"But it's in the shop."

"Shit!"

Ethan ran to the center of town, asking everyone he came across, each time being rejected. "Does no one own a car in this town!" he shouted. He slumped against the market cross and slid onto the ground, placing his head in his palms and beginning to cry.

"Why has this happened to me? What did I do?" His thoughts drifted into a thick cloud of anger, frustration, and sadness. The only thing to break him out of his mind was the gentle tapping of something against his shoulder.

"Ave a good Samhain, Ethan?" Up he looked to catch the gaze of Owen, who was now back in his usual pirate-looking outfit, a wide grin on his face.

"You! You did this!" Ethan directed his finger toward the old man.

"Me? I didn't do a thing. It were the fairies."

"You, the fairies, the fucking May Queen, I don't care! I want it undone!"

"Undone? What is it they did to ye?"

"I can't leave the town!"

"Why would ye want to leave then?"

"I have to get back to London."

"Why?"

"For my bloody job, that's why!"

"What is a job, anyway?"

"It is everything! Without it, who am I?" Ethan said, tears welling in his eyes.

"Exactly. Ye don't know who ye are, Ethan, and goin' back to that job won't help a bit." Owen placed his hand on

Ethan's shoulder. "Embrace Glastonbury, son. She will heal you."

"Who will heal me?"

"Avalon, the Caelliach, the Tor itself. Ye know it, Ethan; this place is always exactly what ye need if ye open yer heart to her. Lucky for ye, she sees somethin' special in ye if she won't let ye leave."

"I thought it was the fairies that kept me here?" Ethan questioned.

"Fairies, Goddesses, spirits, the bloody Virgin Mary herself; it don't matter. It's all the same here."

"Are the Goddesses going to pay my bills then, sea captain dipshit?"

"No, Goddesses don't tend to like money very much, I'm afraid."

"Then what do I do?"

"Give yerself to the land, Ethan. Trust in her and her people."

"Load of fucking good that does me."

"I will tell ye this, Ethan: spend a little more time listenin', and less time runnin' your flap. You may find the answers to all yer problems."

"Fuck off, you old bastard!" he mocked.

"Think on what I said; I think ye would be surprised." Owen paused to look up the road. "Friends of yers?"

Ethan looked up to see Matteo and Jasper riding two bikes down the High Street, looking right at him below the market cross. Ethan looked up toward Owen to see he had already exited quickly around an alley and out of sight.

"Ethan! What are you still doing here?" asked Matteo, who slowed his bike and dismounted in front of him.

"I am trapped in this stupid town," he replied.

"Oh no. Did you not get the car out of town then?" Jasper asked.

"Couldn't find the guy from last night. Now I am going to lose my job, lose my flat… fuck me, man. I will have nothing if I can't get back to London."

"There is still time. When do you need to get to the train station in Bristol?"

"I need to be in London today, maybe tomorrow, to save my ass."

"Then take my bike, ride to Wells, pick up the bus there to Bristol, and get your ass back to London," Jasper said cheerfully, rolling his bike over to Ethan.

"Yes! What an amazing plan! I will ride with you, then I can take both bikes back on the bus this evening. I would love to see Wells anyway. I heard they filmed a movie there!" Matteo exclaimed.

"Are you sure?" asked Ethan.

"Of course. Get going; I will go find Owen. I want to talk about last night anyway. See where I can improve for Beltane!"

"Would this work? I can't seem to walk out of town. Maybe I can ride out of town. And with Matteo there… perhaps it'll work…" he thought. "It's worth a try," he said. Ethan took the bike from Jasper, who waved to him as he and Matteo took off up the High Street toward the bike path that led to Wells.

It took only a few minutes to reach the edge of town and the paved road that snaked its way through the countryside northward. The colors of autumn were at their peak in the sparsely wooded fields of the Glastonbury countryside. The town of Wells was obscured by a series of low hills that surrounded the Tor.

"Do you really think Glastonbury is stupid?" asked Matteo, who was riding alongside Ethan's brisk pace.

"What? No, I mean… sometimes, yeah. Don't you find it a bit odd? The people as well?"

"I love everything about it. This is the most I have felt free since I left Italy."

"How long ago was that?"

"Many, many months ago. I have wandered ever since my brother's death. This place, it feels like home."

"Would you leave?"

"I cannot stay forever! But sometimes… it feels like Glastonbury doesn't want me to leave either," said Matteo.

"You have no idea how right you are…" Ethan said in a low voice. They were now approaching the boundary of the small hills separating the fields of Glastonbury and Wells. "This is the furthest I have made it… perhaps this is my chance. Maybe I will make it!" Growing excited, Ethan sped his bike faster up the path. There was a small depression between the hills that led to the other side. Matteo was now several yards behind him as he rounded the small rise to see Wells in the distance.

"Yes! I can see—" Ethan felt a humming in his ears once more; his vision began to swirl, and the view of Wells in the distance quickly shifted into a view of the Glastonbury Tor, his bike going from rounding the small hill of the bike path to now rounding the top of the second hill of the Tor. He lost his balance and fell off the bike, his face landing on the soft grass of the hill, eyes fixed on the tower before him.

"No!" he screamed at the top of his lungs. "Why won't you let me leave? Curse you, you stupid tower! This fucking place, all this fucking magic. It's all bullshit!" He was now up and gesturing profanity toward the tower, shaking with rage, tears running down his face. The Tor stared down at him like a benevolent god, unmoving, showing no emotion, mocking him in his fit of anguish. "Everything is ruined! My life… it is over."

"Or is it just beginning?" came a voice from the tower.

"What did you fucking say, you stone cock? Did you just speak to me?" he questioned in confusion and hatred. "What will I do for work? Where will I live? Do you have those answers for me, Avalon? Huh?"

Silence from the Tor.

"That's what I thought! Useless, can take. But you won't give a thing!"

"I know, I know. But can we really start a family now?" The voice was now coming from behind him; it belonged to Hamish, who was walking with Isla up the path behind Ethan.

"Not like we have much of a—Ethan? Is that you?" Isla asked, startled.

"Did ye bike up here, lad?" Hamish asked, looking at the bicycle overturned in the grass. "Never seen someone bike up the Tor before. Were ye no meant tae be leavin' this mornin'?"

Ethan was lost for words; he had no concept of reality or what to do in this moment. He simply fell to the soft earth in desperation; his body, mind, and spirit exhausted from the struggles of the last twenty-four hours. Isla approached him and gave him a hug.

"I don't know what ye're goin' through. But I feel yer hurt. Let me take it, but for a moment." Ethan embraced the hug, allowing his tears to dampen the sleeve of Isla's jacket.

"What—what brings you both up here?" he managed to ask.

"Definitely wasnae a casual mornin' bike ride up the Tor, that's for sure!" Hamish joked.

"Well, we got some great news this mornin'; we—" Isla was cut off.

"Should we speak of it already?"

"To Ethan? Why not?"

"Bad luck it is tae speak of before the first month."

"You're pregnant?" Ethan asked.

"Aye, yes I am. Just found out this mornin'. A Samhain blessing," Isla confirmed. "We've tried for so long."

"But it's a hard blessing. It'll be a complicated pregnancy; the doctor said it'd be nearly impossible for us tae conceive. And even more dangerous for her tae deliver."

"Is that why you came here? To Glastonbury?" Ethan investigated.

"It is. I thought Avalon might grant us a wee one, and I was right," Isla looked down, holding her stomach.

"It's gonna be a long nine months o' worry, and I don't want ye tae overextend yerself. Ye'll need plenty o' rest and checkin' up on," Hamish injected.

"Expect me tae sit up in bed all day? Tough chance o' that! I'm pregnant; I ain't ill."

"Soon, I will need help though. Runnin' the shop alone is hard work. And I want ye tae be able tae dae whatever witch things ye need tae make sure ye survive this. Shame our friend Ethan here is so eager tae leave. Could use the help."

"Well, doesn't seem I am going anywhere. Can't seem to leave." Ethan said.

"Can't? Or don't want to?" Isla smiled at him.

"Doesn't matter tae me! If it takes work off ye, I'll gladly take the lad, if he's set on stayin'."

"Set on staying... forced to stay. Does it even matter anymore?" Ethan thought looking up toward the Tower with a cautious and inquisitive eye. "Your plan? Fine."

"No need to decide now—"

"I'll do it," Ethan replied.

"Ye will?" Hamish asked, shocked.

"Yes, but—I need a favor. You can cut my wages if you need, but I need a place to stay. Can I stay in your spare room?"

Hamish thought for a moment, looking to Isla, who nodded her head. "Aye, you can stay with us until the wee baby is born. But then ye'll need tae move out."

"It is a deal then." Ethan stood up and extended his hand to Hamish, who gladly took it. Isla quickly hugged Ethan as well.

"Should've asked, do ye even ken how to make a proper coffee?" asked Hamish.

—

Isla and Hamish told Ethan to meet them back at the shop in the afternoon to get more permanently settled in the flat above. Hamish told Ethan that they would start him promptly the next day, training him on how the business worked—Hamish kept referring to working with his "Scottish meat" and laughing every time he said it. Ethan said his goodbyes and left to return the now-damaged bike back to Jasper, wherever he was. As he left, Isla and Hamish went into the mouth of the Glastonbury Tor to give thanks to the spirits for granting them this opportunity. Ethan could hear the sound of both of them singing a happy song in a foreign tongue he could only assume was the old Scottish language.

It was now properly November; the skies had darkened early in the day and gave way to rain, soaking Ethan from head to toe, his few remaining personal items in his backpack now soaked through.

He managed to find Jasper at the library with Lila, they were both in the heat of discussing the details of the previous night. Ethan apologized for the state of the bicycle, but it did not seem to bother Jasper a bit; he merely shrugged and told him not to worry. The cold had soaked through Ethan at this point; luckily, a small wood furnace was blazing in the library, which allowed him to warm up just in time to receive the first series of phone calls from back in London. First came his boss, who, of course, chewed him out for missing his return day. Ethan attempted to defend himself at first, but what could he have said? That Glastonbury wouldn't let him leave? That a magical vortex was containing him in the Somerset countryside? That some crazy old man had put a spell on him? No. Nothing could be done; the result of the phone call was as Ethan predicted and feared: he was sacked. The click of the other line hanging up left him with an eerie feeling of emptiness, but also a small layer of relief.

"Fuck that place," he said, tossing his mobile back into his jacket pocket.

His flat's rent was due in just under a week; his bank account was already low from his time spent in Glastonbury. He had little option but to try to call and beg for an extension for the next payment.

"I don't even know how long I will be here. What are the rules to this? What are the parameters? It could be days, weeks, forever. I don't know."

For the time being, Ethan decided to push aside the responsibility of dealing with his old flat until he had to. At the moment, his most pressing issue was the wet and soggy clothes that made up his now very limited wardrobe.

"Where are you staying now Jasper?" Lila asked him.

"Weirdly enough I am staying with Christine now!"

"You shagging?"

"No, no. Not in that way. She is dating Josh now."

"That prick?

"Are there any clothing stores in Glastonbury?" Ethan butted in the conversation.

"There are some in Wells. Wait, weren't you meant to be there now?" Jasper was so enthralled with his conversation about the previous night that he had completely neglected to notice that Ethan had returned to Glastonbury and not to London. Lila seemed to also gain interest in the realization that Ethan was still in town as well. As with his boss, Hamish and Isla, and everyone else who would ask, Ethan was lost on what to tell them.

"Decided London is too big. Might stay here a while to see if the country suits me better," Ethan replied.

"A right proper decision in my opinion, wouldn't you say, Lila?" said Jasper.

"The countryside isn't for everyone either. Are you sure you don't want to go back? It's easy to get stuck in a place like this," said Lila, who seemed less than enthusiastic for him.

The word "stuck" rang through Ethan's ears like the chime from a church bell. "Yes, well we will need to see how I get on, won't we? About those clothes, where can I find some in town? Dreadfully wet out for travel."

"Right, there are a few charity shops in town you can try. Always a few pieces from old estates to find. Lila, you should come too. You are the one who designed the whole bloody display last night after all. We can find Ethan's unique Glastonbury look!" Jasper replied.

"I am working today. I have to watch the library," she replied. Just then the chime to the front door rang as it swung open to the dark and dreary High Street. In came Matteo, completely drenched, shivering, and shaking from his long bike ride through the torrential countryside.

"Ethan! You are here! How did you get around me?" Matteo's voice was different than usual; it was shaking from the cold, but it had an air of anger rather than the joyfulness that it often contained.

"Well, I uh—crossed the hill and realized I wanted to give Glastonbury another shot, I guess," Ethan attempted to lie.

"You left me! In the cold rain! I looked everywhere for you!" Matteo said with even more hostility in his voice.

"Matteo, I am sorry. I just took a different way. I lost you. I got wet too, see!" Ethan gestured to his damp jacket and windswept hair, the lie continuing to grow.

"I am cold," Matteo stated harshly. "I will sit next to this fire, warm my bones, then I will forgive you," he glared at Ethan with a subtle smile, collapsing in the armchair next to the stove and taking off his waterlogged shoes.

"Perfect, Matteo can watch the library. Lila, you come and turn Ethan into a charity shop fashion icon!" Jasper exclaimed.

"I still—Matteo, could you?"

"Yes! Leave me here; I will die next to this fire. But I will watch the books," Matteo's eyes were already closed, head slumped against the cushions of the chair.

"Sorted! Let's get shopping!"

Despite Glastonbury's size, it boasts more than ten different charity shops of various sizes. Most contain a mixture of old CDs, board games, books, watches, jewelry, electronics, and small sections of clothing—most of which are from generations long out of fashion. Ethan was used to the fashion of London, which did not seem to reach the streets of Glastonbury. At the first shop, they were able to find two pairs of pants that fit well enough to be excused with the use of a belt. In the following two shops, they tackled the need for shirts; Ethan typically wore pop culture shirts that referenced vintage movies, shows, bands, or classic food brands, none of which could be found. What Lila was able to find for him was a mixture of plain shirts of singular fading color palettes and occasional "hippie" shirts with messages such as "Say Yes to Love" or "Sunshine, Happiness, and Crystals." Ethan opted for the plain shirts over the cringe-inducing messages of the latter.

Finding socks and undergarments at charity shops was proving increasingly difficult; it took until the eighth shop at the base of the High Street for them to find an unopened package of white undergarments and several pairs of warm socks. As each shop passed them by, Jasper seemed to procure more and more necklaces, rings, and oddities—so much so that by the ninth store, he had to purchase a bag to carry all of his new finds.

"Jasper, if you don't mind me asking, what do you do to make money here?" Ethan asked.

"What does anyone do to make money here? We dance, we sing, we play for the tourists!" Jasper answered in a theatrical tone.

"You're a street performer then?"

"One of the best!" Jasper bowed.

Lila came close to Ethan to whisper, "He's shit."

"Do you know what you'll do here, Ethan?"

"Well, Hamish has asked me to help at the café for a bit."

"Wow! In town for a day and already have gainful employment!" Jasper seemed jealous.

"I'll be working at a café; it is hardly glamorous," Ethan replied.

"Actually, it is quite hard to get a job here, Ethan. It took me a long time to secure this library position. There are more people in Glastonbury than jobs. Most people barely get by here," said Lila.

Ethan had not thought until that moment that there were hardly any factories, warehouses, or other such places of work around Glastonbury. Outside of the one grocery store, the High Street shops, and the small cafés and pubs, there were very few places to work in Glastonbury itself.

"Perhaps I owe Hamish and Isla more than I realize…" he thought. "How do people survive then?" he asked Lila.

"They find a way… or they don't," she replied ominously. Jasper was distracted by another oddity in a display case.

"So if he's a shit street performer," Ethan whispered, "how does he survive while also buying all this useless shit?"

"Jasper is a good guy, but he fits into an ever-growing population of young people here…" she started.

"Population of what?"

"Bored rich kids."

"Jasper's rich?"

"Well, not exactly. Look, I shouldn't say more. He is looking for something… he is just trying to buy it rather than earn it, you know?" She sorted through a rack full of jackets, clearly wanting to avoid discussing the subject further. "Here, this ought to do you nicely." She handed him a large wool jumper.

They managed to find the remaining items Ethan needed in the final shop. The day was now getting late, and the sun was barely visible through the clouds on the western horizon. Ethan thanked Lila and Jasper for their help; having two large bags full of clothes felt much better after being broken down to what remained in just one small backpack. Luckily, the cost of the clothing was lower than expected, so he offered to buy everyone dinner for their assistance, which they all gladly accepted. They went to check on Matteo, but he was fast asleep next to the warm glow of the wood stove within the library. Lila locked up the shop.

"I will wake him later; best apologize to him later, Ethan. I have never seen him upset before," Lila lectured.

With so few options for food in town, they were lucky to find space in the local chippie to grab a warm meal before the remaining Samhain tourists ran the shop out of fish, sausage rolls, and even the curry sauce.

"How much longer will the tourists be this many in town?" asked Ethan.

"Not much longer. Samhain is kind of it for the year. They will all be gone within two days. Then, as the Caelliach said: winter takes hold!" Jasper animated between bites of mushy peas.

"He isn't joking. This town completely dies in the winter. We all go a bit mad," added Lila.

"Great. Seems I was given the perfect time to get stuck here then."

"Thought you wanted to stay?" asked Lila.

"A bit of both. Here I am going to see what's left for Matteo; do you mind taking it to him as a peace offering?" Ethan asked Lila, who agreed.

After supper, they all went their separate ways. It was time for Ethan to check in with his new flatmates and get his new possessions in their proper places. The flat entrance of The Andrew's Cross was locked when he approached the door. He knocked several times before Hamish appeared and let him in. They had already rearranged the spare room to a more manageable state for him to place clothing into a wardrobe. The previous night, Ethan had been so tired he did not even observe the room he was sleeping in; now he could see that it was rather outdated, damaged, and in need of a good coat of paint.

"Aye, it'll be one of our projects together!" Hamish said in reference to seeing Ethan's expression toward the walls. "First for you, and then it'll be for a wee baby… a dad. I am trying not to be excited. But it's hard not to be."

"I am happy for you," Ethan said genuinely.

"Thanks, lad. Now let's get some rest. Tomorrow, half-past five, we wake up so ye can begin yer new life as a Scottish barista! And I'll show ye how tae handle me—"

"Yes, your Scottish meats…" Ethan droned.

"Ha! We'll have fun together. Now, rest. Trust me; half-past five is bloody early," Hamish disappeared down the hall, turning off the lights along the way.

8
Medicine

Hamish was punctual. At half-past five in the morning, the lights in the hall came on, waking Ethan from a restless sleep. It was barely midnight before he managed to quiet his racing thoughts. He had done well to distract himself with his wardrobe purchases, a busy dinner, and the quick transition into the flatmate of a married Scottish couple, but it all had caught up to him. He was stuck in Glastonbury, a town far away from everything he knew and all he had once dreamed his life would be. Today, he would start making coffee for next to nothing an hour, adding next to nothing to his near-empty billfold. Had he not gotten this job, he would have been broke, homeless, and asking Jasper for help on how to be a street performer.

"I am grateful," he groaned to himself, blinking at the fluorescent lights of his room. "Half-past five is bloody early."

"Aye, it is. But ye'll see, it isnae all bad. Come, wear one o' those dark-coloured shirts ye got yesterday and come wi' me. Today ye'll take Isla's place runnin' the register."

"So, I am your wife, and handling your Scottish meats now?" Ethan joked.

"Ha! Ye're gettin' it now. I knew ye'd work out! Mostly, I need ye tae worry about the front, get those chairs outside, coffee brewed, and tidy up any mess. I'll handle the prep—

unless I ask ye tae help. We don't usually get busy until eight. By that point, ye better hold onto yer nipples; we get busy quick."

"So, about the espresso. I honestly haven't a clue…"

"Christ, boy! I thought ye were jokin'. I haven't the time tae show ye!"

"Hamish," came Isla's voice, "I'm barely pregnant; I'll show him how tae dae it today. There will be plenty o' time tae rest when he's got it more figured out."

"Fine, but I mean it. I don't want ye overdoing it!" Hamish insisted. He came to give his wife a kiss on the cheek, then went back to work behind the counter.

The rest of the morning until eight, Ethan was given a crash course in the preparation of various espresso drinks, from cappuccinos to skinny lattes, cortados, and flat whites. He managed to retain most of what Isla was telling him; however, he ruined several of the first drinks for the early morning customers. One of the first people to see him was Lila, who had stopped in to see how he was getting on his first day. She quickly left as other customers began to appear. For two hours, Isla and Ethan worked alongside Hamish to serve a very busy café.

"Last day of the tourists, I hear," said Ethan to Hamish between rushes.

"Better no be! We need more business before the cold takes hold, I'm afraid. Especially if I have tae feed ye now too." He handed Ethan a small plate o' food. "Go on then, take a rest. Ye've earned it."Ethan took it gladly; he had not eaten yet that morning. When he sat down in a corner seat, he checked his phone to see he had a missed call from his mother, who had left a voicemail asking where he was. He promptly returned it to deliver the news that he was, in fact, giving up on London and had moved to the countryside to pursue his dreams—or so he told her. She reacted as expected, telling him he was throwing away his life, blaming his father for being too soft on him, and then quickly hanging up before Ethan could say another word.

"She will calm down… but I am starting to sound convincing even to myself that this was my choice. But I can't lose sight. I have to find a way out of here."

Ethan had just finished his food and brought the plate to the counter when in walked Matteo and Zoe with three dogs in tow.

"Zoe!" Ethan exclaimed.

With all that had happened in the last two days, Ethan had completely forgotten his awkward encounter with Zoe only two nights prior. The feeling of embarrassment washed over him once again.

"Zoe… and Matteo!" Matteo pushed forward to hug Ethan. "Yes, I have forgiven you after my long rest yesterday. So… you are working here now! Lila told me when she kicked me out yesterday from the library."

"Yes, living here too."

"Very close to my shop as well," added Zoe.

"Not by design, I assure you. Only out of the kindness of Hamish and Isla."

"Don't worry, Ethan, all is good between us, I promise," said Zoe.

"Oh, even after…"

"You snogged me?" She said with a serious face.

"Yeah, after that…"

"You are not the first unsolicited snog I have gotten in my life, Ethan. Must be my charm!" She snorted.

Matteo and Zoe ordered drinks and sat down inside. Ethan was asked to help with the remainder of the morning business by Hamish, who was up to his nipples in black pudding and haggis. Occasionally, Ethan would stop by to eavesdrop on their conversation:

"…and then he—"

"Really? What next—"

"…was horrible."

"…I am sorry; is there anything—"

"Shit, they have to be talking about me. This is the worst," Ethan worried.

Eventually, the business slowed enough for Hamish to allow Ethan to sit down for a minute to talk with Matteo and Zoe.

"Hey, what are you guys talking about?"

"Mushrooms!" Matteo smiled.

"Oh. That is all?" Ethan prodded.

"Yes," Zoe insisted. "Now, Ethan, have you ever done mushrooms before?"

"Like, the psychedelic ones? Or the ones you put on toast?"

"You could technically put psychedelic ones on toast!" Zoe joked, "but yes, the psychedelic ones."

"No, just some party stuff in uni, a little pot, but never mushrooms."

"Oh, my brother, they can change you. Zoe, is there anyone here that has some?"

"Probably every other person on the High Street, but you shouldn't trust just any fucker 'round here. They might give you portobellos instead if you don't watch 'em."

"I would like to do this; perhaps all of us, Jasper, Lila, and Isla—"

"Probably not Isla—" Ethan started.

"Why not?" asked Zoe.

"Shit. She hasn't told anyone else about the baby yet… try to deflect," he thought. "Heard she doesn't like mushrooms of any kind. Makes her ill or something…"

Zoe was not convinced; she got up to speak to Isla, who was outside cleaning tables. Meanwhile, Matteo shared his first mushroom experience with Ethan. It was only a few months after the death of his brother in Spain when he met a woman who ran mushroom retreats.

"Was this the grandmother that led you here?" Ethan asked.

"No, no. That was grandmother ayahuasca—similar but more intense! My first trip with the mushroom medicine helped heal me of my pain and my rage from the death of Leo."

Their conversation was interrupted by squealing outside the shop. When they both turned to look, they saw Zoe hugging Isla while jumping up and down. Keeping the baby a secret did not seem to be a possibility; Zoe came in with Isla and hugged Hamish as well.

"Hamish, I need to steal your wife! We have so much to talk about. Isla, come with me to the shop. We have planning to do! And sisters to call upon!"

"Aye, I feared ye'd be stealin' ma wife. I thought I would have more time… well, luckily, that's why I've got ma new manservant, Ethan! Ethan! Come, time tae become ma wife. Take over for her so she can gather the coven—or whatever the witches dae."

"You heard him, Matteo. Gotta get back to work," said Ethan.

"Ah, well. I know where to find you now! How often will you work?"

"I think being Hamish's wife is a full-time job…"

"Don't fear; I will keep you company! And I will find us someone to do mushrooms with. I will keep you updated!"

With that, Zoe and Isla left to discuss preparations for the pregnancy. Matteo left after finishing his cappuccino, and Ethan returned to work. The next few days blended together and largely repeated similar patterns:

Ethan would wake up early to open the shop with Hamish. Each day, he became more efficient at his basic duties, and eventually, he was given more responsibility by Hamish to help with prep work. He grew to appreciate the early mornings with Hamish; if they finished before the eight o'clock rush, they would share a small meal and a coffee together, where Hamish would share stories from Scotland. Ethan rarely spoke of himself and found that the stories Hamish told enthralled him. Before long, the first customers would arrive, and the day's work would set in. Matteo was often an early guest who would sit close to the counter to talk with Ethan between customers—always keeping him updated about his search for mushrooms. He would leave within an hour to climb to the top of the Tor every single day. Zoe would arrive shortly after to retrieve Isla from the flat to escort her somewhere in town to discuss all matters around birthing, cycles, and babies. The café would slow down in the afternoon, which meant that there was cleaning to be done. At around half-past four, they would close the doors, and Ethan would be allowed to do what he'd like for the rest of the day.

He was falling into a dreamlike haze in Glastonbury. His savings had dried up, and he was now completely reliant on the under-the-table wages from Hamish, which were small but enough for daily needs. He received a phone call from his landlord a week after starting the job, stating he was past due on rent in London and that he would be evicted within sixty days if he did not make a payment.

"To hell with it!" he said.

On one particular evening, he took a walk up to the top of the Tor to speak with the Tower as he had done at the end of the Samhain festival.

"I have learned your lesson, great Tower!" he would start. "Thank you for the lesson; now I would like to be able to leave the town! I will not go back to London, but I would like not to be a prisoner here."

Thinking this would appease the tower and end whatever spell still had a hold on him, he took the familiar path out to the countryside and to the border between Wells and Glastonbury. He took a deep breath, then crossed the boundary which had previously kept him trapped. When he opened his eyes after stepping over the line, he saw he was in front of the Tor once again, trapped as he was before.

"Why? Why am I still trapped here? I love it; can't you see? I am grateful, I am happy, I am a good friend! I have clearly learned my lesson! So why do you keep me against my will?"

The Tower stared at him in silence, not speaking as it usually did, just like those evenings ago.

"Owen said I needed to listen. So I did. Why? What now? What's the next thing I need to work on?"

Silence still.

"Fine, screw you!"

Ethan was battling within himself as he followed the familiar path of the Tor down to the valley. His thoughts ran and raged while he walked toward the border of his prison. He carefully studied the landmarks to find the invisible line he was unable to cross. There, he built a small pile of rocks so that he would know how far he could go from now on. As he placed the last rock, he realized that, in a way, he was accepting his fate by creating such a symbol of his captivity. He stood up and looked around at the wind-battered countryside. A feeling of lostness and loneliness overtook him in that moment.

While he was not missing London nearly as much as he expected, he was, however, missing the variety in its food, people, and scenery. He ate the same things every day, saw the same people, and even smelled the same smells. He only wished to see the next town over, a different hill, or different faces. Each day, he repeated his routine; each day brought a different feeling: one day of peace in the country, the next of longing for the city, some days an emptiness toward both. November was quickly coming to its final days, and Ethan was feeling particularly low as he unlocked the door to the shop, with Matteo already at the door with an eager smile on his face.

"I found some!" he declared first thing as he walked in from the dark, cold street.

"What? The mushrooms?" Ethan responded.

"I found many people with the mushrooms, but I wanted to find the right person as Zoe had said. And my brother, Ethan! I found that right person."

"Well, who is it then?"

"The Lady of the Garden!"

"Selene?"

"Well, the woman from the garden AND the Winter Caelliach, but yes. Her."

"She has mushrooms?"

"Yes, she harvests them herself from the countryside and runs her own ceremonies."

"Wait, don't you live in the same building as her? Shouldn't she have been one of the first people you asked?"

"That is not important! But, as they say: what you search for is often right in front of you the whole time!"

"Ye really goin' to do this, Ethan?" asked Hamish. "Don't trust nothin' that messes with my mind."

"You can do them with us, Hamish!"

"No, thank ye. I will stick with me portobellos. Far as I know, they don't try and mess with my mind." He took a bite of a raw mushroom that he had in the cooler before returning to work.

"Alright then, when do we do them?"

"This Friday, we meet first at the White Springs in the evening for a private cleansing. Then we make our way to a place of ceremony where we will take the medicine and journey together!"

Ethan had always assumed that Matteo would never come through on finding someone to do the ceremony with. Now that it was more a reality, he felt a certain apprehension about going through with it.

"Damn, I am not sure what to say…"

"You should be excited! This will change your life! Probably," Matteo seemed more excited than usual.

"Yeah, well. If you say so. I am looking forward to doing it… I guess."

"I will accept that answer! Now, how about a coffee?"

—

"Hey Zoe, do you mind if I ask a few questions?" Ethan had stopped by Zoe's flat after finishing work for the day. He knocked on her door, which she answered only partially open.

"Right now? In this moment, right now?"

"Well, not right now. But Matteo has found mushrooms and —"

"Oh good! Thought he would never find them. He asked me two days ago if I knew anyone. Well… this is important business then. Come, come!" she swung the remainder of the door open to lead Ethan upstairs. In the living room were Isla and Lila, as well as Claudia who was from the sharing circle —even more pregnant looking than she had been before— hey were all having tea and cakes.

"Oh, sorry. I didn't mean to interrupt whatever this is…" said Ethan.

"We are just talking about the miracle of birth!" Zoe said, patting his back as she entered the room.

"Yes, the miracle of blood, shit, and vaginal tearing…" Lila added, seeming slightly horrified as she sipped her tea.

"Well, yes. Claudia here has decided to give birth completely naturally. No doctors. And she is due any day now," said Isla.

"Do you think you are going to do that as well? All natural? Is it safe?" asked Ethan.

"Aye, maybe! I'm no' sure, really. Seems magical either way tae me,"answered Isla.

"Best to wait and see if she lives or not first," Lila said darkly. Sensing Ethan was made uncomfortable, Lila added: "Babies scare me. I am not the most maternal type."

"Clearly," answered Ethan.

"It's alright. I'm well aware o' the risk. But this might be the only baby I ever have, and I want tae have it the way ma ancestors did. I want tae feel what the old mothers felt. I don't want tae cheapen that."

"Hamish won't like this…" Ethan thought. After spending several mornings now side-by-side with the Scot, Ethan had been told many times by Hamish that he was worried about what Isla was plotting with "the coven" all day. Natural birth being one of his greatest fears.

"That is why I am thinking about it. Tae me, child birthin' is both horrifyin' and beautiful; it is the most spiritual experience in life! Because I am creatin' life in this world. I don't want to lose that opportunity… Ethan, I am sorry. What brings ye here? I am sure ye don't want to hear all of this," asked Isla kindly.

"Ah, well. Yes, I was here to ask for Zoe's advice. It looks as though I will be doing mushrooms with Matteo and Selene soon."

"Selene! She hasn't done a ceremony in years I think, not since—" Isla started.

"Since I last did it…" Lila finished her sentence.

"Since we all last did them with her," added Zoe. "Matteo really found a powerful person for this. Almost worrying so. Ethan, you came to the right people. Selene is the real deal."

"Alright, you have all turned quite serious. Is this really going to be that big of a deal? They are just mushrooms." Ethan was seeming more worried now.

"With Selene, it's quite serious. She doesnae invite just anyone tae her ceremonies. I wonder who'll help her?"Isla pondered.

"I bet it will be Owen; ol' bat was the head of the Wild Hunt after all," said Zoe.

"No, I heard they are in a spat since Samhain," gossiped Claudia.

"Ethan, she is going to fuck you up," Lila joked.

"Fuck me up? Shit. What am I getting into?" Ethan thought. "Yeah, I will be fine. I am sure!" Ethan feigned confidence.

"Ethan, this is important. What is your intention?" asked Zoe.

"Intention? I don't know. To have a good time?"

"That is not good enough!" Lila taunted Ethan with a cackle.

"I did a mushroom ceremony right before I got pregnant; I saw my future child in the vision given to me in the ceremony. Two months later, I found out I was pregnant… it is powerful medicine," added Claudia. "The more powerful the intention, the more powerful the medicine."

"Agreed," said Isla.

"Well, what should my intention be then?" asked Ethan.

"Doesn't work like that; you need to make it yourself. This is a very personal experience," Zoe said directly.

"Well—what were your intentions then?" asked Ethan to the room.

Silence.

"Can't you share?"

"Yes… but they are personal…" Claudia said.

"I will share," said Isla. "When I first came tae Glastonbury, as ye know, I was a bit lost. Hamish and I were together, but we'd failed so many times at havin' a child; Scotland felt as though it was rejectin' us as well. I'd heard about Glastonbury from the few pagans I knew there; they said it was a place o' pilgrimage. So I came, without knowin' what it was I wanted. I spent two weeks here… and then a month; I couldnae leave, ye see. No' that I didnae want tae! Hamish was horribly worried that I was gone for so long —"

"Stuck? I wonder… was she kept here against her will too?"

"—and then I heard about Selene's mushroom ceremony from an Italian friend I'd made here. She'd walked here from Italy—"

"Wait, she had a crazy Italian friend too? That walked here?"

"—ma intention was 'how do I find love again?' No' for Hamish or Scotland, but for life. I… realized that I no longer loved life. The joy was gone."

"What happened? During the ceremony?" asked Ethan.

"I saw Avalon; I saw the Goddess o' this land. She came tae me and showed me joy once again. Joy within this very land here. I knew when the ceremony was over that I had tae come here, that the joy o' ma life would be found here. So I was able tae finally leave the town, return home, and convince Hamish that I had tae come here. He saw it too, as the only way. After that, we made plans and came here. So ye could say that the ceremony changed ma life—it saved ma life."

Claudia scooted on the couch to hold Isla's hand. "I had no idea," she said, both of them now teary-eyed from the story. Lila began to speak about her experience with the ceremony, but Ethan was lost in his own thoughts:

"If Isla was stuck here the same way I am now, perhaps this ceremony is the way to get out? Selene was one of the first people I met here; she always seemed a bit odd. Maybe she's the source of the magic. Maybe she's the way out… this is all making sense. But wait, what about the Italians? Why did we both find Italian friends? Is she also Matteo? No, that's fucking crazy… or is it? No, doesn't matter. What does matter is that this ceremony is the key to escaping this place."

"—and then I woke up. I realized that I was never going to amount to anything, and now I am here. Cheers to that sad fucking story!" Lila finished speaking and raised a bottle of vodka that she had stashed behind her. "Who wants a drink?"

"Lila, you lush! This was supposed to be a tea party with two pregnant women!" Zoe scolded in a joking way.

"Well—that means more for you and I to drink then! Didn't it! Finish your tea and give your cup here. Let's have a Russian tea party!" Lila took another drink straight from the bottle.

"Zoe, what about you?" Ethan focused his attention toward her, waiting for an answer.

"Oh, well. I guess I will need this vodka then," she filled her teacup and took a sip. "Well, ladies, as you know, Ethan tried to kiss me a few weeks ago—"

"Oh, fuck, here we go. Here comes the embarrassing scolding I have been waiting for."

"—and Ethan, you remember how I told you it couldn't be anyone? That I needed to be alone. I came to this realization during the mushroom ceremony. After I had my heart shattered into a thousand pieces, I was shown the way to heal… and part of that was to not be with anyone else for a very long time."

"Was it also to start training an army of tiny dogs?" Ethan joked while petting one of the several dogs sleeping around the room.

"Nah, I already had most of them by that point. But they are much better than boyfriends," she wiped away a tear while petting one of the dogs herself.

"So… I will either see visions of joy, pregnancy, or celibacy? Not the best options." Ethan continued to joke.

"You joke, Ethan. But this is serious," Zoe looked at him, another tear at the corner of her eye. With seeing this—and the serious expressions of everyone in the room—Ethan felt the heaviness of the conversation.

"Right. Sorry. I don't do well when things turn serious," Ethan apologized.

"If I had advice for you, Ethan, it would be to really spend the time leading up to the ceremony in reflection of your intention. No jokes, but a real intention of why you are doing this," Zoe pressed.

"My advice?" Lila started, "Take a drink of this, hold on tight, and prepare to get fucked!" Lila laughed.

"Not the best advice… but there is something serious to what she said. Everything may change for you, like it did for me…" Claudia said, pressing her hands to her swollen stomach.

"I don't have advice. But I have a favor tae ask," said Isla.

"What's that?" asked Ethan.

"Convince Hamish tae go wi' ye…"

—

After a few more questions—and a little vodka—Ethan left Zoe's flat to find Hamish. Before he left, Zoe gave him a hug and a kiss on the cheek.

"Sorry for that. Probably didn't help much."

"I am absolutely petrified now, thanks," he answered with a smile.

"There ye go! That's what we were aiming for. How many weeks do you have?"

"Weeks? We do it this Friday."

"Shit, that's fast! Well, everything has a reason. Good luck if I don't see you."

"Thanks; I am sure I will be fine. See you on the other side?"

"I will have tea waiting—no vodka this time." She smiled, gave his arm a quick squeeze, and headed back upstairs.

"She is such a tease. I swear!" Ethan thought to himself, a gentle grin on his face as he walked down the street to his flat above the café.

Hamish was upstairs watching the small television in the living room when Ethan sat down to talk about the ceremony with him.

"No bloody way!"

"She thinks it'll help you, the way it helped her," Ethan attempted to persuade.

"She wants me tae dye ma hair, grow ma armpit hair oot, and join the wee hippie cult here, I see!"

"Hamish, your armpits are already hairy…"

"Exactly! Imagine if I stopped shavin' them!"

They both laughed and then sat in silence for a time.

"Do ye think I should, lad?"

"What? Do the mushrooms?"

"Aye. Do ye think it'll help ye?"

"Help me? Shit, I don't really know. I am a bit nervous myself."

"Then why are ye doin' them?" Hamish asked.

"I guess… I am doing them because I feel called to do it in a way."

"Called?"

"To help me feel myself again… or perhaps I really have never felt myself before…"

"Aye… they have already recruited ye, I see. Findin' yerself? Right from the hippie manifesto!" Hamish laughed and taunted Ethan.

"I guess so… I guess I want to find myself," Ethan admitted.

"I suppose we all are in the end…" Hamish looked down at the floor and thought for a moment. "Alright, I think I will do it. If ye are, that is."

"What does it matter if I do it or not?"

"Because if I'm gonna join a hippie cult and drink their mushroom-flavored Kool-Aid, I'm gonna dae it wi' a friend," Hamish said with a smile. Ethan felt his heart warm over. He never thought Hamish considered him a friend before this moment; after knowing him for some time, he knew this meant a lot for Hamish to say.

"Aye, we will dye our hair together! Might even put some bells and sparkles in your beard after we are done," Ethan joked, mimicking his accent poorly.

"So, how many weeks dae we have to prepare?" Hamish asked.

"Two."

"Weeks?"

"Days…"

"Christ."

9
The Ceremony

"You, Hamish, myself, Rasmus—Claudia's husband—then there will be two others I don't know, and I believe Silus is helping in some way."

"What about Jasper?" Ethan asked Matteo, who had stopped by the café the next morning to share more about the ceremony the following evening.

"Jasper had asked me, I asked Selene, and she said 'no' without hesitation. I tried to ask why, but she wouldn't say. She is taking this process very seriously. I have not seen her this way since living in the abbey."

The weather had turned cold quickly; nearly all the leaves were now gone from the trees surrounding Glastonbury. The once-busy streets had turned quiet, with tourists nowhere to be found. "Bad for business, good for us," Hamish had said in response to the quiet morning. He decided he would close the shop for two days while they participated in the ceremony. It was nearly half ten, and there wasn't a soul in the café besides Hamish, Matteo, Ethan, and Isla. When Isla learned he had agreed to go through with it, she was elated and couldn't stop pestering Hamish with advice about what to expect.

"Where do we meet?" Ethan asked Matteo.

"You will love this, I think. We will start off in the White Springs!"

"Bloody well hope we're no' gettin' into the freezin' water. Aren't we gonna be there all night?" questioned Hamish.

"Yes, all night long! We will go to the space above the White Springs where Silus lives; apparently, there is a small home there. But what's the fear, Hamish? Your people are from the cold, mine are from the land of sun. I will surely freeze before you!"

"I think he is just worried about missing me too much," Isla said, giving him a small kiss on the cheek.

"Aye, I will miss ye dearly."

"Now, what do we do till tomorrow?" asked Ethan.

"I believe… we wait! Selene told me to take it easy and reflect on my intention for the next day."

"Funny, we said the same tae poor Ethan when he came tae us yesterday. Have ye thought further on it, Ethan? Yer intention?" Isla asked.

"Yeah, got it all sorted," he replied, tapping his finger to his head, knowing that he had, in fact, not found his intention. "What about you, Hamish? Any thoughts?"

"I think so…"

"What's that then?" Ethan wondered, thinking that he had not been able to find one, much like himself.

"I think I want tae connect tae ma ancestors—both known and unknown tae me. The Macleod name goes back far but doesnae carry as much weight as it once did. I'd like tae know more about ma blood, how far it goes,"Hamish responded.

"Shit, that's good. Maybe I will steal that one…" Ethan pondered.

"That is beautiful; I hope it is everything ye need, my wild haggis," Isla placed her head against his chest.

"Been a while since ye called me yer wild haggis…" They looked into each other's eyes. Matteo and Ethan, knowing to take a hint, both got up and went for a walk in the cold village streets, leaving Hamish and Isla to spend some time together before he would need to leave with them to meet the medicine and let it take them on a journey.

Their walk led them down familiar paths, first to the library to find it closed for the day, and Lila was nowhere to be found. They then took an alley path to the back street of Glastonbury where they came across a large mural on the back of a flat that they had not seen before. Similar to the mural that they had seen on their first days in Glastonbury, this one was clearly from the same artist and depicted the Samhain festival, complete with the May Queen and Caelliach in confrontation with one another. There were several figures placed around the image, including a dragon breathing fire into a cloud, the Wild Hunt and its riders, the Glastonbury Tor with a bright fire burning from its top, and a heron standing proud above a frozen lake with cracked ice.

"The heron… I haven't thought of him in a bit."

"You know the heron personally?" asked Matteo in a joking way.

"Yeah, well—not like a friend. But I saw it several weeks ago… strange that it is in this mural. Who makes these?"

"Not sure; there are several others in town by the same artist. Some going back for a few years. Every one of them beautiful. Have you tried to read the letters?" Matteo pointed out the same symbols from before. "Ah! These are the same runes as the necklaces I bought us all! They must spell something…"

ᛏᛁᛚ: ᚦᛊᚨᚾᛁᛜᚨᚾᚾᚨ: ᚢᛖᚱᚦᚢᛗ: ᚢᛁᚦ: ᚨᚦ: ᚠᚨᚱᚨ

Matteo tried for several minutes to decode the riddle but was only able to remember a few of the runes from his brief lesson before Samhain.

"Till… something 'um' something 'ara' and then there are some more letters. That is all I have."

"Really cracked the code on this one."

"Hey! I remember as much as you. We will ask Zoe; she knows everything!" Matteo said. "Come, let's go to the Tor and stretch our legs. The lack of sun is killing me!"

The two left the mural behind, the runic inscription quickly lost in their minds as they both returned to thoughts of the coming day. The walk up the Tor was cold, windy, and isolated. There were no other brave souls climbing the Tor this time of year, leaving the two of them with a rare chance to enjoy the views of Avalon to themselves. When they reached the tower, they ducked inside for a brief break from the battering winds. The pressure inside the hollow tower was strikingly different from outside. Matteo was sharing what his previous ceremonies were like with other psychedelics when Ethan thought of a question to ask:

"Matteo, what is your intention with this ceremony? If you have done them before, what is it you are still looking for?"

"Oh, you shoot straight for my heart with this question," he said with a saddened smile.

"I have had two other such ceremonies. I will share with you my intention for both," there was a square bench in the hollow chamber of the tower that Matteo rested upon. He took a deep breath and prepared to tell his story…

"My first experience was with the mushrooms; this was only two months after my brother's death. It was a small ceremony in the mountains of Italy. We took the medicine under the stars, and I cried out to the mushrooms to bring my brother back. Can you believe it? I thought they could do such a thing! Back then, I really thought it. I thought that they had the magic in them to do such things. But, as you can imagine, they do not. So, I became angry as I always did then. I yelled, I cried—so much that they had to separate me from the others—"

"Did you have anything good happen then?"

"Yes… my brother did come back, but only in a vision. After they got me to calm down, I returned to the group and closed my eyes. These flowers were blooming in my mind when one of them became my brother Leo, but as a small child. I cried tears of joy! I asked him questions, but he never responded to me. No matter what I did, he just looked at me. A few minutes later, I lost the vision, but I could also taste and smell memories of our childhood. I could smell pasta, tomatoes, and fresh basil from our mother's garden. These memories were very powerful. They were the final experiences for me before I fell into a deep, dark sleep."

"And the other experience?"

"This one you know! It is why I am here. Just a few months ago, I took the ayahuasca, and grandmother told me to come here, that I would heal from Leo for good."

"And have you?"

"No, that is why I go to the mushrooms… I go to learn what I do now. This is my intention."

"Well, my brother, I hope you are able to find the healing you need and the answers you seek." Ethan put his arm around Matteo.

"Ethan! This is the first time you have called me brother!"

"No, I definitely have before," he took his arm away, feeling embarrassed, and called out.

"Trust me, I would remember this! And now, I will always remember. Today, I do mushrooms with my brother!" Matteo grabbed Ethan by the shoulders and brought him in for a hug that he had no intention of letting go. He began to howl like a wolf again, just like the day they had first met.

"Doing mushrooms with a crazy Italian, a mad Scot, and a Glastonbury witch. Not where I thought I would be a few months ago."

"And you want to be anywhere else right now?"

"Honestly… can't think of a place I would rather be," Ethan said to Matteo, fully feeling the words in his heart.

—

The sun had now fully set over the hills of Avalon when they arrived in front of the White Springs gate. Looking inside, they could see the candles were still lit and there was movement from within; the ceremony was about to begin. Ethan looked to see Hamish and Matteo were taking drinks from the fresh water near the entrance, and the others who were invited to the ceremony were arriving to do the same. Jasper was also there, attempting to sneak his way in with everyone else.

"Hey, guys, we about to get started?" Jasper came up, an eager expression on his face.

"My friend, you know that she has already said no. I cannot say she will change her mind," Matteo said, placing a hand on Jasper's shoulder.

"Once she sees me, I know she will change her mind!" he said with confidence.

"Hamish, how are you feeling?" asked Ethan.

"Feel like a fuckin' sheep during butchering season. Not sure if I will be for wool or shepherd's pie by the mornin'."

"Which would you prefer?"

"I would prefer no' tae feel like a scared wee sheep!"

"I will make sure they don't shear your wool off," Ethan said, pointing at his red beard.

"Aye, best no'. Isla may never recognize me without it. Protect it wi' yer life, Ethan. And don't let them put any curses on me either!"

"As long as you do the same for me."

"Agreed." They shook hands. The gates to the White Springs were unlatched behind them, and Selene emerged, cloaked in black, carrying a lantern that gave off a faint golden light.

"Good evening! For those invited, you may enter the space now and prepare for the night's ceremony. For those not invited," she looked specifically at Jasper, "please refrain from entering the space."

Matteo, Hamish, Ethan, and the others slowly shuffled into the dark chamber while Jasper approached Selene and began to make his case for being invited. Within the White Springs, Silus was at the front of the altar with a large stone bowl that was smoking as if a fire was lit in its center. Hamish was visibly nervous.

"Have you ever been in the White Springs before?" asked Ethan.

"No, always been too scared of it. Too bloody dark."

"Baaaaaa," Ethan attempted to make his best sheep noise.

"Shut it!" Hamish said in a scared tone. Ethan let out a small chuckle but was quickly silenced by the sound of the closing gate behind him —Jasper locking it on the other side, not permitted in.

"With the closing of the gate, this space will now be kept sacred. There will be no joking, laughing, or horseplay allowed further." Ethan felt her gaze upon him. "Tonight is a night of healing. Of ceremony. Of medicine. This night is one I only perform when the medicine allows it. Tonight, we will be partaking of a sacred plant used by the Druids of old to seek guidance from the natural world. These plants

—these fungi—were harvested from the roots of Avalon herself and bear her gift to all of you."

Selene walked to the center chamber next to Silus. She then procured a small basket containing a large selection of small mushrooms that had been dried.

"We shall be drinking a tea made of these mushrooms, ginger, and honey—all grown or harvested in this sacred land. We will also be using purified water from this very spring to make our holy drink. Silus, the keeper of the spring, has generously allowed us to enter this space for the beginning of our ceremony. He will be opening the space, calling to the magics of the land, and leading us through the cleansing. Then we will be leaving for the space above us where we will partake of the tea and allow the visions to come to us. This ceremony will take place throughout the night, and we will leave for the top of the Tor for the first light of the new dawn…the new dawn of your new life. Thank you all for trusting us with this ceremony, thank you to the medicine, and thank you to the spirits of Avalon. May they bless us all." She bowed and stepped back for Silus to begin to speak.

"Thank you, Selene. My name is Silus. Many of you have never heard me speak. It is on rare occasions that I open the Springs for such a ceremony. This night is the new moon; the darkness of the night will allow for the deepest visions to come to you. We, as the new moon, will be open to receive, to give, and to heal. My story begins as you: I awoke from a vision of an old life—a life of sin, of drugs, of alcohol, of sexual desire. In Nigeria, we know no other life. Our Gods are dead, our culture is dying. Our people are sick. I go to the sacred springs of my people; I cried for a vision. The ancestors came to me and said: 'Go to England. Go to Avalon.' I had never heard this word before… Avalon. It is strange, foreign to my lips, but familiar to my soul. I felt it. So, I found a way to come here. It took me years. But I found a way to this Avalon. I found a way to these White Springs. I bathed in these waters, and they took my breath—"

He removed his robe to reveal his naked body in the low glow of the candles.

"—and as I cleansed myself, as I lost my breath. You too will be cleansed. Join me in the waters."

Silus stepped into the central well. Looking back to communicate that he was waiting for the others, one by one, people began to enter the well. First was Rasmus, who eagerly approached the water and stepped beside Silus. Next came two women—one older, the other younger—that Ethan did not recognize. Then Matteo, and only Hamish and Ethan were left waiting outside. Hamish was frozen with hesitation. Ethan began to remove his clothes; he looked to his companion.

"You got this. It sucks at first. But you will make it. Together now." Ethan finished undressing and moved toward the water. Hamish pulled together the courage and did the same. They both placed their feet into the icy waters of the central well, the water only coming up to their knees. Ethan could tell right away that the water was now far colder than the first days he arrived in Glastonbury. Instantly, everyone was shaking from the temperature.

"Breathe with me, into the belly, then into the chest in one big breath. Quickly, we create the fire within us."

They all listened and began to follow in the breathing: in through the belly, then filling the chest, then release.

"Faster now, become the fire!"

Ethan felt his lungs burning from the intense breathing, but soon he felt that burning move from his chest to his limbs. Within a minute he no longer was shaking.

"Good! Now that we have created the fire, we give the breath to the waters." Silus moved up to the deep basin at the top of the White Springs. "Come, one by one. Jump into the deep waters. Give your breath, and maintain the fire within."

A line formed, and they all began to climb their ways to the deepest well. This time, Matteo was first in line. He took the plunge, and his lungs released all their oxygen to the abyss around him. He gasped for a moment before returning to the breathing pattern.

"Good! The water has accepted your sacrifice. Come, Brother. Next."

Matteo left the waters and went down to Selene, who was waiting with towels and a hot drink for everyone. Next went Rasmus, then the two women, and then Hamish came next to take the jump. Confidence seemed to have been given to him from the breath of fire; he kept in without hesitation—

"CHRIST!" He shot up out of the water, a large cloud of cold vapor leaving his lungs. "I can't bloody do this—bloody freezing!" He went to get out of the water.

"No! Find the breath, find the fire. You have this!" Silus would not allow him to pass.

"Let me out, ye fucker, before I freeze to death!"

"You will not freeze; find the fire within, as I did! Return to the breath."

Hamish looked into the eyes of Silus with murderous intent, but he eventually found the breathing once again. He stayed in the water for a minute more to find the rhythm and eventually the fire within.

"See, Brother? You have the fire within. Come, you are cleansed." Silus offered him a hand, which he took. Hamish let out a war cry that echoed off the walls with an aggressive effect. "The warrior has been released!" Silus said with a proud voice. Hamish left the water to find a towel and the warm drink that awaited him —leaving Ethan the only one to take the plunge.

"Just like last time. This will help you." He encouraged himself, though he hesitated upon seeing the abyss of black water in front of him.

"It is time to heal," Silus said gently.

"It is time to heal…" Ethan repeated, stepping forward into the freezing waters. He fully submerged, feeling his veins turn to ice as he was covered in the water. Time froze for him. In that moment, he was in the womb—a faint memory of a human once again. He felt the calling of a heartbeat thudding against his ears. The pressure of the water pushed him deeper into the well. The abyss grew into a bright light; he was becoming one with the water; life escaped him.

"Wait. You need to breathe! Release to the water!" His mind entered survival mode; he was losing consciousness. He let go of his breath into the water and went to resurface, his breath propelling him upwards into the air above. He gasped for the warmth of the outside air. Silus was next to him, hands ready to grab him.

"I was ready to grab you, but you have come back yourself. Deep goes the well; heavy is your spirit."

"Am I… cleansed?" asked Ethan.

"Your body, but now we must work on your soul. Now breathe the fire." Ethan found the breath of fire and took in the cool air to warm it again within him. Soon he felt warmth come from his chest, signaling Silus to lift him out of the water so he could walk down to Selene, who quickly wrapped him in the soft, warm towel. She handed him the hot drink.

"Is this the mushroom tea?" he asked.

"No, only something to warm you." Ethan took a sip of the warm brew to find it had notes of cinnamon, pepper, and lemon—a slightly pungent but warming drink that helped. Silus had taken a plunge into the deep water, then came down to warm himself as well. He was quick to place his robe on once again and began preparing the stone bowl, from which smoke soon billowed. Ethan found Hamish and Matteo, who were sitting against the wall with calm expressions on their faces.

"See, Hamish? You made it," Ethan smiled.

"Please, come with us to the womb," Selene gestured for them to enter the tight tunnel of the chamber that had a statue of a pregnant woman at its deepest point. She then procured a small drum and began to beat a pattern similar to a heartbeat against it. Silus appeared behind them with the bowl of smoke, which he began to wave against them with a bundle of feathers fastened together by leather.

"After the waters took my breath, I came here to the womb of Avalon. It is here that I prayed for the vision once again. Why was I here? Why did the springs call to me? It is here my freezing body found peace in reflection of the statue's eyes. I then smelled what you are smelling now, the sweet scent of herbs, of smoke, of salvation. Behind me stood a woman; she was the keeper of the White Springs at that time. She said: 'I see the sickness. I see you are sick. Come, let me cleanse you.' I thought her crazy. What was this smoke to do? I was not sick; I felt well and had never had a cough. But then, I felt the smoke cover me, envelop me with love. And I felt that my body was heavy—not with tiredness, but with life. My blood was thick as honey. I was a young man in those days, but I felt then an old man. I fell to the floor and cried."

The smoke was now being blown around Ethan, who could detect the sweet smell of the burning herbs entering his nose. He felt his blood thicken as it entered him; his heart began to race from the heaviness he felt. He bent his knees to carry the added weight of his body.

"This heaviness? What is this? This is society, this is cities, this is money, debt, sadness, pollution. We do not feel it most days, we do not feel it because we cannot. If we felt this way every day, we would not work for society. But it is there, weighing on our souls…" Silus came to the statue of the pregnant woman. Selene beat the drum faster. "—Great Mother! We come to you! Heavy and weak from this world! The world of humanity! We wish to heal with the medicine of the mother. Be with us! Hear our prayers. Feel our love."

Ethan felt the heaviness slowly lift from him as the drumming continued to increase in rhythm. He felt energy extend outward from his heart and radiate toward his feet.

"You feel that? The energy? Look around you; you will find drums, rattles, flutes, bells, chimes. When you feel the energy come to you, take up an object of expression. Let us offer our spirit to the Great Mother!"

Matteo looked to find a small rattle, which he began to play. Hamish took a large drum, Rasmus found a flute, and the two women found bells. Ethan looked behind him to find a hand drum with a bird painted on it in a foreign style. He took up the instrument and found the rhythm of Selene. The energy he was feeling from his heart was now being expressed in his handling of the drum. Silus had now procured a large wooden tube he was blowing into to create a deep vibration that reverberated off the floor. The womb became alive with music and expression from everyone. Ethan closed his eyes and felt the vibrations around him. Soon, he felt light and began to sway with the beat. He peeked his eyes open to see Hamish was jumping up and down slightly with the beat of the heart coming from the small chamber. Matteo was on his knees, hands raised to the ceiling in reverence of the moment. Selene raised her drum in the air to reach a climax of speed. The heartbeat now became a steady and fast rhythm; she built it to the highest point and then crashed with a final thunderous beat of the drum. They all followed suit and ended their rhythms, leaving only the low drone of Silus to clear the space. All around them, smoke from the stone bowl obscured their vision.

"The womb is prepared; now we must be reborn…" Silus said in bated breath.

Selene led them out of the womb and to the central chamber. There, they all put on their clothing and were led out of the White Springs, where Jasper was still waiting. The gate was unlocked, and they were ushered to the side of the Springs, where another gated path led up to the space above the building. Silus was the last to follow, locking the springs behind him and keeping Jasper from sneaking up to the space above.

Above the White Springs was a flat surface with a small green space. A small fire was burning in the center, beyond which were two small buildings that were lit with candles. The small group came around the fire in a circle where they could look up to the clear night sky and see many stars twinkling faintly. Selene left them to attend something in one of the two buildings.

"After I was cleansed by the smoke and had prayed to the Great Mother, I sang and danced as we just did together. The woman attending the well was the same woman who is now preparing the teas behind you. Selene was the first person to welcome me to Avalon. She took me in, showed me the ways of the Springs, and introduced me to the medicine. Now, I watch over the White Springs. And tonight, I guide you through this journey with her for the first time. For now, I'll leave you to speak together before we take the medicines."

"Thank you," everyone said meaningfully. Silus bowed and left to assist Selene.

"I honestly didn't know he could speak," said the older woman.

"I've only heard a word from him in the past!" Rasmus added.

"What are your names?" Matteo approached the two women, offering a greeting and a hug.

"Oh, yes. Sorry we haven't had the time. Now we have been naked, danced, and frozen together without knowing each other's names. My name is Helena, and this is my daughter, Mari." They both went around and began to give hugs. Hamish, Matteo, Ethan, and Rasmus all exchanged greetings and introductions as well. Helena was a tall woman with greying hair, few wrinkles, and kind eyes. Her daughter, Mari, was equally tall and slender, with long blonde hair.

"Where are you from?" asked Ethan.

"We're from Sweden. We know Selene from when she lived there."

"Selene is Swedish?"

"We don't know if she is, but she used to visit our village often," Mari answered.

"How old is the ol' woman? Silus must be at least fifty, if not older. Has she been here that long?" Hamish pondered.

"I always thought she was from Glastonbury; her accent seems English," added Ethan.

"She's been different since Samhain as well, more serious, even when we speak," said Matteo.

"I'm from all over," Selene said, standing behind them with a tray full of teacups. "And it's not polite to ask my age, Hamish." She winked.

"Sorry, miss! I meant no offense, only curious is all. Ye're a striking beauty, regardless of the age!" He tried to recover.

"You'll make this old woman blush. But, it's time to begin our ceremony. Please, everyone, take a cup. Each one has been appropriately portioned for the right experience. Once you have your cup, speak to the tea and the spirit within. If you have intentions, now is the time to speak them. We have two spaces for you to choose from. This space here, outside around the fire, or within this building, where there's a warm space with beds for rest. We ask that you refrain from speaking during the ceremony. If you're outside, look to the stars or the fire. If you're inside, we have blindfolds for you to use, and we recommend keeping your eyes closed for an internal journey. Out here, you'll travel externally. Does that make sense?"

"What's the difference between the two—external and internal?" asked Rasmus.

"Good question. The internal journey will take you deep into your past, deep within yourself, where fears, traumas, joys, and memories are stored. This is a great way to dig into what needs healing. Out here, in the external space, you'll have your eyes open to seek answers from the spirits around us. This is for those seeking a vision from the spirits and what's to come."

"We also ask that once you choose a space, you stay there for some time. If you feel it necessary, you may switch from outside to inside, or vice versa. But do so not out of boredom, but with intention. The medicine will last most of the night," Silus added.

"Yes, very well said. We're here for you all night. Whether you're worried, scared, happy, crying, or even vomiting—no matter the need—Silus and I are your guides. We'll keep you safe and help you," she said as everyone took a cup of tea. "Any other questions? Please, there are no bad questions."

"What are the risks?" Hamish asked, eyeing the cup in his hand with suspicion.

Silus answered, "Another good question. There are risks, but none you aren't meant to go through. People take these medicines with great caution and respect. This isn't a party drug or a way to get high. I've abused false medicines before, and I've also abused good medicine. Look at the Glastonbury festival, with its music and drug culture. This isn't that culture. This comes from history. As Selene mentioned, history shows us that this medicine is bitter, not sweet, no matter how much honey you put in the tea. The lessons can be—and often are—bitter going down. But it's medicine because, when taken properly, it can heal despite the flavor. If you begin to have what some call a 'bad trip,' come to us, and we'll help guide you to a better place. Surrender—that's key. Give yourself to the experience; you'll live, you'll be safe, and you'll learn much, even from what's bitter."

"How do we speak our intention to the tea?" asked Helena.

Selene answered, "Yes, so—take the cup, admire the liquid, the porcelain, the smell, and whisper words of gratitude to the tea. Then ask the mushroom questions, speak intentions, and treat them like a friend. They're our friends; they'll help us. But we must respect them. Everyone, go ahead, find a space here, and take a moment. Whisper your intentions now."

Ethan looked down at his cup—four little mushrooms floated at the bottom of the cloudy liquid. He went to the edge of the green space and thought, "Okay, this is it. You need your intention…" He thought in frustrating silence for two minutes before leaning his lips against the rim of the cup.

"Hello, mushrooms… thank you, I think? Or thank you for what you're about to do? Honestly, I have no idea what to say. But, I hope you help me? I need your help… yes. I need help… help to… help—I'm stuck here. For some reason, I'm stuck. Why? Why am I stuck here? Please, help me see why I'm stuck here in this place… great and powerful mushrooms."

Ethan rejoined the circle, and he and Mari were the last to settle in around the fire.

"Now, we drink," Selene said, sipping a cup of her own. Hamish looked at her with concern, "Don't worry, Hamish, ours aren't as strong as yours." This seemed to calm Hamish slightly, who now sipped the brew himself.

Ethan took light sips of his tea, finding it more pleasant than he'd expected—strong sweetness, mild spice, and a faint earthiness. There wasn't much liquid, so he soon reached the spongy mushrooms at the bottom.

"Do we eat the—"

"Yes."

"Great." He looked down at the mucous-like spores, closed his eyes, and gobbled them down. Luckily, they required no chewing, because what little Ethan tasted was dreadful. He let out a small belch and quietly waited for everyone to do the same.

"How long does it take?" asked Rasmus.

"You should start to feel something in about thirty minutes. Until then, relax," said Silus.

Selene finished her cup and left for one of the houses behind her. She returned with a large harp and began to pluck lightly, finding a rhythm before starting to sing.

"Glen of cuckoos and thrushes and blackbirds,
precious is its cover to every fox;
glen of wild garlic and watercress,
of woods, of shamrock and flowers, leafy and twisting-crested.

Sweet are the cries of the brown-backed dappled deer
under the oak wood below the bare hilltops,
gentle hinds that are timid lying hidden in the great-treed glen.

Glen of the rowans with scarlet berries,
with fruit fit for every flock of birds;
a slumbrous paradise for the badgers
in their quiet burrows with their young.

Glen of the blue-eyed vigorous hawks,
glen abounding in every harvest,
glen of the ridged and pointed peaks,
glen of blackberries and sloes and apples."

As Selene continued to sing, each person found their space inside or out: Matteo, Rasmus, and Helena chose to stay around the fire. Hamish, Mari, and Ethan found their way to the warmth of the small round building not far away. Inside were six cushioned mats with pillows, blankets, and blindfolds waiting for them. Silus followed behind them and procured his own stringed instrument, which he began to play softly from a small stool in the back of the room. Hamish looked as though he was about to fall asleep; his eyes were so heavy that Ethan could not see them under his brow. The singing continued outside as Ethan felt lighter…

"Is this it? No, I am not sure?" He battled his mind, trying to determine what counted as a psychedelic experience.

"Silus, is there something we should be doing? To help?" Ethan asked.

"Repeat your intention in your mind. If you feel lost, return to the intention."

"Why am I stuck… why am I stuck…" Ethan closed his eyes and lay gently on the cushioned mat. He felt his body melt into the floor, the music carrying him away in a dream-like state. Then a color overtook his thoughts: blue, then purple, then green—soft colors mixed and folded into one another. They began to take shape into flowers, blossoming in his mind's eye.

"Holy shit, this has to be it."

He felt as though he was watching a television program on nature. The soothing sound of the harp and dulled singing in the background filled his mind with various plants growing under his eyelids. The colors began to cascade from natural to cosmic to psychedelic. He watched the flowers turn from petals to vines that wrapped around him like a blanket. Thorns began to run their way through his mind like sandpaper.

"Oh, I don't like that. Back to the flowers, please…"

The thorns twisted, multiplied, and bled into images of technicolor forest—radiating with a light from the center of his mind—he dared not open his eyes to ruin the vision that was before him. For several minutes, the images were of beautiful elemental presences: water, fire, earth, air, and what could only be described as the essence of spirit. Ethan felt like melted butter running over the side of a slice of toast. He could smell the sweet scent of flowers, smoke, and leaves as they rustled around him in a symphony of sensations. The gentle harp slowly faded from the exterior world to turn into the gentle thumping of a drum. The drum changed the visions: from gentle flowers of radiant color to deep reds of echoing thunder. Nature gave way to visions of space and time.

"Fuck… when they say trip… they are not kidding…" Ethan's body was comfortably tucked under the comforting duvet. He felt safe, cuddled, and warm as his mind experienced the adventure of a lifetime. The visions seemed to become thicker with each infinite second. As the visions grew in density, so did the speed of the low drum echoing in the room. The rate of drumming was now increasing Ethan's heart rate: "Woah, okay. Maybe we need to slow down now…" Ethan's thoughts could not penetrate into the creation of words, and he was lost in the ever-growing cacophony of sensations that were now overwhelming him. Time was unknowable, escaping; seconds were uncountable, minutes unknowable, and hours unpredictable. He felt as though he was on an elevator that kept going up to the next floor—each time a new floor appeared, another rapid vision of color, space, and energy was revealed to him. His ears and mind started to play tricks on him… sounds of birds chirping, bees buzzing, and stars expanding were throwing themselves at his head. He felt his blood, tasted his breath, and could hear his lungs expanding—he also felt as though he was beginning to panic.

Ethan threw off his blindfold to see that the room was more normal than his internal visions. He could clearly see Mari and Hamish curled into their duvets—slightly twitching, but otherwise unmoving. He saw Silus in the corner of the space beating his large drum. He looked up to meet Ethan's vision and motioned for him to lay back down. Feeling weak, Ethan could only nod and follow his command. He could feel the presence of the room shift as Selene entered the room with Matteo, who was crying tears of gold from his eyes. Their faces morphed and shifted between swirling emotion and incomprehensible Picasso paintings. Matteo lay next to Ethan; Selene wrapped him in the covers and placed the blindfold on his face. She looked to Ethan, who was staring blankly into her expressionless face. She whispered something to him before he closed his eyes and drifted back into the dreams of euphoria.

Within his visions now, the colors of space were taking form into memories from his childhood. His father was there, kissing his mother, looking down toward her belly and rubbing his hand over a small bump.

"Wait, is that me? This isn't a memory?"

The vision shifted to his mother—fully pregnant now—he moved closer to see that within her womb was a single seed that had taken root, the seed of his life. Heart beating, he saw roots coming from her womb, wiggling and pulsating for attention. Ethan reached out to touch the roots that were throbbing for his affection. As he wrapped his fingers around the dry and dusty veins, he was pulled within to see the depths of creation inside the womb of his own mother.

He saw the face of himself as a baby, whose face was covered in scales and melting water.

"Are you… me?"

The eyes of the child shot open to reveal a deep blackness contained within that pulled Ethan's visage into them like black holes in outer space. He screamed out for help from his mother, from his father, from God. No one came to save him; he was pulled into the abyss of his fetal eyes. Darkness engulfed him. The drum was vapid; sweat was overtaking his physical body; a scream tried to escape but found no way past the void of the soul into the reality of life. Time froze within the void of his fetal soul. Ethan felt naked among the inky black; he cried and sobbed through the loss of all vision… but then a light began to shine from afar, a beacon to his lost soul. He had to swim as if in an endless sea. The light flashed to the beat of the outer drum. He swam hard against growing waves of anguish that came over him. No matter how hard he swam, he was so far away from the light. He cried, he panted; he felt useless within himself.

"I am worthless. I cannot make it…"

He slowed down his swimming so that he was now floating in the black sea of infant sorrow; he sank inch by inch into the thick liquid. As he sank further into the ooze around him, he felt the panic, anxiety, and fear that he had felt his whole life overtake him. His face was being engulfed by the salty fluid when he heard the cries of birds above — opening his eyes, he could see the heron above, screeching and crying for him to reach up— he lifted his arms to try and grab a foot but only managed a feather. Through the feather alone, the heron pulled him from the black sea into the sanguine air of the vision. The beacon beyond was now visible to him once more. Ethan panicked and began to lose his grip on the heron feather:

"Please, don't let me go. Please, I don't want to go back."

"Then you never need to," replied the heron.

"How? How do I never go back?"

"Follow the light…"

The light ahead was closer now; its shape was becoming more visible to him—a lighthouse.

"What is the light? How do I find it?" Ethan asked the bird but was given no answer. Ahead of the lighthouse was growing closer and closer—but this was no lighthouse… it was the Glastonbury Tor. But not the one Ethan was used to; the land where Glastonbury would be was under the sea. The hills had sheep, trees, and small buildings among them. The Tor was surrounded by men in rainbow-fluctuating robes, hats raised high, chanting:

"Beannachtaí do'n talamh chumhachtaigh, cloich-mhealláin, caillígh na draíocht. Chun an fhae, an bhandia, an glas, agus ár n-anamacha athchóirithe."

"I don't know what they are saying!" The heron lowered him to the ground before the cloaked figures. Then, they turned to look into Ethan's eyes. Each one bore the face of someone he knew: Matteo, Zoe, Lila, Jasper, Hamish, Isla, Selene, Silus, and Owen —Owen being the one in charge.

"What are you here to tell me?" Ethan cried out.

The figure that was Owen kneeled down; his face changed to Ethan's father, then to his other, then to his old boss, then to his first girlfriend, then to a demon, then to fire—Ethan was terrified. The figure then raised his arms to the sky to point out the stars, which became faces of unknown beings. The stars fell upon the earth in quick meteors that shook the land. The tower was lit on fire, the sea turned from black to brown, and the smell of coffee filled Ethan's sensations. The vision swirled, lost its form, and returned to shapes. The shapes became the city; the city rushed around him like traffic in London. Faceless people looked at Ethan from all directions. The noise of nightclubs, news stations, radios, and car horns pierced through him.

Ethan shot up from his bed; the world was swirling around him. He could see nothing through the shapes, colors, and patterns in his visions. He launched himself outside the hut to find the soft texture of the grass. When he reached the cool night air, he purged his guts over the earth. He felt the hands of someone behind him lift his torso and gently carry him to the fire. A warm towel was used to clean his face. The fire was the only light in the dark of the night air; the warmth soothed him, gentle singing lulled him, and he found a steady rhythm in his breath once again. He stared into the fire, still feeling the sensations of the mind run behind his pupils —the inky black fetal sea not far beyond his memory— he looked to see Hamish was now outside with him, looking into the fire with a thousand-yard stare of his own.

Ethan's thoughts were still racing; he felt as though he was having several conversations with himself at once—none were comprehensible. With his gut empty, his mind cluttered, and his body used up, all he wanted was to sleep and make it all go away. He laid down around the fire pit and curled his body into a fetal position. A duvet, pillow, and glass of water were brought for him by Selene, who was singing once again about sweet glens and meadows.

Time was still lost to Ethan, but he felt it was early morning as he heard the first chirps of the few birds left in the autumn weather. He closed his eyes and drifted away to a half-sleep state of pulsating colors and visions that became the whispers of faint dreams.

10

Integrations

The morning sun rose lightly over a clouded horizon, enough warmth filtering through to rouse Ethan from his restless slumber. His head was still swimming, but his vision had returned to normal. Hamish was awake—clearly, he had not slept. His beard was ruffled, and his eyes glazed over, lost in the thoughts swirling in his mind. Silus emerged from the round hut, with the others behind him.

"Come, we end the ceremony on the Tor."

The walk up the Tor was slow, cold, and cloudy—both in mind and in the morning skies. Selene trailed behind near Hamish and Ethan. Matteo, on the other hand, was at the front with Silus, a stern expression on his face. Each of them was wrapped in the duvets from the ceremony, the cold biting through as they climbed the final steps, the wind whipping them with torturous intent. When they reached the Tower, they set up near the eastern-facing hillside, toward the low rising sun—hidden for the moment behind a line of clouds.

"To the eastern skies!" cried Silus, arms wide open. "To the medicine! To the Gods! To the Spirits! We ask that the new dawn's warmth brings blessings from our visions. Bless us, Great Spirit!"

Selene stepped forward. "I ask you, Brigid, Frigg, Nehalennia, Minerva, Avalon, Freya! Grant us healing hands, grant us healing breath, and healing thought. We thank you for the medicine of the Earth Goddess. May she work through us in our process of healing!"

Mari and Helena now stood in front with Selene and Silus, arms open to the east, tears streaming down their cheeks. Matteo was shaking; Rasmus was kneeling, and Hamish was now yelling toward the horizon. Ethan felt out of place, confused by the visions he had received.

"I do not feel grateful. I do not feel healed or at peace," his thoughts soured. He remained apart from the group, leaning against the Tower with a bitter expression on his face.

Silus held a large horn hidden beneath his robes. He pressed his lips to it and let out a loud siren across the eastern valley. He walked to the south and did the same, then to the west, and finally the north. With the final blow, he looked to the east one last time and bowed. As he lowered his head, the sun cracked through the distant clouds, bathing everyone on the Tor in a warm glow that seeped into their very bones. Even Ethan felt the joy of the light enter his spirit.

"With that, the ceremony is complete. We hope you all journeyed deep and far and came back whole. Before you leave, we have a small breakfast for you back at our space above the Springs. There, you may share your journey if you wish…" Silus bowed once more and was embraced by Selene. Soon, all but Ethan took part in a circle of hugging and light chatter. The group then made their way back down the hill to warmth, food, and conversation.

—

"So, would anyone like to start? Any observations? Questions?" Selene looked around the small table where they all now sat, bowls of fruit, bread, and warm porridge among cups full of tea, coffee, and juice.

"Aye, where's the bloody milk for my coffee?" Hamish muttered between mouthfuls of porridge.

"You are welcome to dairy, but after this morning, your stomach needs to ease into certain foods," Silus answered. "Would you like to share anything from the night?"

"No meat, now no dairy… killing me! But, yes, there is something I would like to share…"

"Perhaps Hamish didn't have a good experience as well. Maybe I am not the only one. I kind of hope he didn't like it either. Then we can—" he thought.

"—I wanted to thank ye. Both of ye. I needed that much more than I needed…"

"Shit."

"Thank you for trusting us. Anything specific you wanted to share with us?" Selene said with a smile.

"Aye, it's hard tae explain. But, as ye know… as ma friend here, Ethan, knows… I didnae come tae this wee town for love o' the mystical, the fairy, or crystals. Certainly no' bloody mushroom trips! I came here a broken man in some ways. No' for ma life, but for the life o' ma father and his father. Ye see, ma father died a horrible death at sea, drowned in the midst o' a storm. His father died in the war —well, the second one—for the first war that killed his father. Before that war killed a father, then disease, then war, war again, the Jacobite uprisin', and basically, as far back as we know, every father has died shortly after the birth o' a son. And… as some may know now, ma bonnie wife, Isla, is now pregnant. So, it has worried me that ma time may be comin' near, even though all I wish is tae see a wee bairn runnin' around wi' us. I cannae help but live in fear. I already gave up drinkin', as it always seemed tae be involved in the deaths o' ma family in some way. Well—I still couldnae shake it. What happened last night… I met ma father, his father, and his father and so on. I saw them; they talked tae me—"

Hamish began to cry.

"—and they told me that our family was cursed. By an evil spirit some thousand years ago. A sea maiden, one that our family had wronged. They told me where we'd received this curse and showed me the exact spot! Of the Isle o' Lewis it was; they told me how tae break the curse! So that I may live, and ma future son will have a father!" His sobs and tears ran down his face into his beard, snot coming from his nose. "Ma son will have a father!"

Ethan felt guilty now, wishing he had suffered as he had. Selene came to Hamish and offered him a hug, as did Mari and Helena.

"Thank ye, thank ye, thank ye. I still think it's all a bit shite, but it was so clear. The faces of my fathers. How do we trust and believe in all of this? Aren't we just high off our arses?" Hamish asked.

"The key to these experiences—to these medicines—is that it is not about belief in what happened or will happen. It is about the experience itself. You experienced this. You saw it, and now you feel it is the truth. There is no belief needed in that," answered Silus.

"Weel, I still think this town is mad, but today… I have tae admit ma eyes have been opened. Now, I'm bletherin' on; someone else talk. And hand me more porridge!"Everyone lightly clapped and thanked Hamish for what he had said.

"Anyone else?"

Mari and Helena spoke as a pair, their experiences intertwined in many ways. They both had come to the ceremony looking for healing for a long history of suicide within their family—Mari having already attempted to take her life once and Helena trying years prior. The visions they both had showed them the doors to the afterlife. Each was offered to end their own life in that very moment of the ceremony. But when they saw one another, they became one person and were strong enough to step away from the doors of death and step forward into a happier life. They asked Selene how to move forward in life and wondered if the vision was enough to end their depression.

"No, this is only a part of your journey—a big one! But only a part of it. You will need to continue to do the work; however, today you are stronger and have gone to the doors of death itself. You know you can beat it, as long as you have each other."

They both hugged, cried, and offered their thanks to Silene and Silus. Ethan was now feeling more embarrassed and left out, still clouded on the meaning of his own vision.

"I would like to speak next," Matteo raised his hand, his face still bearing an angry expression.

"Yes, please share with us, Matteo," answered Selene.

"In my vision, I saw my rage, my anger and hatred. It was behind a thin wall of paper; the wind blew and completely tore it down, leaving me face-to-face with the fire. It burned me, caught fire to all I loved again. I saw my brother burning in Hell; I saw my brother Ethan burning in Hell. The worst part? This was not God's Hell. No, this was my Hell; I caused it; I fueled the fire. Within my vision, the fire of my Hell kept spreading from one memory to another. From one friend to another, until it reached my mother. Her face turned into the Virgin Mary—she held out her hand and denied the fire. She stopped it from spreading further…" he trailed off in thought.

"What does this mean to you?" asked Selene.

"What this means… I must go see my mother. She is the only way to stop the fire, to stop my rage. I cannot keep a happy face when below is so much pain."

"A powerful message to receive," said Selene.

"When will you go?" asked Ethan.

"Soon, before winter."

"Will ye come back?" asked Hamish.

"That depends on my mother and what answers await me there… please, no more questions. I must continue to think, to write, and to process. Thank you for your ears." Matteo bowed lightly to everyone in the room.

Rasmus then began to speak. His vision involved several animals. First, he saw a fish in the sea who told him to visit the birds of the sky. Then the birds told him to search the earth for a sign, which led him to the dirt and the worms. During his time as a worm, he burrowed into the grave of his own self and began to eat his own flesh as a bug. Rasmus seemed disturbed by the whole thing, but Silus sought to comfort him. "This vision is quite common. The view of eating oneself is a good thing; it means that you have grown past one chapter of your life and are entering a new one." This seemed to make Rasmus slightly less concerned; however, he quickly went silent and ate nothing from the table before him. This left Ethan as the only one yet to share. Selene and Silus gave him no pressure, but he could feel the eyes and attention of everyone slowly growing impatient as he worked his way up to speaking.

"Well, I am a bit confused, I think. Everyone else had such concise visions. But mine were confusing, dark, and do not mean much to me," he said, his eyes downcast onto the table. "Perhaps you can interpret for me?"

"It is not helpful for us to interpret; we can, however, help guide you to the meaning," answered Selene. Ethan then proceeded to share the majority of the vision, from the eyes of his youngest self all the way to the fire at the Tower and the confusing message he received from the robed figures. Selene and Silus were very alert after he shared the chanting that he could remember.

"So, yeah… I don't know. I can't make heads or tails of it at all."

"This heron, have you seen it before?" asked Silus.

"Yes, a few times now."

"When was the first?"

"A few nights before Samhain, after a night of drinking."

"And did it lead you somewhere?"

"Yes—to Owen."

Silus and Selene exchanged a glance, as if communicating something in secret. "This bird is special. It is a part of your spirit," Silus spoke.

"I thought you weren't supposed to interpret?"

"There is no interpretation needed. We all have spirit animals that guide us; clearly, this bird is one of yours. There are ways to connect with it deeper," said Silus.

"I think… maybe I should do mushrooms again?"

"Absolutely not," Selene said sharply and quickly. "This is rarely ever the answer."

"But I think now that I know the heron is helpful, I can ask it more questions."

"There are more ways to speak to spirits than through plant medicines," said Selene.

"How?"

"Through the drums, as we did in the Springs."

"Can we do it today?" Ethan asked.

"No, we should wait for you to come down off the medicine. Perhaps in a few weeks, once you process all that you have seen tonight," Selene said.

"Great, I will just keep wasting time making bloody coffees then..." His thoughts remained negative, and he still felt very confused by the other images of his vision. "Are you sure it will work? The drumming?"

"We will see..."

"Not good enough..."

"Ethan, is there anything else you would like to ask us?" asked Selene.

"No, I think I just need a proper rest now."

Selene stood to address the room. "Wonderful. You bring up a good point. After breakfast, you are all welcome to stay here and rest for the rest of the day. Or you may slowly leave for your homes and your own beds. We ask that you take it easy for at least two days, reflect on what you have seen, and do not make any hasty decisions. The mushrooms are going to be a part of you for some time now, and they will continue to do their work within you. They will whisper these words to you, rather than shout them as they did last night."

Silus now stood. "As Selene has said, we are here for you for the rest of the day. Please take your time. Otherwise, thank you all for going through this experience with us. It was our pleasure to host and guide you." He placed his hand to his chest and bowed. All but Ethan clapped and offered words of thanks to the evening's hosts. Their breakfast took only a few minutes to clean up before people began to leave for their own beds. Mari and Helena were renting a room in one of the pubs, meaning that they left first to enjoy the accommodations they had paid for. Rasmus was next to leave to check on Claudia, which inspired Hamish to do the same.

Hamish nudged Ethan. "Hey, mate, are ye ready to go?"

"Yes, let's see how Matteo is doing first." Ethan walked over to Matteo, who was in a serious conversation with Silus near the fire pit. "Matteo, are you staying? We are about to leave."

"Yes, I will stay for a while longer. Please do not wait for me. I will see you at the café soon," Matteo's expression still bore an intensity that was alien for Ethan to witness.

"Alright, well. See you then." Matteo did not offer his usual hug and only returned directly to his conversation with Silus.

"Both of yous going to be okay?" asked Hamish as they walked down through the entrance gate.

"What do you mean?"

"What do I bloody mean? I have never seen yous two so serious in the wee time that I have known ye. I saw the faces of my long-dead fathers, and I feel perfectly fine. Ye see a bloody bird and a wee bit o' fire, and it seems someone has shot yer dog."

"Well, at least one thing didn't happen."

"What's that?"

"We didn't come out with our hair dyed, nor did we have to rub any crystals on our nipples."

"Ha! There ye are. Good to see you are the same Ethan I knew before."

"Maybe not entirely the same… I know someone who hasn't changed, though…" Ethan looked ahead to see Jasper walking up the street from town toward them both.

"Well, lads! How did it go? Was it everything you dreamed and more?" Jasper had a cheery attitude and a joyous rhythm to his step.

"Aye, blew our tits off. And we ain't telling ye a thing," Hamish smacked Jasper on the back.

Jasper looked to Ethan. "Sorry, Hamish is right. We were sworn to secrecy."

"Oh, come on, you two. At least tell me how they did the ceremony! I have always wondered what Silus sounds like. I have never even heard him speak before! Didn't know he could until recently!"

"Silus speaks? I donnea ken him speakin' at all last night, do ye, Ethan?"

"Nope, in fact, I'm not sure I remember him being there at all, really."

"Aye… was he the bloke with the long blonde hair?"

"You both stop this; it isn't funny," Jasper chased after them.

"Just messin' with ye, ye wee bawbag. Come, I am bloody tired but could use a proper fatty breakfast. Join us, Jasper?"

"Promise to share a little from last night?"

"Christ, offer ye free breakfast, and you are asking for more?"

"Please—"

"—don't ye start begging. I am sure Ethan will give in to yer puppy eyes over a good meal. Come along."

The trio made their way slowly back into the sleepy village of Glastonbury. The warm sun that had greeted them in the morning had now faded into the dim grey clouds of the English autumn weather. When they arrived at the base of the high street at Andrew's Cross, Isla was outside to greet Hamish.

"Ye look shite, husband," she said to him.

"And ye look beautiful, wife." They kissed deeply, then ushered Matteo and Jasper inside for a quick second breakfast of sausages, coffee, and proper milk. "Don't worry, Ethan, won't tell Selene we decided to have milk from a cow if you don't rat us out either."

"Promise." Ethan helped himself to another link of sausage as Jasper continued to pester about the details of the previous night. Ethan was forced to get up and make several drinks while Jasper rambled on.

"I don't think they gave you a high enough dose," Jasper had told Ethan.

"What do you mean?"

"Well, you see, from what you told me about your vision, I think if you'd had a higher dose, you would have found your answers. When everything got cloudy, it was because you needed to go a little deeper. How many grams did they give you?"

"I have no clue."

"Honestly, can't believe how amateurish they were! Didn't tell you how many grams? You need at least eight for a true shamanic journey. That's what you need. Trust me."

"Maybe… I'm not sure," Ethan pondered what an even higher dose would feel like.

"I am not a wee man, and they sent me back several dozen generations with whatever they gave us. I don't want to go meet my caveman ancestors—so, I think I am perfectly satisfied," Hamish said from behind the counter, making their drinks with real milk.

"When are yous going tae share wi' me what ya saw?" asked Isla.

"Aye, we have a lot to discuss… perhaps we'll take our coffees for a walk. I have much to tell ya." Hamish handed a takeaway cup to Isla. "Ethan, mind keeping an eye on the shop while I talk to my wife?"

"We are open today?" Ethan reached for his coffee while looking at the empty streets of Glastonbury Square.

"O' course we bloody are! Closed yesterday to trip on magic mushrooms; can't close two days in a row. Got a baby on the way! Now, there shouldn't be many customers. It's only a Saturday." He winked at Ethan, grabbing his coat off the wall, and walking out into the street with Isla by his side.

The time was near ten in the morning, and Glastonbury had not quite woken up from its autumn slumber. Ethan worked slowly to get the store into a somewhat organized state while Jasper continued to discuss the ins and outs of psychedelic usage. Slowly, customers began to show up after seeing the doors open and two people sitting inside. Ethan was forced to get up and make several drinks while Jasper rambled on.

"Jasper, man, I really appreciate you trying to help, but I am exhausted. If you're going to hang around, mind helping a bit?" he pleaded.

"Oh, well, you just reminded me; I need to get to work myself."

"You have a job? Where at?"

"Think about what I said. I can get us some great psychedelics. I have a guy who knows a guy whose sister grows them. So it's practically already sorted. See you later?" Jasper grabbed his coat and quickly hurried out the door.

"No way that fucker has a job…" Unfortunately for Ethan, the café was unusually busy. The weekend brought several people in for a quick holiday to the shops of Glastonbury.

"So grateful for you, mate. All the other shops are shut!" cheered one perky father, ordering five drinks for his eager family.

"Are you all by yourself? Poor dear. I will take two hot chocolates, three lattes, and a cup of tea for myself," another woman said with a devilish polite tone. Ethan endured hell for three hours of business before Hamish arrived back with Isla, both of whom helped him with the cleaning up and finishing of the day's work. After everything was settled, they asked Ethan to sit down for a biscuit so they could share something with him.

"How long have ye worked with us now, Ethan?" Hamish asked.

"Few weeks."

"Do ye like it? Really understand it an' all?"

"Yes, I think so. Maybe not the cooking part of things."

"Aye, ye won't need to worry 'bout that," said Hamish.

"Why are you asking me this?" Ethan said nervously.

"Weel… I talked it o'er wi' Isla. Shared ma visions and all… we agreed we need tae go back tae Scotland for a couple o' weeks."

Isla continued, "and we were wonderin' if ye wouldnae mind watchin' the shop while we're away. Honestly, it seems like fate that ye're here wi' us durin' this time!"

"Me? Alone in the shop? For a couple of weeks?"

"We trust ye, lad."

"Why do you need to go right away?"

"Have ye been tae the Isle o' Lewis in the bleedin' depths o' winter? Miserable weather, even on a good day. And we need tae handle ma business wi' the sea there before our bairn is born,"said Hamish.

“As soon as Hamish told me what he saw in his vision, I knew right away the ceremony—and the right people—to call upon. Luckily, all o' which are available tae us in Scotland.”

“When do you leave?”

“Monday.”

“Two days Monday? Not two weeks Monday?”

“Aye, that’s right, two days Monday. Think ye can handle it?”

“What about the cooking?”

“No cookin', just coffee. Stay open frae seven till four, and close up on Mondays—after this week, o' course,” Hamish said directly and confidently. Ethan paused for a few moments tae think about what was bein' asked o' him. Hamish clearly thought he was takin' too long when he said, “I’ll pay ye double yer normal wages, plus ye get the whole flat tae yersel' for two weeks… no wild parties, but feel free tae bring anyone ye’d like up.”He emphasized the anyone. “It was Isla’s idea, actually.”

“If ya need—“

“—I will do it,” Ethan finally said. “Not like I have anywhere else to be after all. Should be grand, lots of fun.”

“We ken we could count on ye!” Hamish slapped him on the shoulder, and Isla gave him a small peck on the cheek.

“Ethan, ye really are such a wonderful person. Ye came into our lives like a gift from the Goddess hersel’.”

"Aye, what she said. But maybe less of the Goddess stuff. More of the: you are a bloody good friend stuff. Also, take tomorrow off. We will watch the shop, get our affairs in order, and let ye rest before you become the best bloody barista in Glastonbury!"

That evening, Hamish and Isla retired upstairs to start packing for their mission back up to Scotland. Exhausted, Ethan crawled into bed and fell into a deep sleep, his dreams a mixture of thick darkness and memories playing over from the visions less than a night before. He woke the next morning when his stomach wretched from the meat and dairy he foolishly dove back into against the guidance of Selene and Silus. After releasing himself, he snuck down to make coffee and lean against the window of the café, reflecting on how he would spend his last day of freedom before becoming a slave to the beans and steam of the four walls surrounding him right now. During this reflection, he saw a figure in a bright blue raincoat walk briskly through the dark morning streets of Glastonbury. The figure was, in fact, Matteo.

Ethan ran out of the front door to meet the briskly walking Italian, who did not even glance at Andrew's Cross, clearly having no intention of stopping. "Matteo! Where have you been? Where are you going?"

"I told you yesterday, I go back to Italy."

"Now? This morning? Were you even going to stop and say goodbye?"

"I am sorry, but my mission has changed for the time. I must see my mother."

"Slow down!" Ethan was nearly running to keep up with Matteo's pace. He hadn't even looked back to acknowledge him. Matteo finally turned, revealing the intensity from the ceremony still in his eyes.

"I am sorry, my brother Ethan. I must do this."

"At five in the bloody morning?"

"There is no bus today. I must make it to Wells so I can find a way to the airport. This cannot wait."

"What happened to you yesterday?"

"Come, walk with me and I will tell you. But I must be quick." Matteo continued marching forward. Ethan followed quickly behind, still only wearing his pajama bottoms and a light jumper. The streets were empty; the streetlights provided the only illumination. A light mist hung over the Isle of Avalon as they brushed through to the top of the high street.

"Well, what has gotten over you? I understand it was intense, but come on, man. You are like a different person."

"Yes, you are correct. I am different. But not as different as you'd expect. This is how I have been since his death. For years now, I have worked to find myself. I thought I had found my peace. I found Glastonbury; I found you, Hamish, Zoe, Jasper, this and that. But this ceremony took all that away. I am now exactly who I was moments after Leo was killed. Why is this, Ethan?"

"I don't know. How could I know?"

"Exactly. You do not know; I do not know. Selene, Silus, Grandmother medicine—no one. But apparently, my mother. She is the key. So I go back to her."

"How did you put yourself together last time? You said you were feeling better until the ceremony. How was that?" asked Ethan.

"Years of work, pain, misery, meditation, reflection. All for what? For it to be stripped away! Like I did nothing!" Matteo was full of anger; his voice boomed over the homes they were briskly walking past. They were reaching the edge of the village, about to walk the path to Wells on foot. "Ethan, turn back. You will catch cold if you keep walking in your silly pants."

"No, I don't like this Matteo. I will walk with you to Wells if I have to! I hate to see you like this. Talk to me about this. Where did you find joy before?"

"Before?"

"Before Leo's death. What made you happy?"

"Oh, you are a therapist, I remember now. That is why you can ask silly questions."

"I went to school for psychology, but you are avoiding the question. List where you found joy. Come on."

"Fine, fine! Well, I like to walk. So we are doing that now. Walking helps, but takes a long time. I like to read; books take a long time to read, so I do not wish to do this now. I liked to cook—"

"You like to cook? You have never mentioned cooking before."

"You never asked."

"You never cooked."

"I haven't, not since that day."

"Then we should cook something together. Come back to the village? Yes, I have the whole flat to myself soon. We will cook something together. You cook pasta, yes?"

Matteo side-eyed Ethan. "You say this because I am Italian?"

"No—I mean, who doesn't like—"

"I mess with you! Ha! Every Italian comes out of the womb with dough in hand, ready to roll!" He laughed.

"See! We are already finding joy again!" They were only a few steps away from the boundary that Ethan had previously been unable to cross. "We can invite everyone—Zoe, Jasper, even Silus!"

"Silus at a pasta party! I would love to see it!"

"Great, so then let's—" Ethan took one step over the mystical boundary and found himself in front of the Tower, on top of the wet and windy Tor once more. "You have to be fucking kidding me. What the fuck! I was trying to help someone! Matteo—" He thought about his friend, who was now looking behind him, abandoned once again by the brother he called friend. "He will be heartbroken! Send me back, you stupid fucking Tower—elves, fairies, whatever! Why! What lesson! What are you teaching me!" Ethan cursed, yelled, spat, and screamed at the Tower, all for it to remain silent—no magic, no mysticism, only a Tower of stone presented itself today. Growing cold as his rage wore down, Ethan flipped the Tower a middle finger one last time before finding his footing down the shrouded path to the warmth that lay beyond in the town below. A dark figure appeared from behind the Tower as Ethan walked away. Owen was now watching—completely unnoticed by the young man who was blinded by anger and determination to counteract the magics that kept him tied to the Isle of Avalon…

—

Ethan found Jasper later that day and only said one thing to him before stomping off back to his room above the café: "Find us some fucking drugs."

11
KRISHNA

The week that followed Hamish and Isla's departure for Scotland was a blur of coffee-filled mornings and lonely nights. With Matteo gone as well, Ethan felt a void within himself without the company of his two closest friends in Glastonbury. One evening, he went to visit Zoe, and while her company was enjoyable, he realized that whatever spark he had felt for her before had vanished. Just as the spark for any enjoyment had left him after the mushroom ceremony, he was now left bitter and angry towards the small town he was forced to stay in.

Jasper came by to say he had found some more mushrooms for them to take the following Monday when the café would be closed.

"Who are we doing it with?" Ethan asked.

"A few of my friends. I will lead the ceremony, and this time, you will get your answers," Jasper seemed confident.

"Is it going to be similar to the ceremony we did before?"

"Yeah, a bit. I've picked up a lot over the years; it should be fine."

"Have you ever put on something like this?"

"Well, not like this, no. But I know my medicines!" Jasper reassured.

In the days leading up to Jasper's ceremony, Ethan felt himself becoming more distant with each cappuccino he made for the few people who walked Glastonbury's streets during the early winter days. Some people would strike up conversations with him that he would soon forget. He had regulars whose orders he couldn't be bothered to remember, and by the weekend, he was unprepared for the small influx of weekenders that did come to the shop, passing out early in the evening from exhaustion. His anxiety was creeping back into his life; his heart raced while waiting in line to purchase simple meal grab-and-gos from the nearby co-op, his evenings spent mindlessly watching Hamish's television, masturbating to vague memories of past partners, and enduring dreamless nights.

Monday brought his only relief from the feeling of emptiness; the prospect of finding a way out of Glastonbury gave him new energy that awoke him early to find Jasper. The ceremony was going to be held at another flat somewhere in the town that Ethan had not heard of; he was only given an address close to where the Temple of Artemis was located. He arrived early and knocked on the door, looking over to see that the faded sign read "The Temple of Krishna." The door was answered by a man who looked as though he had just woken up, his eyes swollen red, the smell of pot rushing out with him.

"Hey mate, are you with Jasper?" Ethan asked.

"Fucking what? Do you know how bloody early it is?" the man replied.

"He said to be here by nine; it's half eight now."

"Fuck, well he's not here yet," they both looked at each other blankly.

"Well, do you mind if I wait around? We are doing it here, aren't we?"

"Suppose so. Take a seat. The temple is right around the corner. Name's Josh, by the way."

"Ethan, thank you." He walked inside to the near-identical house he had stayed in during his first weeks in Glastonbury. This house, however, was nowhere near as tidy or as elegant as the Temple of Artemis. Layers of dust, grime, and neglect lay on nearly every surface. The "Temple" was nothing more than a living room with psychedelic posters on the walls, cheap pillows on the floor, and a litter box long overdue for cleaning.

"Do you have a cat, then?" Ethan asked across the room.

"Did. Fucker died a few months ago." Ethan looked at the litter box, realizing what that meant.

"Sorry to hear that..."

"Fucking bastard he was. Always getting on the altar space, probably got himself cursed." Josh came in with a cup of coffee for Ethan while pointing out the altar space at the back of the room, a large poster of who Ethan assumed was Krishna behind it. The altar had various crystals, bowls, bells, bones, runes, tarot cards, and plates of offerings on a tattered rainbow cloth—it was surprisingly the cleanest space in the entire house.

"Live here alone?" Ethan asked while accepting the coffee. He took a sip and felt the lukewarm burnt coffee touch his tongue and turn to regret.

"No. My girlfriend, me mate, my other mate, Jasper, of course, a couple of me mate's kids."

"Always wondered where Jasper lived…" Ethan attempted to take another drink from the bitter coffee before discreetly putting it down on the nearby fireplace mantle. "Is everyone doing the ceremony today?"

"Ceremony? Shit, is he making this a whole thing? Bet that's why he left in a hurry this morning…"

"Do them often?"

"What? Mushrooms? Yeah, 'bout twice a month, man. Great shit."

"Man, fucked me up a week ago," Ethan was attempting to create conversation; otherwise, he felt quite awkward in the space.

"Have you done bufo?"

"Fucking what?"

"Bufo, the frog venom."

"Frog venom?"

"Yeah, now that will send you fucking flying, man. Crazy trip. Similar to DMT."

"Haven't done that either."

"Mushrooms are like weed, man; easy shit. Speaking of, want some weed?"

"Yeah, not sure—" Just then, the door was unlatched, and Jasper came inside in a panic. "Thank God," Ethan thought.

"Ethan! You're already here. Great. See you've met my mate, Josh. You getting on well? Had to grab some things for the ceremony."

"Yeah, 'bout that, mate. You didn't say we were making this a whole thing. Christine ain't even up yet. She ain't going to be happy to hear we have to do a whole thing," Josh groaned.

"Come now, Josh! You know I have always wanted to do it with ceremony, and my friend Ethan here needs help from it. You'll love it! It's the same trip with more meaning!"

"Fine, fine. But you gotta be the one to tell Christine and the others. They'll be pissed; we didn't get to bed 'til a few hours ago."

"Fine, fine. I will! Ethan, do you mind grabbing my bags? Please help yourself to anything in the kitchen too!" Jasper left his bags on the floor and headed upstairs with nervous energy. Ethan took the bags into the "Temple" before heading into the kitchen to rummage around—unsurprisingly, the kitchen was as filthy, if not worse, than the rest of the house. He stepped into something soft and squishy that sent shivers up his spine; nearly every dish and piece of cookware was sitting around the sink, with old food crusted to it, leading to many flies soaring around the space. The fridge held little that looked edible besides a bag of apples, which looked recently purchased—Ethan helped himself to one and quickly made his way back to the "Temple" space. Jasper was coming down from the stairs in a hurry, now wearing a blue robe with a hood. He began to unpack the bags containing different occult objects, bundles of dried plants, and several musical instruments. Jasper then made a fair effort to clean the space, make it more presentable, and even made a circle of pillows and blankets in a similar fashion to the space above the White Springs.

Movement could be heard from above as the rest of the house was now in motion. First to come down were two children—two girls with messy hair and oversized jumpers on—followed by who Ethan assumed to be their father, who looked quite young to have two children at least four years old. Next was Christine, who was wearing a green robe of her own, her breasts hanging half out of the large opening in the front. The final one to come down was an overweight man—appearing to be from somewhere in the Middle East—he had a scruffy beard and his own ill-fitting robe. Josh had changed into a tattered robe as well, also green, his bare chest visible like Christine's, revealing a mixture of tattoos that Ethan did not recognize. She looked at Ethan with an expression that appeared as though she both remembered him and had no idea who he was.

Slowly, the "Temple" space filled with the exhausted faces of the various housemates and the two little girls who had the most energy out of anyone.

"Dad, dad, dad, dad…"

"What!"

"What's for breakfast?"

"Grab some cereal or something. We have to do some work today," the young father responded to their nagging.

"What will we do then, Dad?" they both said in unison.

"You can play upstairs, watch as much television as you want until we get done." The young father took them into the kitchen and continued the conversation away from everyone else. Jasper was still busy preparing the space to his liking; he closed the window curtains, lit candles, and sparked incense that had a cheap, pungent odor. He then grabbed a small bowl and placed bundles of herbs inside that he lit on fire, creating a thick cloud of smoke that choked the air out of the space.

"Okay… is everyone— is everyone ready to begin?" Jasper's hands clasped the smoking bowl, shaking with nerves.

"Get on with it, then," said Josh.

"Right, today we are participating in a sacred… uh, tradition that goes back to the peoples of… where was it— shit. Well, the people of America used similar traditions and ceremonies too…"

"I am so fucked…" Ethan thought to himself. He was growing more nervous; he did not know the names of half the people in the room. The smoke was making him light-headed, and the two girls were making tons of noise upstairs, which made him uncomfortable. "I should just leave; this isn't right…" He was building up the courage to stand when Jasper moved in front of him, blowing the thick smoke in his face. Jasper then came through with a rattle and shook it around Ethan's head, his rhythm broken and disjointed. He then produced a drum and encouraged everyone to take an instrument around them to play. Ethan grabbed a string of bells nearby with hesitation.

"This song was taught to me by my guru; he said it was passed down in his family by Krishna himself."

"You went to India?" asked the overweight flatmate in a sarcastic tone.

"No… well… we never met in person. But I learned a lot from him… anyways! This is for you, Krishna," Jasper bowed in front of the altar. Light chuckling could be heard from Josh and the overweight flatmate.

"Hey Krishna, teri muskurahat kitni pyari,
Mera moja dhoondho, mat chhupaao itni saari!
Ek yahan hai, par joda kahaan?
Sab kone mein dhoondha, phir bhi na mila wahan."

His singing was off-key and lacked cadence of any kind; he restarted several times after losing his chain of thought. Some of the others attempted to play music in tune with what was being sung, but harmony was never found. After a few minutes, Jasper stopped singing and began to prepare several bowls in front of him, filling them with mushrooms. They were then passed around; the one placed in front of Ethan contained over a dozen mushrooms, far more than what he had consumed during the night with Selene and Silus.

"Do I eat all of this?" Ethan asked, looking around the room to see everyone had similar bowls.

"Yes, this is considered the shaman's dose. This is how you break through the wall that is your ego!" Jasper seemed more confident now.

"I don't know—"

"Come on, mate, you'll be fine. We do this all the time," said Josh.

"Yeah, won't kill you," Christine added, already shoving a handful into her mouth.

"I am here for you. You will be safe," Jasper reassured, a large bowl in his hands as well. Ethan saw that everyone was quickly eating the mushrooms. He sighed and began to do the same. The tea he had previously was passable and palatable; the opposite was true for the taste of the mushrooms. The flavor was that of dried dirt, with the texture of week-old chewing gum. Small bits got stuck in his teeth, forcing him to fish around his mouth to get it all down. Eating the whole bowl felt like a monumental task—one the others in the space had already finished. He felt his stomach wretch as he closed in on the last two spores. He looked around for anything to help wash down the dry and unpalatable flavor on his tongue. Luckily, Jasper had bottles of water he handed to everyone, giving some relief to Ethan's struggle. After getting the last of it down, he felt ill and wanted to lie down. Jasper procured a large wooden flute and began to play it for the space. Luckily for Ethan, he was a much better flute player than a singer.

Ethan closed his eyes and hugged his stomach, the soothing notes of the flute calming his nerves. Just as last time, the effects took around twenty minutes to begin—first as color changes, light flashes, and swirls under his eyelids, and finally as mosaic tiles appearing in his vision. He was pulled out of the trance by the others in the circle. The young father had left to check on his two daughters, Josh and Christine were laughing to one another, and Jasper did his best to play the flute through the growing noise of the room. Despite the distractions, Ethan entered a deep flood of images; thick were the colors and sensations. He could see the Heron once again, its wings flapping around his eyes. The Tor shone a light over the dark sea as it had before. This time, however, he could not focus for long before another image overtook the previous one. He saw a dragon, a car, a child, a bee, the moon, the sun, Owen, a cheeseburger, and his mother… the vision floated back and forth constantly. Soon he was seeing the hooded figures; this time their faces were all his own, each one a different age. He was able to call out to them:

"Why am I here?"

The hooded figures wrapped themselves into cocoons and turned into butterflies before his eyes. The sky turned red, then black; the trees withered and died. The Tor transformed into a cave that opened up before him, beckoning him in… he descended the stone steps leading into the depths of the hill. Ethan felt his stomach wretch and his mouth taste of bile; the room was spinning, and he was having trouble breathing.

"Fuck, I feel like shit," he said aloud.

"It's fine, Ethan. You are okay; it is part of the medicine," Jasper rushed over to him. They were the only two left in the Temple; the Middle Eastern man was now in the room next to them watching a movie on his laptop, laughing at a high volume. Josh and Christine could be heard upstairs having rough sex. Ethan could smell the old cat litter wafting ancient feces over to his nose. His sensations were heightened; the room was spinning, and his thoughts were running a million miles a minute.

"I am freaking out, man! What is happening?" Ethan could feel his heart racing; he could barely breathe. Everywhere he looked, he was bombarded with images: red cars, blue demons, yellow clouds, racing rainbows, old faces, dead bodies, flying spears, spaceships, green slime—he was completely overwhelmed and felt horrible. His face turned pale white; he couldn't breathe at all.

"Shit, shit, shit. Hold on; I will be right back!" Jasper ran out of the temple space, leaving Ethan alone on the floor, his universe spinning into darkness. He felt like death; his body lay motionless despite his mind disappearing into the void.

In the distance, as if a mile away, he heard: "Gave him too much, mate; you fucked up…"

"Help him! I don't know what to do!"

"Hold him up; I will—"

Ethan faded from time and space, no longer present in the room, no longer within his own body… darkness completely took him.

—

For what seemed like an eternity, Ethan lay in that void that he only knew could be death. From the void birthed a single flickering light. The light became a candle, the candle became a bonfire, the bonfire became the earth, the earth became the sun, and the darkness was cast aside to reveal immaculate light. The sun's face became the face of an elderly man:

"Hello, my son," came the voice of the sun. "You have found me."

"Who are you?"

"I am life."

"Are you God?"

"You do not believe in God, Ethan."

"I do not. But am I dead?"

"Do you feel dead?"

"Yes."

"Then this is the first time you are alive."

"That doesn't make any sense."

"Does your life make any sense?"

Ethan paused. "What the fuck is happening?"

"You are trapped."

"In Glastonbury."

"No, in yourself."

"How the fuck do I get out?"

"Find the key to the cage."

"Where is the key?"

"It is close, but you are blind."

Ethan looked around as if it were literally nearby. He saw no key but could feel the wind against his face, the feeling of freedom. "Where do I find it?"

"In Glastonbury, of course," said the sun.

"I have searched for it everywhere!" Ethan cried.

"Not everywhere..."

"Wake up and see."

"How do I—"

"Ethan, wake up!" The sun's voice turned into that of Jasper.

Ethan opened his eyes; he was in a car, and Jasper was next to him. "Where am I?"

"You passed out again; we are in Street. We got dinner."

"What street?"

"Not a street; Street, the town nearby. You know it."

"Wait, we left Glastonbury? How?" Ethan shot up, fully alert. He was out of Glastonbury! Outside, he could see the countryside was different than he had seen before—they were driving fast. In the distance, he could see the Glastonbury Tor growing closer; they were on their way back. "Stop the car!"

"Are you going to throw up again?" said Jasper.

"He better not throw up curry in my fucking car!" shouted Josh from the front seat.

"Let me out of this fucking car!" Ethan could see they were getting closer to the roundabout that led back into Glastonbury.

"Calm your friend down, Jasper! He is freaking out again; he has ruined my entire trip with this shit!" Christine called back to them from the passenger seat.

"Lock the doors!" Jasper shouted back as Ethan clawed at the door handle.

"Please, you don't understand!" Ethan cried, seeing they had now crossed the threshold back into Glastonbury, the sign "Isle of Avalon" welcoming them back to the small village—back to Ethan's prison. The ride back to the Temple of Krishna was short; Ethan was pawing at the window and door, wailing at the top of his lungs. When they finally stopped and unlocked the door, Ethan burst out and ran a few steps before falling down and hitting his head on the pavement, knocking himself out cold.

—

Ethan awoke with a throbbing headache. He felt the soft surface of a couch below him and the familiar smell of coffee coming from below. He was back in the flat above Andrew's Cross. He opened his eyes to see it was not dark out; his vision was still clouded with mosaic tiles from the effects of the mushrooms—the major effects now giving way to a feeling of lightheadedness. Jasper was sitting in the chair across from him.

"Hey mate, take it easy. You bumped your head something nasty earlier."

"What the fuck happened?" Ethan asked.

"You kind of… freaked out on us."

"Tell me everything… I don't remember a thing."

"Well, we did the ceremony. Ate the mushrooms. Everything was good for a bit, but then you started to spin out. I was tripping pretty hard too! The flute and mushrooms really get me far. Well—I had to get Josh to help. So we gave you some ketamine to calm you down, just like—a bit…"

"Ketamine? The fucking horse medicine?"

"Just a little to calm you down. And when you came to, we went and got some food on your stomach."

"What did we eat? My stomach feels shit."

"We went to the Indian place in Street," Jasper said, bringing the memories back to Ethan. He was outside of Glastonbury; he escaped. "What did you see on your trip?" Jasper asked.

"I don't really know… but I think… I think it helped, actually."

"Really? Didn't seem like it at the time."

"Well, I felt shit. Still feel shit. But I got out…" Ethan stared at the corner of the room.

"Got out of where?"

"This place…"

"Oh, you mean the self. The ego! You had a true ego death then, man! Congratulations. I told you that this would work!" Jasper seemed relieved.

"I need to see; I need to get out of here," Ethan pushed his way past Jasper.

"Leave? Mate, you are in no condition! Take a night off, and then tomorrow we can go wherever you want to." Ethan was unable to make it to the door without feeling the world spin. He went to sit back on the couch.

"You might be right… I will just rest a bit longer." Ethan closed his eyes.

"Are you okay for me to leave then, mate? Are you going to stay here the rest of the night?"

"Yeah, sure thing."

"Promise me you won't leave."

"Fuck off, fine," Ethan assured. Jasper, feeling satisfied, grabbed his coat and left the flat. The room was still spinning for Ethan when he began to drift away into a hazy sleep. "I got out… I fucking did it…" he said to himself as the darkness overtook him again, this time long into the night.

—

His phone was ringing when he awoke again, this time to the low sun of a new day. Ethan walked over to his coat to find his mobile in one of the pockets, 'Hamish' flashing on the screen.

"Hey, what's up, Hamish?" he said groggily.

"What's up? Sorry, didnae realize I was callin' a bloody teenager. Good mornin' tae ye too, mate."

"Sorry, sorry. Long night—day. Good morning."

"That's better. How's the shop been this morning?"

"Morning?" Ethan looked at the clock on the wall to see it was well past nine. "Shit… I am so fucked," he thought. "Store? Yeah, slow today. Been a slow start as usual!" He lied, grabbing his pants from the floor and shoving them on.

"Not surprisin' at all—last week? Slow as well?"

"Not bad; good weekend, actually," Ethan was talking from the bathroom, throwing deodorant on and fixing his messy hair. "You look shit," he thought in reaction to seeing his face in the mirror.

"Good tae hear, weel—we're settled in Scotland. Out tae take care o' our business in a couple o' days. Just checkin' in; any problems?"

"No, not a problem so far!" He was running down the stairs to open the café doors.

"Alright, well I won't keep ye from the beans. Get to it, make some money, and stay in touch, yeah?" Hamish said.

"Sure, yes. All is well. Enjoy Scotland for me!" Ethan clicked the phone closed, dashing inside to get the store ready for business. Luckily for him, little needed to be done to open the café; unluckily for him, there were several customers right away. His head was still sore, and his balance was a little shaky. "Am I still tripping?" Ethan thought several times, seeing the occasional swirl or shift in color within his vision. He slowly rallied throughout the day, pondering his next move. After shutting the doors for the day, he decided he was going to take a walk towards the town of Street to see if he could break through the magical barricade that had him trapped in Glastonbury. Unsurprisingly, when he crossed the familiar threshold on the south side of town, he was twisted around and transported back to Glastonbury, the Tor looming in the distance.

"So what's the bloody answer then!" he grunted to himself, stopping by the chippy for a platter of grease-covered supper—ever since the morning, his stomach was craving a deep-fried disaster. While looking out the window, he spotted Jasper walking across town.

"Ethan! You are alive. Nasty bump on your chin, I see," greeted Jasper.

"All better now. The healing power of the chippy is already working its magic. Sorry about last night."

"No bother, mate; my fault, honestly. Probably should have prepped you better for how mental mushrooms can really be."

"When can we do it again?" asked Ethan.

"Again? Really? Thought you would never do them again after yesterday."

"The opposite, man. I got so much closer to breaking free; another time I will surely get there."

"Shit, well. Yeah, I think I can do another 'round. Week from now, work?"

"What about Sunday? That way I won't need to open the shop the next morning."

"Fine, that'll do. See you Sunday then?"

"Ace, man. See you soon. Come by for a coffee in the morning? On me." Ethan dashed away to finish his supper from the warmth of the flat.

Sunday came around quickly; soon, Ethan was back at the Temple of Krishna. When asked if he wished to do the ceremony again, Ethan replied with, "Don't bother, mate. Let's just get it done. Is Josh doing it again?"

"Just us. He is a bit pissed at you for ruining his trip," replied Jasper.

"I will make it up to him. Anyway, got any peanut butter or something for these nasty fuckers? Think that's what made me ill last time." Jasper was happy to oblige his request; they made peanut butter sandwiches filled with dried mushrooms, which they quickly downed. Later, Josh arrived with several cans of beer that he offered, which Ethan was happy to take as the mushrooms began to work once more. This time, he was able to control the waves of sensations—as well as the wooziness—when the effects began to come over him. Ethan suggested they head off to Street again for supper at another restaurant. Josh only agreed to once Ethan offered to pay, which he happily accepted. Ethan was fairly lucid when they got into the back of Josh's car. The visions were not as heavy as they had been less than a week ago. As the car approached the roundabout towards Street, Ethan awaited to see what would happen and was surprised when he was able to cross the threshold once again.

"No fucking way, man! This is how I do it!" he said excitedly. "But how do I leave the town for good?" Josh parked his car beside the Chinese restaurant, and they all hopped out. But when Ethan turned around, he was staring directly at a sign that read: The Andrew's Cross. He was back in Glastonbury once again! "You gotta be fucking kidding me!" He rushed back to the Temple of Krishna and waited for Jasper and Josh to return from Street.

"Sorry, guys; left my wallet here. Needed to run back," was his excuse.

"You ran all the way back here, tripping your balls off? In less than two hours?" Jasper said, unbelieving.

"Yes, I ran back in university."

"You owe me sixteen quid, by the way, fucker," Josh pushed past him back into the house.

"Yes, of course." Ethan handed him the cash from his wallet. "I don't feel the mushrooms that much this time. Did we do less?" he asked.

"Actually, we did more. You build up a tolerance," replied Jasper.

"How long do I have to wait to go deeper again?"

"Month to build back up the chemicals in the body."

"Shit, what else can I do?"

"What do you mean?"

"I have come so far; how do I go deeper now?"

"Bufo?" Josh said from the kitchen.

"No, I fucking hate that stuff," Jasper replied.

"Will it get me there? Get me back?" asked Ethan.

"Yeah, it'll get you there. But it is not gentle."

"I will do it. Tomorrow?"

"Buy me dinner again?" said Josh.

"Deal."

The following evening, Ethan returned and smoked Bufo from a pipe. He fell against the floor from a seated position and went deep within himself. He did not see the visions as he had with mushrooms, but he felt pure euphoria radiate from around him. He felt his visage, his ego, his self vanish from his body. He was so entrapped with the sensation that he lost track of time and never left the house to try and escape the city again. Ethan slept over at the Temple of Krishna on the ratty sofa in Jasper's room. He was nearly late again to open the café; while there, Hamish called:

"Sorry, mate, we may need another week. Think ye can handle it on yer own?"

"No problem."

For another week, Ethan spent every night at the Temple of Krishna, partaking of drugs he no longer knew—or cared to—know the names of. Half the time, he was on the floor drifting deep within himself, filling his body with chemicals, spending his meager wages on chippies, Chinese take-out, and greasy pizza from the kebab shop. He always managed to wake up and open the café, but little effort was put into the daily work, his mind only thinking of the night and the escape from his own mind. The drugs provided him peace; he was no longer in Glastonbury, he was no longer Ethan, he was free.

One evening, he came over to find everyone had left the Temple of Krishna for an event at one of the pubs in town, everyone except Christine, who was now standing at the door wearing a low-cut shirt and little else besides panties and socks.

"Sorry, didn't know everyone was out. I will just head back to my flat," Ethan said.

"You can stay. Was looking for some company anyway."

"I'm good, thanks."

"Look, Ethan. You come here all the time; we are friends now, right?"

"Sure, yeah. Friends."

"Friends that do drugs together."

"Yeah, I guess."

"Well, I got some molly here. And I'm pretty sure you have never tried it before," she said in a teasing tone.

"What the fuck is molly?"

"You'll see; trust me. You are going to love it." She took Ethan by the hand and led him inside, finding a small bag of pills that she put onto the coffee table in the adjoining room to the temple space. She poured two glasses of tequila and brought them over. "Molly and a Mexican. That's what I call this. Always leads to a good time." She handed him the glass and small pill. "Cheers." They drank together the drug and shots of liquor, then another shot, another, and finally, Ethan was feeling floaty, and Christine was feeling flirty. She placed her hand on his leg and leaned in close to him.

"What are you doing?" he asked.

"Don't worry; Josh and I do this all the time," she whispered.

"I am not Josh," Ethan started to get up, but was moved back down by Christine's grip.

"We aren't exclusive; he's probably fucking someone right now. So, are you going to fuck me or just stand there stiff as a fucking board?" She pulled her loose-fitting shirt down to reveal her breast to him. Ethan felt himself get aroused, desiring to be touched by her. He sat back down and allowed her to come closer to him once again; the gentle touch of her fingers against his neck sent cascades of chills down his spine.

"So... Christine, molly makes—"

"—makes everything feel better," she kissed him and bit his lip. Ethan was overcome by the rush and the feeling of pleasure and pressed his hands under Christine's shirt. They fucked on the couch, and now they lay together under an old dusty quilt.

"I think I like molly..." Ethan said, eyes dilated, his chest covered in sweat.

"When you fuck on molly... it's always a threesome!" Christine laughed.

"Well, if it's molly and a Mexican, sounds more like a foursome!" Ethan laughed with her, but then a sound came from the front door; Josh was now standing across from them, another woman wrapped around his arm.

"Christine, with Ethan? Really?" Josh said with disgust.

"Don't be jealous. Do you even know her name?" she said as Ethan panicked to put his clothes back on.

"Well—no. What's your name?" he asked the woman beside him.

"Bethany. Who's that?"

"Just my girlfriend Christine and the deadbeat who does all my drugs."

"Hey, I buy you dinner!" Ethan protested.

"Suppose you do. Now, maybe you can buy me dinner for fucking my girlfriend?"

"Are you jealous? You were about to fuck this 'Bethany' in our own bed!"

"Better to fuck 'Bethany' than to fuck you again, slut!" he yelled at her.

"Oh, I fucked up…" Ethan thought to himself, now putting his pants back on.

"Where are you going, Ethan? Don't listen to Josh; he's a fucking burnout anyway," Christine gripped onto him.

"I think I should probably go."

"No, sit the fuck down. You know what? Since we are all about free love, why don't we all go get dinner together?" Josh shouted. "You, me, Ethan, and Becca."

"Bethany…" she corrected.

"Sorry, Bethany. Would you like to get dinner with my whore of a girlfriend and the piss fuck named Ethan? It'll be great."

"Look, I am going to leave. I do not want a part of this," Ethan put on his shirt and moved towards the door, only to be stopped by Josh.

"Oh, you wanted a part of my girlfriend but can't fucking go to dinner with us?"

"Let him go!" shouted Christine, who was now standing only in her underwear.

"You don't tell me what to do!" Josh shouted at Christine but let his guard down, allowing Ethan to sneak past him.

"Want to get the fuck out of here?" he whispered to Bethany.

"Yes, please."

They both snuck out the front, still hearing yelling behind them. The door to the Temple of Krishna clicked shut when Ethan realized that his coat was still inside.

"Fuck. My keys are still in there."

"Do you want to knock and see if they will let you back in?" asked Bethany.

"I doubt that will go well. Shit, what am I going to do?"

"Don't take this as an invitation that you can fuck me too, but you can stay with me. You did save me from making a mistake too."

"Thanks, trust me. You do not want to get involved with that. Where do you live?"

"The campsite. I have a small van there."

"The campsite? Lila told me about that… shit. What other option do I have?" he thought about other options… "Zoe? No, not on a night like this… Selene? And suffer the judgment? No, thank you. Fuck, I wish Matteo was back." With no other viable options coming to mind, he agreed to Bethany's hospitality and ventured to the campsite on the edge of town. The walk was long, and Bethany had little interest in conversation—without his coat, he was freezing cold as well. When they reached the edge of the camp, Ethan could see several dozen tents, vans, and run-down RVs lining a loosely organized field of various sites. Bethany's van was located near the back; she unlocked it and hopped inside. When Ethan went to do the same, she raised a hand.

"Sorry, changed my mind."

"What the fuck do you mean? I came all this way because you invited me."

"Decided I don't trust men after all that."

"What the fuck am I supposed to do?"

"Sorry, really tired. Mind closing the door?"

"You gotta be fucking kidding me…" Ethan stared at her and her determined expression. "What can I do? Force myself into the van? No. Fuck." Seeing that there was no way to change her mind, he stepped back and closed the door, leaving him alone in the cold dark night of early December—no coat, no mobile, no keys, half-tripping on molly. "Fuck."

Ethan looked around the camp to see that no lights were on at any of the tents or vans. The hour was late, and no fires were going either. In the distance, he could see the dim glow of the village lights, the dark Tor looming close by on the path back from the east. He rubbed his hands against his arms and placed them into his pits before marching off in the direction of Glastonbury, feeling shame, regret, and worry clouding his face. He felt the cold wind whip from every direction, cutting through his thin clothing and causing him to shiver and shake.

He was now getting closer to the Tor, following a small path from behind it and through the woods around the base of the hill. He felt hope that he would make it back to town growing faint. "Where will I even go? To find Jasper? Check the library? Go to the pub? I have no money?" His thoughts continued to race. The cold burrowed deep now, as did his fear of something bad happening. Just then, he saw a flicker of light from the corner of his eye… a fire! In the distance was a flame coming from the middle of a field. Ethan felt a rush of energy come to him at the thought of the promise of warmth. He rushed quickly to the glowing flame; as he grew closer, he could see that the flame was contained within a triangular structure… one he recognized as a teepee. "A fucking teepee in Somerset? Who am I to question?" he thought. As he approached, he looked inside to see that there was no one within, yet the fire was roaring as if it had been recently stoked and refueled. He did not question the welcoming flame; he dove in and curled up in the fetal position around the fire, shoving his hands and feet as close as he could without burning them.

"Thank you, fire. Thank you, thank you!" he cried aloud. "I do not know who built you! But thank you! Thank you to this fucking teepee, to the tree that is burning. Thank you!" Tears of both sorrow and gratitude ran down his frozen cheeks. He cried from deep sorrow but also incredible appreciation as the fire slowly warmed his body; soon, the shaking ceased, and he lay unmoving on the hard ground of the teepee. Sleep soon took him, and a thick blanket was laid upon him sometime in the night.

As he slept, Ethan drifted between dreams of warmth and visions of the Tor, its majestic form towering above the landscape like a guardian of secrets. In one dream, he stood at the base, feeling the energy of the earth pulsate beneath him. He reached out to touch the soil, and the ground shimmered with light, revealing countless paths spiraling into the depths of the hill. Each path whispered of possibilities—some leading to places of healing, others to dark corners of his own mind he had yet to confront.

12
Eagle Dancer

Bum...bum...bum...bum...dum...dum...bum...bum...bum...
dum...dum

The distant drumming grew louder from the depths of Ethan's dreams. He peeled his eyes open to the low smoldering fire in the center of the teepee. A man sat on the other side, a drum in one hand, a mallet in the other, and a cigarette in his mouth.

"So, you are finally awake," said the man. "You have slept for a long time in my teepee."

"Shit... I didn't think it was real... the teepee. A dream—a nightmare."

"This teepee is no dream, nor is it a nightmare. What you put into your body, that was a nightmare." The man smoked between puffs on his cigarette. Ethan now saw that he was, in fact, a Native American man in his later years.

"Are you an Indian—sorry, I mean an Indigenous... person?"

"We are all indigenous from one place or another. But we Indians remember our native land. Where is yours?"

"Here, in England. I think."

"You think? If you must think, then you do not feel it. Do you feel this land?"

"Look, Mister—thank you for the teepee, but my head is pounding, and I don't think I can have a talk like this today."

"Ah, yes. Because of what you put in your body."

"How do you know that?"

"Because the Great Spirit told me…"

"Really?"

"No, because you look like shit," he laughed, finishing his cigarette only to light another in the same breath. Ethan sat up and realized there was a blanket on him and a bowl of water sitting close to where his head had laid. "Yes, that was me," the man said, seeing Ethan's confusion.

"I mean no offense by this, but why is there a teepee and a Native American man in Glastonbury?"

"Because I was invited here by a good friend of mine."

"Who is your friend?"

"You do not know my name, and yet you ask the name of someone else? How odd." The man's face had been expressionless throughout the conversation.

"I am so sorry—what is your name?"

"His name is William Eagle Dancer," came the voice of someone from outside the teepee, revealing none other than Owen.

"Good to see you, my friend. Are they ready?" asked William Eagle Dancer.

"Aye, 'bout to be here. When did you catch him then?"

"Last night. He wandered in half-frozen, half-high, and half-stupid." They both laughed. William handed a cigarette to Owen, who gladly obliged.

"I am sorry—I should be getting out of here…" Ethan began to gather himself to leave, only to find his legs would not support him.

"Should we let him stay, ye think?" Owen asked William Eagle Dancer.

"Sweat could do him some good. But he is dehydrated. He will need lots of water."

""He do know the girl, I reckon. Could be good for 'er."

"I wish they wouldn't talk about me as if I weren't here…" Ethan thought, feeling embarrassed.

"If he passes out, he will be your responsibility. And he needs no medicines. Only what the lodge will provide."

"I am sorry, but what are you talking about?" Ethan asked, running out of patience.

"William Eagle Dancer is 'ere to put on a sweat lodge for one of yer friends, no less." Owen answered.

"Sweat lodge? Wait… which friend?"

"Zoe."

—

The morning was still early as Ethan was put to work by Owen and William Eagle Dancer. He was given two liters of water and told to drink it slowly over the course of the morning. He was then put through a series of tasks: taking wood out of a nearby truck bed, piling stones, collecting small green sticks from the nearby forest, and digging a deep hole in the middle of the field near the teepee, all while Owen and William sat in the teepee and talked through two packs of cigarettes.

"Why am I doing this again?" Ethan asked, panting at the entrance of the teepee.

"Because ye volunteered," Owen said sharply.

"Well, yeah, to help Zoe. But I didn't think it would mean I would be made a slave!"

"Were you not a slave to the bad medicine you put into your body?" William said directly.

"I wouldn't say a slave. I just had a bad night," Ethan backpedaled.

"'Ow many nights 'ave you been high this last month?" Owen asked.

"I—don't know."

"Then get back t' diggin' an' drink that water, lad. I want it all gone by the time they get 'ere."

Ethan took his shovel and liter jugs of water and went back outside to continue digging, taking breaks to rest and finish his water. He felt like shit but slowly felt life enter him once again as the work continued. As he neared the limits of his digging abilities, he looked out to see a group of people approaching the field, carrying small bags. At the head of the pack was Zoe. When she caught sight of Ethan—covered in dirt, dressed inappropriately for the weather, with bags under his eyes—she ran over and smiled, "Ethan! I didn't know you would be here!"

"I didn't know I was going to be here either," he smiled.

"It's so good to see you actually," she said genuinely.

"Yeah, good to see you too. So—sweat lodge, eh? What's this about then?"

"Owen up to his old tricks, I see. Signed you up without letting you in on what was happening?"

"Yeah, basically that." One of the women behind Zoe approached her and beckoned her to go inside the teepee with them:

"Sorry, Ethan. I have to go. But thank you for helping with this. It really means the world." She reached her hand out and grabbed his, then headed inside. Ethan climbed out of the hole and approached after her but was stopped by Owen.

"Mate, where do you think you're going?"

"To the teepee; I assume we are starting."

"Aye, we are starting. But this first part we ask you to stay out of. You are too full of the bad medicine to receive this ceremony."

"What ceremony?"

"It's sacred tobacco, but William is insisting that you can't do it. Not in your state."

"But I can do the lodge?"

"Yes, yes, you can."

"What is it?"

"I'll tell ye all about it while ye help me build it."Owen took Ethan by the shoulder and led him over to the pit he had just dug.

He then had Ethan assist him in tying the green limbs together to form something resembling a round structure. While they worked Ethan could hear various noises coming from the teepee: crying, coughing, wailing, gentle talking, and occasional laughter.

"Okay, so what's happening?" Ethan asked, wrapping strips of cloth around two small sapling branches.

"A sweat lodge is a sacred tradition of the Native American tribes. Goes back, maybe thousands of years. William, in there, is one o' the best at 'em in the world. He came to Europe about ten years ago, doin' 'em."

"What are they for? Is it like a fancy sauna?"

"No, fuck no. Saunas are much different. 'Bout all they 'ave in common is the sweatin'. A sweat lodge is a prayer, Ethan."

"A prayer? For what?"

"Anythin', really. But it typically is for a singular purpose—or person."

"Zoe..."

"Aye, Zoe is the prayer today."

"What is she praying for?"

"That I can't tell ye."

"Because you don't know, or because you won't say?"

"P'raps both; p'raps neither. Ye can ask 'er if she wants t' share. But it's none o' our business to know. We're 'ere to support 'er."

"How do we do that?"

"By sweatin', singin', and workin', so let's get back to it."

Owen put together the final piece and lifted the structure up to show its final form. It was a low dome skeleton—no more than a meter high—with one gate-like entrance, placed over the deep hole that Ethan had dug. Next, Owen handed Ethan several large blankets, sheets, and curtains that they stretched over the structure into several thick layers that went down to the ground. Owen then had Ethan place stones on the edges to create a seal while he fashioned a type of flat that could hang over the entrance. Ethan stepped away and stood next to Owen, both of them sweating through their clothes:

"So, that's the sweat lodge..." Ethan said panting.

"That it is."

"Glad that's over with, so when do we start?"

"Start? Ha! We still gotta start the fire, lad!" Owen laughed and placed his hand on Ethan's shoulder, showing him the large pile of wood and stones that awaited them.

"Fuck me…"

Owen explained that the fire had to be aligned perfectly with the entrance to the lodge they had just made. He said it would allow the energies to travel freely between the two. Ethan was more preoccupied with the large stones he was lifting into the ever-growing pile of wood and rocks being created. Standing now nearly to Ethan's head, it was an impressive sight, one that left Ethan completely exhausted. He fell to the grassy earth and looked up at the rare autumn clear skies. Owen sat next to him, looking up towards the sky as well.

"Ye did good, Ethan. Didnae think ye'd have this work in ye."

"I am pretty sure I am dead."

"Not yet; still 'ave use for ye."

"I am afraid I don't have much left, mate."

"You will. Fire'll give ye energy once it's lit. Ever kept a sacred fire before?"

"No."

"Well, ye can add it to yer CV today! Come, it's almost time," Owen offered Ethan a hand, which he cautiously took. From the teepee, the group, led by Zoe and William Eagle Dancer, formed a circle around the unlit bonfire.

"Please, once the fire is lit, I must ask that you do not cross the sacred line between the grandfathers and the Inipi. I also ask that no one besides Owen—"

"And Ethan," Owen said proudly, smacking Ethan on the back.

"—and Ethan, add wood, touch, or manipulate the fire in any way. Once the fire is lit, we will make our way into the Inipi. Myself and Zoe will be in the center; everyone else will need to squeeze together. It will be tight; you will be uncomfortable, you will be dirty, and by the end, we are family—family who are praying together. That is powerful. While we are in the lodge, we will sing sacred songs: fire songs, water songs, tobacco songs. I assume only myself and Owen know these songs. We will guide you, but feel free to sing if you begin to understand. They will add to the prayer—"

Ethan was losing focus, his body still tired from the work he had done and the previous night of regret. He looked to the circle; he could not notice anyone he knew Zoe, he was transfixed. She was in a red dress, bare feet, and had her messy hair in a tight bun, revealing her angular face. "She is as beautiful as ever…" he drifted away into thought. First, about Zoe, then to other things far away from where he was standing. He was brought back to the moment when Owen smacked him on the back, "Come on, that's our cue."

William Eagle Dancer had started the fire from the base and had now procured a large fan of feathers that Ethan could only assume was from a turkey—despite him never seeing one in person. As William Eagle Dancer fanned the base of the wood and stone, flames began to shoot out, warming the barefooted participants.

"Alright, Ethan, this is very important. Take this."

Owen held out his hand containing dried herbs. "This is a sacred mixture of tobacco, mugwort, cedar, and hawthorn. We must feed this to the fire and pray—"

"I still don't know what we are praying for…"

"Are ye deaf, boy? We are prayin' fer Zoe!" he whispered and yelled simultaneously.

"About what?"

"It doesn't matter; she needs praying, and we are here to pray," Owen poured the herb mixture into Ethan's hands. "Now, first present the blend to the East; pray to the East. Then to the South, West, and then the North. We then present it to the Sky, to the Earth, then place it to yer head and then to yer heart. All while ye best be prayin'! After all that, then ye can feed it to the fire—but wi' intention and love! Got all that?"

Ethan's head was spinning from all the information he had just received. He looked down at the dried herbs. "I think so…"

"And fer fuck's sake, boy. Pray!" He smiled and then began to pray with his own handful of dried herbs. Behind him, William Eagle Dancer was doing the same, except he was placing the herbs on the hearts and heads of all those in the circle. Ethan stood staring at his hand…

"What to pray for… what does she need… fuck. I don't know!" He tried to think of everything they had talked about over the last couple of months, searching for what it is that she may need within her life. "I pray for Zoe… I pray for her to heal. From whatever she is hurting from…" he whispered. Ethan looked to the East and presented his hand:

"To the East, I pray for Zoe…my friend.
I pray for her to heal. I pray for healing…whatever that is from.

To the South, I pray for Zoe, my friend!
I pray for her to heal. I pray for healing for whatever her need.

To the West, I pray for my friend Zoe!
I ask for healing to be brought to her, no matter her need!

To the North, I pray to you! My dear friend Zoe, my friend!
She needs healing; I do not know what for. But please be with her!"

Ethan fell to his knees, tears running down his cheeks. He raised his hand to the sky:

"To the Sky, please. I beg of you. Help my friend Zoe.
She means so much to me. Please! Help her!

To the Earth. I pray to you. I pray that you bring her healing. Please, she needs you. I pray for her!"

He placed the herbs to his forehead:

"Zoe, I am so sorry. I wish I knew you better.
Please forgive me. I am here for you now. I pray for you."

He placed them to his heart:

"Zoe, forgive me. Today I pray for you.
I pray for your healing. Whatever that is. I love you."

He kissed his hand and looked to the fire, gently letting the herbs run from his hand into the crackling flame, which seemed to whisper to him as it consumed the leaves and powder. The words had been half in his mind, a quarter said aloud, and the rest felt only in his heart. He sobbed now in front of the sacred fire, feeling the gentle touch of a hand on his back. He looked, expecting Owen, but saw Zoe. "Thank you, Ethan." She was crying, her nose red and cheeks flushed. Ethan got up and hugged her, feeling her shoulder grow wet from her tears.

"Zoe… I am so sorry. Please forgive me."

"As long as you forgive me."

"After this, let's agree to actually want to see each other again and not pretend. Deal?"

"Deal," she smiled. "Now, are you ready to sweat your balls off for me?" She snorted and poked his chest. They hugged one more time, and then William Eagle Dancer said it was time for them to enter the lodge while Owen motioned for Ethan to join him.

"Well done, Ethan. Ye see, ye don't need to know what to pray for in order to pray for someone else," Owen said with a twinkle in his eye.

"Yeah…" He wiped his face with his shirt.

"Take that thing off; it's about ta get a lot hotter." Owen took his shirt off and handed Ethan a brush. "Yer gonna brush the stones; I'll carry 'em into the lodge."

"With your bare hands!?"

"Don't be daft! I've got a pitchfork for that. Come on, the Grandfathers are waitin'."

The Grandfathers were the stones, which Owen carefully procured out of the fire. He then brought them close to the ground without touching, for Ethan to brush the soot and ash from the glowing red stones. Owen slowly crept toward the entrance of the lodge; as he lifted the stone inside, he yelled:

"Tunkasila!"

And William Eagle Dancer responded:

"Pilamaya!"

This process was repeated four times, each time with the same movements, reverence, and words said. After the final stone was brought into the lodge, Owen waved to Ethan and beckoned him to enter. "When you enter a lodge, you must bow and say thank you. Follow me."

"What language?"

"Any that ye know." Owen kneeled to the ground and placed his forehead to the earth: "Pilamaya!"

Ethan approached and placed his forehead against the cool earth. "Thank you!" he said, not knowing any other way to say it. Inside the lodge was incredibly dark; he could barely see the pale faces of those inside except Zoe and William, who were in the center around the glowing stones. It was already quite warm inside compared to the outside autumn air. Owen squeezed in tight to the left, where the other men of the circle sat. To the right, all the women were lined against the edge of the circle. Ethan barely fit next to

Owen; their sweaty skin rubbed against each other as the flap behind him was closed, bathing them in total darkness.

William Eagle Dancer began to speak from the center:

"Once, there was a woman who had five sons. One day, the four elder brothers went hunting and never returned. After a long time, the mother became very sad and mourned for her lost sons. Her youngest son, who was still a boy, heard his mother's cries and felt her deep sorrow. Wanting to help, he decided to find out what had happened to his older brothers. One day, the boy found a stone and began to play with it, carving it into a round shape. As he played, he heard a voice coming from the stone. The voice told him, 'I am Inyan, the Stone. I have great wisdom and power. If you listen to me and follow my guidance, I will help you.'"

William then poured water onto the glowing stones, creating a sizzling noise followed by thick steam that traveled to the top of the lodge. The steam then traveled down the edges of the walls and down the necks and backs of everyone inside. Ethan felt the sweat pour out of his skin; he felt weakness leave his body.

"Today, we learn from Stone; we learn from Inyan; we learn from the Grandfathers. Today, we pray for Zoe. Owen… you may begin."

Owen took a deep breath and produced a small rattle from his pocket, beginning to play along with a drum that William had with him as well:

"Wakan Tanka, unsimalaye,

Oyate kin, heya yelo.

Tunkasila, Unsimalaye,

Anpetu kin le, iyokipi kte.

Makha sitomniya, unsimalaye,

Niya kin le, wicozani kte.

Wiyohpeyata, unsimalaye,

Tatanka oyate, ohitike kte.

Mitakuye Oyasin, Tunkasila,

Wakan Tanka, Le miyeye, heya yelo."

Ethan tried to pick up some of the words; he could hardly focus with the heat and sweat pouring over his body. After the singing ended, William Eagle Dancer said:

"Wíiyu, WíyakA Wíiyu!"

And opened the flap to let in the cool air, leading to a collective sigh of relief. Owen ushered Ethan out, both glowing a deep pink color, glistening from their own sweat. "Ethan, go to the teepee, grab the bowls of water and bring them in for everyone. Take a drink yourself. I will tend the flames."

He rushed off to the teepee and found huge bowls of water inside with little wooden cups hanging from their sides. He dipped a cup into the cool liquid and guzzled deeply two full ladles before leaving to bring the bowls to the entrance of the teepee. William Eagle Dancer greeted him and took the first large bowl inside to distribute to everyone. Ethan then returned to Owen, who was manipulating the large fire to a more manageable size. The heat emanating from it was incredibly intense. He looked over the field toward the Tor in the distance when Ethan arrived beside him.

"How are you holding up then? Did you get water in you?"

"Yes, I did. I am holding up. That song, what language was that?" Ethan asked.

"It's a Lakota prayer."

"You speak Lakota?"

"No, just know a few songs. William has taught them to me over the years."

"How do you know him?"

"Lived in America some years ago; William put on a lodge for me when I needed it. I have sought to learn from him ever since."

"How many lives have you bloody lived?"

"Ha, losing count…"

"Tunkasila!" came a shout from the lodge.

"Break's over; back to the stones, Ethan." They returned to the ceremony, bringing four stones in the same ritualistic manner as before. As before, they climbed back in after the last stone was delivered to the center chamber; the flap was closed, and darkness returned once more.

William Eagle Dancer began to speak again:

"The boy, who became known as Stone Boy, listened to the stone's teachings. The stone taught him many things and gave him spiritual power. The stone also revealed to him that his older brothers had been killed by an evil spirit. Determined to avenge his brothers, Stone Boy set out on a journey.

Along the way, Stone Boy encountered many challenges but always remembered the wisdom of the stone. With his courage and spiritual strength, he was able to overcome every obstacle. Eventually, he reached the place where his brothers had been killed and faced the evil spirit. Using the power of the stone, he defeated the spirit and brought his brothers back to life.

When he returned home with his brothers, Stone Boy's mother was overjoyed. However, Stone Boy felt the need to purify himself after the battle with the evil spirit. He remembered the teachings of the stone and built a small, dome-shaped structure out of willow branches, covered with hides. Inside, he placed hot stones in a pit and poured water over them, creating steam."

He poured water on the stones, creating another cloud of steam that enveloped the tight space once again.

"My brother was killed... but unlike Stone Boy, I did not have the magic to bring him back to life. But I had the steam. I asked my uncle, who was the real shaman. I am no shaman. My uncle, he healed me through the steam of the lodge. For nearly a full day, we prayed to the steam…"

He poured even more water on. The heat was now even more intense than the previous round.

"Today, we pray for Zoe. As my uncle once prayed for me…" Owen saw this as his cue:

"Tunkasila, woiyaksape,

Wakan Tanka, woiyaksape.

Tunkasila, tokatakiya,

Woiyaksape, wowakan ni.

Pilamaya, Wakan Tanka,

Cante wasteya, unsimalaye.

Pilamaya, Wakan Tanka,

Cante wasteya, unsimalaye."

Owen sang this two times. By the second round, several people were able to pick up the words and joined in the song. Even Ethan managed to say "Tunkasila," which he recognized as "Grandfather," and "Pilamaya," which he now knew as "Thank you." The ground was now wet with sweat and spilled water, and many people were no longer sitting up, lying instead on the ground of the lodge. Zoe, however, was still sitting tall, only inches from the rising steam. William Eagle Dancer shouted:

"Wíiyu, WiyakA Wíiyu!"

The flap was opened once more to let in the cooling breeze of the outside world. Once again, Ethan and Owen stepped out to tend to the fire and gather more water. They spoke briefly around the fire and then were summoned once more to bring the stones into the lodge. The rhythm and flow were becoming second nature to Ethan; he barely thought between actions. He sat back in the lodge after the four new stones were brought in and added to the small mountain of glowing rocks in the center of the lodge. The flap was closed once more:

"As he sat in the lodge, Stone Boy prayed to the Creator and the spirits of the four directions, asking for purification and guidance. He felt the heat and the steam cleansing his body, mind, and spirit. When he emerged, he felt renewed, healed, and spiritually connected.

Stone Boy shared this ceremony with his people, teaching them how to build the sweat lodge and conduct the purification ritual. He explained that the lodge represents the womb of the Earth Mother, and entering it is like returning to the source of all life. The hot stones are our Grandfathers. They carry the wisdom of the Earth and the ancestors. The steam represents the breath of life and the prayers rising to the Creator."

He poured water onto the stones.

"This is the tradition of my people, carried from grandfather to grandfather, from father to father, and from my uncle to me. All so that I could be here for Zoe. Our bodies are weak, but pure. And now we sing pure songs of prayer to the Creator!"

*"WíyakA wíyakA, Wíyak
A wíyakA,*

Tȟokáta wíyakA, WíyakA wíyakA.

WíyakA wíyakA, WíyakA wíyakA,

WíyakA wíyakA, Tȟokáta wíyakA.

Mní wíčhóni, Mní wíčhóni,

Tȟokáta Mní, Mní wíčhóni.

Wíyaká wíyaká, Wíyaká wíyaká,

Wíyaká wíyaká, Tȟokáta wíyaká."

They sang it two times again, and by the second round, nearly everyone in the lodge was singing every word. Their bodies were collectively exhausted, but their voices still carried power. Ethan could hardly hold himself up. But whenever he saw Zoe's sweat-covered face, he remembered why he was there—for her—and he found new energy to hold himself and raise his voice louder. As the last note faded, Ethan heard:

"Wíiyu, WíyakA Wíiyu!"

And the flap was opened one last time.

"This will be the final round. Please drink deeply of the water, breathe the cool air, and prepare for our final song, our final story, and our final prayer. Brother Owen, Ethan, please go and find our final stones. Be careful, for we have a mountain in here," William Eagle Dancer said, gesturing toward the large pile of wet rocks that now lay between his legs.

One last time, Owen carried four stones into the lodge; one last time, Ethan brushed the ash from their molten surfaces; one last time, he bowed his head to the muddy floor of the lodge; and one last time, they were covered in darkness.

"Please, brothers and sisters, listen closely. I have a message to share. A message of love, of prayer, of family. I was asked to come here by Owen—brother, a friend—who begged me to come pray for dear Zoe here. Owen said: You must come! Zoe here, she is a beautiful soul. One in need of healing, as you once healed me. I said: Brother! I will come if she is in need as you once were. Then the prayer must be heavy and require strong medicine. And to you, my brothers, my sisters… this has been good medicine. But we have one final prayer. Let us give the good medicine one last time to Zoe!"

Ethan could hear the water come in contact with the stones, their sizzling rang across the ribbed walls of the lodge and deep into his bones.

"May I sing the song?" asked Zoe.

"Do you know the prayer song that I taught you?" William answered.

"Yes, I remember."

"Then sister Zoe, please sing us your song." William began to beat his drum in a slow rhythm, followed by Owen with his rattle, both preparing for Zoe to sing:

"O Corn Mother, sacred and wise,
Wíŋyaŋ Ptehášska, hear our cries,
Your gifts of life flow through our hands,
Bless us, heal us, upon these lands.
Roots that grow deep in the earth below,
Sky above where gentle winds blow,
Your spirit within every seed,
Heal us now, in our time of need.
Bring your strength to our hearts and hands,
Guide us gently through life's demands,
O Corn Mother, help us to see,
Your wisdom, love, and unity."

William alone sang the next part:

"Wóčhaŋtognake kiŋ, wóčhaŋtognake kiŋ,

Háu, háu, woíyokiphi!"

The ground was now wet with sweat and spilled water; many people were no longer sitting up and were laying on the lodge's ground—Zoe was still sitting tall, only inches from the rising steam—William Eagle Dancer shouted:

"Wíiyu, WíyakA Wíiyu!"

"Everyone, please step inside the teepee for some water, fruit, and dry clothing." Owen announced.

William Eagle Dancer and Zoe stayed behind to hug and discuss something in private. Ethan followed everyone into the teepee to find three bowls of various fruits waiting for them in the center of the space. He took three grapes and popped them in his mouth, feeling the refreshing juice fill his soul with joy; he had never tasted a better grape. Everyone around him seemed to be having a similar experience with the apples, bananas, and mangoes that were also in the bowls.

There were fourteen people in total crammed into the small teepee, each person shoulder to shoulder as they had been within the lodge. Zoe joined them soon after—Owen and William Eagle Dancer were discussing something outside. Zoe came next to Ethan, and they both sat down together. She held him close for a moment. "Thank you," she said, her cold sweat still fresh on her dress.

"No, thank you. That was somehow the worst thing I have ever done…and the most amazing."

"You made a good firekeeper, you know?" She looked at him and smiled, filling him with confidence and pride.

"I am sure I was shit, but damn, Zoe! Your singing was incredible."

"Helps when you have something to sing for."

"And what were we singing for?"

"…for my husband." She said with hesitation.

"You are married!" Ethan said, completely shocked.

"Well, not any longer. My husband, you see, he died a few years ago…" She had a tear forming in the corner of her eye.

"Now… everything is making sense…" Ethan said aloud. "This is what she meant; this is why she won't date. And…I am an asshole," he thought.

"The song, it was to let him go… finally."

"Zoe… I am so sorry. Had I known, I would have never—"

"No, Ethan. It was a good kiss. Actually, when you kissed me, it made me realize how much I needed to let him go." Zoe made eye contact with Ethan. In that moment, time froze. Ethan felt the kiss they had shared weeks ago. He thought of this moment and all he had now been through. What he realized, staring into her beautiful eyes and magical smile, was that he did not feel love for her in a way he expected—in a way that he had ever felt for a woman before. He did not desire her, but he still somehow deeply loved her.

"Zoe… can I confess something to you?" he asked.

"Of course."

"This might sound crazy. I love you. But, not in a way I have ever loved anyone… I love you truly, deep into your soul. Just, not in a way that I want to sleep with you or be your boyfriend. None of that, I just care for you… sorry, this is sounding crazy."

"Ethan! Look at you; you finally realized that all women aren't for sleeping with!" She nudged him and snorted her familiar laugh. "Am I your first? You know—your first friend who's a girl?"

"Oh, shut it now! I am opening up here!" Ethan both laughed but felt embarrassed.

"Sorry, sorry. You are right. You have actually done what most never do. I am happy for you. And I love you too! Also, very happy you have started to take that stick up your ass."

"Yeah, I guess I did have a pretty big stick up my ass, didn't I?" He smiled.

"Only a really big one. But at least you always stood up straight?"

"Would have made a pretty good scarecrow, wouldn't I have?" They continued to laugh and embrace one another despite the crowdedness of the room; luckily, everyone was busy with fruit, conversation, or too exhausted to care.

"Wait!" Zoe stopped laughing and looked at Ethan seriously. "Are you saying you have never loved anyone as a friend? Not a single person your whole life?"

"I mean… I had friends. But never anyone that I felt… you know, this way before." He scratched his head, trying to think back to his earliest memories of friends in primary school and beyond.

"Not even Matteo? He fucking loves you, man!"

"Matteo…" Ethan had not thought of Matteo since losing himself in the Temple of Krishna. The feeling of love he was now feeling radiated to his mind. He thought of all the things he and Matteo had discussed, done, and experienced together in such a short time. "Shit… Zoe. I think I love Matteo!"

"Wow, you will be such a happy couple!" She joked.

"Oh hush, not like that. I mean, fuck. I love him. That crazy fucking Italian. I… haven't told him." Ethan now felt guilty; as he thought of his memories with Matteo, he realized how cold he had been to him since he first arrived. What started with thoughts of Matteo turned to thoughts of Hamish and all that he and Isla had done for him. "Zoe, I have a lot of people I need to talk to. I have been such a prick."

"Like who?"

"Everyone! Hamish, Isla, fucking Jasper—well, maybe… no him, yes! Owen, where is that fucker—"

"Lila?"

"Lila? Yes, her too. Zoe, I think I have to go. I need to run with this. Will you be okay?"

"Yes, I love seeing this side of you. Go; I have plenty of people here to keep me company and to rub my sweat on.

Go on," she smiled and pushed him away. As Ethan stepped out of the teepee to look for Owen, Zoe leaned toward Lila, who was sitting on the other side of Ethan, and began to grab her hand.

Outside, William Eagle Dancer and Owen were standing over the sacred fire, which was burning low into embers now that all the stones had been removed. "Ethan! Bloody good job, mate. I was just telling William here about you," Owen said, still wearing no shirt and glowing bright red.

"Owen, I have been a real prick to you," Ethan stated clearly.

"What d'you mean by that?"

"From the moment I got here, you have only ever tried to help me. I see that now. This, the fire, the lodge, all of it. Thank you."

"All right, all right. Don't go kissin' my ring then. But I'm glad t' see you comin' around. Glastonbury'll chew ye up an' spit ye out faster than folks realize."

Ethan turned to William Eagle Dancer: "William, I don't even know where to begin. This morning, I woke up, and you gave me a fucking blanket, let me sleep in your teepee—which probably saved my life—and now the lodge. I just… I am grateful beyond words. For everything and more."

"The lodge is powerful medicine. Not just for the person we are praying for. It breaks us down, shows us who we really are. And you—who you really are—is someone who is grateful, as we all are. What will be difficult is not losing that."

"How do I stop myself from losing that?"

"Be grateful every day... find something to be grateful for—because there always is in this life. I have something for you to try: each morning, when you drink your coffee, think of the lives that touched it before it reached your hands and offer thanks to them all. First, think of the coffee itself—the plant—and the earth that cradled its roots; the rain that gave it strength to grow. Think of the farmer who tended it, the hands that picked each bean, the one who roasted it, the one who shipped it. But do not stop there. Think of the ship, the boat and those who built it, the gasoline that carried it over waters, and the ancient ones who gave their bodies long ago to become that oil. See, we walk a long journey of life for even the smallest things, like our morning coffee. And so, we always have something to be grateful for... and many, many lives to thank for what they have given us, so we can live and learn in this world."

"Holy shit…"

"Yes, it is quite a powerful practice—"

"No, not that. Coffee… I have to go! William, Owen. Thank you, thank you!" Ethan took off across the field towards town and the Andrew's Cross, which he had completely abandoned without realizing over the last two days of good and bad medicine.

"Ethan!" shouted Owen. "Drink lots o' water, rest, and be grateful! Be seein' you!"

13
Winter Solstice

It was half-past one when Ethan came running down the high street toward the town center where the café sat. What he expected to see was a shut-up business; instead, he saw tables placed outside, the inside lit up, and customers coming out carrying drinks from the Andrew's Cross.

"Fuck," he said as he got closer and saw Hamish in the window, looking across the square toward him—Scottish fire in his eyes. Isla could also be seen cleaning a table inside, her pregnant belly now beginning to show slightly through her clothes. Ethan walked up to the front door and prepared himself for the worst. Hamish met him at the door.

"Where the fuck have ye been?! We get home, doors shut, café dark, flat's a bleedin' disaster—place is dirtier than a rat's brothel! And dinnae even get me started on the state o' that bloody espresso machine! Did ye even fuckin' clean it —" Hamish glared at him for a few more moments, breathless, which gave Ethan just enough time to lean in and give him a tight hug around the waist.

"What in the name o' fuck! Ah, ye reek as well! Have ye no' had a wash fer the past week?"

Ethan let him go. "Sorry, sweat lodge."

"A fuckin' what? Also, Ethan. Ye look absolute shit as well! Ye lost at least two stone, and yer face! Jesus Christ, ye look like a ghost!"

"Hamish, I love you. I am sorry I have never said it before."

"Oh, shit. Comin' here lookin' like a Sunday mornin' in Glasgow, and now ye have been converted by the fuckin' witches! Went off an joined their cult have ye?" Hamish took him by the shoulders to inspect him further.

"Hamish, I am so sorry about the café. I am so sorry I have let you down. Please, let me explain. It will never happen again."

Hamish looked him up and down, studying his sincerity closely. "All right… it's no' the end o' the world. We only got back this mornin', and it was quiet as a mouse. But, Ethan… what in the blazes has happened tae ye? Are ye al' right?"

"I will be. I just need a shower. But after, I will clean this store top to bottom. I promise."

"Aye, I believe ye, I do. Go on, get yersel cleaned up. After, we'll all sit doon and hae a wee blether." Hamish ushered him to go upstairs to the flat, a worried expression on his face. He went back inside to his concerned wife and the disheveled café.

Ethan went to the washroom and looked at himself for the first time in what felt like weeks—if not his whole life—his face was gaunt, shadowed, beet red, and his eyes had little white left in them. His hair was unkempt, greasy, and still damp from the sweat; his facial hair was longer than it had ever been before—long, shaggy, and wild. He smiled, showing his dry and sour mouth: "Fuck, I really do look shit," he said to himself before getting to work trimming, brushing, and bathing every part of himself that he could. By the end of the long, hot shower, he looked back at the mirror to see some resemblance of his past self.

Feeling tired and dehydrated, he had to fight the urge to drink a gallon of water and pass out on the bed, but he knew that Hamish and Isla deserved an explanation of why he had been skipping out on his duties around the café. So he mustered his strength and prepared himself for the "wee blether" with his Scottish landlords below.

"Ethan!" Isla announced first, "I cannae believe how horrid this place looked, but when I saw ye and yer face, I kent right away that what was goin' on wi' ye was even worse. Come here, tell me whit happened tae ye?" She pulled out a chair for him to sit down; a fresh coffee and a glass of water waited for him, which he gladly began to sip and enjoy.

"I am so sorry; I really can't say it enough. I have only missed a day—I think. I cannot say. I don't know when it all went pear-shaped, but… it just happened…" he trailed off.

"Which o' these freaks got tae ye?" Hamish asked defensively, sitting up from his chair.

"Hamish! We dinnae ken what it was."

"Aye, but it had tae be somethin' in this bloody town. We werenae gone a month an' he went from a good lad tae shite real quick—no offense, Ethan." He turned to put his arm on him in consideration.

"No, he's right. I fell into something bad… real bad. I just wanted to find a way to escape… and it led me to some bad characters, bad places, and some bad choices. All that led me to wandering alone in the dark the other night… I was nearly a goner, I think, at least until I saw the fire last night. Then today, with the sweat lodge—"

"Sweat lodge?" asked Isla. "Zoe's sweat lodge was today?"

"Yes, this morning. Sorry, I meant to ask—what brought you back to Glastonbury early? I thought you said you'd need a few more weeks up north?"

"It was Claudia, actually! Her wee bairn was just born! A wee lass, fat as a cow in the summer! As soon as I heard she was in labour, we headed back right awa'. A bairn born on the solstice is powerful magic."

"How did everything go with you both in Lewis? Before you had to leave?" Ethan asked.

"Aye, it was good for us. Good for my family, that is. We went tae the shores an' found the spot where I was shown the vision. I had tae bury an auld family relic in the rock at low tide—sing my father's names tae the sea—and then, as the tide came in, a seal appeared right where we buried it… Ah cannae explain it… the seal… it wasnae a seal… Ah swear it became a lass—"

"A selkie it was!" Isla finished.

"Ah'm no' convinced it was one o' these selkies, but it was somethin' unnatural. Whit it was… it looked at me. An' in that moment I kent somethin' had changed… the curse was broken… I think."

"That's good, right? You seem a bit grim about it?"

"Aye, it was hard goin' home. Hard memories up there…" he responded. "Now, back tae you! Are ye alright, lad? Is there anythin' we can dae for ye?"

"I think I am good. I am just staying away from any fucking drugs from now on. They have not agreed with me."

"You aren't the first to get wrapped up in the drugs of Glastonbury; nasty things, them. Have you spoken to Lila about it? She fell into them heavy a while back as well."

"You are the second person to mention her to me today…"

"Aye, now ye're sorted. I can get back tae bein' pissed at ye. Put on some gloves an' let's get tae scrubbing this place from top tae bottom!" Hamish laughed.

"Right, that's my cue tae leave. Goin' tae check on Claudia an' the wee bairn. If ye lads think o' it, an' see Rasmus, be sure tae offer him congratulations, an' maybe a stiff drink. From whit Claudia said, he was pretty traumatized from the birthin'. Off now, talk later." Isla stood up and gave Hamish a kiss, creating a big smile on his face before he turned to set eyes on his neglectful employee, the look of hard work and consequences painted across his brow…

The rest of the day, Ethan and Hamish worked together to get the café back to its original—and clean—state. Ethan struggled to keep up, taking many breaks to sit down with a glass of water; the sweat lodge was not far from his mind. Hamish took pity on him often, allowing him to rest as long as he needed. Often, he would sit down with him and recall their time in Scotland. By the evening, the café was closed, and Hamish made a quick supper for them both. Ethan retreated to the flat, where Isla later joined them. Ethan had little left in him other than the energy to throw himself onto his bed for a quick journey to dreams and deep sleep.

The time on the nearby clock flipped to 12:01 in the night when Ethan awoke from a sound below his window… what seemed like two banshees screaming at the top of their lungs. He launched out of bed to see what was happening. In the street below, two women in white woolen robes were screeching at the top of their lungs in the town center; many others were turning on their lights across the town center to see what was going on.

"Cardea… Vesta?" Ethan observed. His previous flatmates, and silent lovers, were now yelling at each other with the most diabolical language.

"What in tae devil is happenin'!" Hamish came down the hall to view the street below.

"Fucking Glastonbury is happening," Ethan answered, half awake.

"Fuckin' Glastonbury…" Hamish muttered before shuffling down the hallway to go back to his bed.

A few townsfolk were shouting at the street now, telling the two women to silence themselves—but to no avail—they were both completely entrapped in their screaming match with one another. Ethan, seeing there was a way to help end the madness, put on his winter clothes and headed outside to try and sort out what was happening.

"Cardea, Vesta. What the fuck is going on?" he asked when he reached the two women below the market cross.

"Oh, Ethan! Was wondering if we would see you again!" Cardea stopped instantly to answer him calmly.

"Yes, so good to see you again," Vesta added.

"You seem to have awoken half the town. What's this about?"

"The end of our silent fast… it's officially the end of the solstice! Which means we can speak again at last."

"And that means we can finally air out every thought we have had the last year," Cardea smiled. "Like how this bitch farts in her goddamn sleep, EVERY FUCKING NIGHT!" she screeched.

"Better than your horrendous chewing! Are you eating sea shells?" They went at each other again.

"Ladies, please. We all just want to sleep!" Ethan tried to calm the situation; townsfolk were now shouting down at them:

"Shut te' fuck up!"

"We are tryna sleep 'ere!"

"What yas doin' that far!" came the echoes down the High Street.

"Ladies! Please—" Ethan started, but then Cardea grabbed Vesta, and they began to kiss in the middle of the town. "What…" Ethan's face was now agape.

"Come, my love. Let us go talk beautiful things together…" Cardea led Vesta away.

"Goodnight, Ethan," Vesta smiled, grabbing her lover's hand and disappearing back down toward the Temple of Artemis.

"Fucking Glastonbury," Ethan smiled as he said it this time. "Can't help but love this weird place… if you don't, you go fucking mad," he thought to himself philosophically. He stood there for a moment, pondering whether or not to head back into the flat. But the adrenaline had woken him up, and now his mind was racing. The rest of the village appeared to be turning their lights out and going back to sleep. A gentle snow had begun to fall around Ethan, despite the air not being entirely unpleasant.

"Beautiful…" he said aloud at the sight of the white flakes dancing in the low light of the street lamps. "A small walk wouldn't hurt." He put his hands in his pockets, tucked his hair under the hat, and took off down the midnight streets of Glastonbury, a look of wonder on his face as he looked up to the first snow of the year.

For the last month, Glastonbury had slowly been decorated for Christmas: a large Christmas tree now stood near the market cross, wreaths hung from all the lamps and many of the doors, and big red bows adorned many of the signs and even the rubbish bins. The pubs—while closed now—were also highly decorated inside and out; the colors of red and green were now predominant over the often technicolor village. The falling snow was loosely sticking to the surfaces around him; snow was so rare in the south of England, and especially in London, it rarely stuck around for long.

Ethan reflected on all the times he had passed by winter without a care for what was around him, often cursing the cold, dreading the rain, and hating the holiday due to the lack of it from his childhood. For some reason, in this moment in Glastonbury, he felt something that he could only describe in his mind as the spirit of Christmas. The magical moment that he was experiencing extended up the High Street to the other closed shops with their winter-themed windows and displays: "Good Yule!" said one, "Happy Christmas!" said another. Peeking his head down one of the alleys, he could hear the gentle sound of holiday music playing from further away. Deciding to follow it, he walked the narrow close toward the jolly sound of winter-themed cheer. He rounded a bend to find a small radio from where the music was coming from and another painted mural on a once bare wall—this one half-finished, unlike the previous two he had seen.

The mural depicted Glastonbury buried in snow, a large cage made of ice trapping several children with tears rolling down their faces. A menacing black figure stood outside the cage; he wore the clothes of Father Christmas but bore the face of a demonic black goat. Around the mural were several incomplete paintings of demons, devils, goblins, and trolls—all wearing similar Christmas-themed clothes, with menacing smiles on their faces. Below the mural were the outlines of more runes that Ethan still was unable to decipher:

ᚲᚱᚨᛗᛈᚢᛊ : ᚲᛖᛗᚢᚱ : ᚠᛁᚱᛁᚱ : ᚦᚨ : ᛊᛖᛗ :
ᚷᛚᛖᛁᛗᛞᚢ : ᛗᛖᚱᚲᛁᛟᚢ : ᛁᚢᛚᛖ

As Ethan was studying the mural, he heard a noise behind him of someone gasping in surprise. He turned to see Lila standing there with a bag full of paints and brushes. Her face was in shock, her eyes wide under her white winter bonnet. For more than a moment, they looked at each other in disbelief.

"Lila," Ethan started. "You are the one who paints the murals?" he asked, looking back toward the painting on the brick wall.

"No—I mean yes. It's whatever, yes. I am."

"What! I have always wondered; they are incredible," he smiled.

"No one else seems to appreciate them… they always get painted over eventually—"

"Well, do you ask permission?"

"No—I always figured they would tell me no."

"Which is why you do them at night?" Ethan investigated.

"Yes, you must not tell anyone. Or—I will just have to kill you," she said in a less-than-joking manner that made Ethan uncomfortable.

"Promise to make a mural of me if you do kill me?" he smiled.

"Of course; I wouldn't want to waste the extra paint from your blood."

"Um—" he was feeling uncomfortable now.

"Shit, sorry. I am shitty at jokes," she said, putting her hand to her head.

"Well… seems like you'd need a lot of blood to finish this one," he tried to go along with it, "what is this one anyways?"

"This one? It's of Krampus, of course."

"Krampus?"

"You know, evil Santa. From German folklore."

"Does he take children—"

"To Hell."

"Right, scary stuff. Quite charming subjects, Ms. Lila!" he chuckled.

"Yeah, sorry. Not my best work."

"It might be scary, but it is still absolutely incredible."

She smiled and bowed her head. "What—brings you out here? In the dead of night?"

"You didn't hear the screaming?" he asked, "in the center of town."

"No, I just left to go get more paint from my studio. What screaming?"

"Cardea and Vesta, the Artemis worshippers or whatever. They ended their silent fast by waking half the village."

"Fucking drama queens, them, honestly." She said. "Surprised you are even alive after this morning."

"What do you mean?" he asked.

"After the sweat lodge."

"How do you know I was there?"

"Because I was sat right next to you, asshole."

"Shit, what? How! I never saw you." He said with a confused expression, feeling horrible for not noticing her.

"Not surprised; you were too busy on Zoe. But, that's okay! We were all there for her."

"No, it's not okay. How did I not notice you?"

"Blessing and a curse, really."

"How can I make this up to you? Honestly, I feel dreadful about this. We have had a few drinks together before; I should never not greet you, even if we are covered in sweat and nearly passed out." He begged, coming closer to her.

"Pay for my coffee next time I come by the café, and I will call it even." She set her bag of art supplies under the mural, her tone suggesting she wanted to be left alone.

"No, really. This was a horrible sin…" he pondered for a moment, "why don't I help you with the mural? I am sure I can color in some lines; I did that as a child, after all—no problem!" he said confidently.

"You can paint?" she questioned.

"Sure, everyone can, right?"

"Fine, but only because it's fucking cold out here. And if you fuck it up, I will start taking fingers." She pointed a brush at him in a threatening manner.

"Right, and then you will use my blood to paint with. Your threats are empty; give me the brush." He smiled, grabbed the brush, and stepped back to observe the mural. "So... where do you want me to start?"

She pointed him toward one particularly nasty unfinished goblin with a bag full of presents and told him to start coloring in his outfit. He was then given a small cup of paint and sent on his way; Lila worked on the other side, finishing another devilish creature. The music from the radio was playing various holiday tracks—many of which Ethan did not know. Lila, on the other hand, was able to hum to every beat of every song.

"You really like Christmas music then?" Ethan asked after a long period of silence.

"Yes; it helps calm me down," she answered, her focus completely on her work.

"You just don't seem the type."

"And what type do I seem?"

"Well... death metal or something violent, or scary."

She turned to look at him. "Every other day of the year, you are correct. But during the Christmas season, I listen to Christmas music. It makes me happy." She smiled innocently, then returned to her work. Ethan stepped back to take a look at his progress on his holiday gremlin, feeling quite proud of himself. At least until he saw how much better Lila's was right on the other side of the mural.

"Don't worry," she said, "it's more well done than I expected."

"Getting bloody cold; how long do you intend on being out here?" he asked, rubbing his hands against his arms.

"I was planning on finishing the mural tonight. That was until a certain person came and started whinging about how cold he was."

"Hey! I just said something!"

"Don't worry; I am getting cold too. Want to head back to mine for a cuppa?"

As far as Ethan knew, no one had ever been invited into Lila's studio above the library—no one except Zoe. He paused for a moment to think.

"Sorry, I didn't mean anything by it. Figured you'd—"

"—I would love to," Ethan said with a grin under his red nose.

The studio above the library was accessed via the staircase inside; the wood-burning stove within the library had low embers when they stepped in from the cold. Lila added a few logs in before she led Ethan upstairs. When Ethan poked his head around the entrance to the studio apartment, he was taken aback by the amount of art pieces that dotted the space: several easels stood with half-finished paintings, photographs hung from wires near the window, a large table sat in the center of the room with various art supplies, drawings of varying degrees of completion, as well as fabric, dresses, and sewing equipment. In the corner of the room near the window was the only evidence that someone actually lived in this space: a small twin bed, a dresser with a hotplate and microwave upon it, and a wardrobe all lined up against the north wall.

"Sorry, it's a fucking mess, I know."

"I didn't know what to expect to be honest, but I kind of love it," Ethan said genuinely.

"How could you love this disaster?"

"This room, this home… it's you! I feel like I stepped into your mind." He said while inspecting one of the paintings made of the Glastonbury Tor in a style similar to Van Gogh. Lila went to the corner of the room to put on the electric kettle and to search for two cups that were not holding brushes.

"You know I don't invite anyone up here," she said, and he nodded in agreement. "So don't think I won't throw you out if you start making fun of me."

"Making fun of you? I would never imagine doing that. Honestly, this space is really cool. Do you have any idea what my flat back in London looked like?"

"Oh, I would imagine it was dirty, old, smelled like gym socks, covered in sticky tissues, old pizza boxes, and unwashed dishes?" she said confidently.

"Hey! I cleaned up the tissues," he thought, feeling exposed. "Well, you got most of it right. But now that I see this room, I see what rooms are supposed to be like. They are reflections of ourselves… and now I realize that wasn't a good sign for me." He looked down, losing himself in thoughts of his life back in London.

She handed him a warm cup of black tea. "Don't worry; my flat in Bristol wouldn't have been much different."

"Sticky tissues as well?"

"Absolutely everywhere," she chuckled, sitting down at the center table. "So, Ethan. Tell me, how's Glastonbury treating you?" She sipped her tea, eyeing him from above the rim of the mug.

"Ha! Something tells me you know something about that already."

"Don't forget, I saw you this morning. You did look like absolute shit. Rough night?"

"Rough few weeks, honestly. Isla said I should talk to you about it, actually… said you could relate." He sipped his own tea, finding it incredibly bitter. Lila, detecting this, found him some sugar under a pile of ribbons.

"Yes… I can certainly relate. I think I told you already." she said sharply.

"You told me no details, only that you had ended up in the camp on the edge of town."

"And did you find yourself there, Ethan?"

"Yes. I did actually."

"What drugs were you on?"

"Fuck, what drugs wasn't I doing? It got me quick; it started with mushrooms, and then before I knew it, I was smoking frog venom."

"Shit! You were hanging out with to smoke frog venom?" she laughed in a way that alluded to her doing the same.

"Jasper at first, then his roommate—"

"Shit, were you hanging out with Josh?" she said with a gasp.

"Yeah… that's the one."

"Found myself down that road. Woke up in his bed a few times too. That's when I knew I was fucking up bad," she said with some shame.

"Can't say I woke up in his bed… but I fucked his girlfriend," Ethan now said in his own shame.

"Fuck! Man, we both are a couple of fuck-ups then. Cheers to that," she raised her cup of tea to him.

"Cheers," he took a sip to pause and think for a moment. "How did you end up a fuck-up then? This doesn't look like the studio of a fuck-up."

"A one-bedroom flat with a mold problem that I can barely afford in a small English town that the world forgot? To my parents, I might as well be selling my body for crack."

"Shit, that's harsh."

"Well, when they supported me through eight years of university to become this big boss lady solicitor—all for me to end up here—I can't blame them."

"What happened?" he asked.

"What happens to everyone, it seems? I flew too close to the sun for too long. I fell, and I fell hard. The pressure of education, of the city, of life alone in England, it… it broke me. And as you know, I followed Zoe here, and ever since then… I haven't been able to leave."

Ethan's ears perked up at hearing her last comment. "Haven't been able to, or haven't wanted to?"

"There's a difference?" she said coyly.

"There's a huge difference."

"Both, I suppose," she answered.

"Lila, I am going to say this in a way that might seem odd. But, I have to tell someone... Me, I haven't been able to leave." He put emphasis on his final words.

"How much have you not been able to leave?" she said with more interest.

"So much that I haven't been able to step a foot outside the boundary of this town since Samhain. Every time I do I—"

"End up right back here..."

Both Lila and Ethan looked at each other in disbelief. "Is she stuck here just like me?" they both thought while studying one another.

"Prove it to me," she said, standing up quickly to grab their coats, throwing his at him.

It was half-three in the morning when they left the library to march out into the countryside of Avalon in the cold of the winter night. The snow was now falling more steadily, building small mounds in the corners of the street. They walked in silence out to the path toward the town of Wells, the gentle glow of the distant villages warmly glowing in the dark of the night sky. When they reached the mounded earthen barrier that had previously served as the boundary for Ethan every time he tried to leave the town, he knew exactly where he could cross before being shot back toward the Tor.

When they approached the boundary marker, Lila stopped and looked at him. "Right, so. You are telling me that when you cross this line, you get magically teleported back to the town center?"

"Well, not the town center. And I wouldn't say teleported; that's a bit too sci-fi. I don't feel like I'm getting beamed up, Scotty, you know?" he said, realizing she was testing him by saying the town center.

"And when did this start?" she continued her interrogation.

"The night of Samhain."

"Did you do anything before Samhain?"

"What do you mean?"

"Did you do anything that might have caused this?" she pressed with more intensity.

"I don't—" Ethan was about to speak when he reflected on the afternoon spent with Owen near the Gog and Magog—the two old trees at the base of the Tor. "Yes, actually I… I was at Gog and Magog with Owen…"

"Enough now—" she cut him off. "Walk over there," she demanded. Ethan looked at her with confusion, then obeyed her orders, walking toward the rock pile he had built. Before taking his step over the line, he looked back toward Lila, who was studying him closely. He completed his step and heard the familiar hum of whatever was taking him away. He felt the spinning of the earth, and then the Tower was before him again, the snow now lightly covering the Tor. As usual, he felt a bit dizzy, but he began to look around for Lila, whom he was not able to spot.

"Shit, maybe she was—" he started to say, but then he looked behind him to see her standing there with the same dizzy expression that he often found himself having.

"Holy shit..." she said.

"You are—" he said.

They walked toward each other and embraced, feeling for the first time in a long time that they were not alone. They both were reluctant prisoners of this strange land, trapped by magics unknown to them in a place once foreign. The feeling they both felt at knowing that they were in fact not crazy—that all the times they tried to escape were not in their own minds—in this moment, they both wept in joy. But the celebration was short-lived as they leaned back and began to think of what this meant for them both.

"It's been so long..." said Lila.

"How long have you been stuck here?" he asked.

"It was three years this Samhain. And you?"

"Well, I guess about two months then for me."

"Right, what have you found out?" she turned serious again.

"What do you mean found out?"

"Well, you've clearly tried to escape; what have you learned?"

"Oh, well so far I know every inch of the boundary, how far I can go… I also was able to get out once. But only when I was super fucked up on drugs. I was not even aware of it until I was back in town."

"Yes! And when you tried again you couldn't do it!"

"Yes!" The feeling of validation grew within Ethan, warming his spirit. Lila was clearly feeling the same.

"Okay, wow. This changes everything." Lila was now pacing around the edge of the Tor's serpent-like pathway.

"I have wanted to say something to someone for so long… How fucking tired are you of the food here?" Ethan asked.

"Ha!" she laughed. "You have only been here two months! Imagine how tired you are after three bloody years! And what about doing the same shit, every fucking week?"

"Honestly, I hate this fucking Tower." He pointed to his right.

"I have sworn at this Tower so many times, you have no idea." she said in agreement.

"So what have you found out?" asked Ethan.

"Well, this year I suspected that Samhain was the catalyst of why I—we—are stuck here. That's why I volunteered to be a part of it, hoping that I could learn more. But clearly I am still here."

"Did you learn anything from it though?"

"Well, much like you, I think. I am not much into the magic side of this place. Despite being kept here by what could only be something magical. Or—maybe aliens. I haven't ruled them out yet!" she said in a way Ethan couldn't decipher if she was serious or not.

"Aliens? Really?"

"Look, I don't have a logical answer for this, so then we are left with the illogical."

"Good point…" he pondered. "Let's head back; we can talk more on the way down." She agreed, and they walked the all-too-familiar path down the Tor, watching their steps on the wet and slippery snow that now covered the winding path down toward the road. While walking, they caught each other up on every detail they could remember from their experience being trapped in Glastonbury—Ethan obviously having much less than Lila.

"Did you do a similar ritual? Like the one I did with Owen?"

"Not quite similar… Owen was not involved. But Gog and Magog were. I was here with Zoe; we were walking the old pilgrim path from druidic times toward the Tor before Samhain. When we reached the trees, she wanted to make an offering and pray to them—as I said, I was not much into it then—but when I went to pray, I remember…"

"Cutting your hand?" Ethan asked.

"Yes, yes I did. On some thorns nearby!"

"What did you say? To the trees?"

"At the time… I was just asking for help. I was finishing university… I was burned out, and I was asking for help. Then I put my hand on the tree. Then when I tried to leave a week after Samhain—I couldn't. Zoe had already decided on moving here, so I stayed with her for a while, making some shit up about falling in love with the town."

"Have you?"

"Have I what?"

"Fallen in love with Glastonbury, in the two years you've been here?"

"No more than anyone can fall in love with their jailer. I have made my peace, but nothing more than someone with Stockholm Syndrome. What about you? Fall in love with Avalon?" she asked.

"Maybe not Avalon… but maybe the people."

"Really?"

"Yeah, honestly, after today I genuinely can say I love Zoe, Hamish, Isla… Matteo… hell, even Jasper. Of course, you!"

"You don't have to lie to me, Ethan. We have barely talked before tonight. At least not alone."

"You are right… but now we have this! Clearly this means something. Maybe we can figure it out together." Ethan seemed enthusiastic.

"I don't know… I have kind of accepted my fate here. I have tried so many things to get out of here."

"Weirdest one?"

"Well, after about a month I made this mad plan to hide away in the boot of someone's car when they were on the way to Cornwall for holiday… I waited in the bushes outside their house and tucked myself away behind some luggage. It took them an hour to finally leave—by the time which I was sweating like a whore in church—but, as you would guess, when they crossed the threshold, I appeared back here."

"Just standing somewhere?"

"No," she laughed, remembering. "I was still in the boot of a car, just not the same one that had left. I saw light come in from the door opening, and it was someone putting grocery bags in the boot. I was in a completely different car outside the market. Gave the woman a terrible fright, had to make some shit up about an abusive boyfriend to get out of it."

Ethan laughed, and Lila laughed with him; she was happy to finally have someone to share stories with. They were now nearly back at the library, the time well past four in the morning. Across from the library was St. John's, the gate often left open in the night for any wayward souls to find shelter in the small garden that awaited out front. As Lila was turning the knob to her building, Ethan noticed someone familiar under the archway of the church…

"Matteo?" he said with shock, running across the street to find his Italian friend asleep against his backpack. "Matteo! Matteo!" he said, shaking him, his body freezing and slightly covered in snow.

"Is he breathing?" asked Lila.

"Yes, I think so. Let's get him inside the library and get more wood on the fire!" Ethan reached down to pick up his friend and began to carry him back across the street and into the front door. Lila ran behind him and found several blankets to place on the sofa near the wood-burning stove. While she added more wood to the fire, Ethan removed the wet outer layers that Matteo was wearing—finding him to be dry in his inner clothing. Lila was stoking the fire to get it glowing hot while Matteo was wrapped like a baby in a bundle of blankets.

"Is he alright?" Lila wondered.

"I am not sure… I can't tell."

"What should we do?" she asked.

"I will sit with him till he wakes up, keep the fire warm for him," Ethan said, determined.

"I can stay too…" she said.

"No, there is no need for both of us to get no sleep. Go upstairs, get some rest. I need to be here for him." The fire was the only light in the library; the warm glow cast shadows across Ethan's serious expression.

"Okay… well, I am glad we are both stuck here. Makes it better." She said, trying to cheer up the room.

"Yes, it is." He looked to her and smiled. "Now go; I will see you in the morning."

Lila tucked down her head and went upstairs to get herself ready for bed. The two teacups from their earlier conversation sat cold in the center of her studio. She removed her scarf and hat and plopped down on her bed.

"I am not alone…" she thought. "And Ethan? After weeks of Zoe begging me to talk with him, after weeks of watching him… he is now like me…" she lay softly against her warm pillow. "Matteo, he's back… had he not come tonight—maybe something would have—no, silly thoughts. Look at you; you don't even have a proper bed. You have more half-finished art than you have charm… just go to bed, wake up, and he will be there. And you can figure this out together. Maybe, maybe we can get out of here…"

She rolled over and turned off the light above, closing her eyes to try and drift her thoughts to sleep. But she kept thinking of every word Ethan had said to her; she kept thinking of his smile, his voice, and the gnawing feeling inside of her that she had felt for years. The feeling she knew now is what kept her here, the feeling that she thought was gone, at least until she met Ethan. Now she knew why he felt different; because he was stuck here too… The last thing Lila saw before she fell into a deep sleep was the quickly falling snow outside her window, which was now leaving behind thick piles against the edge of the building and onto the street outside. In the distance, the Glastonbury Tor was becoming a globe of white, the footprints left behind from their climb down only an hour before were now covered like a distant memory lost to time.

14
Yule

Lila awoke some time after eleven to the sound of gentle conversation in the library below. The room glowed a soft white from the low-hanging sun illuminating the rare winter wonderland that now existed outside. Lila was not a morning person, often staying up late into the night working on her projects and fighting the insomnia that had affected her all her life. She preferred warmth, and winter days like this rarely offered it to her. Luckily, she had a thick woolen robe and a large pair of slippers—found at a charity shop, they were made to look like smiling sheep. She slipped on her comfortable clothing and went to investigate what had become of Ethan and Matteo over the course of the morning.

"—I arrived, and the snow was thick! We never receive such cold in Italia. When I got to Glastonbury, I was so tired; I found the church to hide from the snow. Before I knew it, I was asleep! If you had not found me—ah, Lila!" Matteo's voice rang joyously. "Thank you for saving me!" He got up from his nest of blankets to hug her as she came to the bottom of the stairs.

"Oh, hey, Matteo. Good morning. Glad you are well." She accepted the hug awkwardly. "Did you get any sleep, Ethan?" she directed his way.

"Only a little; mostly I waited for Matteo to stop shivering," he answered. She shook off Matteo and took a seat close to Ethan on the sofa across from Matteo's nest.

"Don't you need to open the library?" he asked her.

"It's winter; no one comes in here. Don't you need to make coffees or whatever?" she sassed him.

"You would think that Hamish would have my hide when I told him I needed the morning off. But when I went and told him Matteo was back in town, he took pity on me. Gave me till noon to make sure he was okay—well, Isla shamed him a bit, I think."

"Now that you are both here, I can ask—what were you both doing out so late in the snow?" asked Matteo from within his nest once again.

Lila looked at Ethan, looking for him to take the lead on the explanation. "We were—out for a—I was helping her with the murals; she paints them, you know?"

"What! You paint the beautiful murals in town?" Matteo's expression was one of excitement.

"Yes… something I said not to tell under pain of—"

"Pain of murder, death, or fingers being cut off. Honestly, I lost track of the threats; you should be proud, Lila. They are great! Just like everything up in her studio—"

"Don't even think of showing him," she said quickly, blushing slightly. "What brought you back to Glastonbury?" she asked, changing the subject.

"Ah, yes, I was just getting to this when you came down. Well, as you know, my brother Ethan, I left to visit my mother after the journey with the mushrooms. I did not walk; this would be crazy. I flew in a few days later. I spent a month at home; I had not done so in a long time. We spoke of many things: of love, of family, of Leo—we had many fights too—about what I had been doing since I abandoned the family."

"Why did you come back?" asked Ethan.

"For the first time in years! I came here, not because I was told to, but because I wanted to. I missed this place; I missed you, Ethan, you, Lila, Zoe, everyone. I love this town. I think I will live here."

"You actually like it here?" Lila objected.

"Yes! Of course! This is the best place on earth. So full of love and energy; the moment I crossed the boundary of the village—right where Ethan left me!" He poked at Ethan. "I stopped feeling it. I have missed it."

"You and Zoe will be even greater friends then. She bloody loves this place," Lila said, getting up to put more wood on the stove.

"How is she?" asked Matteo.

"I have so much to catch you up on! There was a sweat lodge, I did a lot of drugs; it was a whole thing." Ethan was full of excitement talking with Matteo again.

"I want to hear about it all, but first!" Matteo eyed both of them. "Are you two—a thing?"

"What!" Lila said in shock. "Why would he ask that? Does he know something? Do we look like one? What does Ethan —" she thought.

"No! We are just realizing we have something in common lately," Ethan said. Lila felt her heart drop at hearing it. "I realized that I am not fit for anyone right now. I didn't even know I could love friends till yesterday!" Ethan said with joy. "I want to explore that some more before I ever worry about loving someone more than that… sorry, Lila."

"Why would I care? Glad you are loving people or whatever," she said coldly, deflecting as she always had, despite feeling hurt.

"Wow! You have changed so much, Ethan!" Matteo said. "Also, changed in appearance. You look…" he searched for the words.

"Shit?" Ethan guessed.

"No! I would say… lean!"

"Speaking of, I am starving. Shall we grab some food? The spot next door has a decent serving for a fair price?" Ethan said, looking at everyone.

"I do not wish to leave the fire; I am still feeling exhausted," Matteo said. "You two go; bring me something warm?" He said with a puppy-dog-like expression.

"Sure thing. Lila, you coming? It will give us a chance to talk about… the mural?" he hinted.

"Yes," she said hesitantly. She rarely left the studio for food and detested the cold and mornings. But she wanted to find out more about why they were stuck and more about Ethan.

"Great, get ready. Meet you outside soon."

The café next door to the library reminded Lila of the diners she had been to in America. Not quite the same, but the way there were booths, diner counters, and waitresses that looked on the wrong side of a pack of cigarettes. They took their seat across from each other at a booth in the back where it was warmest. Ethan ordered an omelette, while Lila decided to order the American pancakes, feeling nostalgic. She rarely missed her time growing up in the United States, but she found she often missed the food—even if it was smothered in butter, salt, and sugar most of the time.

"Have you ever left England?" she asked Ethan.

"No, actually I never have."

"Fairies always keep you here?" she joked.

"No, can't say they have. I just never had the opportunity. What about you? If we can get out of Glastonbury, where would you go?"

"Honestly, I have given up hope; I rarely think of anywhere else. Somewhere fucking warmer would do nicely."

"Back to the States?"

"No, I can't say I love it there. I'd like to go to Greece for a while. Or maybe I will travel or go back to school. I don't know." She was feeling embarrassed at how open she was being with him.

"Why not Paris? Try for your art there?"

"I have been to Paris, and I would be eaten alive there."

"Why?"

"I play at being an artist. They take it far more seriously there."

"Why do you hate your art so much? Have you ever been to school for it?"

"Well, no—"

"And you are that good at it? Bloody brilliant," he said in a way that she believed him. Their food was now in front of them, which Ethan quickly tore into.

She picked at her pancake and then asked, "What about you? If we can escape, where will you go?"

"I don't know either…"

"Back to London?"

"Honestly, I never want to see London again. That has been the greatest gift, even if I am trapped here. I feel like a different person."

"Agreed; we won't go to London," she said, not realizing what she implied.

"Agreed; we will go somewhere warm. Maybe Morocco?" he played along with a smile.

"Morocco…" she fantasized in thought.

"Now that I think about it… maybe I would like to go back to university. Really try to be a therapist again. I need a bit more schooling before I can actually do it."

"A therapist? Wouldn't you need to live in a city?"

"I wouldn't try to be that kind of therapist. Maybe with kids or people in the countryside. I don't know. Just a thought." He tore off a piece of toast and dipped it in butter. "Maybe even I will stay here."

She nearly spit out her food at the thought. "Why? Why would you stay here after it has kept you here against your will?"

"I don't hate it honestly. Like I said, I love the people. Matteo, Zoe, Hamish, YOU. I don't know anyone better from the city?"

"What about your parents?"

"We've never been close."

"Sorry, I didn't know," she said, feeling ashamed.

"Don't be. I accepted it a long time ago. What about you? You say they don't approve of the way you live?"

"Yes, well when you leave your university to live in the countryside, it tends to create issues—especially when you haven't visited in over three years…"

"Oh, right. You haven't left Glastonbury in three years. I almost forgot. I'm not used to the idea that I am not alone in this. Three years, wow." Ethan said, growing quiet afterwards, clearly lost in thought. Lila too was lost in her thoughts of the last two years—all the times she begged to be able to leave, all the anger, pain, and anxiety it had caused. All the times she thought about ending her misery for good—

"Alright, I agree. I will help break you out of here," Ethan said, his face lighting up as he looked at her.

"Wait, what do you mean?"

"Well, like I said, I am starting to like it here. But I can't imagine what three years would be like; I want to help you leave. So you can see your family, go to Greece, find Jesus; I don't care. All I know is that I want to help you do it." He seemed determined, his smile reassuring Lila that perhaps all was not lost.

She swallowed due to nerves. "Alright, how do we plan on doing it?" she said with more conviction than she expected.

"That! I do not know. But I will think about it," he said with an even brighter smile that filled her with infectious confidence.

"Okay, I trust you. Let's do this." She allowed herself to smile vulnerably. "So, first we should—"

"Shit, I am sorry. I just looked at the clock; I need to be going. Hamish will have my head if I don't make it there on time." He pulled out his wallet and threw £20 on the table. "That should pay for everything. My treat. Why don't we all meet at the pub later? You, me, Matteo, Zoe; we can have a proper catch-up?" he asked, quickly throwing on his coat.

"Yes, let's—"

"Fuck, Matteo's food! Do you mind bringing him something?" He pulled out £10 more and put it on the table. He was full of energy like Lila had never seen before. "See you later?" He gave her shoulder a quick squeeze before running out the door and down the High Street towards the café. Lila felt as though she were in a daze from how quickly he had just left the building, bits of omelette left on his plate, £30 laying in front of her, pub later, food for Matteo? She felt overwhelmed by it all. So overwhelmed, she got up from the table and just walked back to the studio without hesitation, a fixed gaze on only what was in front of her.

She walked into the library, Matteo sitting up eagerly from the couch: "Ah, my food!" he said with excitement.

"Next door, back booth. £10 for you. We are going to the pub later, by the way."

"Oh, how was—"

She continued her marching orders up the stairs into her studio space and bolted the door. The voices in her mind were growing in intensity; the only way to silence them had always been for her to pick up the brush and focus on the canvas. She flipped on her portable radio, turned it from holiday music to the nearest rock station, and got to work. The painting in front of her did not reflect the music, however; bright, bold colors were loaded onto her brush, which she then dragged across the white space in emotional and expressive patterns. What she was feeling was not what she was used to; it was not anxiety from fear, but anxiety from what could be… from a future promise. She might actually get out of here; she might actually be free.

—

Matteo had left some time in the afternoon, only to return with Ethan to fetch Lila from her studio around the time the sun was beginning to set. The painting was complete, and the voices had been silenced enough for her to put on some proper clothing before heading off to the Dragon's Treasure, a dark, cheap, and empty pub at the opposite end of the High Street from the Market Cross. Zoe was there to meet them; she was dressed in a traditional wool sweater that had snowflakes woven into the pattern. Despite the Dragon's Treasure being darkly lit, it had been decorated quite spectacularly for the winter season, and each table was illuminated with several waxy candles that made the reunion of friends feel as intimate as it deserved to be.

"Matteo, I heard you had a nasty run-in with the cold!" Zoe said while greeting everyone. "Lila, thank you so much for sweating with me the other day. We were nasty little witches afterwards, weren't we?" She snorted. "And Ethan! Come, let us share a drink and celebrate Yule together!"

"What is this Yule?" asked Matteo.

"It is like Christmas, but with more of a focus on family, I'd say. And a bit more magic than just Father Christmas," Zoe said cheekily.

"Krampus involved?" asked Ethan.

"How do you know about Krampus?" Zoe said with surprise.

"Lila was—telling me about him," Ethan said. Lila appreciated his attempt to cover up her nightly activities.

"Krampus isn't quite about Yule, but he is certainly from the same area. I don't think he makes stops in Glastonbury, luckily."

"Is there anything done here in Glastonbury for Yule?" asked Ethan.

"In times past, there was quite the party, but sadly that was with all the old guard, so to speak. You see, Glastonbury has been around for ages, and you have waves of people who kind of steward the celebrations each generation. And we just had a big wave of the old generation die off. Silus, Owen, Selene, Dex, and a handful of others remain," Zoe responded.

"So, it is up to us then!" Matteo declared. "We are the ones who must start the traditions again."

"My my, you are quite excitable," Zoe said.

"He has decided he loves it here, for some reason," Lila added.

"I think it's a fine idea," Ethan smiled. "How do we do one of these Yule feasts then?"

"Well, we don't have a lot of time if we want to pull it off. It is already three days past the solstice," Zoe pondered.

"When do you usually hold the feast?"

"The solstice traditionally… but historically, Yule was celebrated on the first full moon after the solstice, which gives us quite a bit more time," Zoe put together.

"Ace! What do we need?" Ethan sat up in his chair.

"We need to canvas the town, make posters, tell people. We will need to find a location to hold it in… then we also need to cook the food, of course. Past that, we need to have a ceremony or something?"

"I think I know where we can have this feast," Matteo said.

"Really? Where?" asked Ethan, surprised. "You just got back."

"Trust me, you will love it," he smiled.

"Great! I think I can figure out a ceremony. We'll need to do some research," said Zoe. "That just leaves the food, canvassing, and decorating."

Ethan glanced at Lila with a mischievous nature that she did not like. "I know who can decorate and do the canvassing! Lila, you will be perfect."

"Me? No, no. Can't be me. I am busy," Lila said.

"Piss off; no you are not. I will help you," Ethan said with his earlier confidence.

"How will we do it?" Lila asked, still with a pessimistic tone.

"We make posters to promote it—small paintings or whatever. Then we can hang them in all the shops, talk to people while we are out."

"I won't do the paintings," Lila said.

"Why not—"

"Because it'll take too long. I have a computer, and I know someone with a printer. We will make far more that way."

"That's the spirit!" Ethan grew more excited.

"Are we actually doing this?" Zoe said with positive disbelief. "What about the food? This will be a lot!"

"Luckily I know a Scot who knows his meat well. And I think Matteo—you and I were discussing cooking together just before we parted," he said with a warm smile.

"Yes! Yes, we were. I will call my mother; I will get some recipes from her."

"Italian recipes?"

"Of course!"

"It's settled then. We will have an Italian-themed Yule feast with Scottish meats in the best town in England!" Zoe announced, as if to the whole pub as the audience.

"When is the next full moon?" asked Ethan.

"Two weeks, I believe."

"Can we do it?"

"Only one way to find out."

"I hate you all, but let's do this."

"It's sorted then—two weeks. We do this together."

Four glasses of mulled wine were raised in celebration, and the planning continued late into the night.

—

Lila presented Ethan with the poster she had designed: a simple red poster with Christmas trees and snowflake patterns around the edges, a round table in the center with images of food placed around it, "COMMUNITY YULE FEAST" in big bold letters, and the information given below. They had also decided to have a cover charge of £5 to pay for the food that they would provide.

"You made this last night? After all that mulled wine?" Ethan said while studying the details.

"Yes… some of us work even better after a few drinks," she answered proudly. "What about you? Did you talk to Hamish?"

"As always, he put up a fight at first. And as always, he caved after Isla talked him into it. Of course, the cover charge helped. It will mostly cover the cost of the food he will find for us."

"And what of Matteo?"

"He is still being very secretive. Said he would go to his secret place today and find out if we can use it. Past that, Zoe is downstairs now, tearing through your books already, I see… and that just leaves us to spread the word around town." Ethan looked to see that there were at least twenty posters printed.

They spent the next few hours approaching each store that was open on the High Street, asking permission to hang the posters in the window. Only one of the various quirky store owners allowed them to do so, each one also showing interest in attending themselves. Even Ethan struggled to approach people on the street to talk about the Yule Feast, which Lila was relieved about. Luckily for them, Matteo could be seen down the street talking to every person he encountered, clearly excited and telling them every detail of what they were planning.

When they came to Andrew's Cross, Isla was resting at one of the tables with Hamish. "How are you feeling?"

"Aye, I can certainly tell there's a wee one in me these days. Growin' by the minute, it seems. I kent I was in trouble when I saw Hamish's bairn pictures."

"I was barely a haff stone when I came out the womb. But I was two stone by the following Wednesday!" Hamish said, clearly growing excited to be a father.

"Canvassing for the feast? Here, hang a poster right on the front door. I love this idea; I really do. What ye were sayin' about bringing the toon together? Exactly the dream I had when I first visited," Isla remarked while Lila hung the poster.

"Aye, I have tae admit, I love a good feast," Hamish agreed.

"Any thoughts on what you want to cook? Well, alongside Matteo and me?" Ethan asked.

"Hmm, been having a wee think about that. We could do several hams; the farmer I get all my sausage from should be able to provide them. Some chickens as well. How many people are ye expecting?"

"No more than thirty, I'd assume. Not many people in town these days."

"Make it thirty-one?" came a voice from the door. Jasper stood there, holding a poster in hand. Ethan had, of course, told Lila about some of the details around Jasper, enough that she wondered if Ethan would even like him to be there. "Been a while, Ethan. I was worried about you."

"Yeah. Sorry I didn't stop by. Needed a bit of distance from everything—everything around…"

"Me?"

"Well, not just you. But yeah, everything from that brief time."

"I perfectly understand; I have decided to move out after the incident with Josh. Things went downhill there after you left. I am living somewhere else now."

"I am happy to hear you got out of there," Lila said genuinely.

"Thank you. So, this feast. Sounds like a good time. Need any help?"

"No, we don't need help. But we would love to have you," Ethan said.

"Really? Wonderful! I thought after everything—"

"Don't think of it any longer," Ethan said with a small grin.

"I know you said you don't need help, but let me take a poster. I will invite some people from the prayer circle I am close with."

"Fine enough. No one… you know?"

"I understand. I will go tell some folk now!" Jasper made his exit and hurried down the street.

"Surprised you wanted him to come," Lila looked at Ethan.

"As you have said before, Jasper is a good guy; he just is a bit lost. Can't blame him for that. With that, we should continue doing our jobs. Got a whole other side of the street to do after all." Ethan said his goodbyes to Hamish and Isla, then walked out with Lila by his side.

Later that evening, they all found themselves back at the library to fill one another in on their progress. Matteo was grinning from ear to ear: "I got it."

"Got what?" asked Ethan.

"Oh, I will not tell you. Not till the day!"

"How will I decorate a place I do not know?" asked Lila.

"That is a good point. Okay, fine. I will tell you! Please, please, some suspense." He breathed deeply and closed his eyes.

"Are you expecting a drum—" Ethan started to say but was interrupted by Zoe proceeding to pat her legs in excitement.

"St. Benedict Church! Where I lived with Selene—well, I live there again now—but she agreed to host the feast."

"Really? That is a huge space!" Zoe said, excited.

"How much does she want for the space? Most of the money is going to Hamish at this rate," stated Ethan.

"Nothing! This is the best part. She loved the idea so much, she offered up the space for free!" Matteo clapped his hands together. "This is amazing!"

"This is getting serious…" Ethan sat back, feeling the weight of what they were doing. "Zoe, any luck today?"

"Yes, actually I found a great bit of information about the traditional heathen feasts of old. It is said that on Yule, pigs would be slaughtered, and men would come to swear oaths for the coming year on the butt. They would then eat the pig to symbolize the taking in of their promises—sort of like a New Year's resolution. So, I figured we can do that with a bit of ceremony."

"Luckily for us, Hamish is getting hams already arranged for us."

"Perfect!"

"Did you call your mom?" Lila asked Matteo.

"This I will do tomorrow. Don't worry," he smiled. "And you, the decorations. Will you need help?"

"Normally, I would say no. But since there is now a massive church involved, I have to say yes."

"Don't worry; I will help you," Zoe said.

"Good, that will allow Matteo and me to bond over recipes," Ethan said.

"Thirteen more days…"

"What's the time?" Zoe asked, sitting up quickly.

"Just past midnight."

"Then it's Christmas Eve! Happy Christmas, everyone!" she smiled and began to hug her friends.

Lila stood up and embraced her long-time friend. "Happy Christmas, everyone!"

—

Zoe and Lila set off over the course of the remaining days gathering everything they could to decorate the massive interior of St. Benedict's. The interior was a large hall with huge stone pillars that stretched all the way to the roof of the nearly four-hundred-year-old church. Most of the decorations came from Zoe's store and from the storerooms that were opened by Selene for them to snaffle various aged Christmas decorations to fill the central hall. Selene had also offered the kitchen of the church for all of their needs, located just across a small alleyway from the back of the building. There Matteo and Ethan had been working together to try and perfect the various recipes Matteo received over the phone from his mother—all of which were shared in Italian. Due to the busyness of everyone, there had been no more nightly meetings over warm drinks. They all had their duties and responsibilities to attend to in order to meet the deadline. So far, it seemed like they would fill all thirty expected seats, which had been arranged around a huge long table put together in the center of the church sanctuary.

Lila was finding great joy in spending time with Zoe. She had pulled out her radio and was playing holiday music every day, which was also lifting her spirits. Due to the large amount of time Zoe was spending decorating, she also had to bring all her dogs with her, each with their own unique holiday-themed sweater that they seemed to wear with a great deal of pride. The only wish Zoe had was that the church was warmer; the stone floors, walls, and high ceiling ensured that the space stayed frigid during the duration of their work. Selene said there was a furnace, but because of the cost, she could only have it on for the night of the feast itself.

It was the final night before the feast when Ethan had ever seen the completed interior of the church hall:

"I have to get away. That Italian is going to kill me," he wiped a thick bead of sweat from his eyes.

"Matteo?" Lila asked.

"That man is not Matteo. It's like working with ten Italians in the same body, each one with blood made of espresso. I don't think he is even speaking English anymore," Ethan said, appearing almost traumatized.

Zoe and Lila laughed at the thought of Matteo being anything but charming and positive. "What do you think?" Lila asked, drawing his attention to the decorations.

Ethan walked to the center of the room to admire all the work they had done: The stone pillars were wrapped in garland around the middle section; big red bows were tied on all sides. The table was originally made up of nine plastic folding tables but had been cleverly disguised with red tablecloths that made it look more elegant. Beautiful arrangements of holly, mistletoe, and evergreen were at the center of each section of seats. The church also featured many sconces that were now holding candles ready to be lit on the big day; several candles were also ready to be lit on both stands on the ground and on the table. A large Christmas tree had also been placed at the central altar space directly center of the table, gold and silver strings hung from the thick branches, also containing red ornaments stretching towards the top where a star had been placed.

"It is everything we imagined and more. Truly amazing job. I can't believe it," Ethan said in wonder. From the back of the church, rapid footsteps could now be heard.

"Ethan! Figlio di un criceto! We still need the mushrooms to be washed! Dove sei scappato? La salsa al baccalà non è pronta. Le patate non vengono sbucciate. And the flour? It is everywhere! E dov'è il mio olio d'oliva? Mi hai nascosto l'olio d'oliva. Does your father fuck goats? La santa madre ti abbatta! Se hai fatto del male al mio olio d'oliva, sentirai l'ira di mille nonne italiane! And you think you can hide from me?" all said at three times speed.

"Fuck, he found me. I got to go. But tomorrow, it'll be worth it! Wonderful job, ladies. Wish me luck…" Ethan marched slowly towards his raging Italian friend with his head held low. "Coming, dear…"

Both Zoe and Lila were laughing uncontrollably.

"Dear? You call me dear! Non c'è niente di caro in un marito che non si lava le mani. You can call me dear after you sweep up the rice from the floor! Come posso cucinare se rovesci tutto? Santo Cristo, abbattimi se sopravvivo a te!"

The sound of Matteo's scolding carried on as they disappeared back into the kitchen; the echo of Italian cursing carried throughout the town late into the night.

The night of the feast finally arrived after an exhausting final morning of preparations.

"Are we ready?" asked Zoe, dressed in a long green woolen dress with a thick fur shoulder piece. Her hair was left loose in the front and gathered tightly in the back.

"Yes, I think so," Lila said nervously while looking at the dresses she had prepared for herself, Isla, and Selene, as well as matching uniforms for the men—some of which she made, other pieces she found in the charity shop.

Ethan and Matteo had just finished helping Hamish carry in the hams —which had been warmed in the kitchen from across the alley— He had procured nine hams and twelve chickens in total. These were laid next to the seventeen dishes that Matteo and Ethan had been finishing throughout the day: lasagna, tortellini in brodo, capon, roasted potatoes, sautéed greens, panettone, pandoro, torrone, carciofi alla giudia, frittata, agnello al forno, piselli alla romana, colomba pasquale, pastiera napoletana, lenticchie con cotechino, struffoli.

While Matteo looked as though he had just won a gold medal in Italian cooking—standing proudly at the front of the table—Ethan, on the other hand, looked as though he had just been on the wrong side of a pub brawl, small specks of flour still present on the cuff of his thick woolen coat.

The time was nearly five in the evening, the marked time of arrival for all those interested. Isla and Selene volunteered to sit near the front to take donations and direct people to seats; Hamish and Matteo were in charge of handing out plates and keeping watch on the levels of food at each table. Zoe awaited nervously at the head of the table to start the feast off with her planned ceremony. Lila and Ethan were acting as helpers to take coats, answer questions, and watch for any issues that might arise—issues they felt relatively underprepared to handle. Despite it all, however, the group of friends could be seen carrying themselves with a sense of pride for pulling it all off. The clock struck five, the doors were open, and the first group of guests were ushered in.

Not only did they fill all thirty expected seats, but the additional eight were filled as well. Lila shared several glances with Zoe and Ethan in disbelief that so many had even paid attention to her posters. Selene and Isla were soon left with a dilemma: all seats were taken, and yet several stood waiting at the entrance, money in hand.

"What do we do?" asked Ethan to Zoe.

"I didn't expect so many," she replied. "Hamish!" she called. "Will we have enough food?"

"Aye, each ham'll feed a fair few. With the chickens and the daft Italians cookin'... we should have enough fer more. Some plates may need tae be found, but seats are a rare commodity."

"I suppose they wouldn't be bothered to stand?"

"I will go tell Isla to let 'em in." Hamish marched off. Ethan went to the front to help collect coats as well.

"Where are they all coming from?" Ethan asked Selene.

"Are you surprised? You offered full meals at five quid a head. I have never seen a better deal," she smiled.

Jasper walked up to the front and found Ethan. "Told you I would spread the word," he said proudly.

"This was all you?" Ethan asked, surprised.

"I have been a part of nearly every group in the town," he smiled humbly.

"What do we do?" Ethan felt a slight panic at the steady stream of Glastonbury locals coming in.

"Good thing we cooked so much!" Matteo came up with a massive smile on his face. "The spirit of my grandmothers is with us tonight!"

The church sanctuary now had well over one hundred people standing and sitting around the long table at the base of the Christmas tree, Zoe defending the seats for her friends who had helped put it all together. At last, the doors of the church were closed, with the final villager coming in from the cold night; Hamish, Isla, Selene, Lila, and Matteo made their way to the front of the table to take their seats, alerting Zoe that it was time to begin before the food had gone cold. The room went silent as all bright and eager faces looked to her in expectation.

Lila knew that her friend was used to public speaking, ritual, and ceremony—but also knew when she was nervous. Tonight she could see the signs well. Despite this, Zoe stepped forward in front of the great table and lifted her hands to the illuminated ceiling:

"Great guests of this most humble house of God. We call upon the spirits of our ancestors to join us at this table as they have for every winter past. Before you, we see the beautiful hams provided to us by one great and gracious Scot. We also see the wondrous bounty prepared for us by an Italian and a Londoner. Around you, the decorations and generosity of an American and a Caelliach. All brought together by friendship, magic, and the spirit of Avalon. I know many of your faces... some I hope to know after tonight. This night is about Glastonbury; it is about community. We are all here for different reasons; some of us by choice, others who have been brought here by the spirits—"

Lila and Ethan shared a look with one another across the candlelit table.

"—originally the plan was for us all to place our hands on the hams. But with so many of you, I think it may be better to place our hands on one another. From one hand to another shoulder, and for those of you at the table, please hold hands to create a circle around this great table."

The room all obeyed and formed a link of hands, arms, and shoulders that created a web of community that was completed when Zoe joined with both Ethan and Lila.

"In times past, oaths and promises would be sworn into the spirits of the ham, which would then be eaten to embody that promise. Tonight, I wish us all to swear those promises within one another. For the spirit of Glastonbury cannot be contained within a ham, or even in the Tor itself. The spirit of Glastonbury, of Avalon, is within her people. And this evening—this Yule—we embody that spirit and our promises. So let us close our eyes, focus on our intention, and allow our goals for the coming cycles to be carried within this great feast. And then, we will eat this glorious meal." Zoe bowed her head, which cued everyone to do the same.

Some murmured aloud, some in a whisper, others within themselves. Lila found herself lost on what to commit herself to… she looked up at Ethan—who had his own head bowed—clearly struggling to think of something as well. "What do I want? What does he want? What should I want? I am shit at this…" she pondered, feeling the pressure of the many bodies around her, who she believed to have clearer intentions than herself. She looked up once again at Ethan, then she looked at her friend Zoe in the center of the room; she looked powerful yet humble, wise yet young, beautiful and free. "Freedom… I want to find freedom. That is my goal. Freedom from this place, freedom… from myself." She closed her eyes tighter—believing it would make her intention even more serious—without realizing it, she was also squeezing Zoe's hand tighter as well, looking up she saw her friend smiling warmly at her, making her feel as though Zoe had heard her intention.

"And with that, great spirits of Avalon, powerful gods of winter, I ask that our goals and intentions be embodied within this succulent ham! Hail to the hearth, hail to the fire, and I wish you a good Yule!" Zoe raised her hands, bringing Ethan and Lila's along with her. As she shouted her final line, she shook her hands, signaling the release to everyone. "Now, please. Let us feast together!"

"Happy Yule!" came the cheer of the room, everyone quickly grabbing plates, cutlery, and spoonfuls of this and that, carving off ham and breaking off legs of the various chickens. While it was chaotic, everyone was respectful and did not overfill their plates—except Hamish, who was quick to load his and Isla's plate to the brim. "Eatin' fer two," he said.

"You are not! I am!" Isla said with a chuckle.

The room had moved from the sounds of clicking plates and focused eating into the noise of low chatter and deep laughs. Lila looked around the room to see the warm glowing faces of people she loved and knew, and people she had never known before. She saw Owen whispering something to Selene while he poured her a glass of wine; they both smiled and clearly agreed on something. She saw the ever-serious Silus laughing with someone she did not recognize at the end of the long table.

"You haven't gotten any food yet," Ethan said, snapping her out of her daze. She looked down to see that she was the only person in the room with an empty plate.

"Oh, I was lost in my mind, I think."

"Here, let me get you some ham before it's all gone—" Ethan took her plate and reached across a very focused Hamish to snaffle a slice of glistening pork for her. "So, what did you wish for?"

"Wish for? Oh, you mean my intention for the year?"

"Yeah, that. It did feel a bit like a wish for a birthday in a way!"

"And just like a birthday wish, I am not going to tell you," she smiled, receiving her plate from him. She looked at all the other dishes and began to assemble her plate slowly; by the time she had her first bite, many had already finished. Zoe finally sat down from her own conversation with Owen, who was now walking around the edges of the bustling room.

"How was it?" she asked Lila nervously.

"Perfection, my dear. I loved it."

"Good, I was a bit worried. Never talked to so many people before."

"What did Owen want?" Lila asked.

"Oh, something about wanting to make a speech at the end of the meal, him and Selene both. Not a problem, of course; I think I am ready for a glass of mulled wine after that anyway," Zoe searched around for her glass and took a sip.

Matteo and Ethan ran off to the kitchen to procure the last of the dishes for the table—as nothing was left due to the extra guests that had arrived—Hamish went to guard the alcohol, which was being pilfered by a few of the town's less savory characters. This left Isla, Zoe, and Lila to talk with one another, mostly about Isla's time in Scotland, how Claudia was doing with her new baby, and the details of the evening that they might have changed.

"Probably should have thought about who is going to wash these bloody dishes," Isla pointed out.

"Is it too much to assume that everyone will think to do it on their own?" Lila said hopefully.

"Oh, there is always a chance. But something tells me we won't get so lucky, especially as the drink continues to flow!" Zoe responded, looking around at the merry faces, which were all beating slightly more red than when they first arrived.

"So, what's the plan for next year?" Isla asked.

"We are already planning next year? We haven't even finished this one!" Zoe snorted.

"Next year…" Lila reflected on her intention of freedom, something that had already drifted from her mind.

"Lila, do you think you could make us—" Zoe had started but stopped when she heard the clinking of a glass behind her, something Lila was grateful for. Owen was standing at the head of the table in front of the Christmas tree, Selene by his side:

"Good Yule to everyone, and blessings to the cooks, the planners, and the helpers. Hail to the good host!"

"Hail!" cried the room, some voices lagging behind the others.

"We have had a truly blessed night, haven't we?"

"Aye!" responded the room, drinks in hand.

"To see a community sprout from the ideas of the young 'uns, well, it does bring a bit of warmth to the hearts of Selene and me, that it does. Same as I reckon it does for all the old folk what've seen this kind of thing come and go in our time, aye. But there's a touch more hope in the air now, there is, more than we've felt in many a year. And that be why we're lookin' forward to spring and to Beltane, we are. Here we be, halfway through winter, but soon enough we'll feel the sun on our backs again and see our green Avalon come back to life, sure as the leaves turn.

What we be wantin' this year, mind ye, is a Beltane like none as has been seen afore in this here community. One where the old pass the torch of Avalon down to the young. One where the flowers keep on bloomin'. And fer that, we'll need ourselves a Green Man and a May Queen that's ready to stand tall and represent that bountiful growth, they will. So, we ask ye, young folk, take a look inside yer hearts and think on who might be ready to step up as the Green Man and May Queen for this comin' Beltane."

Lila felt Ethan's gaze shift to her; looking up, she saw a dangerous grin on his face that she knew she did not like.

"I will be your Green Man!" shouted a voice from down the room; it was Jasper.

"Thank God," Lila whispered under her breath.

"Now then, Jasper, ye was already the Green Man last year, weren't ye? We be lookin' fer someone new this time 'round. Ain't no sense in havin' the same face up there every year, now is there? Spread the honor a bit, lad. Let someone else take a turn dancin' 'round the maypole, eh?" Owen stated clearly. Jasper sat down in disappointment, and Lila became worried once again…

The room was silent as the village folk looked from left to right, searching for someone to stand up and raise their voice.

"Trust me…" came a whisper from behind Lila, a gentle pressure applied to both of her shoulders.

"No, don't—"

"We will volunteer!" Ethan raised his hand, the other resting gently on Lila's back.

"Ethan, I was hopin' ye'd speak up. I had ye in mind," Owen said with a smile.

"And you, Lila. You have already helped us at Samhain. Are you ready to step forward as the May Queen this year?" Selene said, directing the gaze of the room upon her. She felt the pressure from all sides; her senses were on fire, and she felt completely exposed. She shot up quickly and ran out of the room, out the back door towards the alleyway to the kitchen. Ethan ran after her.

"How fucking dare you, Ethan? What made you think—" she started to scold him.

"I know. I know. But please, trust me—"

"Trust you? How can I do that? What a stupid idea!"

"My wish was for you," he said calmly.

"What?"

"My wish, or my intention… or whatever, it was for you to be free of this town."

"Why would you do that? Why waste your intention on me? You are stuck here too."

"I am, but you have been here longer. And I want to help you find a way out of here. I want you to be free, more than me."

She didn't know what to say; she leaned against the stone wall of the church, searching within herself for how to feel.

"And after the ceremony, I was thinking of everything we have discussed about why we are stuck here, and what you have tried made sense. Samhain is how we got stuck here, so—Beltane is the opposite of that, right? So maybe that's how we break the spell that has us stuck here. So, when they came up and mentioned the Green Man and the May Queen… well, it felt meant to be. I think we are meant to be in that ceremony."

"Well—I just…" Lila still was lost for words. Everything he was saying made sense, but the thought of her standing like Zoe just did in front of even more people terrified her.

"Think about it? I am sure we can let them know later." Ethan said.

"Just leave me alone," Lila said, not looking him in the eye.

"Okay. I will. Whatever you choose, I am not changing my intention. I want to help you in any way I can." He smiled one last time and headed back inside, leaving Lila alone with her thoughts…

"I have no clue what a Green Man is… what have I just volunteered for?" Ethan thought to himself as his eyes adjusted to the warm glow of the feasting hall. Owen stood patiently waiting for him.

"Well? She coming?" he asked.

"I am not sure…" Ethan said quietly.

"Well, we shall see then, won't we?" Owen placed his arm on Ethan's back and turned to the room. "Does anyone else wish tae take on the responsibility o' the Green Man? Speak now!" Owen addressed the room, scanning every corner.

No response.

"Then, let us raise our glasses tae Ethan. May he bless us wi' good harvest and green earth this summer! Hail tae Ethan, the Green Man!"

"Hail!" screamed the room. Ethan felt it resonate in his chest.

"Owen," he whispered.

"Yes?"

"What do I do as a Green Man?"

"Dinnae worry; Ah'll help ye. It'll be a long winter till Beltane yet." He patted him on the back, which made Ethan feel better.

"We are still in need of a May Queen," Selene raised her voice, looking now to the room, her eyes meeting the gaze of several women who quickly turned their heads away. She landed her gaze on Isla, who held it for a moment, then shifted down towards her growing belly. Then Selene looked to Zoe, who stood straight up and proud; she began to sit up to acknowledge the feeling of responsibility for the community, but then…

"I will do it," came a voice from behind Ethan. Lila stepped beside him. "I will be the May Queen," she said confidently and loudly to the room.

"What changed your mind?" Ethan whispered.

"Freedom."

"Let us raise our glasses to our May Queen!" Selene said in a heavy voice to all corners of the hall.

"Hail to the May Queen!" came the cheers.

Lila took Ethan's hand subtly, feeling his hand wrap around hers. Her face grew red, but not from the feeling of his soft palm against hers, but from what she knew from the previous Beltanes in Glastonbury. She blushed because at Beltane, the May Queen and Green Man share a kiss.

15
Winter Preparations

Once the celebration of Yule was complete, a cold winter settled across the rolling hills of Somerset. Unprecedented snowfall blanketed Glastonbury, with many calling it the prophecy of the Cailleach being fulfilled. The streets were coated in white, the snow piled high on the edges of the sidewalks, forcing the townsfolk to stay inside for fear of the unnatural chill in the air. Ethan, Hamish, and Isla were no different; for the first few days of the winter weather — despite the warm drinks they served— no one dared brave the walk for more than they had to. Glastonbury was in a deep hibernation.

Matteo was shacked up with Selene in the church dormitory once more. After the intensive cooking from Yule, he was not seen by anyone until nearly the end of January when he arrived at the front of the café with two letters in his hand—one for Ethan, the other for Lila.

"Selene has sent me on a mission to deliver these letters! Quickly, let me in; it is freezing!" Matteo pushed past Ethan to sit near the radiator against the far wall. "Perhaps I have made a mistake choosing Glastonbury. Is it always this cold?"

"Nah, this isnae usual for anywhere in the UK. Even back hame, it ne'er freezes o'er this long," Hamish said in a stern tone, gazing oot the windae at the deserted village streets.

"It's meant tae be. At least for me. This bairn is takin' its toll on me, an' I'm in need o' the rest," Isla said, laying across the seat of the booth along the outside wall.

"What's this letter then?" asked Ethan, who was making a coffee for his freezing companion.

"It is from Selene and Owen. I do not know what it is about." He replied, graciously taking the warm drink from Ethan, who in return took his letter.

"It seems Owen wants to meet…" Ethan read through Owen's handwriting. "Seems I will see where the mysterious old man lives. He wants me to meet at his home. To discuss plans for Beltane. In this bloody weather?" he said, looking back outside into the white world that existed beyond the safety of the radiator.

"When?" asked Hamish.

"Tonight, it seems."

"Good, I was gettin' tired of lookin' at yer ugly mug anyway. We've been shut in for nearly two weeks now, after all!" Hamish joked, but said it in a way that he meant it slightly.

"Mind coming with me?" Ethan asked Matteo.

"And go back out in this cold?!" Matteo exclaimed. "In the night as well!"

"I would feel better being there with a friend. Owen is kind of intense, after all."

"How far does he live?" Matteo asked.

"Looks like somewhere near the Tor, unsurprisingly."

"So, far."

"Haven't you walked across Europe? This will be nothing for you!" Ethan pleaded.

"Fine, but if I freeze to death, then I will haunt you and give you never a night's peace!" Matteo finished his coffee. "Now, I must make the hike to the library to deliver this message."

"Meet here at half six, okay?"

Matteo wrapped his scarf around his head, only leaving a small slit for his eyes to see. "Remember, I will haunt you if I die!" he said before opening the door to brave the arctic weather once more.

Later that evening, Ethan learned that Matteo was not exaggerating the temperature or the severity of walking across town. Their walk to Owen's address was difficult, with the uphill climb on the slippery streets while facing the cold blast of wind coming from the Tor. Owen lived along the street leading to the Tor, just before the White Springs, in a building that appeared to be leaning slightly from its age. A placard with "1653" was posted on the edge of the building. When the door opened for them, they were greeted by Owen, whose beard seemed to have grown tremendously since even Yule, now hanging long and gray at the center of his breastbone.

"Ethan! Don't reckon I said nothin' 'bout bringin' an Eskimo wi' ye, did I?" He raised an eyebrow at the tightly bundled Matteo beside Ethan.

“Nor did you say to bring an Italian, but I wasn’t going to make that walk alone.”

"Aye, smart move. The Wild Hunt be ridin’ fierce in these winds. Best come in, quick like.”

Matteo was first to shuffle inside; Ethan followed next, closely inspecting the contents of the home within. The crookedness of the house continued inside, where the hallway seemed to bend in an unnatural way through the center of the building while leading to a staircase at the far end. From the crooked hallway led four other rooms—one a study with a large dark wooden desk surrounded by bookshelves containing just as many books as the library where Lila worked and lived. Across the hall was what would have been a formal dining room at one point in the home’s history, now containing several small tables filled with various occult objects, idols, crystals, charms, and many unrecognizable things to Ethan’s quick eye. In the back rooms, a small kitchen of equally mysterious and aged quality could be found, with a sitting room across from there that held four large armchairs in front of a roaring fire. From what Ethan could tell, the home had no electricity and was only lit by numerous candles on the surfaces of tables and placed on sconces along the walls. Despite the fireplace being the only visible source of warmth—as no radiators could be seen—the home was very cozy. Additionally, the age of the home and its contents did not lead to it feeling decrepit, unsafe, or unpleasant. Ethan felt comfortable and quite transfixed by the many objects of mystery scattered on nearly every surface and hanging from every wall.

“This house is like a museum!” Matteo admired, unraveling his scarf from around his face.

"How long have you lived here?" Ethan asked.

"As long as I can remember. My family's always lived 'ere too: me dad, me dad's dad, an' so on it went. Fairly certain one of me dads built the bloomin' thing. But we've lost track o' so many dads ago. Now, come join me by the fire, 'ave a drop o' whisky and let's 'ave a natter." Owen ushered them into the sitting room. Three glasses were sitting neatly by a bottle of amber whisky perfectly centered on the table.

"Thought he wasn't expectin' a third?" Ethan wondered, hanging his coat on a nearby wall peg. Matteo took the closest chair near the fire, quickly pouring himself a drink of warming whisky.

"I never had whisky in my whole life before coming to Glastonbury, and now I understand why you drink it here in England. It keeps your soul warm," he sniffed the drink deeply.

"Best be appreciatin' that drink. It's older'n I am." Owen winked while taking his own seat opposite Matteo, pouring Ethan a glass as well.

"Thank you, Owen. Why have you invited me here?"

"To discuss Beltane, o' course! Winter'll be breakin' soon, so it's time to get ready. Unless ye've forgotten, ye're s'posed to be the Green Man?" He eyed Ethan, expecting him to say he had forgotten.

"No, I haven't forgotten. And I am very curious what all this entails."

"First, let me ask: why are ye doing it?"

"Why do you ask? No one else seemed to be stepping up, is all." Ethan took a sip of the strong and warming drink.

"Was it te girl?" Owen asked.

"Yes and no. Not in the way you'd expect."

"And how would I be expectin'?" Owen questioned.

"Well, you know. A guy does a thing for a woman, and it's expected he is sweet on her. In the past, sure… but not this time."

"So, you are not sweet on 'er then?" Owen cocked an eyebrow up.

"No, I made that mistake before."

"Right, well, regardless o' intention, we've got a ceremony to prepare for. What d'you know about Beltane?"

"Hardly anything," Ethan admitted.

"And what about ye?" Owen eyed Matteo, who had his eyes closed with a smile near the fire.

"Me? Oh, I know nothing! This is all new to me. Why are you asking me?"

"You'll be helpin', o' course. As one o' te Green Men!"

"There are more than one Green Man?" Ethan wondered.

"Aye, o' course. Can't be carryin' that pole by yerself. But ye'll be the main Green Man."

“The pole?” Ethan was beginning to realize he had no idea what he had volunteered for.

"Right, gather ’round, lads. I’ll tell ye a tale ‘bout how Beltane come to be, and the Maypole, the Green Man, and the May Queen. In the time o’ olden days, when the world was a bit different, the ancients celebrated the turning of the seasons. Come springtime, when the earth was wakin’ up after winter’s chill, they’d gather to mark Beltane. They believed that on this day, the veil ‘twixt the worlds was thinnest—much like at Samhain—and the fae folk, the spirits, they’d be about in full force. So, it was a time for great joy and magic.

Now, the Maypole, that’s a symbol of the world tree, a mighty oak that stands at the heart of all creation. They’d plant it in the ground, tall and proud, and decorate it with ribbons. The pole represents the axis o’ the world, the point where the heavens and earth meet. The ribbons, they’re for weaving together the old and new, the seen and unseen. This year, we will focus on the coming together of the masculine and the feminine.”

“The Green Man and the May Queen!” Matteo said, showing he understood some of what was being told to him.

“Right ye are! The Green Man, he’s a spirit o’ the woods, a symbol o’ nature’s rebirth. They’d dress up in leaves and branches and dance ‘round the Maypole to celebrate life returning to the land. The Green Man’s got roots in old Celtic traditions, where he’s seen as the guardian o’ the forest, blessin’ the fields and the folk n’ such.

And then there’s the May Queen. She represents the fertility of the land and the abundance of the year ahead.

She'd lead the festivities, wearin' flowers and a crown made o' fresh greenery. Her role's to honor the goddess of spring, to bring new life and prosperity to the community.

So, every year, they'd gather 'round, dance 'round the Maypole, and give thanks for the coming warmth and growth. The Green Man and the May Queen would be at the heart o' the celebrations, bringin' life and light to the festivities. That's the story, lads. It's not just 'bout the old ways, but about celebratin' life, love, and the joy o' the earth's renewal." Owen leaned back, a satisfied smile on his face.

"Wow! What a story. So, I will be one of these Green Men! With you, Ethan!" Matteo was excited, his eyes alight with ideas.

"So, let me get this straight. We carry a pole, to where?" Ethan seemed confused.

"The ladies, they dig the hole for yer pole! Get it?"

"Sounds… sexual?"

"'Cause it is! It's spring; the ancients might 'ave been magical, but they still thought 'bout one thing all the time. Especially in the spring…" he held up a finger while saying "one thing."

"Sex," Ethan said plainly.

"Sex, fertility, holes n' poles—all of it." He giggled and seemed proud of himself, now sitting up from his chair, beginning to shake his legs. "Beltane, unlike winter, is 'bout fun, energy, an' new life. Just like spring."

"Wait, am I bloody dancing?" Ethan said.

"Right ye are! Not only that, ye'll be leading the dance!" Owen grabbed Ethan by the hands to lead him around the room.

"Oh, fuck me!" Ethan cried as he was led around the room by Owen.

"Matteo, grab yer lad here. Dance like the fairies!" Owen tossed Ethan to Matteo so that he could grab a fiddle that was on display above the mantle of the fireplace. He began to play a tune, one similar to that heard in an Irish pub.

Matteo was surprisingly quite the natural at dancing; Ethan, on the other hand, was not prepared at all and was tripping over his feet.

"We have a lot o' work to do with ye, don't we, Ethan!" Owen picked up the pace and stepped on top of his armchair to give room for Ethan and Matteo to dance. "Now, Matteo, be the girl for this next bit!"

"What?" Ethan said in shock.

"At Beltane, ye will be dancin' with the May Queen; can't be havin' ye dance like that to celebrate such an occasion!" Owen slowed down his pace, cueing the two lads to dance slower in each other's arms.

"You look handsome, my Green Man!" Matteo joked with Ethan, laying in his arms.

"I bloody hate this…" Ethan droned.

"Best get used to it! We'll practice three times a week 'til Beltane. Also, ye'll need to convince a few others to be yer Green Men, to carry the pole and dance with the May Queen and her maidens."

"Who in Glastonbury will I convince to go through this shit with me..." Ethan pondered as he and Matteo danced slowly together in a way taught to them by the fiddle-playing Owen. They practiced late into the cold of that winter night. On their way back to their homes, they noticed the air seemed warmer, and the wind had shifted directions... warmer weather was on the horizon.

"Absolutely fuckin' not," Hamish said bitterly, unlocking the door to the café early the next morning in response to Ethan's request for him to be a Green Man.

"What's a bit of dancing?"

"Bit o' dancin', he says. Only that I'll be covered in green, freshly grassed up by the fairy folk o' Glastonbury. I've done a lot wi' ye, Ethan—th' mushrooms, th' feast, all th' other shite. But this? Naw, I cannae be bothered. The conversion'll be complete! I might as weel turn in ma kilt an' put on ma flower skirt!"

"You won't be dancing with me! You can dance with a lady."

"A lady that is not my wife!"

"Actually, I will be dancing as well. Lila asked me last night to be a maiden for her at Beltane."

"And you will be expected to dance with another man? Another one of the Green Men?"

"As is tradition, unless you don the green yourself, husband."

"Ye two devils've got me cornered. Think ye're both so clever, movin' me to this town, makin' me put a bairn in ye! Now I'm trapped!"

"Hamish, I think you actually love it here," Ethan said with a smirk.

"Love it? How could I love it! There ain't a proper chippy, water tastes like pennies, an' me wife's only become more o' a witch with that damned coven!" he carried on.

"And?" Isla looked at him questioningly.

"And… well—I… couldn't be happier. Fine, I bloody admit it. But I don't like havin' to dress up in green."

"We won't tell yer brothers ye did any o' it. Ye can act all manly 'round them on holidays up North." Isla grabbed him 'round the neck.

"Aye, best not. They'll have ma bollocks if they know I let ma witch wife paint me green."

"I'll be painted red meself."

"Everywhere?"

"Absolutely everywhere."

"What's happening?" Ethan was growing concerned he shouldn't be in the room any longer.

"What color will it make when we rub that paint together?" Hamish looked at his wife and grew closer to her lips.

"So, Hamish, are you in? If so, great, and I will get out of here." Ethan said, backing away towards the door.

"Aye, I am in. Get out of here so I can kiss my witch wife in peace." He gestured with his waving hand towards Ethan, closing the distance between his wife's mouth and kissing her deeply. "I love ye, ye she-devil."

Ethan nodded, grabbed his coat, and walked outside into the streets of Glastonbury. The snow was beginning to melt, and the air no longer had the familiar bite to it. January was nearly at an end; come the end of April, spring would be fully set in and Beltane would be celebrated on the 31st. Ethan was making his way toward the library to see how Lila's meeting with Selene had gone the previous night. When he arrived at the unlocked door, he found her on one of the couches, hard at work in a journal.

"Hey, it's good—" he started.

"You! Are you happy with yourself?"

"Sorry, what?"

"Are you happy with yourself? Look at all of this!" She pointed at a table containing dozens of scrap pieces of paper scattered around.

"What's all this?"

"Ideas, sketches, notes—all for this damned May Queen role you have thrust onto me!"

"Hey, this is going to be difficult for me too!" He snapped back.

"Oh, so you have to dance?"

"Yeah, actually."

"Sing to?" She continued.

"We have to sing?"

"Sing, dance, start a fire, climb a bloody mountain, might as well bring down the moon closer to us too." She rambled on.

"I take it your meeting last night went well then?" He joked to try and change the tone.

"Well, ha! Selene met us here and we talked for hours about what was expected of me as May Queen. Expected, ha! I expect to lose my fucking mind!"

"Who else was there? You said us?"

"Zoe, Isla, and Christine."

"Christine as well?"

"Yes, she was the previous May Queen, which means she gets to partake if she wants to at Beltane."

"How does Zoe feel about that?"

"Horribly, of course. But that's not my problem. What is my problem is trying to make this dress."

"How can I help?"

"Help? Do you sew? Do you draw? Do you have an idea of what a May Queen should look like?"

"No, but I have two hands. I have a mind that's half functional, and I am sworn to help you. So I will." He said, sitting down next to her. For the first time since he walked in, Lila looked up from her notebook and studied his expression to see if he was serious.

"Fine, if you want to help. Take a look at all those papers; see which of those sketches you like the most." She pointed with her pencil. Ethan looked over and grabbed a handful of the half-finished drawings, thumbing through them. Some were nothing more than a rough outline; others were even colored to show details. One caught his eye that he showed to her.

"This one. I like it." He said.

"And why do you like it?" She pressed.

"Honestly, I haven't a clue…" He studied the image more. "What do I like about it?" he thought. "Well, last year they had the sun behind her back; it was reflective."

"Yes, I know. I designed the bloody thing."

"Right, well this year. Let's not go with a sun theme. So this one, it has lots of flowers. I like that, and then we can also match that with the Green Men and have lots of bright colors along with the green paint. And earlier Isla said something about being painted red? What's that about?"

"Well, I was jealous of you getting to be painted. It helps disguise who you are. I want to be able to hide under something."

"I don't think you should," he said plainly.

"Shouldn't what?"

"Hide."

"Rubbish."

"I am serious. You are a beautiful woman, and spring isn't about hiding, but about blooming. Someone as beautiful as you shouldn't hide under a coat of paint. Leave that to us ugly men, yeah?" He looked at her confidently.

"Fine, I will think about it." She smiled at him briefly, then went back to her drawings. "Who else are you having help you with the pole?"

"Matteo, of course."

"Of course."

"Hamish, naturally. Then I was thinking Jasper, actually."

"Really? Even after everything?"

"Yeah, he came through at Yule. Not to mention he was the Green Man at Samhain; he is eager for it."

"Who else?" she asked.

"Silus maybe? I am not sure. I don't know many people that well, really."

"Claudia is going to help us; invite her husband, Rasmus."

"Yeah, I know him. Speaking of, isn't Isla going to be VERY pregnant by then? Will she dance okay?"

"She seemed confident enough. I trust her."

"And they all have to dance together, right?" Ethan asked.

"Around the Maypole they do."

"So that means Hamish and Isla, Jasper and… Christine? Claudia and Rasmus, Matteo and…"

"Matteo and Selene; she's helping as well."

"Right, okay then. That's everyone."

"You and me," she said sharply.

"You and me… shit." He had nearly forgotten that they were both going to not only be involved but also leading the celebration. "We should probably practice then." Ethan sat up.

"Practice what?"

"Dancing."

"You are supposed to be helping me, not making me dance."

"This is helping you; come on now! I have one night's practice with Matteo; I think I might have charmed him a bit." He extended his hand to hers. She studied it for a moment, then took it gently.

"Wonderful, now place your hand here on my waist, like Matteo did. Then your other hand here…" Ethan showed her everything he had been shown the previous night. They both danced slowly to the sound of crackling fire in the library, Lila's drawings scattered around them.

"This isn't so bad…"

"Well, at least until Owen speeds up his music… he will play the fiddle, I am guessing."

"And how do you dance then?" she asked him.

Ethan leaned back from her and smiled. "Like this!" He began to run around the room, her hand still in his. She started to laugh uncontrollably as he ran between the bookshelves, jumping on the sofas and chairs, even leaping over the center table a few times. They laughed, ran, and danced as long as their breath held out. They both collapsed onto the couches, panting heavily. Ethan looked out the window to see the windows had fogged up. Beyond, the snow was dripping like rain as the early winter sun shone onto the streets of Glastonbury.

February quickly passed by for Ethan and Lila, both of them settling into the routine of work, practice, and preparations for what lay beyond them on the other side of winter. Ethan continued to meet with Owen weekly to learn everything he could from him about the role of the Green Men during Beltane. Matteo, Hamish, Jasper, and Rasmus were also brought up to speed during several meetings at the café to discuss details of the ceremony. They agreed that when the weather warmed, they would meet in the pastures around the Tor to go over dancing with the May Queen and her Maidens.

Lila insisted on making all the dresses for Beltane, as she had done for Samhain. Zoe and Claudia assisted her as much as they could. Christine was unsurprisingly uninterested in helping in any extra way—jealous that she was not asked to be May Queen again—Isla, of course, wanted to help, but her pregnancy was proving to be more exhausting than she had expected. She often needed to take long mornings preparing for the day, sometimes never leaving the bed. Hamish was growing more worried by the day, insisting that they back out of the dancing, always reassured by his wife that she was going to be capable.

As March unfurled in Glastonbury, the village began to stir from its winter slumber. The ancient oaks, their branches still bare, started to show the first hints of green as buds swelled and tiny shoots pushed through the frost-kissed earth. In the heart of the village, the cobblestone streets were gradually cleared of the muck of winter. Children, wrapped in woolen scarves and mittens, ventured out to play, their laughter mingling with the calls of early birds returning from their southern migrations. The scent of damp earth and fresh shoots filled the air, a reminder of the life stirring beneath the surface.

“It’s finished,” came the familiar voice of Lila from over the counter. Ethan looked up to see her smiling.

“What’s finished?” he asked, glancing at the clock to see it was only a quarter past seven.

“My dress—the one you helped me pick out. I finished it last night… well, not last night. More like an hour ago. Anyway, make me a coffee and come look at it with me.”

“Are you sure you need coffee? You seem a bit shaky as it is.”

“Yes, I am being kept alive by caffeine right now, and I won’t rest until you see this work. It’s… good.”

“You, liking something you made? Alright, this does have cause for checking out.” He looked to Hamish, who was by the small grill on the other side of the café counter. “You mind?”

“No bother, still early anyways. Be back in an hour.”

Ethan made Lila a coffee—decaf—and headed out to meet her. She was jumping up and down slightly. "Happy first day of spring, by the way," she said, greedily taking the takeaway cup from him.

"It is the 21st already? I have lost track of time; we have been so busy."

They arrived at the library and went inside. "Now wait here, no peeking! I am heading upstairs to get changed."

"Promise no peeking," he said, sitting down to wait.

After around thirty minutes, Ethan began to wonder if she was going to come down at all. He even thought of going up to take a peek to see if she was okay. But right as he started to get up, he could hear her footsteps on the staircase. He sat down quickly.

"Alright, here it is…" Lila turned the corner, her green dress clinging to her form with a sensual elegance. A delicate layer of gold, embroidered with frilly floral patterns, draped loosely over the fabric, shimmering as it cascaded over her skin. The long, billowing sleeves, reminiscent of a robe, were made from a silky material that caught the light in a way that made them glow with an exotic allure. Her figure was accentuated at the bust and waist, with the dress flowing gracefully from her hips and loosening around her knees, where it fanned out dramatically at the back. A daring slit, starting at her left ankle and ending mid-thigh on her right leg, revealed thigh-high stockings adorned with a checkered pattern. Though she wore no shoes, a gold-laced girdle wound around her ankles, keeping the stockings snug. Ethan sat, mouth agape, lost for words.

"I look fucking incredible, don't I?" she said with pride.

"I honestly don't know what to say. You made this yourself?"

"Of course! Who else in this town could make such a thing? Also, not like I could leave to find one on my own anyway. Do you like it? Or is it too much?"

"Like it? I love it. I never knew something could look so elegant and yet so…" he was lost for the word.

"So… sexy?"

"Well, I was trying to think of something more appropriate, but yes. You are very sexy." He blushed, and so did she.

"It's not complete. There will be real flowers woven throughout to match a crown that I will make with Zoe in the days leading up to Beltane."

"Sounds incredible." He couldn't take his eyes off of her. "So, I see you decided not to wear any paint?"

"No, I am taking your advice. No hiding. But don't let it go to your head now. Can't let you think you are right often." She smirked. "So what are you doing for the Green Men to outdo this?"

"I don't think there is any outdoing you, but I thought we'd take our shirts off, paint ourselves green, and put some ferns in our hair," he said pridefully.

"Is that it? Are you serious?"

"No— I am only joking!" he said, knowing he was not. "I will need to think of something else now…" He looked back to her. "Are all the dresses going to be like this?"

"Not as nice, of course—I am the May Queen, after all—but they will be close. But, as Zoe reminded me, this time of year isn't about the dress or how beautiful I look. It is about summer, the new sun, and new life. She honestly doesn't shut up about it."

"Yeah, neither does Owen, I am afraid. But beauty can't hurt," he smiled.

"Are you confident in what you will be saying for the ceremony?" she asked.

"I think so."

"Are you going to share anything with me?"

"No, not unless you do."

"Fat chance, Green Man." She winked. "We are nearly a month away from it…" Lila trailed on.

"I know. You nervous?"

"A bit, but honestly, we have prepared as much as we possibly can at this point. Sure, we still need to get the others to dance together… but at least we have had plenty of practice." She smiled, sipping her coffee. "Ethan, do you think we have done enough?"

"Yeah, we can always dance more beforehand."

"No, not dancing. I mean, have we done enough to make it out of here? To break the spell?"

"Oh, I don't think about it much anymore, to be honest with you."

"I just want the choice, the choice to leave," she said.

"Before it was beaches and anywhere but here; now you sound like you are thinking about staying?" he asked.

"Not what I said. I still want to leave this place, but I cannot deny that I have enjoyed working as a May Queen—a little at least…"

"Well, it is an honor to be your Green Man, no matter what happens."

"Thank you, Ethan. It is an honor to be your May Queen." She looked at him warmly and then squinted her eyes to yawn. "Right, time for you to leave; I am exhausted. We still have a lot to do!"

—

Over the final few weeks of their preparations, the Green Men and the May Maidens all met once a week in the fields under the Tor to practice and go over their routine. Owen and Selene supervised them on the dance of the Maypole and their after; they also ironed out the details of the ceremony and what would happen before and after. Ethan worked with Zoe in secret to create his speech and make changes to the Green Men outfits to try and match Lila's work. Hamish and Matteo worked in their spare time on creating the Maypole for the festivities from an old fallen elm tree they had found in the abbey, all while Claudia and Christine gathered flowers in the final days before the event for all the flower crowns and decorations.

It was the night of the 29th, the final evening before the celebration began when Lila awoke to Ethan knocking on her door.

"Have time for one last mural?" He held up a box full of paints and some brushes, as well as two aprons he had taken from the café.

"This is a surprise. What did you have in mind?"

"You'll see. Come on." He held out his arm to offer it to her to hold; she gladly took it, and they walked off in the cool spring morning to a spot behind the town hall, which had a large blank canvas ready to be covered.

"Here, this is what we will be painting." He handed her a picture he had clearly taken out of a book at some point. She studied it to see that it was of a tarot card—the Fool—specifically.

"Do you even know what this means?" she asked.

"It symbolizes infinite possibilities; at least that's what Zoe told me. I wanted something we could paint together that would hopefully give us a leg up tomorrow. New life, new chances, and all that. Do you like it?"

"Yes. It's perfect." She put on an apron and tied back her hair. "Try not to mess it up like you did that goblin."

"Hey, I liked my Christmas goblin!" They both laughed and painted together late into the night. Lila finished the mural with the runes:

ᚠᚱᛖᛖᛞᛟᛗ

Happy with their work, they retreated back to their homes for one last night of restless sleep before the day of the Beltane celebration was upon them…

16
Beltane

Lila dug her hands into the cold earth, removing a large layer of soil that she scooted aside. Above her stood Zoe, who began the song:

"Rise with the sun, the morning's gold,
Earth in our hands, the tale is old.
Circle we stand, sisters so true,
Beltane is calling, the light breaks through.

Dig, dig, dig for the Maypole high,
Roots of the Earth and the sky draw nigh.
Turn the soil, with heart and soul,
Beltane fires make us whole.

Morning dew clings to our feet,
Feel the rhythm, hear the beat.
In every stroke, a prayer we weave,
Life returns, and we believe.

Dig, dig, dig for the Maypole high,
Roots of the Earth and the sky draw nigh.
Turn the soil, with heart and soul,
Beltane fires make us whole.

With every breath, the earth awakes,
With every swing, the old spell breaks.
Lift your voice, and raise the cheer,
Beltane's spirit, ever near.

Dig, dig, dig for the Maypole high,
Roots of the Earth and the sky draw nigh.
Turn the soil, with heart and soul,
Beltane fires make us whole.

Now the hole is wide and deep,
May the Maypole's roots take keep.
Dance we soon beneath the sun,
Beltane's song has just begun."

With the hole deep and the morning dew beginning to simmer in the early sun, the ladies ran down the hill to clean the mud from their hands and prepare for the afternoon when the Maypole would be raised high.

Meanwhile, Ethan was up early. He and his fellow Green Men had slept outside under the sky the night before. Hamish was just now waking up after hearing the sweet sounds of the women's songs coming from above.

"Still can't believe ye are goin' to get me to bloody sing like that," he said, half-awake.

"Come now, Hamish, it'll sound more manly when we all do it together," Ethan said with a grin.

"Doubt it." He rolled off his back and looked to the sky. "But at least it looks to be a perfect day for caroling."

Ethan went to awaken Matteo, Jasper, and Rasmus, who had all slept near the fire. "Come now, lads, we have plants to be picking."

"What are we doing again?" asked Rasmus.

"We have to pick mistletoe, hawthorn, bluebells, and oak leaves if we can find them. Otherwise, we just need some bushy leaves. And lots of them. Also, remember to only use these—" he pulled out a small box of golden scissors that Owen had given him, "—to cut the plants. No pulling, no yanking. And always say thank you to the plant."

"Owen never told me any of that when I was Green Man!" Jasper said, yawning on his way out of his sleeping bag.

"Trust me, it took a lot of evenings listening to that old fool to learn all this, and for some reason, lots of dancing." Ethan handed Jasper one of the golden scissors. "Right, Matteo, time to get going, so you better wake up."

Matteo stretched his arms. "Morning already? Can you believe it? It's Beltane already…"

"Yes, it is… and no, I cannot believe it. But what I do know is we need to get to work before noon. We need to be at the Abbey Gardens then to complete our transformations into —the Green Men!" He raised his arms in a cartoonish manner, trying to motivate his troupe. Then he started to sing:

"In the morning's silver glow, we rise,
Underneath the dawning skies.
Through the fields of dew we tread,
Gathering herbs with the light ahead.

The Green Man whispers on the breeze,
Through the branches, among the trees.
He guides our hands, he leads the way,
As we prepare for Beltane's day."

"And yer transformation is complete, Ethan! You have become what I have always feared! One of them, singing about the bloody trees!" Hamish scoffed jokingly.

"And you are coming with me, as always, my friend," Ethan smiled. "Now, chorus please!"

"Oh, Green Man, Green Man, guardian of the land,
We reap the bounty by your gentle hand.
With flowers and leaves, with herbs and vine,
We weave the blessings of Beltane's sign."

"That's the spirit, lads! Come, to the forests and fields we go!" Ethan marched off, gesturing for his Green Men to follow him:

"We take the sage, the rosemary sprigs,
And dance among the willow twigs.
Lavender blooms, thyme so sweet,
The Green Man's gift beneath our feet.

The earth it hums with ancient song,
As Beltane's fires won't take long.
We gather now, in morning's grace,
For in the night, we'll find your face."

"Who made this song anyway? Was it Owen?" asked Jasper, who was shearing off a small twig of hawthorn.

"Zoe and I made it together. Chorus, please!" Ethan shouted.

"Oh, Green Man, Green Man, guardian of the land,
We reap the bounty by your gentle hand.
With flowers and leaves, with herbs and vine,
We weave the blessings of Beltane's sign."

"Can't let the women show us up; put some spirit behind the next one!"

"In the heart of spring, the earth awakes,
The Green Man stirs, and the old ground shakes.
We honor him with what we find,
In Beltane's light, our souls unwind."

"This is so fun, singing with my brothers!" Matteo exclaimed while climbing an oak tree.

"Chorus, please!"

"Oh, Green Man, Green Man, guardian of the land,
We reap the bounty by your gentle hand.
With flowers and leaves, with herbs and vine,
We weave the blessings of Beltane's sign."

Ethan sang the final verse:

"So sing his song in the morning air,
And know his spirit is everywhere.
For in the plants and in the trees,
The Green Man lives in you and me."

"Lives in ye and me, load o' shite!" Hamish shouted as he struggled with a large bush to try and harvest its leaves.

"Feel the Green Man within you! Become the forest!" Ethan said in a sarcastic voice. "Chorus!"

"Oh, Green Man, Green Man, guardian of the land,
We reap the bounty by your gentle hand.
With flowers and leaves, with herbs and vine,
We weave the blessings of Beltane's sign."

"Now we do it again, this time without the attitude and back talk. Sing with me, boys!"

—

"Do you hear them down there?" asked Zoe as they made their way down the Tor toward the village. "They sound surprisingly good!"

"Always have said Hamish was a bonnie singer," Isla said proudly, walking slowly and holding her swollen belly.

"I think we sounded even better," Lila smiled proudly.

"What's next? I feel filthy," Christine complained.

"The White Springs, of course!" Zoe responded. "You won't feel dirty after that."

The women met up with Selene, who was in a conversation with Silus at the entrance of the White Springs. She was already in her dress, ready for the day's celebration.

"You ladies look beautiful," Silus said plainly.

"Shut it. We are covered in mud. Let me through!" Christine shoved past them into the chamber of the springs.

"Feeling ready, Lila?" asked Selene with her ever-pleasant smile.

"For once, I think I am."

They all disappeared into the dark of the springs, the echoes of the men's song still hanging in the branches of the trees.

—

"Whit's this paint made of, anyways?" Hamish asked as he rubbed the thick, bright green paint over his chest.

"You know… paint," Ethan responded.

"Obviously it's fuckin' paint. I meant, will it come off?"

"Should."

"When?"

"Couple of weeks, more than likely," Jasper jumped in, helping Rasmus rub some on his back.

"Make sure you get between your toes as well, Hamish. I want everyone to be an authentic Green Man!" Ethan jested with him.

"I am about to make you a black n' blue man if you don't lay off m' bullocks!" He threw flecks of paint at Ethan.

"Come now, let me get your back, ye jolly green giant!" Ethan came toward him with a handful of paint, Hamish lightly sprinting away.

"Ah'll do this masel'! Only ma wife gets tae rub ma back."

"We are closer than brothers now, Hamish!" Matteo was now chasing him as well.

"Stop this right now!" Hamish did his best to evade them.

Rasmus and Jasper were laughing as they watched the two much smaller men chase around the burly Scot with the green paint. The sounds of music began to be heard from the village beyond the walls of the Abbey; only a few short hours remained before the procession would begin up to the Tor…

—

"Hurry now; music is already starting in town! We need to get these flowers together!" Lila said to her rapidly working maidens who were weaving together flowers that had been collected around the village.

"How many is that?" asked Christine.

"We need… four more. Each of the men gets one as well!" Zoe said, the one who had made the most so far.

"Ow!" Isla said, grabbing her side.

"Should you be doing this? You are only a few weeks away from popping out that baby," Lila asked Isla for not the first time today.

"Aye, Ah telt ye already! Ah'll be fine, ye ken. Still got plenty o' time afore the wee bairn comes out tae see us. Just need tae take it slow, is all."

Lila was focused on getting Claudia into her dress—one that needed to be resized several times due to her ever-changing weight after giving birth herself. "You are next, Zoe! We are running out of time. The procession starts an hour before sunset. That's soon!"

"I love seeing you this way," Zoe smiled at her friend.

"What way?"

"Happy."

"Shut it, and get over here so I can stuff you in this dress!" Lila said, embarrassed but focused on the task ahead.

—

“Perhaps we should have practiced carrying the pole?” Matteo said, perplexed at looking at the large timber rod decorated with wreaths, ribbons, and flowers that all came together in a large wreath at the top.

“There are only five of us?” Jasper said, worried, he and Rasmus being quite thin men.

"Dinnae worry yersels; this is why ye brought a real man wi' ye. Ye ken, Ah used tae take part in the Highland Games! Threw cabers like this yin for fun on a Tuesday afternoon… in the bloody rain," Hamish said with pride.

“Wow! So you are saying you could lift this—right now!” Matteo said, egging him on.

“Move aside, ye wee Italian; I will show yous.”

Ethan stood from afar, nerves beginning to build in him. He watched as Hamish tucked under and did, in fact, lift the entire maypole by himself—but only for a moment. Their outfits were complete: painted green, wreaths of oak leaves hung around their necks, their hair woven together with mistletoe and bluebell. Hawthorn branches acted as primitive arm guards on each of them. “It isn’t quite as majestic as what Lila worked on… but you pulled it together. You have your Green Men. Now… we wait for—“

"Put that bloomin’ pole down, ye mad Scot! ‘Tis a long walk t’ the Tor, fer ye t’ be wastin’ yer energy like that!" came the voice of Owen, who had appeared with his fiddle and his own suit of green.

Hamish dropped the pole rather quickly, nearly onto the barefoot of Matteo, who was standing rather close.

"Are you lads ready? If so, I will guide you down to the street and we will start the festival…"

Ethan looked to each of his Green Men, who all looked back at him the same. Each one had lost their humorous expressions and now bore looks of focus and determination. Ethan knew in that moment that they were all there for him, his friends… and some, even his brothers.

"Yes, let us begin," he nodded toward Owen, who happily raised his fiddle and began to play.

—

Preparing for Beltane is not the duty of just one person, or even the May Queen or the Green Man; it takes a village to make this celebration happen. As Lila looked over the green hill that sat below the Tor, she could see all the effort put in by the dozens of villagers who made this festival possible. Beautiful flags of gold and white were on long poles around the ceremony area, wooden tables had been brought up under colorful ribbons. A large fire was being built near the spot for the Maypole, with banners, fires, and decorations flowing from the path at the base of the Tor all the way to the Tower itself. Zoe came up beside her, her face painted red with white accents, the beautiful green dress flowing magically over her figure. She placed a flower crown on Lila's head.

"Proud of you; you have come so far," she said seriously.

"I would have never made it without you, Zoe."

"You would have—"

"Please, I mean it. I wouldn't be alive without you," Lila said, putting more emphasis on how serious she was.

"I understand, and I am glad you are here," Zoe smiled faintly, then grinned widely. "And now you are the bloody May Queen! Ah! Look at you!" She laughed and went to hug her friend.

"Wait! The paint!" Zoe stopped her.

"Oh, close call there! Almost forgot I looked like I am covered in the blood of my enemies." She laughed and snorted.

The noises from the town below began to pick up; the sound of fiddles, drums, and excited cries signaled that the procession had begun. "Start the fire," Lila stated. Zoe gave her one last look for good luck, then headed over to the rest of the maidens to start the large bonfire atop the hill…

—

"Even with Hamish taking most of the weight, this thing is bloody heavy!" Ethan thought to himself as he led the Green Men with the Maypole resting tightly on his shoulder. Hamish was beside him, with Matteo, Jasper, and Rasmus all distributed down the length of the pole. Owen danced around them gracefully in his suit of green, now sporting a top hat that matched several other dancers, musicians, and performers that made up the rest of the procession. Much like Samhain, they worked their way up the same path through the village—also like Samhain—thousands of people lined the streets of Glastonbury to get a look at the half-naked men covered in green paint carrying the large tree trunk up a hill to a group of beautiful women who waited for them.

"Fucking Glastonbury," Ethan said so that only Hamish could hear him.

"Fucking Glastonbury," he replied. Then all the men joined in turn, sharing a laugh at the audacity of it all.

"Wouldn't do this with anyone else in the world, lads!" Ethan shouted.

"Aye, no one else in the world could have made me!" Hamish declared.

"Brothers for life!" Matteo replied.

"Sing, ye bastards!" Owen danced close to them. "How else will the Green Man hear ye?"

"Oh, Green Man, Green Man, guardian of the land,
We reap the bounty by your gentle hand.
With flowers and leaves, with herbs and vine,
We weave the blessings of Beltane's sign!"

They sang their song all the way up the hill, each step becoming harder and harder to make. The crowd made it difficult for them to weave in and out to reach the top. As they got closer, Ethan could feel Matteo and Rasmus dragging them down, rather than pushing them up. But Hamish stayed strong, despite the beads of sweat washing away some of the green on his face. "Come on, lads!" he shouted. "Sing with me!"

"Oh, Green Man, Green Man, guardian of the land,
We reap the bounty by your gentle hand.
With flowers and leaves, with herbs and vine,
We weave the blessings of Beltane's sign."

Ethan felt the weight become lighter as Matteo and Rasmus gave them more help. All they needed to do was finish the climb… and dance with the May Queen and her maidens.

—

"There they are! Look at ma husband! Strong as a bull! Father of this fuckin' kid!" Isla shouted with pride and joy at seeing the group of green-painted men ascend past the final rise of the hill.

"They look tired, but I will give it to Ethan; they actually look quite convincing as Green Men…" Lila said, standing regally in the middle of her maidens in front of the roaring bonfire. The sun was setting over the western horizon, creating a brilliant display of red and purple colors across the sky.

As the Green Men reached the hole that the women had dug earlier that morning, they all went down to their knees—which seemed a hard task for all of them—and then wedged the edge of the pole against the rim of the earthen hole. "Heave!" shouted Ethan. They all pressed up and got the post to stand erect in the earth, the ribbons releasing to create a brilliant effect as the wind carried them toward the south. Cheering from all around them could be heard as the crowd had made their way into a semi-circle around the bonfire and the Maypole.

Ethan and his Green Men were winded, but still needed to perform their duties. They formed a circle around the pole, leaving space for the women to come between them. Owen stepped forward, his fiddle still in hand.

"Are ye all ready t' celebrate the May Queen an' the Green Man!" he shouted wildly into the crowd. Cheering, hollering, and screaming could be heard from all around. Ethan knew this meant his time had come…

He left his circle of friends and made his way to the line of women in their brilliant dresses and flower crowns, each one with an additional flower crown in hand. His eyes met Lila's; her unpainted skin glowed with beauty and grace, and she bore a powerful smile under black lipstick. He stopped and bowed before her, then turned to the sea of people behind him and began to speak:

"Good folk, as we stand beneath the eve of summer,
On this sacred day of Beltane, when the earth awakens and life has just begun.
Here in Glastonbury, where the ley lines flow,
We call upon the spirits of the land, the seeds we shall sow.

I am the Green Man, keeper of the woods,
With roots deep in the soil, where the wild things brood.
From the ancient oaks to the blossoming glade,
I dance with the winds, in the sunlight, unafraid.

Today, we honor the May Queen, radiant and fair,
With her crown of blossoms, she'll lead us with care.
As she bestows her wreath, a symbol of fertility and grace,
We welcome the bounty of life, in this hallowed space.

May her spirit rise in the flowers that bloom,
Bringing joy to our hearts, dispelling all gloom.
With each petal that falls, may our wishes take flight,
In the warmth of the sun and the coolness of night.

So come, gather close, as we weave our intent,
For love and for laughter, in nature's content.
As the fire's flame flickers, let our spirits entwine,
In the magic of Beltane, let our hearts brightly shine.

If you give your wreath to me and mine company,
O May Queen, we pledge our devotion,
To nurture the earth, like a flowing ocean.
Together we stand, in this dance of the season,
Bound by the earth, love, and ancient reason.

Let the blessings of nature, the sun, and the rain,
Guide us in harmony, through pleasure and pain.
For today we are one, in the cycle of life,
Embracing the joy and the ending of strife."

Ethan had practiced that speech countless times over the last weeks, worrying about every detail. Now that he had said it, he wasn't sure he had spoken at all! He looked back to see Zoe nodding at him in approval. He then looked to Lila—it was a ceremony, so he knew that she had to give him the flower crown—but he still feared rejection now that he was in front of such a beautiful visage of Lila. Luckily, she picked up her flower crown and moved forward to place it upon his head:

"O Green Man, keeper of forests, and all that is wild,
In your strength and your spirit, we find nature's child.
You dance with the winds, and you sing with the trees,
Your essence awakens the earth and the breeze.

As I place this wreath upon your noble brow,
We celebrate the fertility of this season, right now.
May these flowers remind us of the bounty to come,
Of the joy that we share and the life that we hum.

With this crown, I bless you, with the essence of spring,
As the sun warms the earth, may our hearts brightly sing.
Together we rise, in this dance of delight,
With love as our guide, through the day and the night.

So take this gift, dear Green Man, as a sign of our bond,
In the cycle of life, we are forever fond.
May your spirit grow stronger, with the roots that we sow,
In this sacred embrace, where the wildflowers grow.

Let the fire of Beltane ignite our sweet dreams,
In the dance of creation, let love be our theme.
For today we are one, in this joyous refrain,
Together we flourish, through sunshine and rain."

Lila raised her arms after finishing her speech, the flower crown resting snuggly on Ethan's head. As he rose and joined her hands, cheers rang out across the land. The maidens moved like wisps over a glen, joining each of the other Green Men in a similar display of devotion as they presented their flower crowns. Isla slowly made her way to Hamish, who could see her struggle with her hands on her belly.

"Isla! My darling, please, let us dance slowly on our own. We have made it further than anyone else would have," he said as he approached his pregnant wife.

"For once, husband, I think ye may be right. Let's wait to dance the maypole until the wee one is with us," she came up to him with the flower crown in hand. "I still want tae hear yer devotion, husband."

He smiled and got down on one knee, his hand resting gently on her belly:

"Ah share this love so true, fer ma dear wife and our wee bairn, soon to be new.
In the warmth o' this Beltane sun, we celebrate life, as we wait fer the joy that'll come with our lad, and the strength o' ma bonnie wife, who carries him near.

Wi' every heartbeat, every gentle kick,
Ah pledge ma heart, ma soul, and all that Ah am,
to cherish and protect ye both, through thick and thin.
Together we'll grow, in love and in light,
as we welcome this life into our world, so bright!"

He struggled with the words, which made it flow poorly, and Ethan could tell he hated some of the rhymes and was ashamed of what he had said. But then he felt the gentle pressure of the flower crown being rested on his head.

"Ah share the depths o' ma heart, fer the man who stands beside me, the father o' our wee bairn, and ma truest friend. In every moment, ye fill ma days wi' laughter and joy, like the sun breaking through the clouds after a storm. Your strength and kindness wrap around me like a warm blanket, keepin' me safe and cherished.
As we await the arrival o' our lad, know that ma love fer ye grows deeper with each passing day. Together, we'll face the challenges and celebrate the beauty of life, hand in hand, heart to heart. Ye are ma rock, and Ah am so grateful to walk this path wi' ye."

Hamish had tears running down his face; he sobbed into her hand before standing up and holding her as close as he could. The crowd cheered from behind them as they shared a wee kiss between them both. As the noise of the audience subsided, the music from Owen and his group of musicians began to play slowly, signifying it was time to dance.

Ethan still had Lila's hand in his own. He looked at her and said, "You ready to dance?"

"With you? Always."

They approached the hanging ribbons of the Maypole, the men on the outside holding the longest red ribbons, the women on the inside holding the short green ribbons. Each dancer looked at one another as the music was halted for a moment, then released in a fast rhythm of fiddle and drum. The dance of the maypole had begun!

The men raised their ribbons high so the women could duck below, and as the women came back around, they too reached their ribbons high. Quickly they all ran in circles around the pole in this rhythm and flow, and they could be seen getting closer and closer to the pole as their ribbons wound their way around the base. Now they were so close they were bumping into one another—laughing as they did—Matteo bumped into Selene and looked worried, but then he saw her laughing. Jasper, on the other hand, bumped into Christine and was politely told, "Fuck off!" by her as he passed. Tighter and tighter they wound until nothing was left besides the final inches of Ethan and Lila's ribbons, which they met in the center and tied together with a bow.

They all stepped away as the music changed and shifted. Each dancer found their partner, joining hand in hand to dance slowly around the pole in a way that Owen had taught them over the last month. The music picked up and they began to spin and twirl around one another, the leaves of the Green Men beginning to blow off of their loosely constructed outfits. The elegant green dresses of the May Queen and the Maidens flowed with the wind. Lila was focused on Ethan and where her hand was placed; between the grasps of his fingers, she held her tight yet free.

"What are you doing to me?" she asked, caught up in the moment.

"What's that, my dear May Queen?"

"Perhaps we are already free..." she said, causing Ethan to skip a beat, stumbling slightly. The music changed once again, the crowd now dancing with one another to the slow song being played by Owen's fiddle.

Selene approached them. "Quickly, time to start the Beltane fires." She brushed past them with Matteo in tow.

Lila and Ethan exchanged a look before following to the entrance to the Tor, where two unlit fires were placed on both sides. The other Maidens and the Green Men came after, hand-in-hand, signaling the dancing crowd to move with them. As they approached the unlit fires, Owen also appeared and put down his fiddle to stand beside Selene, waiting for the audience to settle; the sun had now fully ducked beyond the horizon, a faint glow hovering above them.

"Good people of Avalon!" Selene shouted. "Today, we gather to celebrate Beltane! The return of the sun, summer, and fun. The Cailleach now rests in her mountain until the return of the next winter. Now is the time for dancing, laughter, and cheer for the first time this year. But, this Beltane is different, dear folk, for new magic has come to our humble land, one that you will take in when you walk through this smoke!" She knelt down to start her fire.

Owen stepped forward. "Good people of Summer, ye who survived the trials of the cold. We are but another winter old, a little more wrinkled we may be, but the time of warmth has returned with much virility. We celebrated the Green Man and the May Queen as they symbolize the return of all that is good, beautiful, and green. As the druids of old have taught us, between two fires we shall step to cast aside the darkness that once covered us like a thick mist." He knelt down to light his own fire, Selene's now roaring quite spectacularly.

"Good people! Step forward and climb the Tor; there we shall witness the union of the Sun and the Earth, which shall come together to bring us a year of prosperity!" Selene shouted last. Ethan and Lila knew this was their time to step forward together.

Hand in hand, they stepped between the smoke of the two flames. Their eyes began to burn, and the smell of burning wood filled their lungs but quickly faded. The path of the Tor was illuminated by dozens of glowing torches along the safest route. They were told to walk slowly to give everyone time to follow behind them as they made their way to the entrance gate of the Tower. Behind them were the other Green Men and the Maidens, holding hands as well—but certainly not as intimately as Lila and Ethan were in this moment.

Neither of them said a thing, but they still felt words being shared between their fingers and in their steps as they ascended. As they approached the tower, they could see flowers lying around the base and along the final stretch of the path to the mouth of the Tower that was now decorated as if a wedding were about to be performed—and in a way —the union of the Green Man and the May Queen was a marriage. Zoe had told them both the legends and traditions of Beltane celebrations going back for hundreds of years. What they were about to do had been done by many others before. Yet, they still felt the moment special, as if no other Green Man or May Queen had ever existed. As they reached the archway of the Tower, there was no one else in the world besides the person in front of them.

They stood for a long time, waiting for Selene and Owen to come on either side of them. The top of the Tor was now filled to the rim with onlookers and celebrants. Ethan looked around to see the familiar faces he drew strength from, and the many endless faces that made him nervous. Then he felt a hand upon his cheek—Lila was looking at him with intensity and love.

"It is here! Under St. Michael's Tower atop Glastonbury Tor of Avalon that we bear witness to the union of Heaven and Earth, of Warmth and Soil!" Owen cried to the sky above.

"It is here that we witness magic and tradition; it is here we honor the memories of those who came before! To witness the sacred union of nature and his bride!" Selene said into the wind.

Ethan brought his hands to Lila's cheeks, and she enveloped her hands over his.

"With this kiss, I bring forth the powers of the green and fertile earth. May our embrace lead to life and fertility."

"With this kiss, I bring the powers of passion and the energy of the sun. May our embrace lead to peace and unity."

The world froze, the silence encircling them. It was as if all the light in the world shone on them for a single instant as they closed the distance and embraced their lips upon one another. Ethan felt his heart skip a beat, and Lila felt hers shoot through her chest. Love was exchanged between them in that moment, a feeling they wished could last forever.

They released, and the sound of hundreds of voices screaming to the skies erupted—heaven and earth—amid the playing of whimsical music and the blasting of horns. The ceremony of Beltane was complete!

Owen clasped his arm on Ethan's shoulder. "Well done! Well done!"

Lila was whisked away by Zoe, Isla, and Claudia; her hand reaching out for Ethan's as they were both swallowed up in the madness.

"My brother! We did it! We are home!" Matteo hugged him and howled as he had done the first day they had met.

"I might be weak because I am green, but I love ye, lad. Good job!" Hamish shouted loudly in his ear. Ethan couldn't hear him as he was looking desperately for Lila.

"I can't believe you remembered everything I taught you!" Zoe exclaimed in excitement to Lila.

"Have you seen Ethan?" she said desperately.

"What do you think we should do for Samhain? Think you will be the Green Man again? How was it?" Jasper started to rapid-fire questions toward Ethan.

"Later, Jasper. Now I have to find someone," he pushed past him.

Lila was feeling overwhelmed; the Tor was unable to fit all who were up there and beginning to celebrate around the small fires that were being made at the summit. Only moments ago she was the May Queen on top of the world, and now she was swallowed in a sea of unfamiliar faces—but then she felt a hand on her side.

"Come with me; I know a way down," said Ethan, who whisked her away to a side path that snaked its way down the Tor. She stopped him and kissed him again, and he looked at her and did the same. The path was dark and difficult for them both with their bare feet. Ethan led the way, finding all the rocks and guiding Lila slowly through the dark.

"Honestly, what just happened?" Lila asked as they reached the base of the Tor, entering a path into the countryside.

"I am not convinced any of this was real," Ethan said in amazement. "The music, the dance, Hamish and Isla, the bloody sky—"

"The kiss…"

"The kiss!" He said, giggling to himself.

"Like I said earlier. What have you done to me! I was perfectly content here, alone with my paintings. I had one friend and little responsibility."

"And now?" he asked.

"And now, I am—happy? Honestly, makes me feel sick to say."

"I know what you mean… when I came here… that was a different person."

"Do you think you'll ever be that person again? The person that came here? Are you worried to lose it all?"

"I am not sure that person was ever really me. Now that I feel this, this life. I never want to lose it again."

"So, how are we going to protect it then?" she asked, holding him closely to shield against the cool night.

"We could build a big wall around our happiness, keep all the thieves out who try to steal it." He said.

"Get a big scary dog to bark at any monsters that try to get us?"

"You mean like Krampus?"

"Krampus and his evil Christmas goblins for sure. They will be very jealous of us," she said.

"Admit it, though," he said.

"Admit what?"

"You cried when Hamish and Isla made their speech to one another!"

"If you didn't cry at that, I am not convinced you are human. I love them. What do you think they will name the wee lad?"

"Haggis, probably."

"Maybe Nessy?"

"When's she due?"

"Soon."

"Should I make them some baby clothes?"

"I think that would be wonderful!"

"When we get back, I will get started—"

The Green Man and the May Queen walked together hand in hand to the summer valleys of Avalon. They were so caught up in conversations of the future and listening to one another dream that they did not realize they had stepped over the small rock pile Ethan had built months ago. The invisible barrier that had once kept them both there no longer existed, and they no longer cared. Ethan laughed as he saw that he had gotten green paint on her face; she kissed him on the cheek, collecting some more.

In the distance, the sound of horns, drums, and singing could be heard for miles beyond, and the warm glow of the fires upon Glastonbury Tor illuminated all that was around, like a lighthouse in the dark of a starless night calling to all the lost souls of the world looking for safe harbor from the storms of life…

Jacob Toddson's other book: A Yule Story
Available on Amazon

Visit www.jacobtoddson.com for his videos, projects, and retreats.